On Bended Knee

On Bended Knee

Brittney Holmes

www.urbanchristianonline.com

Urban Books, LLC
78 East Industry Court
Deer Park, NY 11729

ISBN 13: 978-1-60162-784-1
ISBN 10: 1-60162-784-X

First Printing May 2011
Printed in the United States of America

10 9 8 7 6 5 4 3 2 1

Distributed by Kensington Corp.
Submit Wholesale Orders to:
Kensington Publishing Corp.
C/O Penguin Group (USA) Inc.
Attention: Order Processing
405 Murray Hill Parkway
East Rutherford, NJ 07073-2316
Phone: 1-800-526-0275
Fax: 1-800-227-9604

On Bended Knee

Brittney Holmes

Dedication

For my best friend for over a decade, Talib X. You have always been there for me and I appreciate you allowing me to be there for you. I've always believed God had a purpose for bringing us together and I know it's being fulfilled each and every day. We've been through so much, and no matter what the future holds for us, I thank God for our blessed meeting.

Acknowledgments

As always, I'd like to give honor and praise to God—my Savior and keeper—for all He has done for me. Lord, I can't thank you enough for all of the blessings and lessons you've allowed me to experience. I thank you for implanting this story line in my heart because I truly believe that someone will receive that undying message that it is all about your timing and your will. I pray that this book blossoms into what you predestined for it to be. Thank you for this gift; I give it back to you.

To my parents, Jonathan Bellamy and Kendra Norman-Bellamy, thank you for raising me into the young woman I am today. I know I make you guys feel old (lol). But seriously, it's because of my upbringing and your support and encouragement of my gifts that I am able to use them to God's glory. I love you both. To Jimmy Lee Holmes: Daddy, I've learned a lot from you through those whose lives you touched. I have truly come to understand what it means to live and not die.

Crystal, my baby sister, you make me feel old. I can't believe you're an "adult" (I use that term loosely ☺). But it truly does seem like we were just sharing a room and fighting only yesterday. . . . It was probably last weekend (lol). I think you've developed into a beautiful individual, and I hope that as you come into woman-hood, I have set a good example for you.

To my grandparents, Bishop and Mrs. H. H. Norman, Mr. Jesse and Mrs. Dorothy Holmes, and the late Elder

Acknowledgments

Clinton and Mrs. Willie Mae Bellamy, and the rest of my extended family (uncles, aunts, and cousins): thank you for always praying for me even when I may think I don't need or deserve it. For your support of my career and your gentle and loving guidance, I am grateful.

To one of the greatest cousins/publicists ever, Terrence Wooten! Of all of the many hats that you wear so well, being in my family is the best fit of all! Thanks for always being there whenever, and in whatever capacity is needed.

To all of my friends at the University of Georgia—you know I wish I could name you all—I really appreciate you making the last three years of my collegiate career the most interesting, fun, spontaneous, life-changing, and wonderful time of my life. To my family within the Black Affairs Council, my lovely Freshman Advisory Board members, the National Association of Black Journalists, the Red & Black, Rocksprings Community Center (I love my kids!), and *InfUSion* magazine—thank you for cultivating me into the leader I am today.

To all of my close and newfound friends (you know who you are), thank you for the listening ear, the laughter, the nights downtown, the all-nighters pulled the evening before the test, the pep talks, etc. etc. You have been there for me for so many things, and I pray that you'll continue to remain the roots in my growing tree of life. May God bless you all in your future endeavors . . . because I know we'll all be successful!

To the Great Redan High School—faculty, staff, and students—thank you all for your continuous support and for seeing me as a member of the Raider family, even though I'm no longer a student there.

All of my love to my spiritual family at my home church, Revival Church Ministries (Bishop Harold H.

Acknowledgments

Norman—granddaddy), and my home away from home church, Grace Place Church of God by Faith Ministries (Pastor Wayne Mack)—I thank you for your prayers, support, and the ministry I've received while participating in both ministries. Your prayers, encouragement, and care packages are not in vain. I appreciate you for all you do.

To those inspirational authors who've paved the way for me—thank you for being great role models in work and in life that I can look up to as I mature. Your literary works have inspired me beyond comprehension, and I pray that my work is continuously blessed through your words.

To my publishers, Urban Books (Urban Christian), my experiences with you have been some that I will cherish for a lifetime. Thank you for making all my dreams come true. Special appreciation goes out to my editor, Ms. Joylynn Jossel. Thank you for your constructive criticism and for challenging my creativity. I know that I am a better writer because of you.

And finally, to my readers, this book is one that hit very close to home for me, so I can only pray that it will touch you in the same way that it did me. It is my hope that you will turn the last page of this book and realize that for every event in your life, there is a purpose designed by God. It is not your will, but God's will be done!

Chapter 1

The constant banging against his front door was working on Devon's last nerve. He stood in his bathroom, brushing his freshly cut fade; then he smoothed down his mustache and applied lotion to his face. Whoever was knocking at his door, as if they had no sense, was about to find his foot up their behind. He wasn't in the mood for any drama tonight, and he definitely didn't have time to handle someone else's problems.

"Trina!" he yelled as he came out of the bathroom and walked into his bedroom. "Trina, get the door."

His girlfriend was sitting on the king-sized bed with the phone positioned between her right shoulder and ear as she chatted with one of her friends and painted her toenails at the same time. She looked up at him and sighed heavily. "D, my hands are kinda full right now. *You're* not doing anything. You get the door."

"What are you good for?" he mumbled as he walked past her and out into the den.

As he got closer to his front door, the knocking became louder and he could hear someone on the other side calling his name. He hastily unlocked the door and swung it open, nearly sending it off its hinges.

"Big D, man, what took you so long to answer the door?" The uninvited guest breathed heavily as he walked into the house.

Devon looked down at the gentleman who wore nothing but jeans and a white undershirt, despite it being only forty degrees outside. "Antwon, what you want?"

"Man, I just had to handle that punk, Lewis. He tried to stiff me." Antwon continued to gasp for breath.

Looking at the sweat pouring from his acquaintance's forehead, and the gun barely hidden in the side of his pants, Devon guessed that Antwon had fired a few shots at his opponent before making a run for it. *Amateur,* Devon mused as he shook his head.

"You mean, Lewis tried to cheat *me,*" Devon corrected. "Or did you forget my cut?"

"Naw, I got you, man," Antwon assured. "So what we gon' do about this?"

Devon looked at Antwon as if he was missing a piece of the equation. "My bad, I thought you said that *you* already handled it?"

Antwon was still pacing, like he was nervous or extremely angry. "I did. Well, kinda. I got him in his leg and then in his side, but he ain't dead."

"Did you get the money?" Devon asked, pinpointing that was all he cared about.

Antwon stopped pacing long enough to pull the roll of cash out of his jeans pocket. Devon took the stash and counted it, giving Antwon his percentage.

"Go home," Devon said, motioning toward the door.

Antwon looked around nervously. "B-but I ain't never shot nobody before, Big D. What if Lewis snitches and the cops come lookin' for me?"

Devon was starting to get angry. He couldn't believe he had a kid like Antwon working for him. He didn't have time to babysit cowards. "Man, get out my house and go home. Lewis ain't no snitch. He knows me. Trust me, he too scared to rat your sorry behind out to five-oh." He pushed Antwon out the door and shut it in his face before the boy had time to whine.

Locking the door, Devon sighed as he went back into his bedroom. Antwon was only sixteen, but sometimes he acted as if he were ten years younger and in need of a pacifier and a blanket. Devon tried giving him the benefit of the doubt, because Antwon was new to the game, but the teen was beginning to irk him to no end. Devon had a few youngsters like Antwon working for him, but none of them acted as scary as Antwon did. Devon knew he would have to work overtime in order to get the boy in line before he screwed up his entire operation.

At the age of nineteen, Devon Omar Torres's life had become hustling. Starting at the tender age of fifteen, he ran drugs for his street mentor, Kane. He quickly got caught up in making money, and by the time he was a junior in high school, he was ready to drop the books and become a full-time drug peddler. With a mother who couldn't do anything with him, and no father, Devon had no one stopping him. So he readily quit what he despised the most and dived, full speed, into what he loved.

Kane taught Devon everything he needed to know about the streets and the hustlers who ran them. He had promised Devon that when his time came to an end, Devon would be more than welcome to take over Kane's territory, and not even a month after those words escaped Kane's lips, he got killed in a drug deal gone wrong. Devon didn't take much time to mourn, because he realized that Kane would want him to get his streets in check before things got out of order.

After moving into Kane's single-level house, equipped with more than enough furnishings and entertainment, Devon quickly established his name and territory. Soon he was Big D to all of the small peddlers still trying to make it in the game. He now had guys ranging from fourteen to twenty-five running his drugs all over the community, bringing in enough funds to keep his inherited roof over his head. His territory ran ten blocks straight, and he made sure that things ran tightly and remained in order.

Devon always tried to keep a low profile, so he rarely ever sold his own merchandise, but when he did, his customers found it a treat to be able to buy directly from Big D's hands. Sometimes he would have to handle the ones who would spontaneously decide that they didn't want to pay up. Customers like Lewis rarely ever walked away without a bullet wound. Devon figured that saving a few bucks was more important to them than their life. His belief was that as long as he received his money, everything would be cool. Nothing in this world was free, and he felt that the people he associated with should be aware of that by now.

Devon had never murdered anyone, but he had crippled a couple of people in his lifetime. Even he had been afforded his fair share of wounds, but as he looked around his house, he knew he wouldn't trade this life for any other.

He walked back into his bedroom, only to find Trina still on the phone. He shook his head in disapproval as he walked into his closet and grabbed his leather jacket.

"Where are you going?" Trina asked.

Devon stuck his head out of the closet and looked at her. "You talkin' to me?"

She looked around the room and replied, "There's no one else in here except you and me, and I'm surely not talking to myself."

"Well, when you start paying bills round here, you can ask me questions like that." He walked out of the closet and moved toward the door.

Before leaving the room, he heard Trina say, "Uh-huh, girl. He's lucky I love him."

Trina's words made Devon stop in his tracks. They had been dating for nearly a year and she had never told him that she loved him. Devon was thankful for that, though, because if she ever said those three words to him, he wouldn't be able to express the same sentiment in return. He carried too much baggage to allow himself to be in love. The last thing he wanted to do was fall for some girl, and then drag her into his lifestyle. If he ever did have a family, it would surely be after he'd retired from hustling.

But hearing Trina say those words about him caused red flags to go off in his head. When he'd first met Trina Williams, Devon had told her that he wasn't looking for anything serious. All he wanted was a girl he could hang out with when he just wanted to kick back and relax. Trina had been okay with that. But things began to move a little too fast for him when she moved in with him almost six months ago, after she got way behind on her rent and was kicked out of her apartment.

"It's just temporary, babe," Trina had told Devon when she and her girlfriends had first brought her belongings into his house. But by the time the girls had finished lugging in six heavy suitcases, Devon knew he'd gotten himself into trouble.

Having Trina living with him hadn't been so bad at first. She cooked and cleaned and took care of Devon when he was tired and worn-out from working, but after about three months, she grew comfortable. She started using his house phone and would be on it for hours at a time. She stopped cooking, which Devon hadn't stressed about since she wasn't all that good at it, anyway. And she'd started using his personal products, like his razor to shave her legs and his toothbrush to clean her teeth. Devon would've kicked her out of the house long ago if it hadn't been for the intimacy that they shared.

Trina was a very attractive woman. At twenty-one years old, she stood five feet ten inches, and every inch of her caramel-colored body commanded his undivided attention. Devon liked spending time with her, especially after he'd had a long day, because she always knew how to make him feel better. However, her declaration of love made him realize that they needed to slow things down, real quick.

Devon walked out of the house, jumped into his black Lexus, and pulled out of the driveway. He needed some time away from the house and from his business. A round of drinks with his boys was what he needed.

Chapter 2

Saturday afternoon sunrays stirred Devon out of his sleep. He turned over on his stomach and looked at the clock that sat on his dresser: 1:30. He sighed as he sat up in the bed.

"Trina!" he called for his girlfriend. "Trina!"

Trina stuck her head out of the bathroom. "What?"

"Woman, why you let me oversleep like that? You know I always check my blocks on Saturdays," Devon fussed.

Trina shrugged. "I'm not your mama, D. You're the one that stayed out till three in the morning last night."

He cursed as he climbed out of bed and looked at Trina, who was dressed in jeans, a fitted sweater, and a pair of snow boots, as if it already was winter. "Where are you going?" he asked.

She sauntered out of the bathroom and moved toward the den. "If I'm not mistaken, I asked you the same question last night. Did I get an answer?"

"You and your mouth are startin' to get on my nerves," he responded as he followed her.

She glanced back at him as she walked toward the front door. "I'll be back later. And don't worry, I ain't takin' your car. Shakia is here to pick me up."

Devon went into the kitchen and perused the refrigerator. "Hey, Trina, hold up," he said before she could leave the front porch.

"What?" she whined as she turned back toward the house.

"There ain't nothing to eat, up in here!" he yelled to her. "I thought you went shoppin' last week."

"D, I did go shopping, and there is plenty to eat in that kitchen. You just want a bunch of junk food that you know I don't buy or eat." She moved away from the door. "If you want something to eat, eat what I have, or go shopping yourself. I'm gone."

Devon walked up behind her and shut the door with a loud grunt. He never went shopping because he always depended upon Trina to buy the food. She used to buy junk until she got on this crazy diet, he complained inwardly.

"Dang, I got too much to do to be tryna go shoppin'," he muttered as he walked back into his bedroom.

Though he was complaining, Devon knew that he had to handle his business. So after washing up and getting dressed, he proceeded to make sure his business was in order. He checked all of his blocks and collected his money. As he was making his last rounds, he ran into Lewis.

Lewis was a senior at Devon's old high school. He'd had a drug-dependency problem for the last year, and it was starting to take a toll on his academics. He didn't care, though. If Lewis needed a quick fix, he'd do anything to get it. And if that meant trying to cheat an old friend, then so be it.

Lewis walked up to him with one crutch under his arm, and a crooked grin on his face. "Wassup, Big D?" he greeted, stretching his hand out to Devon.

Devon frowned and pushed Lewis back a few steps, nearly knocking him off his feet. "Step off me, man. I heard about you tryin' to step out on my li'l man last night."

Lewis laughed nervously. "Oh, man, th—that was nothing. I ain't meant to cheat him. I just took out the wrong amount."

"Yeah, whatever." Devon moved around the crack-head. "You just better be glad I got my money or else yo' mama woulda been buying that black dress today."

Lewis anxiously chuckled again as he hopped out of Devon's way. "A'ight. You take care, Big D."

Devon shook his head as he got into his car. He almost felt sorry for Lewis, but he'd chosen to live this life, so Devon couldn't mourn too much for him. Besides, guys like Lewis kept his lights on and his water running, so he definitely wasn't going to gripe.

With all blocks checked, Devon headed to the grocery store. It was nearly four o'clock in the afternoon and he hadn't eaten since last night's hot wings, so he was starving. His hunger became obvious when he grabbed a buggy and began throwing any and everything into the basket. Chicken wings, hot dogs, frozen fries, potato chips and dip, cookies, sodas, artificial juices, and anything else he knew Trina wouldn't buy due to her strict diet. As he moved toward the next aisle, Devon narrowly escaped being hit by a shopping cart that was hurriedly making its way to another aisle.

"Dang," Devon said as the woman pushing the cart tried to steady it before it toppled over.

"I'm sorry," she said genuinely, and her soft voice nearly knocked Devon off his feet.

He looked down into her brown eyes and almost tripped as he tried to move out of her way. In his eyes, the young lady was absolutely gorgeous, and he could not move his gaze away from her. She looked to be about eighteen. Her mocha brown skin glistened, and her slim yet shapely frame was one he hadn't seen in a long time. She could definitely knock Trina out of her first-place slot, Devon thought. The girl seemed to become uneasy under his intense gaze, so he literally had to force himself to stop assessing her assets.

"It's cool," Devon finally said. "I shoulda been lookin' where I was goin'."

She smiled. "It's okay. I'm just in a hurry. My mother needs these things for dinner and I'm . . ." She stopped as if she was wondering why she was telling him all of her business.

"I'm Devon," he said, without thinking, as he extended his hand.

She smiled softly and took his hand. "Hi, Devon. I'm Shaniece."

"You can call me D," he offered, realizing he'd revealed his birth name and wanted to make it clear that he preferred to be identified by the initial.

"Okay . . . D." She laughed, and Devon deemed it music to his ears.

They stood with their hands still linked. It was as if they momentarily had forgotten where they were as they stared openly at each other. Devon didn't know what had come over him, but he honestly didn't care. He'd never fawned over a girl like this before. It seemed as if he was attracted to more than just her outer beauty, even though he didn't know anything deeper than her silky smooth skin, soft brown eyes, and captivating smile.

"Niecey," a male voice called out.

Two towering bodies, running down the aisle, caught Devon's attention and broke the connection that he'd been sharing with Shaniece. Shaniece turned toward where Devon's eyes had moved and immediately took her hand out of his. She ran the palm of her hand across her head nervously as she gave her complete attention to the two people.

"Niecey, tell Rainelle that she can't have them cookies," a young boy, who was about six feet tall, only a few inches shorter than Devon's six-foot-four frame, said as he stood next to Shaniece.

The girl who was with him was only a couple of inches shorter. "I *can* have these cookies. Basketball season doesn't start until the end of November." The girl's eyes landed on Devon and her entire demeanor changed. "Who is *this?*" she asked with a smile.

Shaniece looked back at Devon and smiled slightly. "This is my little brother, Keith, and my younger sister, Rainelle." She turned her attention back to her siblings. "Guys, this is Devon."

Devon felt as if "little" and "younger" contradicted the siblings' appearance. Both were taller than Shaniece; however, her mature beauty revealed her seniority. "Wassup?" Devon nodded in their direction, but immediately returned his gaze to Shaniece.

"So, Niecey, tell Rain she can't have the cookies," Keith insisted as if Devon's presence meant nothing to him.

Clearing her throat and forcing her eyes away from the chocolate gentleman before her, Shaniece said, "Rain, put the cookies back. Mama didn't put them on the list, so we can't get them because she only gave us enough money for what she wrote down."

Devon noticed Rainelle's disappointed whimper. He could relate to the young girl because he knew how it felt not to be able to eat whatever he wanted when he wanted. As he was growing up, his mother struggled to keep on the table the little bit of food that they had; so when he wanted something sweet, he would have to settle for sugar water.

"Here, let her get the cookies," Devon suddenly said as he took a money clip from his pocket and offered a twenty-dollar bill to Shaniece.

Shaniece's bewildered expression amused him. "N-no, I can't take this from you. I don't even know you."

"It's cool. I don't mind," he stressed, still holding the money in his hand.

Rainelle was smiling from ear to ear, but Keith's face showed his disapproval. "And what do you get for giving that to my sister?" he asked.

Devon shrugged as he smiled down at Shaniece. "Her phone number would be nice."

"Deal," Rainelle said as she took the money out of Devon's hand. She looked toward her sister. "Well, go on, Niecey, and give him your number."

Shaniece glared at Rainelle in disgust. "I feel like I'm being auctioned off and I *know* I'm worth more than whatever amount of money he can give y'all."

Her sudden confident tone made Devon's smile widen. He concluded that she wasn't as quiet as she appeared. She definitely had a little attitude about her, and he liked that.

"Tell you what," Devon cut in, "you keep the money and take my number and call me whenever you want." As soon as the compromise left his lips, Devon knew there was something special about this girl. He hardly ever gave out his phone number, cellular or home, to anybody who wasn't a part of his business.

Shaniece curiously glared at him as if trying to see what his motive really was. Devon could tell she was trying to read him, and that attracted him to her even more. Not only was she confident, but she was also cautious.

"If you take my number, you have all the control," he added. "It's your choice. You can call me or forget about me, but I'd be disappointed if you dissed me like that." He pouted playfully.

Shaniece unsuccessfully hid her smile when she said, "Okay, I'll take your number." She pulled a small black cell phone out of her purse and handed it to him.

Devon quickly punched in his name and number before handing it back to her. "Please don't disappoint me," he said as he backed away.

"Wait," Shaniece said as she snatched the money out of her sister's hands. "What about your change?"

Devon shrugged. "Keep it and buy as much *junk* as you want."

"Aww, thanks, man." Keith, seemingly over his earlier apprehension, took the money from his oldest sister.

Devon laughed as he watched Rainelle grab the money from him as if to say that it all belonged to her. He left the siblings to fight over it as they ran off toward the snack aisle, with Shaniece calling after them. Before leaving, she opted to take one more look at the handsome stranger who had made a notable first impression. Devon knew she hadn't expected him to be looking in her direction still, but when she turned around, their eyes locked. She afforded him one last smile and a thank-you before walking away to find her siblings. Devon watched her until she was out of sight. He shook his head to gain control of his thoughts as he grabbed his last grocery item and headed for the checkout counter.

Chapter 3

Natalie Simmons studied the grocery receipt and frowned when she noticed the total amount of money that had been spent. She then began going through the groceries that her children had just lugged into the house, but she couldn't find the two bags of Doritos, the box of crackers, the package of marshmallows, and the pack of Oreo cookies that were listed on the receipt.

"Shaniece, get down here," Natalie called.

Her call to her oldest daughter drew all of her children down the stairs, signaling that something was definitely out of order. Once they stood in the kitchen, Natalie held up the receipt.

"Why are these on this receipt?" Natalie pointed out the listed snack items.

Rainelle and Keith looked toward their sister as if she had the answer written on her forehead.

Shaniece pretended as if she didn't know exactly what her mother was asking, "What do you mean, Mama?"

Natalie placed her left hand on her hip. "Don't act stupid, Shaniece. I gave you fifty dollars for a few items that I would need for dinner. The last time I checked, I did not need cookies and chips to make gumbo." She shoved the receipt in Shaniece's face. "Now, where are these snacks that are printed out on this receipt, and where did this extra money come from?"

Shaniece shifted her feet as she looked at the receipt as if studying it. "Umm . . ."

"Mama, me and Rainelle wanted some cookies and stuff, because we knew we can't have them no more after this month is over, so I took some extra money with me so we could get something." Keith spoke confidently, as though telling the honest truth. "They're upstairs in my room."

Natalie glared at her son and then moved her gaze to her youngest daughter. "Rainelle?" she called.

Rainelle nodded. "He's telling the truth."

Her mother raised her eyebrows. "Did I ask you if he was telling the truth?"

"Umm . . . no, but—"

Natalie shifted her eyes toward Shaniece. "Where did this money come from? And the next person who lies to me is in serious trouble."

Shaniece sighed deeply. "This guy gave it to us because he heard me telling Rain and Keith that we didn't have enough money to get the snacks."

"What guy?" Natalie questioned, with both her hands now on her hips.

Shaniece shrugged. "Just some guy who was grocery shopping."

"And this guy is a complete stranger to you?"

Shaniece lowered her eyes, not wanting to answer her mother's question.

"So what did you give him?"

"Huh?"

Natalie's eyes narrowed. "Don't 'huh' me, Shaniece. Now, I've always told you to never, *ever* take anything from any guy because he'll always want something in return," she began to yell. "Was he so *fine* that you forgot everything I've ever told you about strange guys who *seem* to be nice?"

"No, Mama," Rainelle broke in. "Niecey didn't give him anything. He just wanted to talk to her, but she wouldn't give him her number, so he gave her his."

Natalie stared at Rainelle as if her explanation did little to calm her temper. "And you plan to call him?" she asked Shaniece.

Shaniece shrugged as she lowered her eyes. "I don—"

Natalie shook her head. "Don't do this again," she warned sharply as she cut her daughter off. "Ooh, Jesus. Y'all done got me all heated. You lucky your daddy's at the church, 'cause he wouldn't have handled this as calmly as I did."

The children exchanged glances, and though they knew that their mother hadn't been as calm as she thought she had, they realized that she was telling the truth.

"Bring that junk down here and keep it down here." Natalie left the kitchen and walked toward her bedroom. "And put the rest of those groceries away."

As their mother walked off, the kids moved into the kitchen and began to finish the job that Natalie had left for them to do. Keith immediately ran upstairs and retrieved the junk food from his room and brought it back into the kitchen, where he placed the items in the snack cupboard, which was usually filled with their father's rice cakes.

As Shaniece put away the vegetables, she released a sigh of relief. She was sure that her mother was about to give her a good tongue-lashing about taking the money Devon had offered her. She wouldn't have taken it if it had required her having to give him her number; but since he'd offered his number, instead, Shaniece hadn't seen any risks in accepting it. For all he knew, she could've deleted his number as soon as they departed from each other.

Shaniece had to fight to keep the smile away from her face as she thought about Devon. Her mother had been right in her assumption that Devon was so fine that she'd almost forgotten all she'd been taught. His six-foot-plus, muscular frame was covered in milk chocolate skin that appeared smooth, and begged to be touched. And his caressing brown eyes and sensual full lips caused her to blush each time he looked into her eyes and smiled. He looked to be in his early twenties, and by the diamond studs in his ears, the platinum chain around his neck, and the expensive-looking watch on his wrist, Shaniece could tell he was a hardworking man.

"Niecey," Keith called out, with a bag of onions in his hand.

"Huh?" Shaniece responded in somewhat of a daze.

He nudged her. "Why are you just standing there with the refrigerator wide open like that?" he asked.

Shaniece hadn't even noticed that she was positioned in front of the open refrigerator, but she welcomed its cool air, needing a reprieve from the heat she felt flow to her face as she thought about Devon. She frowned as her brother pushed her aside and shoved the fridge door closed before placing the bag of onions in the corner of the counter, along with the potatoes he'd placed there earlier.

With her hands on her hips, Rainelle looked at her sister. "She thinking 'bout that boy from the grocery store." She smiled. "So are you gonna call him, or do I have to do it?"

Shaniece avoided looking at her fifteen-year-old sister. Rainelle was five feet nine inches and 140 pounds, with slim curves and long legs. While Shaniece's five-seven and 130-pound frame attracted more attention from guys, it was Rainelle's loud and boisterous attitude that gained her many friends—male and female alike. Her status as the only sophomore on Riverside High School's Lady Jaguars varsity basketball team had made her one of the most popular people in school. Shaniece loved her sister because Rainelle didn't care what people thought about her; she was happy as long as she was being herself. Shaniece felt the same way and thanked her mother for passing that trait down to them.

"Hel-lo," Rainelle said, gaining her sister's attention. "Are you going to call the boy or not?"

Shaniece frowned. "I don't know, Rain. I don't even know him."

Rainelle rolled her eyes. "That's kinda the point of calling him."

"Rain, please. Whether I call him or not is my business."

Keith gathered the empty grocery bags and placed them in a narrow cabinet that held a box of garbage bags, in case they could be used later. "Well, personally, any guy who will just give a girl he's only known for five minutes twenty dollars is bad news. He probably does crap like that all the time and got girls coming in and out his crib 'cause of it."

"Keith, you were all for taking that money," Shaniece pointed out.

"Yeah, 'cause I wanted some chips, but that don't mean you should do that all the time."

Shaniece shook her head. Rainelle and Keith were a lot alike. They both were tall, loud, and very opinionated. At fourteen, Keith was a freshman at Riverside, and he held a starting position on the school's junior varsity boys' basketball team. With his smooth coffee-colored skin, thick brows, and long lashes, Keith was known to attract a few girls of his own, and he believed that made him an expert when it came to the games guys played.

"Like I said, whatever decision I make is my business," Shaniece said as she left the kitchen and went upstairs to her bedroom.

She turned on the radio, which sat on her dresser, before going over and lying back on her bed and settling into the coolness of her pillows. Saturday was always her day of relaxation. Her mother would usually have her run errands in the early afternoon, but by four o'clock, Shaniece would be settled in her room, away from the rest of her family members.

Her father, Cedric Simmons, usually spent Saturdays at Creekside Church of God in Christ, finalizing his Sunday morning sermon, so he wouldn't be seen until late in the evening when it was time for dinner. Keith and Rainelle would soon leave the house for the park to play a couple rounds of one-on-one in order to prepare for the up-and-coming basketball season. Natalie would start on dinner and laundry, which would keep her busy for the next several hours. So Shaniece was free to do whatever satisfied her mood.

She hummed along with Chrisette Michele's "Love Is You" as she flipped through her assigned book of the month. Her book club, Ladies of Literature, was scheduled to meet on the first Saturday in November, and she had two weeks to finish *Lady Jasmine,* a novel by Victoria Christopher Murray. The *Essence* multiple best-selling author was one of Shaniece's favorites. She'd read all of the woman's books and had met the Delta Sigma Theta Sorority member twice. She made a mental note to be at the author's next Atlanta event.

She sighed as her cell phone began to ring. *As soon as I get into the book, somebody wants to talk,* she thought as she grabbed her phone off her computer desk. She glanced at the caller ID and smiled, despite her annoyance.

"Hey, Tati," Shaniece greeted her best friend.

"Hey, girl. What's goin' on?" Tatiana asked.

"Same old, same old," Shaniece answered, although her mind revisited her encounter with Devon.

"Well, I'm going to the mall tonight because Macy's is having this sale and it ends today. I was calling to see if you wanted to come with me."

"You know we have church in the morning and have to be up early for that," Shaniece said. "How late are you planning to stay out?"

"Well, it's about five o'clock now, and I wanted to get there and back home before eight."

"All right, I'll ask my mom about it. I'm sure it will be okay." She smiled as she added, "And, boy, do I have something to tell you."

"So, is he cute?" Tatiana asked as they arrived at the mall.

Shaniece climbed out of the passenger side of the car and shut her door. "He is *fine*, but I still don't know if I should call him."

"Why not?" Tatiana asked as they began walking toward the entrance of the mall.

"Because I don't know him," Shaniece stressed.

As they passed through the Macy's entrance door, Tatiana interlocked her arm with Shaniece's. "Girl, the boy gave you twenty dollars just to hit him up."

"And that's another thing. What guy just gives a girl some money without any motive behind it?"

Tatiana smiled. "Craig gives you money all the time," she said, speaking of their mutual friend.

"A dollar for a soda and twenty dollars for a bag of cookies and a phone call are two different things," Shaniece pointed out. "Besides, I've known Craig since the sixth grade; I just met Devon today."

"Look, I don't see the problem." Tatiana began looking through winter sweaters. "You said he was fine and he was nice. I'll admit the money thing would've turned me off a little too, but you didn't give him anything for it, so it's cool. He put you in complete control of initiating a relationship, so this is all up to you."

As she stood with her hands on her hips and her lips pursed in disbelief, Shaniece glared at her friend. "Are you telling me that you don't have an open opinion on this matter?"

"Oh, I ain't sayin' all that," Tatiana said, with exaggerated hand movements. "I think you should call him just to see what he's all about. But like I said, it's up to you."

Shaniece watched her friend pick up two of the same sweaters in two different colors before moving toward a rack of blue jeans. Shaniece stifled a laugh as she watched a man, who was visibly old enough to be Tatiana's father, nearly trip over his own feet as he tried to watch the movement of her best friend's hips as she sauntered around the department store.

Tatiana Knowles, at five feet five inches tall, carried enough confidence and attitude for at least three people. Her dark cocoa-colored skin was clear of acne and blemishes, and her nearly jet-black hair was either pulled back in a slick bun or combed down, bob style. Tatiana always kept herself looking her best because, as she put it, she never knew when Mr. Right was going to come along.

Well, I hope Grandpa doesn't think that he's Mr. Right, Shaniece mused as she watched the man play off his stumble and continue toward the exit doors. She moved quickly to catch up with her friend as Tatiana grabbed more and more clothes as if they were going to disappear, along with the sale, at the end of the day.

"Tati, why are you buying all of these winter clothes now?" Shaniece asked. "It's still fall."

Tatiana tossed Shaniece an irritated glance that spoke volumes. "You don't need to worry about what I'm doing. You need to be worrying about that Devlin boy."

Shaniece laughed. "It's Devon, and I'm not even thinking about calling him," she declared.

"Yeah, right," her friend retorted. "If you aren't thinking about him, why are you walking around with your cell phone out as if you're about to call somebody?"

Shaniece looked down at her right hand, which Tatiana was pointing to. She hadn't even noticed that she was holding her phone. She'd taken it out long ago to check the time, but as she looked down at the device, she noticed that she had opened her contact list and the highlighted name read, D (Ur Man).

"Confident, ain't he?" Tatiana chuckled as she looked at the screen name Devon had chosen. "You're blushing," she pointed out before walking away.

Shaniece tried to force the smile off her face, but it only grew wider. Devon was a man who was very sure of himself. Part of Shaniece liked that, but she prayed that it did not foreshadow any cockiness. She couldn't stand a cocky man, but she could get comfortable with a confident one.

Chapter 4

Every Sunday, it had become routine for Devon to pick up the phone and call his mother. He didn't know why, but Sundays seemed like the right day to check in on her to make sure she was okay. Maybe it was the fact that on most Sundays, Devon would find his mother sleeping restlessly in her bedroom after shedding endless tears the night before because he hadn't come home. That had been years ago, though. After he left home, almost four years ago, his mother, then thirty-two years old, had stopped crying, but she continued to pray for him.

Since he'd left home, his mother had gotten back into going to church regularly, which she wouldn't do as often when she had been worried about Devon running the streets. She would frequently invite Devon to the eleven o'clock services, knowing he wouldn't want to accompany her; he never had.

Though they lived within twenty minutes of each other, Devon could count on one hand the number of times he'd seen his mother. He had been adamant about her not visiting him in such a rough neighborhood for the sake of her personal safety. And since he was always so busy with running his business, he rarely made the trip across town to check in on her.

Their last reunion occurred when he'd stopped by her house to give her a birthday gift back in August. He remembered Yvonne Westbrook kindly refusing the diamond earrings because she knew they had been purchased with illegal money. He wanted to hate his mother for silently judging him, but he could only love her because of how hard she'd worked to give him a stable home.

Devon's biological father had abandoned him and his mother when Devon was just three years old. Devon always despised the fact that he carried the selfish man's last name. His mother had her share of male friends, but none stuck around long enough for Devon to deem him "father." So he turned toward the streets for his role model. Living without a steady male role model in the house hadn't only been hard on Devon; it had its effect on Yvonne also. She worked two jobs to keep food on the table and clothes on her son's back. Christmases and birthdays weren't filled with gifts, but Devon knew his mother had tried her hardest, when, on his birthday, she would purchase a Little Debbie snack cake from the vending machine at her job and bring it home for him. There were no candles, but Yvonne would always ask her son to make a wish. Year after year, Devon's wish was always the same: a better life than the one he shared with his mother. Christmases were just the same. No family or material gifts to enhance the holiday. The only gift his mother could afford was her gift of song as she sang carols, but Devon had always been thankful for her effort.

It wasn't until he got into high school and saw how all of his friends sported the latest designs in clothes and shoes that his desire for a better life became stronger. When he was introduced to Kane, everything changed—everything, except the way he felt about his mother. He worked his hardest on the streets with the image in his mind of his mother sitting in a large living room of a four-bedroom, two-story brick home. Every time Yvonne fussed at him about the life he was becoming addicted to, Devon would pull a wad of money out of his pocket and say, "I'm doing this for you, Mama." Yvonne tried holding on to him for as long as she could, but once Devon dropped out of school, she had to let him go.

Devon knew that putting him out of the house was one of the hardest things Yvonne ever had to do, but in the last few years, he'd realized that it was the best thing she'd done for herself in years. Yvonne had put her life on hold for him, and it wasn't until he was out on his own—and his mother began to participate in things for her own enjoyment—that Devon realized he had been holding her back. He was glad that she'd done what she had. In the long run, her putting him out had helped both of them achieve the goals that they'd set for themselves.

"Hey, Mama," Devon greeted after the phone had rung several times. "You just gettin' home from church?"

"You know it," Yvonne answered, a smile in her tone. "And Reverend preached a good Word that reminded me of you."

Devon rolled his eyes heavenward. He wasn't in the mood for a sermon today; he just wanted to make sure his mother was alive and doing fine.

Noticing his silence, Yvonne laughed. "Boy, I'm not about to preach to you. I know how you feel about that."

"'Preciate it," he said in all sincerity.

"So how you been?" she asked.

"Good," Devon replied. "What about you? How you been doin'?"

"Blessed," Yvonne said. "God's been good to me. Are you still with that girl, Tina?"

"Trina," he corrected. "Yeah, I'm still wit' her."

"So, are you serious about her, or is this just some prolonged temporary arrangement?"

Devon could hear the disparagement in Yvonne's voice, and he wasn't in the mood for a lecture either. "It's not serious. I'm just chillin' wit' her." As he'd done in the last six months, he decided against telling his mother that Trina was now living with him.

"Boy, you're nineteen, going on twenty in a few months," Yvonne said as if she needed to remind her son how old he was. "You need to do something with your life and *chillin'* ain't gon' get you anywhere with a decent girl."

Devon was silent as he thought about Shaniece. She seemed to be above and beyond a *decent* girl, but he hadn't heard from her and was sure that she'd forgotten about him. She could probably tell that all he was up for was *chillin',* but Devon wasn't about to change for anybody, so he figured the best thing she could do was forget about him. Now all he had to do was stop thinking about her.

Instead of replying to his mother's statement, Devon turned the tables on her. "So what about you? You found a man yet?"

Yvonne laughed. "Honey, I don't need a man to complete me. The last guy I dated thought I should put him before God, and he got kicked to the curb real quick. As far as I'm concerned, God is the only man I need in my life right now."

"I hear you," he agreed. "Besides, I don't wanna have to come over there and beat some old dude down 'cause he tryna run game on you."

"You know me. I can definitely handle myself, but I don't mind calling on you if need be."

The line was silent for a few moments, and Devon knew his mother was about to return him to the center of the conversation.

"So, are you still trappin'?" Yvonne asked quietly as if someone would be listening.

Devon never felt comfortable discussing his job with his mother. He was so uncomfortable with sharing his lifestyle with her that he made her promise never to set foot on his side of town. It was for both their well-being.

He was well aware of the fact that she knew where all of his money came from, but it still didn't make the conversation a pleasant one for him. His mother always tried talking him out of hustling and would voice her desire for him to go back to school, but Devon would never hear of it. Dealing had gotten him the lifestyle he'd always dreamed of, and he didn't want to let go of that.

"I guess that's a 'yes,'" Yvonne assumed aloud after the lengthened silence.

"Ma, I don't wanna—"

"I know," she interrupted. "I'm not going to say anything, except that I'm always praying for you, and I love you no matter what."

"I love you too, Mama," Devon replied, relieved. "I gotta go, but I'll talk to you soon."

"All right. You take care of yourself."

"Always," he said before saying good-bye and hanging up the phone.

Devon climbed out of bed and went to use the bathroom. Once he was finished, he washed his hands and went out into the den to watch television. Trina was sitting on the couch, eating a bowl of fruit and talking on the phone. He was glad that his home number was listed as private. The way Trina used his phone, everyone on the west side of Atlanta would be calling his house, otherwise.

Devon was not in the mood to watch any type of Lifetime movie, so he took the remote out of Trina's lap and flipped through the channels. He saw the distasteful look his girlfriend threw at him, but she didn't bother to argue. Devon felt she had made a good choice.

After flipping through the channels several times, he settled for watching *Paid in Full* on BET for the millionth time. The movie was one of his favorites, probably because it somewhat mirrored the way he lived his life: on the streets, with nobody but gangsters and drug dealers to have his back. He actually understood why by the end of the movie, the main character, Ace, gave up his gangster lifestyle and turned to what was most important: his family. But because Devon had no family, other than his mother, to rely on, he had no motive to stop living his illegal lifestyle. Though his mother openly disapproved of what he did, Devon couldn't see how it directly affected her. Unless he saw otherwise, he would continue to make his money the only way he knew how.

"Baby, let's go somewhere."

Devon was almost fast asleep on the sofa when he heard Trina's soft request. He opened his eyes and looked at her, momentarily caught off guard when he saw Shaniece's beautiful face staring back at him. "Huh?" he mumbled, shaking his head to get rid of his disoriented thoughts.

"I said, 'Let's go somewhere,'" Trina repeated, looking into his eyes.

Devon didn't feel like going anywhere, but he settled for asking, "Go where?"

Trina shrugged as she sat up straighter on the couch. "I don't know. Anywhere is fine with me," she said. "We don't go out anymore, and I'm bored just sitting in the house all day."

"Well, you shoulda called my mama and went to church with her this morning," he said jokingly.

"And speaking of your mother, when am I going to meet her?" she asked curiously.

Blaring sirens and flashing red lights began to go off in Devon's head. He saw the big sign that read, STOP BEFORE IT'S TOO LATE! He had to find a way out of this one. "Why do you want to meet her?"

Trina looked around, taken aback, because the answer was so obvious. "Because she's *your* mother." She moved closer to Devon. "Baby, come on. We've been dating for a year, and I think it's about that time."

Devon's eyes opened wide as he struggled to keep from screaming out in fear. "About *what* time?" he questioned knowingly.

"D, don't play," Trina fussed. "Now, I'm tired of playing house. When are we gonna step this relationship up to the next level?"

Oh, it's time to get rid of this chick, he thought as he looked at Trina as if she were out of her mind. "Trina, I told you that I ain't lookin' for nothin' serious."

"But it's been almost a year," she countered. "You have to have had a change of heart by now."

"Baby, look," he said as he pulled her closer to him, trying to find a way out of this conversation without losing the level of comfort he shared with her. "I'm fine with the way things are, right now. I been wit' you for a year, and I ain't goin' nowhere, so why complicate things by getting caught up?"

"I'm not talking about getting caught up. I'm talking about a commitment, D," she said, looking into his eyes so he could see how serious she was. "Shoot, I'm twenty-one and I want to have a family . . . as in a husband and some children. And I want that with you." She poked him in his chest to add emphasis to her words.

Trina had never seemed so serious about anything before, and Devon hated that marriage would be the first thing she ever considered with a sincere heart. As far as Devon was concerned, both he and Trina were way too young to be thinking about having such a serious relationship. He had no plans to settle down anytime soon, but he liked having Trina around, no matter how much she worked his nerves.

Before he could respond to her heartfelt words, Trina leaned forward and kissed him softly. Devon pulled her closer and deepened their kiss, secretly thanking her for rescuing him from a response. He knew that this wouldn't be the end of this conversation, though, and he mentally prepared himself for those that would follow.

Chapter 5

Shaniece locked the doors to her Ford Fusion as she and her siblings exited the car. She had just received the used car from her uncle, who felt that because she was such an excellent student, and an even better niece, she deserved to ride to school in style, instead of in an old, dingy yellow school bus.

She tightened her grip on her books as she followed her brother and sister into Riverside High School. The two-story building was a fairly new school. Shaniece was amongst the first group of students to be enrolled into the educational institute, nearly four years ago, and she loved the school and the people that she interacted with on a daily basis.

"Good morning, Mr. Hutchinson," she greeted her principal, who stood at the front door.

The man returned her smile and said, "Good morning, Ms. Simmons."

She continued walking and laughed when she saw her siblings give her a disapproving look. "What?"

"You are such a principal's pet," Keith said.

"I know," Rainelle agreed. "What self-respecting student actually holds a conversation with the principal, or any other administrator for that matter?"

Shaniece raised one arched eyebrow and replied, "One who wants a good recommendation for college. Y'all better get with the program."

They walked into the commons, where many of the students convened until the first bell signaled their release to their first-period class. While Keith and Rainelle went to socialize with their friends and teammates, Shaniece took a seat at her usual table, with Tatiana and some of their friends.

"Hey, Niecey," a few of the females sitting at the table greeted.

Shaniece smiled as she waved at them. "Hey."

"Wassup, Shaniece?"

Shaniece smiled as she looked across the table at the male who had waited for everyone else to give their greetings before offering his. "Hi, Craig. How was your weekend?"

"It was a'ight," Craig replied. "It would've been better if you woulda came to the movies with me on Saturday night." He pretended to pout. "I had to go by myself."

Shaniece laughed softly. "I'm sorry, but when you called, I was out with Tati. *She* wanted to catch some sale at the last minute." She cast a sidelong glance at her best friend, seated next to her. "Maybe next time, okay?"

He smiled. "I'ma hold you to that."

Tatiana discreetly elbowed Shaniece in her side, and Shaniece didn't even have to look at her friend to know what she was thinking. Anyone with common sense knew that Craig Davidson had a serious crush on Shaniece. They had been friends since middle school, but it wasn't until their junior year in high school that Craig openly began to show interest in her. Shaniece had to admit that Craig was very handsome. He was a little over six feet tall, with intensely dark eyes. He kept his thick, curly hair cut low, and his fair complexion was always radiant. Hardly ever without a pleasant attitude, Craig always kept a smile on Shaniece's face, but in all the years she had known him, she hadn't thought of him as anything more than a friend.

The first bell rang, releasing the students to their first-period class. Shaniece and Tatiana went to their lockers to retrieve their Advanced Placement Macro-economics books.

"Have you finished reading this month's book?" Shaniece asked as she slipped out of her jacket and placed it in the locker.

Tatiana gave her friend an amused glance. "*Girl,* that book is a mess," she indirectly answered with a laugh. "I'm glad that Jasmine girl is just a fictional character, because if she weren't, I think I'd want to find her just to knock some sense into her head."

Shaniece laughed also. "Hey, some people do crazy things for love."

"Yeah, like paying somebody twenty dollars to call them." Tatiana was laughing as if she'd just told the most hilarious joke ever heard, but Shaniece only glared at her friend with her mouth open wide in disbelief. "So, have you called him yet?" Tatiana asked after she'd caught her breath.

Shaniece closed the locker and they began walking toward their class. "No. I haven't had time."

Tatiana rolled her eyes and chuckled softly. "I bet you, he won't be handing out money to random females anymore. As he can see, it doesn't get him anywhere."

Shaniece decided against telling her friend that she'd tried dialing Devon's number several times last night, but she couldn't get up enough nerve to allow the call to completely go through. She wasn't sure if she should call him. She was positive that he'd forgotten about her already. He probably had females doing any and everything to get his attention; Shaniece was just one in the number. Though she desired to have a relationship in which she could share her time with a guy who was genuinely interested in her, she didn't want to be just another notch in a man's belt.

By the end of the day, Shaniece was ready for the week to be over. She had been assigned two projects, and they were both due within the next week. She hated when teachers assigned multitudes of work without taking into consideration that their students had other classes, with other work to complete and turn in.

As the last bell rang, Shaniece grabbed her books and headed for her locker. She smiled when Craig walked up beside her and offered to carry her books.

"That's okay," she said. "I've got it."

"You sure?" he questioned with extended hands, illustrating his offer to help.

She laughed. "It's only two books. I'm sure I can handle it, but thank you, anyway."

The hall was crowded and those students walking in the opposite direction of Shaniece continued to bump into her, causing her to nudge Craig in his side continuously.

She looked up at her friend. "I'm sorry, Craig," she offered. "I guess these underclassmen haven't been taught any manners." She glared at a young boy who was practically running and pushing people aside in order to get wherever he was going.

"It's okay. I'm not complaining." Craig smiled down at her.

Shaniece turned away from his stare and sped up her walk so that she could get to her locker. She was anxious to rid her arms of the heavy books she'd been determined to carry so that Craig wouldn't mistake an acceptance of his offer to help as a return of his affections.

"Are you coming to the NHS meeting this afternoon?"

Shaniece looked back at Craig as her eyes widened in horror. "There's a National Honor Society meeting *today?*"

Craig nodded. "They said it during the announcements. It's an emergency officers' meeting."

She sighed as she went to her locker and entered the combination. As she put her books away, she pulled out her cell phone so that she could call her parents and let them know she wouldn't be home for another hour. She silently prayed that she wouldn't be reprimanded for not having informed her parents of the meeting prior to this afternoon. As Shaniece waited for someone to answer her call, Tatiana walked up to the locker. She had the most annoyed look on her face.

"Did you know about the NHS meeting today?" Tatiana asked in an irritated tone.

Shaniece rolled her eyes. "Craig just told me," she said as she pointed toward Craig, who was still standing next to her. "I couldn't hear the announcement because of those noisy kids in my class." She held up one finger to stop Tatiana's response as she said, "Hello? Ma?"

"What is it, Niecey?" Natalie questioned as if she had something better to do than to carry on a conversation with her daughter.

Shaniece noticed her mother's tone and knew that she had interrupted something important. "Sorry to bother you, but I have to stay after school for a meeting. I should be home by five o'clock."

"That's fine," Natalie said. "But remember you still have to go back out to the school to pick up Keith and Rain from basketball practice."

Shaniece had forgotten that her siblings were staying after school today also. "Okay, bye."

Her mother barely said good-bye before hanging up the phone. Shaniece stared at her cell phone for a moment as though looking for something to jump out of it.

"What's wrong?" Craig asked.

"I must've interrupted something, because my mom was acting like she wanted to rebuke me for calling her." Shaniece gave a small laugh as she placed her phone back into her purse.

"Mmm," Tatiana grunted. "I guess we know what the reverend does in order to release stress after exhausting Sunday services."

"Ooh." Shaniece held her right palm up in her best friend's face. "Please don't say that. I don't need that image in my mind."

They laughed as they headed toward the NHS sponsor's classroom. While Shaniece was the treasurer for the honor club, Tatiana was the president and Craig was the historian. The club was well known throughout the school for its academic successes and community service. Shaniece liked being a part of the association, but it annoyed her that their club adviser, Mr. Patwell, was known to schedule impromptu meetings.

When they arrived at the classroom, they found that the rest of the officers—the vice president, Tony; the recording secretary, Constance; the corresponding secretary, Rosa; and the parliamentarian, Frank—had already arrived and were waiting for them. Greetings were exchanged as Craig, Tatiana, and Shaniece took their seats.

"Okay, now that everyone is here, let's get started," Mr. Patwell said from his position behind his desk. "I called this meeting because we are a little behind schedule this year. It's nearly November and we have yet to induct the new NHS members. So we need to get on top of that. Mark your calendars. . . . Induction for the new members will be next Monday."

Shaniece opened her notebook and calendar and wrote down the date.

"So basically we're going to have to skip preliminaries," Constance insinuated.

Mr. Patwell shook his head. "Not at all. The nominees have already filled out their forms, and Tatiana, Tony, and I went through and selected the ones who qualified for induction. We've just been so busy with other things that we haven't been able to let them know that they've been accepted."

"So when will that be handled?" Shaniece questioned.

"Between tomorrow and Wednesday," Mr. Patwell replied. "We want to send home notifications no later than Thursday. It's short notice, but it is much better than having the students go home on Monday afternoon and inform their parents that they have an induction ceremony to attend that same evening."

Tony raised his hand and was acknowledged by Mr. Patwell to proceed with his question. "I know that you wanted the display board to be a part of the decorations for the induction ceremony, but it is still incomplete."

Mr. Patwell nodded. "This meeting is only about induction, so if a few of you could stay afterward, I'm sure we could get the display board complete by five o'clock."

"I'll stay," Shaniece immediately volunteered, since she'd already told her mother that she wouldn't be home until that time.

Shaniece's willingness to stay behind prompted Craig to do the same. Shaniece ignored her best friend's stare when Craig suddenly raised his hand and offered his assistance.

"I don't mind either," Tatiana said as she glanced at Shaniece. "I think it would be good for me to keep watch over things."

Shaniece cut her eyes at Tatiana, who was trying to suppress a smile. Tatiana had nothing to worry about, because Shaniece could handle Craig's subtle advances without her help.

After Mr. Patwell offered to pick up the celebration cake, they discussed who would bring the cups and sodas for refreshments. Balloons and banners would be placed on display in the auditorium immediately after school on Monday. Once they agreed on dressy attire of black and white, the meeting was dismissed. Mr. Patwell left the volunteers to work in his classroom, requesting that they have a janitor lock up his room before leaving.

"Okay, so let's get started on this board," Tatiana said after everyone had departed. "I am not trying to be here all night."

Shaniece chuckled as she listened to Tatiana complain, acting as if someone had forced her to stay behind. She walked into Mr. Patwell's closet to retrieve the unfinished display board. "All we have to do is finish the service and leadership sections, so this shouldn't take long."

"Craig, do you see those pictures from last year's Festival of Trees event in that box?" Tatiana asked as Craig looked through a box that was full of the club's history. "And also the pictures from the Atlanta Food Drive we did. For the leadership section, we can just put up the pictures of each of the officers we took earlier this year."

Craig retrieved everything Tatiana had asked for and handed them to Shaniece.

"Thank you." She smiled.

"You are most welcome," Craig replied, smiling widely.

As they began to work, both Shaniece and Tatiana took notice of how Craig complimented everything Shaniece did. When she placed the colorful borders around each of the pictures, he remarked how great of an idea that had been. And when she had used a ruler to mark where each picture would be placed on the board, he praised her for her precision.

"So, Craig, how do you like the letters *I* made," Tatiana suddenly asked with exaggeration. "Aren't they *wonderful?*"

Craig looked at the large letters that Tatiana had stenciled and cut to near perfection and nodded, with a slight shrug. "Yeah, they're straight."

Tatiana rolled her eyes and laughed as she glanced at Shaniece, who had caught on to what she had been trying to prove.

"Okay, you guys," Shaniece said, "we're almost done. All we have to do now is glue down the officers' pictures."

As they wrapped up the project by placing the officers' photos on the board, Craig acknowledged how photogenic Shaniece was.

"Thank you, Craig. Your picture is nice too," Shaniece said, smiling slightly.

It was only four forty-five by the time they had finished, and they were all proud of the completed product. They left the board by Mr. Patwell's desk so he would be able to see it first thing tomorrow morning. After asking a nearby janitor to lock up the room, Craig followed Tatiana and Shaniece to their locker and waited for them as they retrieved their belongings; then they proceeded to leave the building.

"So, do you have any important phone calls to make this evening?" Tatiana asked Shaniece as the trio made their way to the student parking lot.

Shaniece narrowed her eyes and wanted to strangle her friend for bringing up Devon in front of Craig. Though she held no romantic feelings for her friend, she knew he would be disappointed to hear that she could possibly be taking up company with another guy. She'd let him down easy before, and though it was apparent that he hadn't gotten the message, Shaniece didn't want to flaunt Devon in Craig's face.

"Not that I know of," Shaniece said tightly, throwing Tatiana a look that told her to drop the subject.

Tatiana obeyed, but only for a moment. As soon as Craig said his prolonged good-byes, Tatiana asked to use Shaniece's cell phone.

"Why?" Shaniece asked cautiously.

"Because my battery died an hour ago and I need to make an important phone call," Tatiana explained. "Please?"

Shaniece hesitantly yielded her phone and watched as Tatiana punched a few buttons before bringing the phone to her ear.

Soon she heard her friend saying, "Hi, Devon. This is Shaniece's friend Tatiana."

Shaniece's mouth fell open in shock as she immediately tried to grab the phone out of Tatiana's hand. "Tati!" she yelled.

Tatiana quickly moved out of the way and continued walking around the parking lot with the phone to her ear as if on a business call.

"I'm gonna kill you!" Shaniece shouted after her friend.

Shaniece watched in pure horror as Tatiana spoke quickly into the receiver. By the way her friend talked without taking a breath, Shaniece could tell Tatiana was leaving a message, but that didn't calm her beating heart. She knew that before the night was over, Devon would return the call. Shaniece had decided that if his name showed up on her caller ID, she wouldn't answer.

Chapter 6

As darkness began to fall, Devon stood in front of the corner store not too far from his house. He leaned against the building with his right foot set against the wall and his left supporting the rest of his body. He watched as kids rode by on bicycles and adults drove by in their cars. Some people walked along the street, and a few sat on the corner as if they were waiting for someone or something.

Standing in front of this corner store brought back many memories for Devon. This had been one of his assigned posts when he was under Kane's mentorship. He'd stood on this corner almost seven days a week, selling marijuana and crack to anyone who wished to purchase or barter for it. He had been frisked by police here, had been chased from, and shot at, in front of this store. Today, Devon was prepared to defend his business in front of this store. He'd been called to "work" because he'd been informed that a frequent customer of one of his peddlers was cheating him out of his money. Devon hated when he received information like this, because it meant that he'd most likely have to beat somebody near death. He hated fighting, but he had no problems doing so if need be.

He had been standing in front of the store for about an hour and had sold a few ounces of his merchandise, but he still hadn't gotten a glimpse of Chester, the guy who was supposedly cheating him out of his profits.

Devon had vowed to stand out by the store all night if that's what it took to catch this guy.

"Big D."

Devon nodded toward a guy in a black hooded sweatshirt who was walking down the street. He didn't bother to return a greeting, because it would distract him from the job at hand.

A few minutes later, Devon spotted Chester walking up to the corner store. Chester was only twenty-seven, but years of drug abuse and alcoholism had caused him to physically age far beyond his years. The cane that supported Chester's limp walk tapped against the concrete as he made his way toward Devon.

"Oh, Big D," the gentleman called out.

Devon cut his eyes toward Chester and didn't bother to smile.

"You takin' care of me today?" Chester asked. "Man, you done made my day," he said, smiling. "What you got for me?"

Devon eased his hand out of his pocket and brought out a small packet of crack cocaine. He held it out for Chester to see and he noticed the longing in the man's eyes. Devon almost laughed when he saw Chester lick his lips hungrily. Chester pulled out his money and the men discreetly exchanged the items. Before Chester could run off, Devon grabbed him by his collar and pulled the man close to him so that Chester could hear his hoarse whisper.

"It's all here, *right?*"

Chester looked at Devon confusedly. "Y—yeah, yeah. It's all there," he stammered. "I . . . I wouldn't steal from *you*, Big D."

"Yeah, but what you don't know is that when you steal from my li'l homie, over there, you steppin' out on me too." Devon nodded toward the other side of the store.

Chester looked to where Devon had indicated and saw a young boy, around fourteen, looking directly at them.

"Q, come over here, li'l man," Devon said, tightening his grip on Chester's collar.

The teen held on to his falling pants as he ran toward Devon and glared angrily at Chester. He stood with his arms folded, posturing like he was just as big and bad as Devon.

"Count this for me." Devon handed Q the money that Chester had just given him.

Q quickly flipped through the bills, and then said, "He's short."

Devon looked toward Chester, who now nearly quivered in fear. Then he looked back at Q and took the money out of his hands. "Handle it," he commanded, releasing Chester from his grasp.

As soon as the words left Devon's mouth, Q shoved his knee in Chester's groin. As Q proceeded to assault Chester, Devon looked around at the children and adults who continued to pass by the store as if nothing was going on. They realized that this was an everyday thing in their neighborhood, so they didn't bother to get involved. Devon knew that at any moment a passing squad car would pull over to investigate the problem, but he allowed his peddler to take revenge for now on someone who had done him wrong.

"All right, li'l man," Devon said, pulling a still wound-up Q off Chester, who lay on the ground rocking in pain from being hit repeatedly with his own cane.

Q's breathing was uneven and heavy as he looked wildly at Devon. "Don't you want a piece, Big D?" He tried to hand Devon the man's cane so that he could finish the punishment.

Devon laughed softly as he looked down at Chester, who seemed to be praying that Devon wouldn't give him what he really deserved. "Naw, I think you got 'em for the both of us," he said. Devon knelt before Chester and looked the man directly into his eyes. "Next time we have to have this discussion, I'ma let my piece do all the talkin', understand?"

Chester nodded his head as a small whimper escaped his lips.

Devon shook his head in disgust before digging his hand into Chester's pocket to retrieve the rest of the money he owed. Once counted, Devon realized that he'd pulled out more than the original total, but instead of giving it back, he held it up for Chester to see and said, "This is for interest."

He stood and handed Q a portion of the money. "Keep holdin' it down right here, a'ight?"

Q nodded. "A'ight, Big D."

Devon walked down the street a few blocks, nodding toward a few familiar faces. As he walked up the steps that led to his front porch, he released the breath he'd been holding during his walk home. Cops were usually all over his neighborhood because it was known for its high crime rates. Devon had gotten caught in a drug bust only once during his time as a drug dealer. It had been two years ago, right before Kane's death. Thankfully, he hadn't been the one dealing that night. He'd just been caught with the wrong people. Devon had spent nearly a month in prison before the police could verify that he hadn't been guilty of possession. Devon remembered being released from prison and seeing Kane waiting for him outside in a black Cadillac Escalade.

"Boy, you need to watch who you rollin' wit'," Kane had said jokingly as Devon climbed into the car.

Devon had laughed with him, knowing Kane was trying to be funny about the situation one of his young and inexperienced peddlers had gotten Devon in. But on that day, Devon vowed never to get busted again, and he had held true to his word so far.

As Devon entered his house and shut the front door behind him, he noticed Shakia and LaNiesha, a couple of Trina's friends, sitting on his black leather sofa with a large bag of baked potato chips and a manicure set opened on his coffee table. The loud music coming from the sound system sent his nerves to an all-time high.

Devon began to curse silently as he asked, "What is going on in here?"

The girls turned toward him and waved, with wide smiles. "Hi, D," they sang harmoniously.

Devon walked toward the stereo and turned down the volume so he wouldn't have to shout in order to be heard. "What are y'all doing in my house?"

"Calm down, baby." He heard Trina's voice coming from the kitchen.

Devon looked up and she stepped into view. "What is going on here?" he asked again, slower this time.

Trina shrugged innocently. "I just wanted to hang with my girls, so I invited them over for the night."

"'For the night,'" he repeated as if he wasn't sure he'd heard her correctly.

She nodded.

"Trina," Devon sighed as he shook his head. "No. I'm sorry, but I ain't up for this tonight."

"C'mon, baby," she pleaded, sauntering toward him with a pouted lip.

"I've had a long day and I'm tired," he insisted.

She wrapped her arms around his neck and kissed him softly on the lips. "Please," she requested, placing more kisses on his cheeks and neck. "I promise we won't bother you." She moved her kisses toward his ear.

Devon hated when Trina did this to him. She knew where his most vulnerable spots were, and once she hit them, she knew she could get whatever she wanted from him. He looked at her friends, who sat smiling like two Cheshire cats.

"Fine," he breathed. "Just let me have the bedroom to myself and we're even."

Trina looked up at him and smiled. "Thanks, D," she said before lightly kissing him again.

Devon walked into the bedroom, shutting and locking the door before falling onto his bed in exhaustion. As he settled against the pillows, he turned on the television, which sat on his dresser against the far wall. Whatever movie BET was showing would have to be his companion tonight. Devon sighed when he heard a round of loud, high-pitched cackling coming from the den. *Yep, it's going to be a long night,* he thought as he pulled his cell phone from his hip.

The screen showed that he had a voice message, and when he slid the phone open, it showed that he had missed one call. When he pressed the button that would allow him to view the missed call, an unfamiliar number showed up. He rarely gave out his cell number to random people, so he knew that this number could only belong to one person. *Shaniece,* he thought as he dialed his voice mail, hoping to hear her sweet voice. As he listened, the voice he heard wasn't that of the soft-spoken, but confident, young lady he'd met at the grocery store only two days ago. The voice coming through his earpiece was louder and seemed to be amused by something.

"Hi, Devon. This is Shaniece's friend Tatiana," he heard the female voice explain just before hearing another female, in the background, scream out, "Tati!"

He could hear the girl leaving the message laugh before continuing. "I'm sure you remember Shaniece. You guys met on Saturday at the grocery store. Anyway, she can't stop talking about you, so I figured that since she was too *chicken* to call you herself, I'd do the honors for her."

Devon frowned when he heard another loud scream. "I'm gonna kill you!" By Tatiana's message, he could tell that the angry screams in the background were coming from Shaniece. It amused him to know that she'd been too afraid to call him after he'd made it very clear he was interested in getting to know her.

As Tatiana began to bring her message to a close, she informed Devon that she was calling from Shaniece's cell phone, so if he wanted to return her call he should dial the number that had shown up on his caller ID when she'd called. But just to make sure, Tatiana recited Shaniece's phone number so that if it weren't on his phone, he'd have it, anyhow. Devon memorized the number she was leaving for him. Afterward, he hung up his phone with a grin plastered across his face and immediately checked to see if the number Tatiana had left matched the number that had shown up on his missed calls list. When he confirmed that they were the same number, he decided to give Shaniece a call.

The phone rang several times until he heard a soft "Hello?"

"Shaniece?" he replied cautiously.

"Yes," she replied. "Hi, Devon."

"So you remember my name," he said, wondering why he wasn't demanding that she call him "D," just like everyone else. He didn't even allow Trina to call him "Devon." Something was definitely special about this girl.

Shaniece laughed. "I do. You left quite an impression for me not to remember, but I gotta tell you, I'm surprised you remembered mine."

"Why?" he asked. "You left an impression on me too."

"Well, I just figured a guy like you had plenty of girls tying up his time," she admitted. "The names could be endless."

Devon was surprised that he was slightly offended. "Man, that hurt," he told her.

"You're hurt, but am I wrong?"

He laughed as he repositioned himself against his pillows. "I mean, I do attract a few females, but I'm just tryna get to know one in particular at the moment."

"'At the moment,'" she repeated. "So you get to know this girl and hang with her until you're tired of her, and then you move on to the next name on the list. Please correct me if I'm mistaken."

"Yeah, you are," Devon said with a smile in his voice. He could already tell that Shaniece was definitely a girl not to be trifled with. He would have to be very careful when it came to establishing a relationship with her. "And if I was a gambler, I'd be quick to accuse you of judgin' me based on the fact that I'm a guy. 'Cause if I said you were only tryna get to know a guy because of what he has, I know you'd be quick to correct me. Right?"

"Hey, you offered the money with no obligations. How could I refuse?" Shaniece chuckled and said, "But you are right, on both accounts. I apologize."

He laughed at her former statement. "It's cool. I was just calling 'cause I got your friend's message." Hearing Shaniece's annoyed, nearly unladylike grunt caused him to burst into laughter once again.

"I apologize for her bothering you. And I assure you that I beat the mess out of her after she left that message."

His laughter became louder. "I can't even imagine you beatin' the mess out of anybody, but you don't have to apologize. I've been waiting for your call since leaving the store on Saturday."

"Really?" Shaniece seemed surprised.

"Yeah," Devon assured. "I don't usually give out my cell number, but I made an exception for you."

"That's nice to know."

"So what you up to?" he asked.

"Well, I'm actually buried in homework." She sighed.

Inwardly, Devon's heart sank and he tried hard to stifle the loud disappointed sigh that tempted his lips. "Do you need to go? I can call you back later if it's a problem," he offered.

Shaniece was quiet for a moment, and Devon was almost certain that she was wrestling with the idea of continuing her conversation with him or ending their phone call and taking care of her schoolwork. "Umm . . . it's mostly projects that aren't due for a few weeks, so I can spare a few minutes."

A few minutes turned into a couple of hours as Devon and Shaniece talked about everything from school to friends to future goals. Devon made sure he skirted around the conversation when it focused on work and his personal life. He was as honest as he could be without telling Shaniece that he'd dropped out of school at sixteen after drug dealing became his life and that he lived in a bad part of town with his twenty-one-year-old girlfriend.

When Devon had asked Shaniece about her dream man, the first words out of her mouth were: "He's got to be a born-again Christian." Devon was immediately silenced by those words, but for some reason, he wasn't turned off. His mother was a Christian, so the religion wasn't foreign to him, but he reminded himself that he would change for no one. He had never been a Christian before, so what was the point of becoming one now? Certainly not because a girl, who just happened to be the most beautiful, sincere, and honest woman he'd met in a long time, had said she wanted to spend the rest of her life with a man of God. Most certainly not.

Chapter 7

Shaniece awoke the next morning with a slight smile on her face and a little pep in her step. She pressed the off button on her alarm clock and climbed out of her bed. She'd had a peaceful sleep after her conversation with Devon. His voice was so mellow and caressing that she couldn't help but smile when he spoke. At one point in the conversation, Devon had asked Shaniece a question, but she'd been so enraptured by his tone that she couldn't respond.

"Shaniece," she'd heard him call her. "You still there?"

Shaniece had opened her eyes and shook her head. "Yes, I'm here," she replied, suppressing the urge to tell him that she'd just wanted to hear him speak without interruption.

She wasn't sure what she was feeling, but something told her that Devon had walked into her life for a reason.

As she prepared herself for school, she hummed a soft melody. She walked into her closet and pulled out a long-sleeved, V-neck soft pink top and a pair of skinny jeans. She went into the bathroom to wash her face and brush her teeth before returning to her room to dress herself. After she completed her attire with a pair of boots to match, she went back into the bathroom and pulled her hair up into a clip.

Since she was a little ahead of time today, and her brother and sister had just decided to get up and get ready, Shaniece chose to spend the spare time with God. She hadn't had a daily devotional since Friday morning, and she knew that God was more than deserving of His time with her.

She grabbed her Bible and flipped through its pages. Lately her father had been talking about love—how to show love, who to love, and when to express love. She pulled out and opened the notebook in which she'd scribbled a few notes and noticed the scriptures she'd highlighted throughout her father's sermon.

Many waters cannot quench love; rivers cannot wash it away, she silently read from Song of Solomon. She remembered her father reprimanding mankind for tossing the word "love" around as if it had no real meaning.

"But love," Reverend Simmons had told them, "*real* love is so strong that it can't be bought, bargained for, or destroyed. It lasts forever."

Shaniece knew her father was trying to relay a message to the younger members of the church. He talked about how many young adults randomly tell their significant other that they love them, when in reality they have no idea what they're saying to one another. Shaniece had to admit that she'd been guilty of using the endearing term on more than one occasion during her last relationship, but she'd been sixteen and infatuated. Now she was eighteen, more mature, and held higher standards for herself. If a guy wanted to approach her, he had to have more going on than a nice smile and sweet words.

The scripture also reminded her that God had set the prime example of everlasting love. He loved her past her faults and sins, which allowed her to love Him in return. Shaniece thanked God every day for saving her and allowing her to understand the true meaning of love.

As she closed her Bible, she recited a silent prayer. *God, I thank you for a brand-new day. I pray that I will please you in my walk and that I will not intentionally do anything to displease you. Keep me focused on my relationship with you and my schoolwork. Everything else comes secondary. I pray for a drama-free and productive day. I love you. Amen.*

She slipped into her lightweight jacket and grabbed her books and prepared to leave her siblings if they weren't ready. "I'm gone," she yelled as she walked down the stairs toward the garage.

As soon as she pressed the button to open the garage door, she heard what sounded like a stampede racing down the stairs. She laughed as Keith walked past her with his shoes in hand. Rainelle was right behind him, holding a pair of earrings in her mouth as she pulled on her jacket. Shaniece shook her head as she followed her siblings down to the garage, closing and locking the door behind them.

They arrived at school nearly ten minutes later and became invisible amongst the crowd of students entering the school building. Shaniece abandoned her siblings as she headed toward her usual table.

"So, did he call?" Tatiana immediately questioned her friend without greeting.

Shaniece tossed an annoyed look in Tatiana's direction before plastering a smile on her face and saying, "Hi, Craig."

Craig smiled his authentic smile and returned Shaniece's greeting.

"Excuse me," Tatiana said with plenty of attitude in her tone. "Niecey, I know you heard me."

With a frown upon her face, Shaniece rolled her eyes and looked at her best friend. She was still irritated with Tatiana for having called Devon last night without her permission. Shaniece had been content in her decision not to talk to the supermarket hottie, but Tatiana acted as if she couldn't function without something exciting happening in someone else's life. Shaniece knew that the only reason Tatiana had phoned Devon last night was to have something to talk about every day. It didn't matter that Shaniece preferred not to get caught up with him.

"Ladies' room," Shaniece said tightly.

Shaniece realized that Tatiana didn't hesitate in gathering her things and leading the way to the restroom because she'd receive more information if she and Shaniece were alone, away from prying ears. Once in the restroom, Shaniece placed her books on one of the shelves that was nailed to the wall above the sinks before turning toward her friend with the same irritated expression on her face.

Tatiana clearly read Shaniece's thoughts and she sighed submissively. "Okay, I'm sorry. It's just that . . . you're this attractive young girl who has everything going for herself and you refuse to share that with a nice guy."

Shaniece relaxed her face, realizing that her friend was only trying to get her to loosen up and give another relationship a try, even though she knew Tatiana still had selfish intentions for doing so. "Thank you," she replied. "But I'm not really worried about sharing my life with a guy right now."

They were quiet for a moment and Shaniece knew Tatiana was dying for just a morsel of information, but she wasn't giving in so easily.

Tatiana sucked her teeth and rolled her eyes simultaneously. *"Niecey!"*

Shaniece laughed. "He called," she simply stated.

When she didn't say anything else, Tatiana ran both her hands through her hair as if pulling the strands from their roots. "God, she's killing me!"

Shaniece laughed harder at Tatiana's antics and decided to divulge her phone conversation with Devon. "When you left that message on his phone yesterday, I told myself that if he called back, I wasn't going to answer," Shaniece explained. "And when I saw his name flashing on my phone, I tried my hardest not to pick it up, but I couldn't deny the fact that I really wanted to talk to him."

"It's fate," Tatiana said in a matter-of-fact tone as she placed her right hand on her hip and nodded her head as if she knew her statement to be a fact.

"Anyway," Shaniece continued. "We talked for a while . . . a *long* while."

"So what did you find out about him? How old is he? What school does he go to? Does he have a job? What about a girlfriend?"

Shaniece reeled her head back as she frowned at her friend's flying questions. Tatiana was acting as if Shaniece were a private investigator who had been on an assignment when she'd been conversing with Devon. Her intentions had not been to find out all of his business, but Shaniece couldn't help but smile at the fact that she did indeed know the answer to her friend's questions. . . . Well, at least one of them.

"He'll be twenty next March—"

"Great, not too much older than you." Tatiana nodded as if in approval.

"And the other stuff he really didn't talk about," Shaniece said as Tatiana's wide smile turned into a deep frown. "I mean, I told him that I was a senior, and we talked about what we looked for in a mate, but he never told me specifically what school he went to, where he worked, or if he had a girlfriend."

"Did you ask?" Tatiana questioned suspiciously.

Shaniece shook her head. "The conversation pretty much revolved around me, but he did say that he would like a girl who was real and down-to-earth. He wants someone who would be supportive of him, and someone who wouldn't take advantage of his generosity. She had to be sweet, smart, and sophisticated. Someone who had class, but wasn't uppity. And, of course, he said that good looks were always a plus." She smiled.

"Umm." Tatiana began to nod again as if approving Devon's taste in women. "He sounds like he has a good head on his shoulders. I'm still not dismissing the fact that he left out basic info. School, work, and baby mamas are a must-know."

Shaniece laughed. "Baby mamas, Tati? I'm sure he would've said something about having a kid."

Tatiana pursed her lips as her brows rose in apprehension. "Don't be so sure. I've known a guy or two to conveniently *forget* that they had a couple of children running around somewhere."

The ringing bell drowned Shaniece's laughter. The girls picked up their things and headed out of the restroom to their lockers.

"Well, if he does have a kid," Shaniece continued the conversation as they merged into the crowd of students moving up and down the hallway, "he doesn't have to worry about me talking to him at all. I don't have time for baby mama drama. Plus, I'm not up for babysitting anybody's Bébé's Kids."

Tatiana chuckled. "Just keep me updated. For some reason, I feel like this one could have serious potential."

Chapter 8

Shaniece walked into the choir room on Sunday morning with a smile on her face. She spoke to those who passed her as she moved around the room, toward the breakfast table. She grabbed a plate and selected a few strawberries, melons, and grapes amongst the trays of fruits and pastries that had been provided for the choir members to feast upon before Sunday service began. Shaniece found a seat at a table near the back of the room and was soon joined by Tatiana and another young choir member, Krystal Powell.

"The joy of the Lord is all over you this morning," Krystal kidded as she sat down with her plate of fruit and bite-sized donuts.

Shaniece laughed as she chewed a strawberry. She watched Tatiana eye her before allowing a wide smile to spread across her face. She knew that her best friend was well aware of the reason behind her happiness. Shaniece had done nothing but talk about Devon for the past two weeks and had spoken or exchanged text messages with him every day since their first phone conversation. Most times he would call her for a few minutes of conversation after she'd come home from school; then he'd say good-bye so that she could focus on her schoolwork, but he'd always promise to talk to her later. Even when she was not speaking with him, Shaniece either found herself talking about him to Tatiana or thinking about him when she should be focusing on homework or chores.

Shaniece couldn't count the times in the last few days that her mother had had to snap her out of lingering daydreams so that she could continue washing the dishes. Last night, Rainelle had nearly knocked the bathroom door down before Shaniece had realized she'd almost drowned herself in the tub of soapy water because she'd been too busy thinking about Devon's soft, caressing voice to notice that she'd allowed the water to run for too long. Shaniece wasn't sure what was going on with her, but she kind of liked it.

As she finished her breakfast with her friends, the choir director came into the room and walked toward Shaniece. Shaniece smiled as the petite, curvaceous woman walked toward her, with her arms and hips trying their hardest to keep up with the hasty stride of her feet.

"Niecey, girl, I need a huge favor from you."

"What's up, Ms. Yvonne?" Shaniece looked up into the woman's eyes and could almost see the neediness in them.

"I really, really need you to lead devotion today," Yvonne requested to Shaniece's surprise.

"The *entire* devotional service?" Shaniece questioned as if the woman had lost her mind. She looked toward Tatiana and Krystal, almost asking that Yvonne choose one of them, instead. Shaniece knew that Krystal's voice was ten times better than hers, and Tatiana was a close match.

Yvonne squatted as though threatening to get down on her knees and beg if that was what it would take for Shaniece to permit her request. "Niecey, please. Ty caught a terrible cough sometime during the week and didn't bother to tell me until this morning," she informed, concerning the choir member who was initially chosen to be the choir's lead singer. "These are new songs that you presented to the choir for selections, and you're the only person I know who can do this without a problem."

Shaniece looked deeper into the woman's eyes and felt as if it were Devon nearly on his knees begging for her help. It had been a two weeks since her encounter with him, but she was certain that Yvonne's eyes mirrored his dark brown ones. She grabbed the woman's hands and smiled. "It's cool, Ms. Yvonne, I'll do it. No problem."

Yvonne seemed to be engulfed with joy as she stood and hugged Shaniece as if her life had depended on the young girl's willingness to lead devotion. "Oh, thank you so much. Girl, God is really going to bless you!" Shaniece laughed as Yvonne released her. "All right, let's get ready for the service," she yelled out to the rest of the group. "Shaniece is leading devotion today, so please give her all of your support and backup as you would've Ty," she said before walking away.

The other choir members clapped and shouted out comments of approval as Shaniece smiled nervously. She stared down at her empty plate and released a deep sigh.

"What's wrong?" Tatiana asked.

Shaniece shook her head. "Nothing, I'm fine."

Tatiana suddenly moved her chair away from the table and anxiously looked up at the ceiling.

Shaniece and Krystal looked at her as if she were half crazy. "Girl, what is wrong with *you?*" Krystal questioned with a laugh.

Tatiana glared at Shaniece. "Oh, I just didn't want to be too close to her when the lightning struck. She just told a bold-faced lie . . . on a Sunday . . . in the church."

Shaniece rolled her eyes. "I can't stand when people say that. What is the difference between a lie being told on a Sunday, in the church, and a lie being told on any other day of the week, outside of the church?" She stared at Tatiana. "A lie is a lie, Tati. A sin is a sin."

Tatiana folded her arms. "Well, regardless of what the difference is or isn't, you still just lied. Something's wrong with you, girl. What's up?" she asked, concerned.

Shaniece shook her head. "I'm okay. I guess I'm just a little nervous about singing."

Krystal laughed, almost involuntarily. "You've sung before. So it's not just singing that's got you shaken up."

Tatiana gazed at her best friend as she searched Shaniece's eyes for the truth. Suddenly she sat straight up, with her eyes and mouth opened wide.

"What?" Shaniece and Krystal asked at the same time.

Tatiana pointed a slim finger in Shaniece's direction as a slick smile spread across her face. "You invited that boy to church, didn't you?"

Shaniece feigned ignorance, but inwardly she smiled knowing she couldn't hide anything from her friend. She had, indeed, invited Devon to church while speaking with him on Wednesday night. He'd turned down the invitation, saying that he didn't "do church," but Shaniece had continued to ask every night since then. When she'd brought the subject up last night and told him that it would be a good time for them to see each other again, he'd laughed at her persistence and told her that he might stop by. It hadn't been the definite "yes" she'd been looking for, but it had been close enough to make her nervous about him walking in while she would be up in front of everyone singing praises to the Lord.

Krystal looked between the two girls. "What boy?"

Tatiana was still staring at Shaniece. "You did!"

Krystal, still confused, asked once again, *"What boy?"*

Shaniece avoided her friend's eyes and shrugged. "He might come through."

"I knew it!" Tatiana sat back in her seat and clapped gleefully.

Krystal rhythmically hit her hand against the table and questioned, "Would someone like to fill me in?"

Shaniece looked at the twenty-year-old fair-skinned woman, whose nose and cheeks were decorated with freckles, and smiled slightly. "I invited a friend to church and he said that he'd think about coming."

"Just a friend?" Krystal asked skeptically. "It seems like more from the way Tatiana is lookin' at you, and that wide smile on your face."

Shaniece nodded. "He's just a friend. I've only known him for a couple of weeks and I've only met him once."

"Please tell me you met him *before* you started talking to him," Krystal pleaded. "We don't need none of that online predator stuff coming up in the church."

Shaniece laughed. "No, I met him at the grocery store and we started talking afterward."

Before the conversation could continue, Yvonne called for the choir to move toward the sanctuary. After Shaniece discarded her breakfast plate, she fretfully wrung her hands together, silently praying that she'd be able to keep her mind on singing to God and not on what Devon would think of her voice.

CREEKSIDE CHURCH OF GOD IN CHRIST. Devon had read the sign nearly ten times since pulling up to the church thirty minutes ago. He couldn't believe he'd agreed to meet Shaniece at a church. Even when he'd told her that he'd think about it, that response hadn't seemed to come from his mouth. It was as if something was pushing him to visit the church . . . and it wasn't just the notion that he'd be able to see the beautiful young lady he'd met at the supermarket two weeks ago.

His own mother hadn't been able to get him to go to church when he'd been living with her. As a matter of fact, the last time Devon had stepped inside a church, he'd been fourteen years old. After taking up business with Kane, he'd been too busy working to accompany his mother on the rare Sunday mornings she decided to attend worship service at a small Baptist church around the corner from their home. Now he was sitting in his car, staring at the church sign as if his glare would make the words, which revealed that he was truly at a church, disappear.

Devon anxiously rubbed his hands together and prepared to step out of his vehicle. First he looked into his visor mirror and ran the palm of his hands over his faded cut. Then he opened his door and allowed one shaky leg to exit his vehicle. It took several moments before his brain transmitted to him that his other leg needed to do the same. Once he was on both feet, he straightened out his suit and shut his car door. As he took a few steps toward the entrance of the church, he power-locked his car and placed his keys into his pants pocket.

He shook his head as he stopped only a few feet away from the door. Laughing aloud, he ran his hands down his face in frustration. "What am I doing here? This ain't my territory," he told himself aloud. He remembered the look on Trina's face this morning after he'd told her that he was going to church. She'd asked him where he was going so early in the morning, and why he was so dressed up to go wherever he was headed.

She'd laughed so hard that she nearly fell off the side of the bed. Then she became serious.

"D, if you're going to lie, you need to come up with a better one than that," she'd said, glaring at him. "Do you think I'm stupid? I know you've been distancing yourself away from me since our conversation the other night."

Devon shook his head. "Trina, I don't want to talk about this. I'm going to hang with the fellas for a few hours and I'll be home later." He'd settled for the lie that was more believable than the truth.

Trina had frowned as she lay back on the bed. "Whateva, D."

Devon knew he'd have to face Trina and her desire for marriage at some point, but now just wasn't the time. If her mind was as sharp as he knew it to be, it would only be a matter of time before Trina found out about Shaniece. Though Devon wasn't dating her, Trina would declare him a cheater regardless of the actual status of his relationship with the young woman. He wasn't worried about that, because though he really liked Shaniece, he wasn't ready to replace Trina just yet.

Now he had to focus on getting his mind to cooperate with his body. Although he hadn't promised Shaniece that he'd be here today, he felt obligated to be present, and he knew he couldn't let her down. He took a deep breath as he walked through the doors of the church. Immediately a balding man dressed in a dark-colored suit greeted him. The man's friendly smile did little to calm Devon's nerves as he was led toward a second set of double doors, which surely led to the sanctuary. He walked down the corridor and inhaled once more before reaching to open the door. As he entered the sanctuary, praise music enraptured him and drew him into the service. He nodded toward an usher, who showed him to a seat near the back of the almost fully occupied building.

He took a seat, deciding against standing as everyone else was, and glanced around the building at the worshippers who were enjoying the service. His eyes focused on the pulpit and he noticed a very robust man, dressed in a dark brown suit, seated behind the podium. He allowed his twenty-twenty vision to zoom in for a better look, and the man reminded him of Shaniece, with his round eyes and bright smile.

Before he could continue studying the man, the fast-paced music slowed down and his ears perked up when he heard a soft soprano voice fill the sanctuary. He shifted his gaze slightly to the left and was shocked to find Shaniece standing in front of the choir with a microphone in her hand. She stood in her black pinstripe skirt suit with her left hand lifted up in praise and her eyes closed in meditation as she sang the soft melody.

Unconsciously, Devon smiled and stood to his feet as he kept his eyes glued to the young beauty across the room. There was something about Shaniece that made Devon's entire street demeanor change. He didn't act like the hoodlum that most people knew him to be. He didn't even talk to her or treat her like he talked to or treated most people he interacted with, including Trina. Devon could only find one explanation for the change, and it was the fact that Shaniece was different, which was something he'd seen in her from the day they'd met. She was as different from the rest of the people in his life as he was from the most sanctified people in this church. The fact that she was different made *him* want to be different . . . at least when he was around her.

Devon sat through the rest of the service, hardly paying attention to the fact that he'd decided to stay, instead of leaving early as planned. The man whom he'd been watching earlier was now standing behind the podium. Devon's eyes showed his surprise when the man commented on how wonderfully his daughter had sung today.

She's the pastor's daughter, Devon thought as the minister began his message. *I knew he seemed familiar. I've got to be careful with this one,* he cautioned himself.

By the time Shaniece's father had reached the climax of his sermon, he had sweat pouring from his forehead and was using a white handkerchief to wipe it away. The parishioners around Devon were rising to their feet and waving their hands while shouting words of praise. The organist was tuning up and the drummer continued to bang his sticks against the cymbals. But all of this went unseen and unheard as Devon kept his eyes on Shaniece seated in the choir stand. From where he was seated, he took the opportunity to study her more closely. She kept her head down as if reading the Bible in her lap. She would periodically nod as if in agreement with the preacher's words, but he'd often catch her eyes wandering around the sanctuary as though looking for someone. He smiled, knowing she was searching for him. He still had to decide if he would approach her after service or escape as soon as the benediction was delivered.

Chapter 9

As Shaniece gathered her belongings and stepped down from the choir stand, several church members came up to her with compliments and words of encouragement concerning her lead in the worship service. She smiled and expressed gratitude for their respects, and then she, Tatiana, and Krystal walked toward the front row of seats and stood off to the side. Shaniece watched as the line of people waiting to greet her father grew longer and longer. She sighed heavily, knowing it would be a long while before she would be able to leave for home.

Shaniece was weary for another reason, and she felt as if it was causing her to be more aggravated than usual about having to stay at church until her father finished greeting his congregation. She'd hoped that Devon would give coming to church some serious consideration. Either he'd just said he'd think about it in order to get Shaniece to stop asking, or he'd thought about it and decided that seeing her was not a good enough reason for him to drop everything he was doing in order to stop through, if even for a few minutes. Whatever the reason behind his absence, she was still disappointed. Even now, Shaniece found herself searching the perimeter of the sanctuary, hoping to spot him. She didn't know what it was about Devon that drew her toward him, but she felt as if she'd been placed in his life for a reason. Though she didn't know what that reason could possibly be, she was determined to continue getting to know her new male friend until she found out.

"Girl, you look disappointed," Krystal pointed out.

Shaniece shrugged. "A little. I thought he would show."

Tatiana looked around the sanctuary still full of people socializing with one another. "Well, it's going to be a while before Mr. Cedric's ready to leave, so you want us to chill outside with you, away from all of these people?"

Shaniece nodded and she and her friends walked outside. Late October's weather continued to consist of mild temperatures and lots of sunshine—just the way Shaniece liked it. She hated extreme temperatures and favored Atlanta's early spring and fall weather. She inhaled the fresh air as she and her friends walked along the sidewalk. A few more people greeted Shaniece and complimented her on her solo during the service.

"I wanna go somewhere today," Shaniece suddenly said.

Tatiana chuckled. "Like where? You know everybody's going to your house for dinner."

Shaniece rolled her eyes. "I know. That's why I wanna go somewhere else. Maybe out to eat . . . with you guys?" Her eyes pleaded with her friends.

Krystal shrugged. "I rode with my mom today, but I know she's headed to your house, so I don't mind."

"I guess I can hang. I drove today, so if you wanna go somewhere, you have a ride," Tatiana offered.

Shaniece smiled. "Thanks. I'm just tired of being around church folk. No offense, but Sunday services, Tuesday night prayer meetings, Wednesday night Bible Study, Saturday afternoon choir rehearsals, and occasional Saturday Youth Nights are starting to suffocate me. I love the church and God even more, but I just wanna do something outside of church for once."

"What you need is a man," Tatiana said. "I've told you that a million times. You wanna have fun? Find yourself a man with a little bit of money and go have some fun."

"You want me to find a boyfriend just so I can use up his money to satisfy my desire to have fun?" Shaniece asked disbelievingly.

"You know what I'm saying," Tatiana defended. "You need to get out more, and what better way to do that than with a guy you like spending time with?"

Krystal nodded in agreement. "Yeah, she's right. I don't really know about the boyfriend thing, but just find somebody you can hang with for a few hours of enjoyment. For you, that could be Tatiana." She pointed in Tatiana's direction.

Tatiana laughed. "Well, I do hang with Niecey and she's still here complaining about not having a life. It's apparent she's not talking about just any old body."

Shaniece tuned out her friends as she searched the parking lot once again, hoping that maybe she'd underestimated Devon. Maybe he had shown up, but hadn't approached her yet. Maybe he was one of the people in line to greet her father. She chuckled inwardly, knowing that wasn't a possibility. Even if he had come, he would've left by now. She had just hoped that if he had come, he would at least speak to her before leaving.

"Girl, you need to get that boy out of your head," Tatiana said, and noticed the shocked, almost innocent look on Shaniece's face. "Yeah, I can see it in your eyes. You keep looking around like he's just gonna pop up out of thin air. He didn't come."

"Okay," Shaniece replied, close to being annoyed with her friend's bluntness. "I can see that."

"Niecey!"

Shaniece rolled her eyes at the sound of her sister's voice calling out her name. She knew that she couldn't be that annoyed by her sister's call and determined that Devon's absence was not only disappointing to her, but she was nearly angry about it. She couldn't explain what was going on with her emotions concerning this guy. It had only been two weeks since they'd met and the status of their relationship was still in the acquaintance stage. *So why am I acting like he's the air that I breathe?* she silently asked herself.

"Niecey, I know you hear me calling you!" Rainelle shouted again.

Shaniece folded her arms, refusing to turn toward her sister. "If she wants something, she's going to have to come over here and ask for it. I'm not about to be *ghetto* and yell across this church parking lot."

Shaniece watched as Tatiana took a step to the right in order to see where Rainelle's voice was coming from. Tatiana's facial expression soon changed; she pursed her lips and raised one elegantly arched eyebrow as if she'd just seen something she liked. She motioned for Krystal to take a look. When Krystal glanced in Rainelle's direction, she had to take a second look to make sure that her eyes weren't deceiving her. Both girls looked back at Shaniece with wide smiles plastered across their faces.

"Nie-cey!" Rainelle's voice had become a teasing singsong tone.

"Girl, I think she has something *you* want," Krystal said.

Shaniece's annoying glare disappeared as a confused expression clouded her being. She turned slowly and looked around for her sister. When she saw Rainelle on Devon's arm, walking toward her, Shaniece couldn't help but smile. Keeping her eyes on the man she'd been searching for all day long, Shaniece became mesmerized by Devon's smile and his sparkling brown eyes. She couldn't deny that she'd noticed the sudden fluttering in her heart. If someone told her that she was blushing, she would know they were telling the truth. She could feel the effect he was having on her.

"Girl, is that *him?*" Tatiana slyly asked through barely moving lips.

"Uh-huh," Shaniece mumbled softly.

Krystal nodded approvingly. "He's fine," she sang in the same slick tone.

When Rainelle stood before Shaniece with Devon only inches away from her, Shaniece tried to regain control of her emotions.

"I thought you might want to see him." Rainelle held a smirk on her face that let her sister know she deserved an offering of appreciation for bringing Devon to her.

Shaniece cut her eyes at her sister and looked at Devon, who was smiling down at her. "Hey, I thought you weren't gonna come."

Devon shrugged. "I told you I'd think about it."

"But that wasn't a 'yes,' so I wasn't sure," she replied, hoping her smile wasn't covering over half of her face, as she felt it was.

Tatiana stepped up and softly pushed Shaniece off to the side. "I'm sorry. My best friend has no manners at all," she said, with her hand extended in Devon's direction. "I'm Tatiana . . . the one who left the message on your phone." She smiled.

His smile revealed that he remembered the message she had left on his voice mail on Shaniece's behalf. He took her hand and shook it gently. "Nice to meet you. And I 'preciate you callin'. If it wasn't for you, I don't think Shaniece would've ever called a brotha," he said as he released Tatiana's hand and looked in Shaniece's direction.

"And I'm Krystal. I just heard about you today, but from the way Niecey was acting all throughout service, I'm guessing you've had quite an effect on her in the past several days."

Devon chuckled as he shook Krystal's extended hand.

"Okay, that's enough from you guys," Shaniece said, trying to keep her friends from embarrassing her any further. "So, are you getting ready to go?" she asked Devon.

"Actually, I was thinkin' 'bout goin' out for dinner, that is . . . if you're not busy?" Devon gazed down into her eyes as if trying to see deep into her soul.

Shaniece boldly returned his intense stare, despite the fact that her sister and friends were watching the two of them very closely. His eyes teased her emotions and she willed herself not to fall too deeply. "Well, we were actually planning to go out," Shaniece finally replied as she pointed to her friends.

"Excuse me," Rainelle's loud voice rang out. "But if you've forgotten, Mama has cooked all that food at the house, and people from church are coming over for dinner. Have you cleared your little plans with her?"

Shaniece narrowed her eyes and glared at her sister. "Not yet, but I'm sure she wouldn't mind me hanging with Tati and Krystal for a few hours."

"And Devon," Tatiana added with a cunning smile. Shaniece looked back at Tatiana, and then at Devon. "If he wants to come," Tatiana continued.

Devon turned toward Shaniece, whose eyes questioned him hopefully. Then he said, "That's cool wit' me." Turning back toward Tatiana, he added, "But only if you call me D."

Shaniece reeled her neck back and raised her eyebrows in response to Devon's request. She wondered why he never asked her to call him "D" before. *Or maybe he had,* she thought, remembering he'd only saved *D* in her phone's memory when he gave her his number.

Devon noticed Shaniece's facial expression and continued speaking. "I asked Shaniece to call me D when we first met, but I guess she likes callin' me Devon." He smiled. "So besides my mama, she's the only person who calls me that. *Everybody else* calls me D."

Tatiana chuckled softly as Shaniece blushed like a young schoolgirl at the notion that she was just about the only person that Devon allowed to call him by his given name. "Well, Niecey, why don't you go ask your parents about coming to dinner with Krystal and me," Tatiana suggested. "And, *D,* we'll meet you at Chili's."

Chapter 10

Devon had figured that getting permission for Shaniece to be able to go out to dinner would be a hard task. She just seemed like the type of girl who'd been sheltered all of her life, and by the way her mother questioned her, he figured he'd been right in his assumption. Natalie had wanted to know whom Shaniece would be with, where they were going, when they would return, why she didn't want to share dinner with her church family, and who was the guy who had been hanging around her all afternoon—that had been the hardest part. For a moment, it looked as if Tatiana was going to save her friend from having to tell her mother who Devon really was, but Shaniece wouldn't have anyone lying for her.

"He's a friend that I invited to church," she said with a strong voice as she looked directly into her mother's eyes. "Krystal, Tatiana, and I wanted to go out to dinner, and I thought that it was only polite to invite him along."

When Devon had looked at Shaniece, he noticed she was nervously chewing on her bottom lip as she awaited her mother's blessing. To Devon, Shaniece seemed to be sweating bullets, noticeably afraid her mother would further question her about her relationship with him. However, she played it off enough for her mother to believe she was anxiously awaiting a positive answer. When Natalie approved of their plans, it was Devon who'd almost sighed in relief, because he truly wanted to spend more time with Shaniece. He definitely hadn't come to church for the sermon. Natalie would allow Shaniece to go to dinner with her friends, as long as Tatiana was driving her *and* Krystal, and she was home by a reasonable hour.

So Devon followed Tatiana to the restaurant and they were shown to a table for four by a male greeter, who secretly complimented Devon for being in the company of three beautiful young women. Devon nodded in the man's direction with a slight smile before allowing the girls to take their seats in the booth. He then took his own. A waiter came to their table and introduced himself before receiving their drink and appetizer orders.

"So, D, how did you meet Shaniece?" Krystal asked as the waiter left the table.

Devon looked at Shaniece, who sat next to him in the booth, before turning his gaze toward Krystal, who sat directly across from him. "She nearly ran me over in the grocery store." He laughed.

Shaniece blushed. "I did not."

"*Yes,* you did," Devon stressed. "See, when I grocery shop, I take my time so I can make sure that I'm not forgetting anything. Apparently, *she's* the exact opposite," he said, pointing to Shaniece. "I was turning onto one aisle and she's coming toward me full speed and nearly hits me with her cart."

Tatiana laughed. "I don't remember this part of the story, Niecey." She smiled toward her friend, whose face was bright red.

"That's because it was not meant to be told," Shaniece responded curtly, cutting her eyes in Devon's direction.

Devon shrugged. "Then we started talkin' and I gave her a couple of bucks to buy her brother and sister some snacks, hoping she'd call me."

"A *couple* of bucks?" Shaniece looked at him for a correction.

Devon placed his hand against his forehead dramatically. "Oh, my bad. What was it again—"

"Twenty dollars," Tatiana answered with a brief laugh.

"And I wouldn't have taken it, had I been thinking clearly," Shaniece added.

"I still would've offered, even if I knew you weren't gonna call me," Devon said, gazing into her eyes.

Shaniece turned away and focused her attention on the menu before her and Devon tried not to smile at the expense of her embarrassment.

Krystal shook her head. "*Twenty dollars?* You acted on faith, brotha."

Devon's chuckle came from deep within. "I guess."

The waiter returned with their drinks and appetizers. He asked for their dinner orders, which everyone was ready to give. After the waiter left, Devon waited for the interrogation to begin. He knew that it would especially come from Tatiana. She was Shaniece's best friend and seemed to have the most dominant personality out of the two. He prepared his answers and hoped that they wouldn't be able to see that he was flat-out lying. He watched as Tatiana clasped her hands together and placed them on the table. Her back became stiff as a board and her stare was bold and immovable. Devon felt Shaniece tense up beside him and he glanced in her direction and gave her a look that told her everything was okay. She relaxed and he continued to prepare himself for anything Tatiana would throw at him.

"So, D, what school do you go to?" Tatiana asked.

"I'm not in school. I graduated last year," Devon responded.

"And you don't attend a college, university, or technical school?"

Devon bit down on his bottom lip and furrowed his brow as he tried to think of a convincing response. "Honestly, I didn't do too well in high school, so I knew college wasn't for me."

Tatiana searched his face and then looked down at the chain hanging from his neck and the watch on his wrist. "So how do you keep a watch like that on your wrist?"

Devon looked down at the nearly $6,000 Frank Muller watch that was on his arm. "I ain't even gonna front," he began, though he knew that was exactly what he was about to do. "This watch isn't as expensive as it looks, but I've been working since I was fifteen with the same company. They put good money in my pocket."

She grunted as she picked up a toasted chip and dipped it in the salsa. She took a bite, chewed, and swallowed before asking, "And what company might this be?"

"Coca-Cola," he said, and licked his lips nervously.

Krystal looked at him in disbelief. *"Coca-Cola?"*

"Yeah, I started out working part-time in the factory. Now I make local deliveries."

Devon couldn't believe he was lying about his job. He'd never lied about the way he made a living before. Not to Trina, not even to his mother, but here he was putting up a front for people he didn't even know. Inwardly, he scolded himself, knowing it would be a nightmare trying to explain himself later on, when being honest would be inevitable. For now, though, he continued to build on the lie he'd already told and hoped that his words came across as truth.

"Oh, okay," Tatiana said. "My uncle used to work for them a couple of years ago, but he made deliveries throughout the south."

"Is driving for them something you want to do for a living?" Krystal asked.

Devon shrugged. "I'm not really sure, but like I said, they keep my pockets deep enough to live decently. So I'm not tryin' to ditch 'em right now." Wanting to change the subject and push all attention away from him, he looked at Shaniece and smiled. "I didn't know you could sing."

Shaniece shook her head and shrugged. "A little."

He laughed. "Girl, you can blow. I was surprised because you seem so quiet and soft-spoken."

As if on cue, Tatiana and Krystal released a round of laughter as if Devon had just told a joke. He looked at them and then back at Shaniece, who was glaring at her friends with a smirk on her face.

Devon was confused. "Did I say somethin' funny?"

"Niecey is not quiet or soft-spoken," Tatiana said.

Krystal shook her head in agreement. "As loud as you heard her singing today . . . she can get louder than that in a regular conversation."

Devon looked back at Shaniece. "Really?"

Shaniece picked up her butter knife and pretended to threaten her friends with it if they didn't stop with their teasing.

"But seriously, Niecey," Tatiana said, still laughing, "I thought you were 'bout to die when Ms. Yvonne asked you to sing in Ty's place this morning."

Devon's gaze shot in Tatiana's direction. "Yvonne?"

Tatiana replied, "She's our choir director. The guy, who was supposed to do the solo that Niecey did, got sick, and Ms. Yvonne was the one to ask her to sing. Niecey looked like she wanted to pee in her pants. I'd never seen her so nervous."

"Yeah, she's sung before," Krystal continued, "but today she seemed terrified. Then we found out that you might be making an appearance during service and we figured out why she was so fidgety."

Devon chuckled in order to hide his nervousness. He had been so busy watching Shaniece during the service that he hadn't even noticed a choir director. He knew his mother was musically involved in her church, but he couldn't remember the name of the church Yvonne had told him she'd started attending a couple of years ago. If his mother was the choir director at Shaniece's church, he was glad that she hadn't spotted him. Yvonne would definitely be upset with him for not taking her up on any of her invites to accompany her to a service, but she'd be glad that he had come, even if it was just to see a pretty girl. He'd have to be on the lookout for his mother *if* he decided to visit the church again.

Their food arrived and Devon was taken aback when all three girls bowed their heads to bless their food, but he quickly followed suit. Shaniece took the liberty of praying, and once she said "Amen," they began to eat.

"So what are your intentions with Niecey?" Tatiana suddenly asked after a few moments of eating in silence.

Devon thought that since their food had arrived, they would be able to move toward more enjoyable conversation. He felt as if he were out to dinner with Shaniece's parents with the way Tatiana continued questioning him about his personal life. He could see why Shaniece called the girl her best friend. *Opposites do attract,* Devon concluded as he swallowed a piece of his steak and wiped his mouth.

Before he could answer, Krystal laughed and said, "Dang, Tatiana. You sound like the reverend."

"I know," Shaniece agreed. "And if I wanted Devon to be grilled and given the third degree, then I would've taken him to my house for dinner where my father, mother, and everyone else in the church could've been all up in his business. I thought this was supposed to be a relaxed dinner, remember?"

Tatiana's eyeballs darted around the restaurant before landing back on Shaniece. "I'm sorry. I was just trying to get to know the guy *you* haven't stopped talking about *since* last Saturday afternoon."

Shaniece grunted. "Okay, but we're just friends, so there's no need for the interrogation."

Devon shook his head, gaining the girls' attention. "It's no big deal," he said, smiling softly. "I just wanna get to know Shaniece," he answered Tatiana's initial question. "She seems like a really nice person and she's been real with me from jump. I like that, and I just wanna continue to get to know her."

Tatiana stuffed a forkful of shrimp and pasta in her mouth and asked, "And what happens after you get to know her? . . ." She left her question hanging in the air.

"Is completely up to her," Devon finished as he looked directly at Shaniece.

He knew that the closer he got to Shaniece, the more he'd want to establish a more permanent relationship with her. Part of him prayed that they'd remain just friends, but she'd been the realest person he'd met in years, and that alone made him want to get closer to her. Getting closer to her, though, would reveal who he truly was, and that was something he'd rather keep hidden from her until he felt it was right to let her in on what his life was all about. He had so much baggage—a girlfriend, an illegal job, and a shameful past—that he wasn't sure if he should continue associating himself with Shaniece, but there was something about her that had captured his heart and it wouldn't let go.

Chapter 11

Ladies of Literature was meeting at Tatiana's home today, so Tatiana had asked Shaniece to come over a few hours before the meeting was to start so that her friend would be able to help her prepare. Shaniece happily consented, wanting to get away from her siblings, who continued to question her concerning her relationship with Devon. Shaniece had told her siblings that she and Devon were just friends, and nothing more, but even she knew that the more she and Devon conversed, the further their relationship would progress.

He'd already asked her out for a date, and, of course, she'd readily accepted, but she'd informed him that he would have to meet her parents before any activity could be arranged. She had been terrified that he'd take back his proposal in order to evade cross-examination from the reverend and first lady, but Devon had been a good sport about the preliminaries that Shaniece's parents had set for dating in the Simmons household. He'd agreed to a Friday night dinner with her parents, and if things went well, they would go out the following weekend.

As time came closer for the book club meeting to begin, Shaniece and Tatiana began to set up the family room so that a relaxed discussion could take place. As Shaniece was cutting various fruits to be placed on a serving platter, Tatiana walked into the kitchen with her baby brother, Samuel, in tow. Shaniece smiled at the two-year-old and placed a kiss on his chocolate cheek.

"Hey, Sammie," she greeted as he laughed.

"Ne-ne," the toddler squealed with a wide smile.

Tatiana placed Samuel on the floor and shook her arms as if trying to get her blood to circulate regularly. She laughed as she looked down at her plump little brother. "Boy, you need to stop eating. You are getting heavy."

"Eat!" Samuel said, holding his hand out.

Shaniece laughed as she sliced a small strawberry in half and gave him a piece. He shoved the fruit into his mouth and smacked as if it was the tastiest meal he'd ever had.

"Has he eaten breakfast yet?" Shaniece asked Tatiana.

Tatiana shook her head. "Mama just woke him up and told me to fix him something. I'm about to give him a banana and be done with it," she said as she grabbed the fruit from a bowl centered on the kitchen table. "So when are you going to ask your parents about D coming over on Friday night?" she asked as she sat down at the table and pulled Samuel onto her lap.

Shaniece shrugged as she arranged the sliced fruit on the platter. "I'll probably ask them after church tomorrow. My dad is always pleasant during dinner, especially if service goes well. I figure if I ask Ms. Yvonne to let me sing one of Daddy's favorite songs during the service, and then he preaches the house down, dinner will be great and he'll at least give Devon's visit some thought."

Tatiana nodded as if approving Shaniece's plans. "That's a good idea. But remember to take it slow with D. I don't want you to rush into anything, and then things don't work out like you plan."

Shaniece laughed. "Girl, you don't even have to tell me. I'm still getting to know Devon and I see some things that I don't like—like the fact that he refuses to go to church. I know he only came last Sunday in order to see me, but if we start going out on a regular basis, he won't have a reason to come to service at all. You know that I have a list of standards when it comes to guys, and being a Christian is one of them. He says he believes in God, the Father, the Son, and the Holy Spirit and has no doubt about Jesus' death and resurrection, but he's not a born-again Christian," she explained, referring to the fact that Devon had yet to invite Jesus into his heart.

"Umph," Tatiana mumbled disapprovingly. "Now, I'm not going to say drop him because of that, because you can always work with him, but don't—as in *do not*—get into a relationship with him until he makes that change. You know I don't believe in lowering your standards for any guy. Making slight changes is okay, but lowering the bar just so they can jump over it is a strict no-no."

"Oh, trust me, my standards will forever remain the same," Shaniece assured her friend as she moved toward the refrigerator and pulled out the ingredients she needed in order to make the finger sandwiches. "I refuse to give my heart to a man who has yet to give his heart to Jesus. That's a relationship bound for destruction."

"Well, you're smart and you know what you want, so I'm not going to even tell you what to do about D," Tatiana said, feeding her brother the last pieces of the banana.

"But that's not going to stop you from offering your opinion," Shaniece said with a soft laugh.

Tatiana tilted her head to the side and gave a sweet smile. "Of course not. Girl, you know me too well." She laughed. "D's a nice guy. I like him and you're nearly infatuated with him. He seems levelheaded, and even though he's come with a few missing pieces, I think you can work through that. Help the brotha out and then help yourself to the brotha." She snapped her head back and laughed at her own statement.

Shaniece shook her head as she continued preparing the snacks for their meeting. "All right, Tati, come help me with this before the girls start coming up in here and complaining about the food not being ready. You know that's the only reason some of them come."

Tatiana laughed as she took Samuel to her mother before returning to assist her friend.

After the book club meeting, Tatiana had asked Shaniece to spend the night at her house so that they could spend more time talking. Shaniece knew that Tatiana just wanted to hear more about Devon, and even though Shaniece had wanted to get away from her own house because of her siblings' continuous questions, she didn't mind chatting about Devon with her friend. So after receiving permission from her father, Shaniece went home to get a few necessities and an outfit to wear on Sunday. She then returned to Tatiana's house.

"So what else do you want to know?" Shaniece asked as she settled in Tatiana's bedroom after taking her shower that evening.

"Whose Lexus is he driving?" Tatiana questioned. "I know he said he works hard and is paid well, but a nineteen-year-old driving a Lexus?" She gave Shaniece a look that said something wasn't right about that.

Shaniece laughed. "Tati, it's an *old, used* Lexus. It couldn't have cost that much."

"A used Lexus can still cost a fortune," Tatiana defended her viewpoint. When Shaniece shrugged, Tatiana shook her head and leaned against her headboard. "So, does he have any siblings?"

"Nope, he's an only child."

"What about those baby mamas?"

Shaniece looked at her best friend and shook her head. "None, and he almost died laughing when I asked him that. And tell me why he knew that you were the reason behind my asking that question?"

Tatiana laughed. "I don't know why he thinks you're too shy to ask him something like that."

"Because I am," Shaniece declared.

Tatiana laughed again. "He'll find out differently in due time."

"Anyway," Shaniece said as she rolled her eyes, "he said he's never been in a serious relationship."

"So what does that mean?" Tatiana asked, confused. "He can't have a baby mama somewhere?"

"Tati!" Shaniece laughed.

"Okay, okay," Tatiana relented.

The room became quiet for several moments and then Tatiana asked, in a soft voice, "So . . . is he a virgin?"

Shaniece picked up her pillow and began hitting her best friend with it. Tatiana screamed for mercy, but Shaniece wouldn't stop until she was nearly out of breath. When Shaniece dropped the pillow onto the floor, Tatiana looked up at her with wild hair and playful eyes.

"So, is he?" she still wanted to know.

Shaniece laughed and fell back on the bed. "No. And to answer any more of your questions: no, I wasn't surprised to hear that; yes, he asked me if I was a virgin; and yes, I told him that I am, and I plan on staying that way until I'm married."

Tatiana innocently smiled at her best friend. "That's all I wanted to know."

Before Tatiana could ask any more questions, Shaniece's cell phone began ringing. Retrieving it from her overnight bag, she noticed the name on the caller ID. With a smile, she answered it just before the caller received her voice mail.

"Hey, Devon," she greeted to Tatiana's delight.

"Hey, yourself," Devon replied.

Tatiana pointed toward the phone and whispered, "Put it on speaker!"

Shaniece frowned and pulled away from Tatiana's hand. Immediately Tatiana picked up the pillow that Shaniece had been hitting her with earlier and threatened to do the same to Shaniece if she didn't comply with her request. Laughing softly, Shaniece pressed the button that would allow her best friend to be nosy, as usual.

"What's so funny?" Devon asked in response to Shaniece's laughter.

Shaniece hadn't known he'd heard her and tried quickly to come up with an excuse. "Nothing. It's good to hear from you," she said, even though she'd just spoken with him the day before.

"Yeah, it's good to hear your voice," Devon replied, causing Shaniece's face to redden.

Tatiana stuck her index finger into her gaping mouth, pretending to be disgusted by the conversation already.

Shaniece elbowed her friend softly in her side. "So what are you doing?"

"Just gettin' off from work," he said with a sigh. "It's been a long day. What are you up to?"

"I'm at Tatiana's house for the night. Our book club met over here today, but she's holding me hostage for the night."

"Book club?" Devon said with a question in his tone. "Sounds interesting. Well, tell Tatiana I said wassup."

Shaniece pretended Tatiana wasn't listening to the conversation and relayed Devon's message to her, just loud enough for him to hear. In response, Tatiana hollered a loud "hello," as if she was across the hall.

Devon laughed. "Is she always that loud?"

Shaniece laughed also—not because of Devon's question, but because Tatiana was looking at the phone as if she wanted to jump through the line and show Devon just how loud she could be. "She knows how to tone it down when it's necessary," Shaniece answered.

"What book were you guys discussing?" Devon asked, to her surprise.

Tatiana gave Shaniece a look of approval in response to Devon's interest in the things Shaniece was involved in.

"Victoria Christopher Murray's *Lady Jasmine,*" Shaniece answered. "The discussion was good, but the book was even better."

"Really? What was it about?"

Shaniece wanted to scream and shout "Hallelujah!" A man interested in literature! She was impressed, especially since reading was her favorite pastime. "Let's just say it's about a woman who'll do anything for love, *except* tell the truth. You can read the book yourself if you're interested in finding out more." She hesitated before commenting, "I'm surprised you called me on a Saturday, seeing as how I could easily bug you about coming to church tomorrow."

He playfully grunted. "Yeah, I know, but I just wanted to talk to you before I turned in for the night. It's nice to go to sleep with something sweet on my mind."

Shaniece looked back at Tatiana, who was biting her lip in order to keep from laughing. She knew Tatiana thought the line was cheesy, but unlike her friend, Shaniece felt that Devon's words were endearing and she bought into the fantasy she was building in her mind. "You do have a way with words," she said softly. "So tell me, why don't you have a girlfriend?"

Shaniece was getting too comfortable because she almost felt as if she were alone, until Tatiana sat up straight as her ears perked up when her interest in the conversation heightened.

There was silence on the line for a few seconds before Devon replied, "I just haven't found that special girl yet. I mean, there's always a girl out there who's just right for the time being, but they come a dime a dozen. A girl who's just right for a lifetime . . . well, they're only one in a million."

"Are you looking for a lifetime kind of girl?" Shaniece asked, secretly hoping that he was, but pretending she was just probing for information. "Because you don't seem like the type that's ready to settle down."

Devon laughed. "Well, I'm only nineteen, and right now I'm really into my work, so I'm not lookin' for a long-term commitment. That might be cool someday, though. So if a one in a million type of girl just happens to come into my life right now, I ain't gon' have any complaints."

"At least you're keeping your options open."

"So why don't you have a man?" Devon asked, turning the tables on her. "I mean, you're an attractive young lady, with a bright future ahead of yourself. I know you have plenty of options. Why are you single? Is it by choice?"

Shaniece paused and thought about her answer. She looked over at Tatiana, who was lying flat on her belly, with her head propped up on her hands.

"Don't look at me," Tatiana whispered. "I'm just listening."

Shaniece smiled softly before returning her attention to her phone conversation. "Well, I do have a few options. Some are actually pretty good ones, but I guess I'm just looking for a particular quality that I have yet to find in any of my prospects. Some days I feel like my standards are too high, and then other days, I take a mental look at my list and realize that nothing on it is too hard to achieve." She paused once more. "To answer your question, yes, I'm single by choice. I'm a busy girl. With school and extracurricular activities, I don't really have time to spend with anyone. Plus, I'm not necessarily looking, but like you said, if what I want happens to fall into my lap, then I'm not going to turn him away, and I'll definitely make time for him."

"Well, we seem to agree on what we're *not* looking for," Devon said with a subtle laugh. "I think you're a really nice, caring, and sweet young lady, Shaniece, and I appreciate having you as my friend."

Shaniece giggled. "Thank you, and the feeling is mutual. You're definitely a breath of fresh air," she almost whispered, with her eyes closed and her mind in another world.

Tatiana thumped Shaniece on her thigh, bringing her friend back to reality. Tatiana shook her head and suppressed her laughter. Shaniece felt her face flush from the embarrassment of being caught in her daydream.

"I'ma let you get back to your girls' night," Devon finally remarked.

Shaniece was still trying to get a hold on her emotions when she quietly said, "Okay. I'll call you about Friday night's dinner with my family."

"All right, I'll talk to you later," he said. "Good night."

"Good night," she said, her voice still gentle.

She flipped her phone closed and looked at Tatiana. Shaniece knew her face revealed every emotion she was feeling on the inside. Tatiana was looking at her friend and shaking her head, almost in dismay.

"I thought I told you to take it slow," Tatiana cautioned.

Shaniece smiled. "We are taking it slow. Didn't you hear him say we were friends?"

"Friends don't talk to each other in soft, sensual voices like you guys were just doing," Tatiana pointed out. "And they definitely don't grin and blush at everything the other person says."

"Tati, we're just friends," Shaniece insisted.

Tatiana laughed. "Okay, well, when we go to school on Monday and Craig compliments you, I wanna see your entire face turn red just like it did when you were talking to D."

Shaniece hastily licked her lips and narrowed her eyes in playful anger. She took her pillow and began hitting Tatiana with it once again. Tatiana decided to retaliate this time and picked up her own pillow, returning equal blows.

Chapter 12

"What is this?"

Devon had just exited the bathroom after having showered and shaved. He was preparing to get dressed when he heard Trina's demanding tone question him. He looked at his girlfriend, standing by the nightstand on his side of the bed, with her right hand positioned against her hip and a torn white sheet of paper in her left hand. He didn't have to look at the paper to know that it was the sheet he'd written Shaniece's address on earlier that day. He glanced at the clock and noticed that he had a little less than an hour to finish getting ready for dinner with Shaniece's family, which meant he had no time to entertain Trina's insecurities. Blatantly ignoring Trina's questioning glare, Devon moved toward his closet to find something to wear.

"Excuse me," Trina yelled. "I know I just asked you a question. What is this?"

Devon glanced over his shoulder at her. "Why are you in my stuff?"

"Don't answer my question with a question, D," Trina said. "You know I hate that." She looked down at the paper in her hand. "Now, what is this?"

He shook his head and continued fishing through his collection of clothing. Shaniece had told him that he didn't have to dress up, but she stressed the fact that both her parents hated the look that most young guys sported: pants that were worn below the waist or without a belt, and a wrinkled shirt that looked like a dress because the guy had purchased one that was three sizes too big. Devon had told Shaniece that she didn't have to worry about him wearing anything that resembled that look because he always dressed to impress.

"Just make sure you look good," he'd playfully told her.

"Excuse me, but don't I always," Shaniece had replied, pretending to be offended.

Devon had laughed. "Yeah, you do."

He chuckled aloud now as he pulled a long-sleeved Sean John shirt out of his closet, along with a pair of dark blue jeans.

"I don't think there's anything funny about this," Trina yelled, mistaking the reason behind Devon's laughter. "D, I'm trying so hard here to make you happy, but you don't even appreciate it."

Devon sighed as he stepped into his pants. He didn't have time to have this conversation. He'd successfully avoided it over the last weeks, but today he couldn't avoid Trina's complaints.

"Trina, why are you trippin'?" he asked her. "That could be anybody's address."

"But it's not just *anybody's* address. You're seeing somebody," she accused. "And don't try to deny it, because I know you too well. For the last couple of weeks, you've been spending *way* too much time outside of this house, and it ain't been all about your business. Plus, you been spending the early evenings away from me, on the phone, for at least an hour a night."

"Trina—"

"No," Trina cut him off. "I want you to listen to me. When we met last year, you said that you weren't looking for anything serious. I agreed because I was still in school, and working and a serious relationship would've been something that would have disrupted my focus." She sat down on the edge of the bed and placed the piece of paper back on Devon's nightstand. "I've got my degree now, but I'm not doing anything with it because you said you'd take care of me. I got used to that and I want to continue to be comfortable with it, but it seems like you're pulling away from me . . . from us. I really do love you, D," she said tearfully.

Devon pulled his arms through his shirt and looked at his girlfriend. She was beautiful, but his feelings for her didn't go beyond physical attraction. Trina was a smart girl, she was caring, and she loved him, but her neediness was wearing him thin. She was becoming insecure and defensive where their relationship was concerned, and Devon couldn't stand a girl who possessed those two qualities.

"Trina," he called her softly. "I ain't gon' stand here and tell you that I love you, because I'd be lying." He heard her whimper, but he continued, anyway. "But I do care a lot about you and I love having you with me. You my girl, and that means somethin', whether you know it or not. I love the fact that you don't judge me and you been holdin' it down right here wit' me. Now, what other girl would do that when it could cost her life? I don't know one, and I don't care to go out and find one." He went back into the closet and found a pair of shoes. "Now, I got somewhere to be. If you love me like you say, you'll be here when I get back."

"And if I'm not," Trina asked defiantly as she crossed her arms over her chest and crossed her legs at the knee, successively.

Devon shrugged. "Baby, you gotta do what you gotta do. I'ma always be me and do what I gotta do to make sure I'm straight."

He grabbed his coat, deciding to leave now before Trina could instigate another argument. He picked up his keys, cell phone, and the slip of paper with Shaniece's address written on it. He looked down at Trina, who continued to sit on the bed with an attitude, and kissed her forehead before walking out of the room.

As he drove toward Shaniece's house, he thought about the situation he was placing himself in. He really liked Shaniece and would establish a relationship with her if the opportunity presented itself, but he wasn't ready to let go of the comfort he shared with Trina. Having Trina around brought back the sheltered living that Devon once shared with his own mother. However, he would never tell Trina that, because she would surely begin complaining about him using her just so he could have someone to take care of him.

But Shaniece was the type of girl Devon would have no problem taking home to show off to his mother. The fact that the two women might already know each other, and that there seemed to be no tension between them, made a relationship with Shaniece seem even more appealing. Though Devon had seen very little of his mother in the last three years, he knew he could trust her opinion concerning the woman in his life. Yvonne had voiced over and over that she didn't care for the meaningless affair Devon was having with Trina, and he could understand that. But until he had more options, he'd settle for what he could take.

Looking down at the address, Devon realized that Shaniece didn't live as far out as he'd expected. Though she didn't live on his side of the neighborhood, where the majority of the community's crime took place, it only took driving past her high school to get to her home where many middle-class families resided. He arrived at her home within fifteen minutes. Devon pulled into her driveway and shut off his engine. He looked at the clock and realized that he was ten minutes early for dinner. His nerves were at an all-time high and he hated the anxiety he felt building up inside him. He had to admit that he was nervous about meeting Shaniece's parents. He was used to turning on his charm when he was around a nice girl, but he'd never met a nice girl's parents before. He was unsure of how to conduct himself. Shaniece had told him just to be himself.

"Act like you act when we talk," she'd said. "Be who you are and they'll be cool with you."

Though he'd agreed that she was right, Devon knew that he'd been partially putting up a front when he talked to Shaniece, and she only knew who he portrayed himself to be. Devon tried, effortlessly, to keep his street mentality on the down low when he interacted with Shaniece. He didn't want her to know what he was all about, because that was a surefire way to lose her. So if he wanted to keep Shaniece in his life and make a good impression on her parents, the masquerade would continue.

He picked up the two bouquets of flowers from the backseat. He'd managed to hide them from Trina by keeping them in his car. He headed toward the house and took a deep breath before ringing the doorbell. Rainelle answered the door, with a wide smile, and motioned for him to enter the house.

Keith came down the stairs and nodded in Devon's direction. "Wassup?" he greeted, giving Devon a brotherly handshake. "Niecey should be down in a minute."

"Are either of those for me?" Rainelle asked Devon playfully as she pointed toward the flowers in his hand.

Devon laughed, which helped to expel some of the nervousness he felt. The flowers were for Shaniece and her mother, but to satisfy the curious look on Rainelle's face, he pulled a single flower from one of the bouquets and handed it to her.

"Thank you," she said as she studied his face. "You're nervous."

Devon looked at her and smiled. "Is it that obvious?"

Rainelle tightened her smile and nodded.

Keith laughed. "Man, every dude that come up in here asking for Niecey has that same look on his face. When you have to go through the *reverend,* Niecey's hard to get at."

"Stop scaring him," Shaniece said with a laugh.

They all looked up at Shaniece, who was coming down the stairs. Devon admired the way she looked in her fitted jeans and black sweater. Her hair was back in a bun, allowing Devon to admire the delicacy of her face.

"Hey," she greeted him with a smile, and surprised him with an innocent embrace.

Devon smiled as she released him. "Hi." He handed her the flowers. "I brought these for you."

"Thank you, Devon," Shaniece replied. "These are really nice."

"He's nervous," Rainelle pointed out with a grin. "Tell him that's a good thing."

Shaniece laughed and nodded. "It is. Daddy likes feeling superior," she whispered to him.

"Hey, is that knucklehead boy here yet? I'm ready to eat," a loud, riotous voice proclaimed.

Rainelle and Keith laughed out loud when Devon's eyes nearly popped out of his head at the sound of their father's voice. Shaniece tried to hide her laughter behind a small cough, but Devon knew he'd become the butt of the joke.

Cedric entered the room with his wife right behind him. Devon assessed the man from head to toe. He could tell where Rainelle and Keith had gotten their height, but all three of the siblings were just as slim as their very attractive mother. Though Cedric was only a couple of inches taller than Devon, he supported a very large frame, and his broad shoulders and muscular chest caused him to look as if he could effortlessly snap Devon in two with his bare hands.

Devon forced himself to pull his emotions together. If his friends ever saw him acting in the manner that he was now, they'd dismiss him so fast, his children would grow up without the respect of the people who lived throughout his community. He reminded himself that he was Big D, the biggest, most respected hustler on this side of Riverside. He feared nothing or no one. He'd been beaten, stabbed, and shot, but continued to live his life, regardless of the fact that any day could be his last. He would treat this situation just like any other—only with a tad more respect and humbleness.

"Devon, this is my father, Cedric Simmons, and my mother, Natalie Simmons," Shaniece introduced. "Daddy, Mama, this is my friend Devon Torres."

"Good evening," Devon said in a sturdy tone. He shook each of their hands and then handed Natalie the other set of flowers.

She smiled. "Thank you."

"What?" Cedric huffed. "No gift for me?"

Devon became speechless as he looked at Cedric, and then at Shaniece, who only shrugged her shoulders.

"I'm just kidding, son," Cedric said, patting Devon on the back. "C'mon, let's eat."

They moved into the dining room and Devon motioned to a seat for Shaniece. She smiled and he saw the impressed look on her face, but he was confused when she declined his offering.

"I have to help Mama serve," she said softly.

He watched as she disappeared through a set of double doors, which he assumed led to the kitchen. Cedric sat at the head of the table, and Devon figured that the seat directly opposite of that would be where Natalie would sit. He took a seat across from Rainelle and Keith, leaving the seat next to him open for Shaniece to rest.

"So, Devon," Cedric began as he settled comfortably in his seat, "how old are you?"

"Nineteen," Devon replied, with a slight nod.

Shaniece and her mother came into the dining room with a pan of lemon pepper chicken, and bowls of yellow rice and green beans, a basket of dinner rolls, and a large pitcher of homemade lemonade. They set the food on the table and took their seats. The scene almost looked like one from the old black-and-white movies that depicted a somewhat distorted image of the contemporary American family.

Devon knew that a prayer would take place, so he didn't hesitate in bowing his head, along with the rest of the family, as Cedric led them through blessing the food. He was slightly bewildered, but even more fascinated, when he saw Natalie fixing her husband's plate of food. He knew, then, that this was a very traditional home.

"White or dark?" Shaniece asked Devon.

"I'm sorry?" Devon questioned, and then laughed. "Oh, the chicken. Dark, please."

Shaniece placed a thigh and a leg on his plate and then proceeded to add the sides. Devon looked at her, almost in surprise, then realized that she was probably following instructions her mother had given her before he even walked through the door. Devon decided that he'd have to show Shaniece that, though the gesture was polite and greatly appreciated, it was unnecessary. When she finished fixing his plate and pouring lemonade into his glass, she started to prepare her own food, but Devon took the large fork, which was being used to pick up the chicken, out of her reach.

"White or dark?" Devon asked, holding the fork in his hand.

Shaniece reached for the utensil. "I can get it."

"I could've gotten my own, but I let you do it for me," Devon said. "So I'll fix your plate, if it's okay with you."

Shaniece looked up at her mother, who shrugged, and then at her father, who nodded. "Okay," she said softly. "Dark, preferably a leg . . . please."

Devon smiled as he prepared Shaniece's plate. Once he was finished, he placed it in front of her and she thanked him.

Natalie chewed a mouthful of rice and smiled at Devon, who knew that her polite gesture foreshadowed the beginning of the interrogation. He remembered the moderate version of the cross-examination he'd received from Tatiana and knew that the Simmonses' questioning would be a lot more intense.

"You met Shaniece at the grocery store?" Natalie asked, as if for confirmation.

Devon smiled toward Shaniece and nodded. "You could say she nearly knocked me off my feet when I saw her."

Shaniece and her siblings laughed knowingly as their parents looked at each other in misunderstanding.

"I bumped into him with my shopping cart," Shaniece clarified after swallowing a piece of chicken.

"Oh," Natalie said, and offered another soft smile. "So, do you give money to every pretty girl you meet in the supermarket?"

Devon shifted in his seat and offered Natalie a sheep-ish grin. "No, ma'am. When Rainelle and Keith were asking for the snack foods, and Shaniece was telling them that they couldn't get any because they only had enough money for what they were supposed to buy, it reminded me of when I was little and my mom always told me I couldn't have sweets because we didn't have enough money for them," he explained. "I figured it would be a nice gesture."

"And a way to impress my daughter," Cedric added knowingly. He watched the anxious look that crossed Devon's face and chuckled. "I know all about it. Tried to get Mrs. Simmons by flaunting my bank account in her face, but it didn't work. I had to show her who I re-ally was on the inside before she even let me approach her."

"That's what we try to teach Shaniece and Rainelle," Natalie continued. "And Keith. A relationship can't be built on material things, because they only last for so long. It must be based upon what's on the inside and, of course, God's will for the two persons in the relation-ship."

Devon nodded. "I know that, and Shaniece is appar-ently listening to you. We're still just friends and get-ting to know each other."

"Do you plan to take your relationship with her any further?" Natalie asked.

"That really hasn't come up," Devon answered, glanc-ing at Shaniece, who was quietly eating her dinner. "We've talked about what we look for in a partner, but we've kinda let each other know that we're too busy to have a relationship." He shoved a forkful of rice into his mouth and tried to suppress the sudden guilt he felt. He and Shaniece had agreed that a relationship wasn't at the top of their priority lists, but right after having that conversation with her, he'd found himself in bed with Trina—and though their relationship was a shaky one, it was still a monogamous bond, nonetheless.

"I won't beat around the bush and pretend that Shaniece keeping *casual* company with you is fine with me," Cedric stated as he placed his fork on his plate. "I want my daughter to focus on her schoolwork. She's graduating this year, at the top of her class as far as I'm aware. Then there's college and possibly grad school, depending on what she wishes to do. Anything that would hinder her from making these things happen on schedule is displeasing to me." He peered deep into Devon's eyes.

Devon kept eye contact and nodded. "I understand, and if Shaniece—or you all—feel as if I'm hindering her from anything, I don't mind backing off for a while. But like I said before, we're just friends, and there are no plans to change that before the time is mutually right."

There was silence around the table for a few minutes as they enjoyed their meal. Then the relaxed atmosphere began to tense as a new conversation began.

"Are you saved, son?" Cedric suddenly asked.

Shaniece's fork hit her plate with a loud clank, and Keith and Rainelle exchanged glances. While Natalie looked at her daughter and could see the answer to the question written all over Shaniece's face, Cedric kept his glare on Devon, wanting to receive a response from the young man, to whom his question had been directed.

Devon had known this was going to happen, and he couldn't make up a lie in order to appease the good reverend. He'd already told Shaniece that he wasn't born-again. He hadn't accepted Jesus as his personal Lord and Savior, even though he did believe in everything he'd been taught about the Christian religion, including the fact that if he didn't commit to the afore-mentioned, he'd be subject to eternal damnation. So he could only be honest when answering this question.

"No, sir, I'm not." He glanced at Shaniece, who seemed to hold an intense interest in the food on her plate. She looked as if she was praying, but he could see her biting her bottom lip, signifying how worried she was about this situation.

"May I ask, why not?" Cedric questioned in a tone that signified he was unhappy with the news, but he was calm enough to discuss it.

"Daddy, can we not talk about this?" Shaniece pleaded, lifting her head slightly.

Cedric sat up straighter in his seat. "I'm sorry, but I think if I'm going to allow you to go out with this young man, I should know enough about him to feel comfortable with you being in unsupervised situations with him. Now, if you have a problem with that, we can end this discussion and dinner immediately, and it wouldn't bother me none," he threatened. "So, may I continue, or would you like to show your guest to the door?"

"Yes, sir," Shaniece said softly.

Devon figured her answer was directed toward her father's request to continue with the conversation, since she hadn't moved from her seat. He could tell that Shaniece was completely uncomfortable, though, by the way she sank her teeth deeper into her bottom lip. He, too, was starting to feel awkward in the situation, and he prayed that he wouldn't become defensive as he usually did when he found himself in an uncomfortable position. Silence resumed, and from the way Cedric was looking at him, Devon realized that it was his turn to speak in response to Cedric's question.

"I guess the main reason is that I haven't really been exposed to the Christian lifestyle in a positive way," he answered. "No offense to you or your ministry, but a lot of pastors I've heard about or seen on television seem to talk about money or live these lavish, unrealistic life-styles. And some of the everyday Christians I've come in contact with seem to be judgmental or hypocritical. It's just not something I want to be a part of." He took a moment to breathe. "Plus, I just feel like I'd be tied down if I fully gave my life to Christ," Devon answered.

"Well, I definitely understand your issues with some Christians portraying less than Christ-like lifestyles," Natalie stated in a somewhat nurturing tone, sounding as if she was trying to ease the tension in the room. "But not every Christian is like that. . . . Just to put that out there. But I'm more concerned with learning what you mean by saying you'd be 'tied down'?"

Devon shrugged. "I like to do certain things that I know would be off-limits if I were to make that change in my life. I believe in God, and I understand the principles and beliefs surrounding the faith, but I'm young and I just want to live without any restraints."

There was silence again and Devon watched Cedric's expression. The man looked as if he wanted to say more . . . ask more questions . . . take the conversation to a deeper level. Then Devon looked at Shaniece and noticed that she had her hands pressed together in her lap, and her eyes were shut tightly, and he knew that she was praying for an end to come to the conversation very quickly. Devon silently joined in with her fervent prayer.

"Well, not to offend you or anything," Cedric began, and glanced at his daughter when he heard her inhale deeply, "*but* it is now my family's, *including* Shaniece's, job to help you get to that point where you can accept Jesus into your life."

When he didn't say any more, Devon heard Shaniece release a lungful of air. She finally lifted her head as Keith and Rainelle began to talk about the upcoming basketball season, a conversation that was a more comfortable topic for both her and Devon.

Shaniece turned toward Devon. Her eyes told him that she was now obligated to help him, and as he fell deeper into her gaze, he felt as if she'd known from the very beginning that was the reason she'd been placed in his life.

From this day forward, Devon knew that he and his relationship with Shaniece would be tested in many ways.

Chapter 13

Two tickets to the hottest play in town. Devon smiled as he placed the tickets into his wallet and shoved his wallet into his back pocket. He looked into the mirror positioned near his closet and straightened out his dark blue dress shirt and adjusted his pants so that they would comfortably rest around his waist. He tightened his belt so that this would be the last time he'd have to adjust them tonight. He glanced down at his watch and realized he only had a short amount of time to pick up Shaniece and drive downtown before the play began at seven o'clock. He'd been anticipating this night for seven days, and he was glad that he could finally spend some alone time with Shaniece. He nodded his head, as if approving of his appearance, and then turned to pick up his keys.

"What's her name?" he heard Trina ask.

Devon sighed as he snatched his keys off his dresser. He didn't have time to sit—or stand—around entertaining his girlfriend's insecurities. He glanced at his watch again, though only thirty seconds had passed since he last checked the time. He needed something to distract him . . . something that would keep him from having to defend himself in this argument for the umpteenth time, but there was nothing. He had everything he needed; now he just had to make it to the door.

"D, why are you doing this to us?"

Devon felt his lip curl in disgust as he turned toward Trina, who was standing in the bedroom doorway. "Trina, why are *you* doing this to *us?*"

Trina moistened her lips angrily and inhaled a deep breath. "Answering my question with a question is not going to get us anywhere and you know it." She walked into the room, toward him. She stood close to him, inhaled, and then she stepped back. "You're wearing the cologne I bought you for Valentine's Day. You hardly ever wear it. This girl must be something special for you to pull a two-hundred-dollar bottle of cologne from the back of the bathroom closet." Her fiery stare pierced Devon's eyes. "What's her name?"

Devon stood before her with his head tilted to the side and a nonchalant expression on his face.

Trina, apparently tired of being ignored, slapped him across his face and demanded, "What is her name?"

He massaged his right cheek and tried to steady his breathing. He was becoming angry, but if his mother had taught him one thing, it was never to hit a girl, even when provoked. "Trina, don't hit me," he said calmly.

She slapped him again, this time against the other cheek. "What is her name?" she commanded, her voice rising.

"A real man never hits a woman." He heard his mother's voice and he tightened his fists, trying to keep from retaliating. "Trina, I ain't gon' te—"

Another slap cut him off. "What is her name, *Devon?*"

Trina knew he didn't allow anyone to call him by his given name . . . at least not without permission. He felt as if she'd just spit in his face and then brushed it off as though it wasn't a big deal. He grabbed Trina by both her wrists and held them tightly as he glared at her. She was unafraid to return his stare. She wanted to know whom he'd been spending his time with; he'd most definitely let her know.

"Shaniece Simmons," he said; a slight smile was on his face. "The most beautiful, intelligent, and talented woman I've met in a long time. We been talking for a little over a month now. . . . We met in a grocery store." He raised his eyebrows in realization as he nodded toward Trina. "Oh, I forgot to thank you for not having any food for me to eat; 'cause if I hadn't gone to the store that day, I woulda never met her." His smile grew. "We talk *every single* day. I met her parents last weekend and they approve of me. As a matter of fact"— he glanced at his watch once more without releasing her wrists—"I'm just about late in picking her up for our *date* tonight. Taking her to a play," he added, with a nod. "She'll love it."

Trina had tears in her eyes, but Devon knew that she would never allow him to see that he was tearing down her self-esteem. "Does she love you? The real *you*, I mean."

Devon's face fell at her words because he knew what she was trying to get at. He slowly loosened the grip he had on her.

Trina's eyes showed her surprise at his unspoken answer. "So you been puttin' up a front for your li'l girlfriend. She don't even know what you're all about, does she? Don't worry. If you tell her, I'm sure she'll still stick it out with you . . . like I've been doing for the last year," she said, unintentionally spitting in his face. "You know, I've been here with you this whole time. Playing middleman with you and your peddlers. Being the lookout while you handle your business. Acting like a worried mother, always afraid of receiving that early-morning phone call about you being locked up or dead somewhere in the streets, while you stay out to three and four in the morning without a care in the world. I've been here for over twelve months putting up with your mess, and you can't even tell me that you love me, but you're all of a sudden infatuated with this girl, who's known you for a few weeks, but doesn't really know the *real you* at all. That's messed up, D."

Devon hated hearing the truth come from Trina's mouth in such a spiteful manner. He knew she was right, though. This situation was a complete mess. He hadn't planned on falling for Shaniece, but he knew it was happening. In the short amount of time he'd known her, she'd been nothing less than honest and straightforward—that enticed him and caused him to want to spend more time with her, getting to know her. But when it came to being himself, he hadn't been as noble as she had been.

How would he look trying to explain to Shaniece that he was a drug dealer? Not only a drug dealer, but one of the biggest hustlers on his side of town? Most people knew him as Big D, and with that name came the descriptions of trapper, peddler, dealer, and trafficker. Trying to explain any of the labels would end with Shaniece walking away from him, and he didn't want that.

"Look, Trina." Devon spoke after several minutes of silence and watching her cry. "I'm sorry about all of this, but I told you that I wasn't lookin' for nothin' serious when I met you, and that hasn't changed. I'm too wrapped up in my business to settle down right now."

"So what are you going to tell your girl when she starts to feel how I'm feeling and you dismiss her like it's nothing?" Trina asked, with excessive hand movements accompanying her words. "What are you going to say to her when she tells you that she wants to marry you and have children with you and spend the rest of her life loving you? What are you going to say when you walk out on her, leaving her with a broken heart to mend all by herself? What are you going to say, D?" she yelled.

Devon shrugged, knowing he didn't have an answer to any of her questions. He never wanted Shaniece to feel like Trina was feeling at this very moment. He never wanted to have to go through this with Shaniece. He wanted her to be happy in his company, and so far, everything was going according to his plan.

"She's different" was all Devon could say. "She makes me want to be different."

Trina laughed. "Yeah, right. D, you're a drug-dealing thug who's never going to change. The streets are all you know, and now some little Miss Perfect from the other side of the tracks is going to make you want to change your whole lifestyle. *Please!*" she spat mockingly. "You're always going to be Big D, never just Devon."

He flinched at his name flowing from her lips. In the last few weeks, he'd become accustomed to only hearing Shaniece's sweet voice say his given name. He'd struggled through dinner last week with her parents calling him "Devon," but having Trina say it was just annoying. He felt as if she was purposely trying to disrespect him.

He reached up, his hands close to her throat, but instead of choking the life out of her, like he wanted, he threw his hands up in frustration. "I'm out," he grumbled, wanting to leave before Trina made him do something he'd regret.

"Well, I won't be here when you get back," she retorted. "I'm tired of this and I *know* I deserve better."

"Good for you," he said as he grabbed his jacket and walked toward the door, unknowingly leaving his cell phone on the nightstand.

She followed behind him. "So this is it? It's over . . .
just like that?" she questioned. "You're giving up someone who loves you *for you* for some girl who doesn't
even know who you are?"

"Trina, I didn't ask you to leave. You made that decision," Devon said as he continued walking until he
stood outside the house. He could hear Trina's loud,
angry scream as he descended the porch and allowed
the door to slam behind him. He didn't have time to
think about her dramatic attempts to keep him home
tonight. He had a date, and he planned to make it on
time.

He opened his car door and got inside. As he started
the engine, he noticed that his gas tank was just above
empty. He sighed heavily. Having to get gas would only
make him later than he already was. Despite the time,
he pulled out of his driveway and headed to the nearest
gas station. He pulled up to a pump and got out of his
car; then he ran into the store and paid the cashier for
the gas, returning then to the pump.

As Devon filled his tank, he noticed a black Cadillac
pulling up to the pump across from him. He didn't pay
much attention to it until the driver stepped out of his
vehicle and stared in Devon's direction.

"Hey, what up, Big D," the driver beckoned. "What you
up to tonight?"

Devon peered at the man. He didn't recognize his
face, but he didn't know everybody in his neighborhood, so it didn't provoke his thought of who the person might be. So he answered as casually as he would
to any other person on the street.

"Just chillin' tonight," Devon replied.

"A'ight," the man responded. "Aye, you think you can
take care of me, real quick?"

Devon sighed. If tonight continued with all of these interruptions, the play would be over by the time he'd get to Shaniece's place.

"Naw, man," he responded. "I gotta get to this spot. I'm already late as it is."

The man looked around nervously. "Aww . . . c'mon, man. I just need a dime. Real quick."

Though he was in a hurry to pick up Shaniece, he never passed up a chance to make some money. Devon silently nodded as he finished topping off his gas tank. He then used his car keys to unlock the glove compartment, where he kept a small stash of his merchandise. He walked toward the man and they made the exchange with a quick handshake.

"'Preciate it, Big D," the man said.

"No problem," Devon mumbled, but before he could walk away, the man grabbed him by his arm and jerked Devon toward him.

Devon tried to reach for the gun he kept tucked in his pants, but the man grabbed his other arm also. The man shoved Devon up against the Cadillac and spoke words that Devon hadn't heard since he was seventeen.

"You are under arrest," the man said, flashing his police badge in front of Devon's face before slapping handcuffs on his wrists.

As Devon was read his rights, he mumbled a string of curses. He looked toward the gas station to see the clerk looking out at him in confusion, but not making a move to come out and help him. He thought of Trina, who was only a few blocks down the street, probably shoving her belongings in her Louis Vuitton suitcase.

Kane was dead. His mother would expect to hear from him by the end of the weekend but if she didn't, she wouldn't think much of it. Shaniece was unknowingly waiting in vain for him to pick her up for their date. Devon was on his way to the county jail. No one had his back. He was left alone to bail himself out this time.

The rhythmic tap of Shaniece's heels against the floor was matched by the ticktock of the clock in the living room. She rested her elbow on her leg and her head in her hand as the clock resounded throughout the house. *Seven P.M.*

Shaniece had been waiting for Devon for over an hour, and she'd concluded that she'd been stood up. She'd tried calling him at six-thirty, but had only received his voice mail. The same happened when she'd called at six forty-five. At first, she'd been worried that something might have happened to him. Maybe an accident had occurred and he couldn't get to a phone, but she figured that he would've at least had someone call her on his behalf to explain what was going on. Now she just felt like he'd abandoned her.

Even still, she couldn't accept that he would just not show up. They talked every day, and last Friday at dinner, he'd gone as far as asking her father for permission to take her out tonight. He'd been anticipating this date almost as much as she had been, and now he just didn't show up. Something wasn't right.

"Hey, Niecey, you're still here?" she heard her sister ask.

Rainelle had asked her that same question nearly thirty minutes earlier, and her parents and Keith had questioned the whereabouts of her date also. Cedric was heated at the thought of Devon canceling his date with Shaniece and not calling to inform her of it. He'd threatened to wait in the living room with Shaniece, so that *if* Devon did show up, he could give the young man a piece of his mind. But Shaniece had asked that her father leave her alone to handle Devon *if* he ever arrived. Sensing her rising disappointment, Cedric left the room after giving a kiss to the top of her head.

"Has he called?" Rainelle asked, not giving her older sister a chance to respond to the first question she'd asked.

Shaniece tried not to cry from the thought of something happening to Devon, but she couldn't stop the single tear that rolled down her rosy cheek. "No, I'm going to call him again, just in case." She pulled out her cell phone and dialed Devon's number. This time, she received an answer, but it wasn't Devon's voice that greeted her.

"Hello?" a cold, unwelcoming tone answered after the third ring.

Before she responded, Shaniece pulled the phone away from her ear and stared at the screen, making sure she'd dialed the right number. "Hi, may I please speak with Devon?"

The line was quiet for a moment and then the woman asked, "Who is this?"

Shaniece's frown deepened, and she almost wanted to respond by asking the woman the same question, but she decided to answer, just in case this woman was Devon's mother or guardian. She couldn't have his family thinking she was disrespectful and rude, though the woman on the other end of the phone line was definitely displaying those characteristics. "This is Shaniece. I'm calling because Devon was—"

"Oh, you the girl who's had *my man* walking on cloud nine," the woman cut her off.

"Excuse me?" Shaniece said in confusion.

"Yeah, you heard me," the woman continued. "You been chillin' with another woman's man."

Shaniece was becoming angry with the woman. She was already upset about Devon's absence, and now this woman was taunting her with this little childish game. "Can I speak with Devon?" she asked evenly.

"There is no *Devon* here," the woman spat coldly. "His name is D, most know him as Big D," she said. "They call him that because he is the *biggest* hustler in town. He has people all over our neighborhood running his operation as tightly as they can. D's all about his business."

"What are you talking about!" Shaniece was nearly screaming.

Her tone caused her parents to come out of their bedroom and her brother to join her sister at the top of the stairs. She refused to look at her family, afraid that they would see the mounting tears behind her eyes.

"D is a drug dealer," the woman informed her. "The biggest this side of town has ever seen since the death of his mentor. He's been running this operation since he was seventeen, but he's been dealing since he was fifteen. He's a high-school dropout and depends on his illegal income to keep a roof over *our* heads and food on *our* table." The woman paused, before continuing. "Yes, I said *'our,'* because I've been living with him for the last several months. *I've* been taking care of him like he needs to be taken care of. *I've* been with him for the last year, despite what he does and how he lives. Why would I stay with him if I know he, or even I, could be locked up or killed at any moment?" she said defensively, as if Shaniece had posed the question. "Because I love him. *I* love him. *I love him!*" she yelled through the phone, loud enough for Shaniece's family to hear.

"Baby girl, what is going on?" Cedric asked as he watched his daughter sit motionless on the couch, with tears running down her face and the phone glued to her ear.

"And who are you?" the woman continued, her voice rising with each word she spoke. "Some girl he just met. You don't even know him! You don't know him!"

"May I please speak with Devon?" Shaniece asked, her voice soft and wavering. "Please?"

The woman was silent for a moment and then said, in a softer, but still icy, tone, "I don't know where D is. We had an argument and he left the house over an hour ago to pick you up for your little *date*. I just noticed that he left his phone behind." She was quiet again.

Before the woman could say any more, Shaniece hung up the phone. She began to cry uncontrollably, ignoring the calls and questions of her family. She couldn't believe Devon had lied to her. Nearly everything that had come out of his mouth had been a lie. Shaniece had been nothing but honest with him, and she despised him for not being man enough to return the favor. Devon had seemed so genuine, and that was what had attracted her to him in the first place. Now she didn't know what to think of him. So many descriptions came to mind, and none of them were positive. She knew what she had to do. It was what she should have done from the very beginning. She needed to get this boy out of her mind and move on.

Chapter 14

Thanksgiving and Christmas had come and gone, leaving Devon without the joy of the holiday season. Within a two-month time span, he'd been tried and sentenced to serve a ten-to-twenty-five-year sentence in prison for possession and distribution of controlled substances. Devon could only lower his head in anguish at the thought of spending another day in jail. It was cramped and utterly disgusting, but it would be his home for *at least* another ten years.

Before the officers hauled him off to his cell in the Fulton County Jail, they'd allowed his mother to give him one last hug, which he could not return due to the cuffs that restrained his arms. When Devon had been allowed his one phone call, the same night he'd been arrested, he'd irresponsibly wasted it on Trina, hoping she'd feel some morsel of sorrow for him and come bail him out.

"Boy, please," she'd spat into the receiver. "For all I care, you can stay there for life. Maybe you'll take the time to think about how you should've appreciated me while you had me." Then she hung up in his face.

He'd been too afraid to call Shaniece for fear of rejection. So the second time he'd been allowed to use the phone, he'd called his mother. Yvonne's tone was full of disappointment as she barely uttered two words during their conversation. He'd been upset when she refused to come bail him out, and he cursed her for deserting him in his time of need. She shed several tears and told him that she could only pray for him. He hurled a few more choice words through the phone line before angrily ending the call; so it had been a surprise to him when he saw her sitting in the courtroom almost two weeks ago.

As Yvonne hugged him, she mumbled a quiet prayer and told him that she loved him. Before they had parted, Devon whispered, "Tell Shaniece that I'm sorry." As the officers pulled him away, he could see the confused look on his mother's face, but he knew she'd figure out his request, come the next Sunday morning.

He sat on his top bunk and stared down at the gift Yvonne had given him for Christmas, just three days ago. It was a picture of her with Shaniece at the Christmas celebration her church had hosted the Sunday before the holiday. He knew his mother had taken the picture especially for him. He hadn't shared with her the details behind his brief, less-than-serious relationship with Shaniece, but somehow his mother knew what was in his heart.

Shaniece had been in his thoughts ever since he'd gotten locked up. He was sure she knew the truth about him, and was even more positive that she resented him for the lies he'd told. He desperately wanted to call her, but fear of being completely forsaken taunted him and encircled him with doubt and many questions. He wanted to explain everything to the girl he'd come to love in the last two months, but he was too afraid to make the first move.

He still wasn't sure how he'd fallen for Shaniece so quickly, but the attraction he felt toward her was so undeniable that it had to be love . . . right? He questioned it from time to time, especially since he wasn't the type to be head over heels for any woman, but he couldn't shake the feeling.

Whether or not he was truly in love with Shaniece, he knew he felt *something* for her. He'd asked his mother to try persuading Shaniece to join her for a visit, but he had yet to hear anything back. He knew he was living in a fantasy world if he thought Shaniece would come within one hundred feet of him. She deserved better than him, and Devon knew it.

The toilet, which sat in the corner of his room, was flushed, and he waited a second before looking at his cellmate, giving Mitch time to fix his clothes. Devon hated times of the day like this when Mitch seemed not to be able to control his bowels. The smell was horrific and reminded Devon of how he took something as simple as his private bathroom for granted.

Mitch looked up at Devon and shrugged. "Couldn't help it, man."

Devon didn't bother to respond.

"Whatchu got?" Mitch questioned.

Devon flashed the picture in front of Mitch's face. The five-foot-eight, caramel-skinned gentleman smiled as he studied the photo.

He cursed under his breath. "The honey wit' the braids is lookin' kinda nice," he said with a wide grin, revealing the small gap between his two front teeth.

Devon's eyes shot toward the photograph and he moved the picture from his cellmate's view. "Man, that's my mama," he said, disgusted; though Devon had to admit that his mother was still young and looked just as good as some of the girls he tried to attract.

Mitch laughed. "My bad, but I call 'em how I see 'em. The other girl look good too. If that's yo' sister, lemme holla at her," he said with a wide grin.

Devon gazed at the picture and smiled down at Shaniece's image. Her smile was wide and full of happiness. It was a smile he'd seen many times, but it was slightly different, though. Her parting lips revealed her anticipation of the holiday season, but it was her eyes that drew his attention. In the few times he'd been in her presence, her smile had been accompanied always by her gleaming brown eyes. But in this photo, her eyes were vacant of that sparkle. He wanted so badly to make her smile like she used to, but how could he do that from an eight-by-twelve room?

He shook his head. "Naw, you can't holla at her," Devon said, responding to Mitch's comment.

"Why not?" Mitch asked, seemingly offended.

"'Cause that's *my* girl," Devon proclaimed as he pointed toward Shaniece's image in the picture. Silently he hoped he could make his dream a reality.

"Devon wants you to know that he's sorry."

Shaniece had spun on her heels and faced the voice that had just delivered the message she'd been longing to hear, but had been pretending as if she could care less.

"Ms. Yvonne?" she had questioned. "How do you know Devon?"

"He's my son," Yvonne had informed her solemnly.

Shaniece's face had revealed her surprise as she gazed into Yvonne's eyes, but then she remembered thinking that Yvonne's eyes were strikingly similar to Devon's enchanting brown ones.

Yvonne had nodded to assure her. "I was sixteen when I had him. But that's beside the point."

"So why are you delivering messages for Devon? Why can't he just call me and apologize for standing me up . . . and for lying to me?" Shaniece had known she sounded bitter, but that was how she felt.

Yvonne's expression had remained somber. "He's been incarcerated for drug possession and intent to sell."

"What!" Shaniece had shrieked. "That woman was right," she had mumbled almost disbelievingly. Devon is a drug dealer, *she allowed her mind to process. She had wanted the woman's words to be lies, but Yvonne's information contradicted her hopes.*

Yvonne had seemed confused. "What woman?"

"I don't know. A woman who answered Devon's phone when I was trying to call him," Shaniece had explained. "I spoke with her the night Devon was supposed to take me out. She told me everything about him and I was hoping she was wrong." The tears in Shaniece's eyes had mirrored the ones in Yvonne's, and Shaniece had known they shared a mutual disappointment.

"Yeah, Devon's been doing this for a long time, and I've been praying for him, but . . ." Yvonne had allowed her voice to trail away. "Anyway, he asked that I tell you how sorry he is. He would like to see you."

Shaniece had longed to see Devon. She wanted to gaze into his enticing brown eyes and take in his alluring presence, but her anger wouldn't allow her to give in to her heart's desires. "I'm sorry, Ms. Yvonne, but I can't."

Shaniece had wanted to ask Yvonne to tell Devon that she would be praying for him or to offer some sort of consolation for his predicament, but she couldn't find a compassionate nerve that would allow her to do so. Instead, she had ended the conversation with Yvonne and promised herself that today would be the last day she'd allow Devon Torres to cross the threshold of her thoughts.

***

That conversation had taken place a week before Christmas, and now, nearly a week into the brand-new year, Shaniece still couldn't get Devon out of her mind. She hated thinking about him because her thoughts only reminded her of the lies their relationship had been built on. *Five weeks is hardly a relationship, Niecey,* she scolded herself, but she knew she'd allowed Devon too much access to her heart. During their late-night conversations, she'd expressed her wants and needs, and somehow he'd been able to cater to them. He was a manipulator and a cheater, and she wanted nothing to do with him.

"Niecey, you've been looking a little down lately," Craig said as he sat down with her at their usual lunch table at school.

Shaniece looked up from her plate of chicken and rice and smiled in her friend's direction. "I'm okay," she softly said before lowering her head again. She could hardly lie to Craig and knew he could tell she was going through something. Her thoughts were confirmed when he reached across the table and lightly placed his hand over one of hers.

"Shaniece," he called, waiting to capture her eyes before continuing.

"Yes?" she answered, almost inaudibly, as she raised her gaze.

He stared into her eyes and said, "I'm here . . . you know, if you ever wanna just talk."

She managed a soft smile. "Thank you, Craig. I appreciate that."

He kept his hand over hers for a minute longer and then pulled away. Tatiana arrived at the table and took a seat next to Shaniece.

"Hey, girl, you feelin' better?" she asked with a concerned smile.

Shaniece nodded, but she remained silent. She knew if she answered that question once more, her quavering voice would contradict what she felt in her heart. She was hurting, not just because Devon had betrayed her trust, but she missed him. He'd been in prison for two and a half months, and he hadn't used any of his call times to phone her. Yvonne had delivered a few messages that begged for her to visit Devon, but Shaniece wanted to hear him ask her for a visit. She wanted him to humble himself and approach her with a sincere apology upon his lips. She needed him to show that he needed her. The possibility that he felt that he was too much of a man to do that pained her to the core.

"How would the reverend feel about me taking you to dinner on Friday night?"

Shaniece's head snapped up and her eyes focused on Craig. He was looking directly at her, with a small smile tugging at the ends of his lips. She stared into his eyes, wanting to see the sincerity that she heard in his voice. His eyes held truth and trust. She'd always been able to trust Craig. They'd been friends for six years, and not once had he ever disappointed her. She'd known Devon for less than a month, and he'd shattered in one night all the faith she'd thought she had in him.

Shaniece didn't see any harm in going out with Craig. He was nice and genuine and he cared for her feelings. Her parents had *approved* of Devon, but they *loved* Craig. She could see a major difference between the two and wondered if she should give Craig a chance.

"I don't know." Shaniece spoke softly. "He might approve." She glanced at Tatiana, who was smiling at the thought of her moving on with her life.

Craig's smile reached his eyes as it grew. "I'll call and ask. I promise you'll have a great time."

Shaniece nodded and returned her concentration toward her lunch. She had about ten minutes left to enjoy her meal, but she wasn't hungry. Devon continued to cloud her thoughts, and she wanted to scream for him to go away. She didn't need to be thinking about him when she could be focusing on a better man—a man like Craig. She looked back up and caught him gazing at her. He smiled and didn't waver in his stare. Shaniece searched his eyes and promised God that if she gave Craig the chance that he deserved, she would take things much slower than she had with Devon. She wouldn't get hurt a second time.

Chapter 15

One visitor per day was all Devon was permitted. His mother had come twice this week, and he was almost tired of coming into the visiting area and seeing her sitting at his table. He loved his mother to death, and would do anything for her, but he'd seen her more in the last few weeks than he had in the last few years. However, when he looked around and saw that he was one of the few who were released during the visiting hour, he was thankful that Yvonne took time out of her work and church schedule to visit him; it showed how much she loved and cared about him.

He'd asked her about Shaniece's well-being, and Yvonne could only shake her head. "She's so angry with you." Yvonne had spoken softly as they sat across from each other. "I can tell that she still cares, though. I can only keep trying, but I'm not going to push her."

Devon understood that Shaniece needed time and space to get over what he'd done to her, but he yearned just to have her near him. He hadn't known anyone to fall in love in a matter of weeks, but he believed he had, and he couldn't shake the feeling. A sense of nausea washed over him every time he thought of Shaniece being with another guy. He knew that had to be love. When he had been with Trina, the thought of finding her with another guy angered him, just because of his pride and reputation. If she had left him for another, he would've been fine. The thought of losing Shaniece to another guy, who probably deserved her love far more than he did, hurt him. It also caused him to take drastic measures in order to make sure that the possibility of Shaniece becoming his girl—once he was released—remained tangible.

Today, Devon relished in the thought of seeing a fresh face. He walked into the visiting area and sat at the table where the fourteen-year-old boy had been told to sit. Devon grinned at Q, who returned the smile.

"They let your li'l scrawny tail in here by yourself?" Devon asked teasingly.

Q laughed. "Naw, man. My mama had to sign me in."

Devon nodded. "Your mom was always cool wit' me, huh?"

"She say you be takin' care of me," the younger boy replied somberly. "Man, it ain't the same out there. You got outsiders tryna take over your territory. We tryna hold it down, but these dudes is rollin' in 'bout ten-to-twenty deep."

Devon's jaw clenched at the thought of somebody wreaking havoc in his neighborhood. He'd made calls to a few of his older peddlers and told them to make sure the business continued to run tightly and had informed one of his most trusted to hold on to the earnings. He knew, firsthand, how sneaky even the most trusted people could be, so he had to find a way to make sure his blocks were taken care of.

"I ain't worried 'bout that right now," Devon said, allowing his jutted chin to relax. "I need you to do me a favor." Q leaned in like Devon was about to reveal a top-secret plan; Devon laughed. "Not that kinda favor. Now sit back before that guard think we up to somethin'."

Q did as he was told and asked, "What's up?"

"You go to Riverside High, don't you?"

"Yeah, I'm a freshman," he said proudly.

Devon chuckled, almost reminiscing about the days when he was a high-school student. "Shaniece Simmons . . . she's a senior. You know her?"

Q rubbed his chin in deep thought and shrugged.

Devon sighed and tried to think of something that would make Q realize who Shaniece was. "Okay, there's this loud, dark-skinned girl she hang wit' all the time . . . Tatiana . . . I don't know her last name, but—"

"Oh yeah, I know her," Q interrupted. "That's my friend's girlfriend's cousin. Yeah, she fine."

"I don't care 'bout all that," Devon snapped. "I'm talkin' 'bout the girl who be wit' her all the time . . . Shaniece."

"*Oh* . . . you talkin' 'bout that girl who be wit' her all the time," Q stated as if he'd just had a revelation. Devon rolled his eyes. "She 'bout my height? Got some nice brown hair? Brown eyes? Yeah . . . she fine too."

"I know," Devon said with a smile. "I need you to look out for her for me."

"Like make sure nobody mess wit' her?"

Devon nodded. "Yeah, just watch out for the dudes that come up to her. Keep me up on who she might be messin' wit'."

Q scrunched his nose. "Don't tell me that's your girl?"

Devon's jaw clenched. "And what if I said 'yeah'? You act like I can't pull that."

Q laughed. "Naw, it's just that you be wit' Trina all the time. I ain't know you had some on the side."

Devon shrugged and shifted in his seat for a more comfortable position. "I was talking to her before I got up in here. See if you can get at her and ask her to come see 'bout me."

Q shook his head. "I don't know, man. Why can't you just call her?"

Devon refused to tell this boy, who looked up to him, that he was too scared to call Shaniece. Q may be afraid to challenge him, but even Devon wouldn't be able to blame him if the teen laughed himself out of his seat. "Why can't you just do like I ask?" he decided to retort.

Q smacked his teeth. "Them seniors be actin' like they better than everybody else. I ain't tryna get dissed in front of the whole school."

Devon pursed his lips in anger. "Man, stop acting like a li'l punk. I know I taught you better than that. You done approached many girls older than you and it ain't like you tryna talk to her. Besides, Shaniece is different; she ain't gonna diss you."

Q nodded. "Well, I'll try, but I guess you should know Tatiana ain't the only person she be hangin' wit'." Devon's eyes questioned him, and Q inwardly smiled, proud that he could provide Devon with a bit of information he already had. "She got this guy friend, Chris or somethin', but they all be hangin' out. Tatiana, her, and him. He feelin' her too—Shaniece, I mean—but she don't really be givin' him no play."

Devon felt the heat rising to his face, but he tried to calm the storm he felt building inside him. "She ain't wit' him?" Q shook his head. "Okay, then. He ain't a problem. Just do what I said and keep an eye on her. If you can get close enough to ask her 'bout me, handle that too." He looked deep into the boy's eyes. "You always got my back, right, li'l man?"

Q nodded. "Always, Big D, always."

Shaniece was sitting on her bed, reading her book club's chosen novel for this month. *The Last Woman*

Standing by Tia McCollors was definitely a page-turner. The only reason she hadn't finished the novel, after nearly a week, was because school kept interfering with her reading. During school, she carried the book to each class, and even to lunch, so that she'd be able to enjoy it during her spare time throughout the day. If she kept up her irregular reading schedule, she would be done with the book in the next few days, a week before the meeting was scheduled.

"Knock, knock," Cedric said as he tapped against her open bedroom door.

Shaniece placed a bookmark in her book and smiled up at her father as he walked into her room. He took a seat at the edge of the bed, and Shaniece laughed when she heard a light squeak.

"I never hear that noise when I sit on the bed," she teased.

Cedric laughed as he looked down at his stomach, which was beginning to settle over his belt. "Yeah, I made a New Year's resolution to lose about fifty pounds."

Shaniece gazed at him skeptically. "That's the same one from last year, right?"

He laughed again. "Yep, maybe I'll stick to it this year. Your mother's gonna try and hold me to it. You see she stocked that cabinet downstairs with more of those nasty rice cakes."

She nodded. "I saw. So what's up?"

"Craig called me at work this afternoon," he stated. "He asked if he could take you out on Friday. He said that he'd asked you about it yesterday."

"He did," she said softly.

"Well, you certainly don't look too happy about it."

Shaniece shrugged and looked toward the mirror that was positioned above her dresser. She gazed at herself and could see the sadness behind her eyes; she could only hope her father wouldn't catch wind of it. "I guess it would be fun to go out, but Craig's just a friend. I don't want him to read more into our relationship."

Her father nodded as if he understood. The room was enveloped with silence for several long moments, and Shaniece knew her father was studying her attitude. He would do that from time to time when he knew she or one of her siblings, or even his wife, was going through something that they had yet to discuss out in the open. He would assess their mind-set and then decide if it would be acceptable to open the matter for discussion.

"Sister Yvonne talked to me after services last Sunday," Cedric suddenly stated. "She told me about her son, who was sentenced to ten to twenty-five years in prison due to drug distribution."

Shaniece's eyes began to tear up. She hadn't known that Devon was serving that long of a sentence. She felt so sorry for him, but that didn't overshadow the anger that still resided in her heart.

"She asked me to pray for him," Cedric continued. "She wants him to come to the Lord and begin a new life before it's too late. I told her that I'd have a few brothers from the prison ministry visit him if he'd like."

Shaniece remained quiet and continued to stare into the mirror, but avoided looking directly into her own eyes. She felt her father move closer to her and take her hand.

"Baby girl," he said softly, "have you been praying for him?"

She bit down hard on her bottom lip and shook her head. She'd tried several times to get on her knees and pray for Devon's safety while in prison. She'd tried to pray that somehow he'd find the Lord. She'd tried to ask God to have mercy on his life, at least until he made that change. But each time she attempted to fall on her knees on Devon's behalf, she could only cry. She couldn't find a prayer in her heart for him. She'd searched and searched as deep as she could for the words that would allow God to have His way in Devon's life, but she had yet to find them, let alone speak them.

"You know, it's always going to be hard for you to pray for him if you continue to hold a grudge against him." Cedric continued to speak as if he knew why his daughter was having such a difficult time with this situation. "I see it in your eyes. You're angry with him, and that's understandable. I was angry with him, but I've forgiven him."

"It's so hard. . . ." Shaniece began to speak, but her voice broke as tears began to flood her eyes.

Cedric's eyes were full of compassion. "You know why it's so hard, Niecey. You're more hurt than angry. When someone is angry with someone else, and they hold a grudge against that person for years and years, it's not because they can't stand the person they're angry with. They usually love the person they're holding the grudge against, but they're in pain about whatever happened. And it hurts more when the person you love with all of your heart does wrong against you. But until you get over that pain, you're always going to be angry.

"You have to let go of this situation. Devon was stupid . . . as most young boys trying to impress a pretty girl are, but he needs your forgiveness. He may not deserve it, but we didn't deserve for Jesus to die on the cross for our sins. . . . He did it, anyway, because He loves us. And you love that boy. Now I don't know if it's just the love of Christ that you have for him, or if it's deeper than that, but I know you love him."

Shaniece lowered her gaze upon hearing her heart's truth divulged in her father's words. She loved Devon.

She loved him with more than just the love of Christ, and she'd known that for a while. Though she was unsure as to why she felt such a deep love for him, her father made her realize that she was in pain about what he'd done to her because she loved him. She wanted to forgive him, but she couldn't—not when the reality of what he'd done was still fresh in her mind.

"Now, that's all I'm going to say about that," Cedric said. "You pray for direction and do as God will have you concerning this situation." He leaned forward and kissed her forehead. "And as far as Craig . . . you don't lead that boy on. Going out as friends is okay, but until you know what you want, and your heart is no longer attached to someone else, don't let it get any further than that. I told him that Friday was fine with me and he said he'd call you about it." He stood to leave and the bed creaked again.

For the first time in the last ten minutes, Shaniece smiled, despite her tears. "Daddy, I'm holding you to your resolution this year."

He laughed heartily and headed for the door.

"Daddy," she called him once more, "thank you."

"You're welcome, baby girl," Cedric said. "I love you," he added before walking out of the room.

Shaniece reopened her book and continued reading, trying to keep Devon out of her mind, but holding on to her father's advice.

Chapter 16

"Are there any other concerns?" Tatiana spoke to the club members as she looked around the classroom. "Okay . . . meeting adjourned." She closed her folder and stood.

Shaniece packed up her things and prepared to leave. Today's National Honor Society meeting had gone on longer than expected. The meeting had lasted thirty minutes longer than usual, and Shaniece was worn-out and ready to go home.

The new members were still having complaints about the $300 they'd have to shell out for the state convention that would be held in April. Tatiana had gotten so annoyed with a sophomore that she nearly bit the girl's head off when she retorted angrily, "Well, if you don't want to pay the money, use the brain that got you into this club to think of a good fund-raiser we could do." The tenth grader was prepared to stand off with the club's president, and Mr. Patwell had to break up the altercation before it could even start. Shaniece wanted to reprimand her friend for her quick temper, but she almost couldn't blame her. She'd subtly snapped at a few of the underclassmen as they continued to complain about the money, but still struggled to come up with a way to raise the funds. She had a headache and was ready to go home and lie down.

"So, are we still on for tonight?" Craig asked as he followed her out of the classroom.

Shaniece inwardly sighed. She'd almost forgotten about her date with Craig tonight. She wanted to tell him that she'd changed her mind or that she needed to reschedule. She didn't feel like going out tonight, but the anxious look on her friend's face caused her to place her desires aside and nod. "Yes."

"Great," he said with restrained excitement. "I'll be by to pick you up at seven."

"What should I wear?" she asked, not wanting to be underdressed or overdressed for the occasion. When Craig smiled, Shaniece knew exactly what his response would be.

"You'll look great in anything you wear," he replied as she mocked the words in her head.

She smiled softly. "Thank you, but should I wear something like what I have on"—she pointed toward the jeans and sweater she was dressed in—"or something more dressy?"

"A little more dressy," Craig said. "I gotta go, but I'll see you tonight."

Shaniece nodded, afraid that her exhausted tone would contradict her acceptance of tonight's date. She watched as Craig walked out the door before she released a depressed sigh.

"Why are you doing this to yourself?" Tatiana asked as she stood next to her best friend.

Shaniece didn't bother to look at Tatiana when she replied, "I'm not doing anything. You were the one that said I needed to move on, and that's what I'm doing."

"That was before I knew you loved that boy."

Shaniece's head snapped in Tatiana's direction. "I never told you that," she said defensively.

"You didn't have to." Tatiana laughed. "Anyway, it's hard to move on when you're in love with somebody else."

"I'm not *in love* with him," Shaniece declared. "And I don't love *him;* I love the person he pretended to be."

"It doesn't matter. There's no way you can give your heart to someone else if it's still with D," Tatiana told her.

They walked down the hall in silence and Shaniece dwelled on her friend's words. She loved Devon, or at least she loved the picture-perfect appearance he'd put on for her, but what could she do about her feelings? She couldn't build upon them because she was not now—nor would she ever be—in a relationship with Devon, and she couldn't make herself stop loving him. She could only keep praying and hoping that God would allow her heart to mend so that she could fully move on.

"Hey, Tatiana," a girl greeted as they walked into the commons.

Tatiana smiled at the girl. "Hi, Whitney." She turned toward Shaniece. "Niecey, you remember my cousin, right?"

Shaniece smiled. "Yeah. Hey," she said, and noticed the boy standing next to Whitney looking at her and Tatiana as if they were slabs of prime rib on his dinner plate.

"This is my boyfriend's friend Q," Whitney said. An annoyed expression clouded her face. "He's been asking about you, Shaniece. Please don't ask me why."

Shaniece looked at the boy, who probably turned many of the freshmen girls' heads with his smooth skin, bright hazel eyes, and pearly white smile. "Can I help you?" she asked him, almost amused at his gawking.

Q composed himself and nodded. "Umm . . ."

Shaniece searched his face in confusion. He looked as if he knew what he wanted to say, but he couldn't find the right words. "What is it?" she urged.

He cleared his throat and stiffened his stance. "Big D . . . wants to see you," he said with assurance.

Shaniece's face tightened; she was no longer amused with the boy. "And how would you know this?" she asked, with one hand against her hip.

The boy now held a higher level of confidence as he spoke. "He told me. I went to see him a few days ago and he told me to tell you that he wants you to come visit him."

Shaniece was tired of Devon sending his couriers to her with messages that begged her to come see him. She still couldn't understand what was so hard about picking up the phone and calling her. He'd had to call both his mother and Q in order for them to know he was incarcerated and they needed to visit him. So what was the problem with calling her and asking her to visit him? Maybe he sensed that she would say no, and having her turn him down in someone else's face was probably easier to handle than having her reject him over the phone. Whatever he was thinking, she wished he would just stop bothering her.

She gazed at Q and tried to smother the fire in her eyes as she replied sweetly, "You tell *Big D* to call me on my cell." Then she gave the boy her number.

"Can I use this for myself?" he asked boldly.

Shaniece laughed. "Sure, if you don't mind explaining to my father why you're calling me."

The boy shrugged and replied, "I'll make sure Big D gets this." He walked away with Whitney waving at them, before he did the same.

"So you're going to talk to him?" Tatiana asked as they walked toward the parking lot.

Shaniece marched with determination as she tried to calm her anger. "Yeah. I'm gonna let him know how I really feel."

Tatiana watched her friend's attitude take over her entire body. Her walk was fierce and she looked like she was waiting for someone to cross her so that she could retort, releasing all of the rage she had built up inside her. This was a part of Shaniece that rarely showed, but when it did, there was almost nothing that could be done to calm her until she confronted the problem head-on. And that was exactly what she planned to do.

"Pappadeaux?" Shaniece glanced at Craig as he pulled his car into the parking lot of the restaurant.

"I thought you might like a taste of some Cajun seafood," he said before stepping out of the car and walking to the passenger side to help his date out of the vehicle.

They walked into the restaurant and waited nearly thirty minutes to be seated. As they waited, Craig apologized twice for not making reservations, and Shaniece assured him that everything was okay. Once they were seated, a waitress immediately served them. She had their drinks and appetizers out within ten minutes.

"I'm glad you decided to come out with me tonight," Craig expressed with sincerity.

Shaniece could only smile. She still had a headache from the club meeting, and it had become significantly worse after her encounter with Devon's little friend. She had had very little time to nap, like she'd wanted to, before preparing for her date with Craig. She had barely made it home from school, with two hours to spare, before Craig arrived to pick her up.

Craig leaned forward and looked deep into her eyes. "Are you okay? You look like you don't want to be here."

Shaniece bit her bottom lip, scolding herself for allowing her true feelings to overshadow the happy façade she'd had on display since she opened her front door to him this evening. "I'm sorry," she said softly. "I'm just a little tired. The new NHS members gave me a headache, and I had planned to sleep if off before tonight, but never got the chance."

Craig's eyes told her he understood. "Would you like to reschedule so you can get some sleep?"

She couldn't think of anything more she wanted to do than just lie down, but rescheduling a date with Craig wasn't an option. She would get through this date if it killed her. She was tired of staying at home, thinking about Devon. She'd promised herself that she would move on, and she would do just that.

"That's okay," she replied. "I want to have a good time with you tonight." Craig's face lit up and Shaniece knew he had read more into her statement than she'd meant. "I like hanging out with my *friends,*" she emphasized. "It makes life less stressful, you know."

Craig intensified his gaze and spoke softly. "Niecey, you know I've been trying to be more than just your friend for the last two years."

Shaniece looked away and forced herself not to chew on her bottom lip, knowing Craig would notice the nervous habit. "I'm not really looking for a relationship."

He relaxed in his seat and squinted his eyes. "So who's Devon to you?"

Her gaze jolted up in his direction and questioned him.

"I used to hear you and Tatiana talking about him all the time," he confessed. "You used to be so happy last semester. Then, like right before Thanksgiving, you became really sad and distant. I figured it had something to do with him."

Shaniece was sure her lip was bleeding by now. She wasn't surprised that Craig knew about Devon. When she was involved with him, Shaniece would speak of Devon almost every day, even during the times when she knew Craig would be around to hear. It was never her intention to flaunt Devon in Craig's face, but she couldn't help it during a time when just a fleeting thought of Devon made her face brighten.

"Did he hurt you?" Craig questioned quietly.

Shaniece had accepted this date in order to take her mind off Devon, and now Craig wanted to make him the topic of their dinner discussion. She was still hurt, and discussing the person who'd been deceptive enough to cause her wounds only made things worse. "Craig, I don't really want to talk about this."

"Okay, I apologize for pushing," he conceded. "I just don't like seeing you so upset. I look forward to seeing your beautiful smile every day and you've been disappointing me lately." He smiled encouragingly for Shaniece.

She couldn't find the strength to allow a smile to form on her lips in return. "I've just been going through some things, and they're really hard to deal with."

Craig reached across the table and took her hands. "Like I've told you before, I'm always here for you."

This time, the ends of her lips curved slightly upward as she replied, "I'll remember that."

Chapter 17

Devon had memorized the numbers and had repeated them over and over as he dialed the digits that would hopefully connect him to the person he'd been longing to hear from since he'd been incarcerated. He waited for the automated voice to ask if she would accept the phone charges. Devon prayed she would, knowing there might be a slight chance she could have changed her mind and wouldn't accept his phone call. He nearly shouted out in joyfulness when he heard her speak.

"Shaniece," he had whispered.

"Yeah," she had replied coldly.

He had been caught off guard by her icy tone. "I'm glad you responded this time."

"Well, I figured since you had moved from your mother to a kid, you must be desperate to hear from me." Usually she'd laugh after saying something like that, but her voice had been as dry as a scorching desert.

"Yeah, I wanted to call you, but I didn't think you'd want to hear from me."

"And how do you think I felt when I had people coming up to me out of the blue asking about you?" she had questioned harshly. "That was a punk move, Devon. I thought drug dealers had more guts than that."

Devon had sighed, disheartened at the fact that she knew who he truly was. He figured she'd found out, but he had hoped his assumption had been wrong.

*"Yeah, your little girlfriend told me everything,"
Shaniece had admitted.*

*"I need to see you." Devon had spoken quietly. "I have
things that I want to say to you that I don't have time
to say over the phone. I'd much rather speak to you in
person, anyway. Please," he had begged, looking over
his shoulder at the line of guys who were waiting to
make phone calls.*

*After a long silence, Shaniece had spoken. "Next Sat-
urday is good for me."*

*"Thank you," he had said. The words "I love you" were
on the tip of his tongue, but he had swallowed them and
said his good-bye.*

"Dang, what time is it?" Devon complained as he ran
his hands over his freshly cut hair.

Mitch laughed. "Why you trippin' today?" he asked.
"Who comin' to visit you?"

"Why you askin'?" Devon retorted with a slight smile.

"You ain't care 'bout what time it was when your
mama was comin' up here. And you been up in here
for almost three months and all of a sudden you need
a haircut," Mitch observed. "It's got to be somebody
new. Somebody you tryna look good for." He paused as
if in deep thought and then a wide grin spread across
his face. "That fine honey comin' to see you?" he asked
as he pointed toward the photograph of Shaniece and
Yvonne, which Devon had taped on the wall above his
bunk.

Devon only smiled as he ran his fingers over his head
once again. He looked at the picture and his grin broad-
ened. Last week, when he'd called Q about Shaniece,
the boy had informed Devon that he'd spoken with her
and had succeeded in getting her number so that Devon
could call her. So the next time Devon was able to use

the phone, he called Shaniece, and though her tone showed she was angry with him, her willingness to visit him showed that she still cared. The six days between his phone call and her visit seemed to pass by as slow as snails. But he tried to pass the time away by playing cards to stack up enough cigarettes and stamps in order to trade them with one of the prisoners in return for a haircut and facial grooming. His neat mustache had turned into a messy beard and he had to get rid of it before Shaniece's visit.

"I just needed to freshen up, that's all," Devon lied.

"Yeah, well, I'll see," Mitch said. "My mama's bringing my son up here so I can see him, so I'ma find out who here to see you."

Devon laughed and shook his head at his cellmate. Mitch had served four years of his ten-year sentence for assisting a friend in a bank robbery. He and Devon had gotten along from day one, because, just like Devon, Mitch wasn't a bad person. They both had just made some bad decisions in their lives.

When visitation time came, Devon nearly jumped in anticipation.

Mitch laughed. "Man, you actin' like the ice cream truck is comin'."

Devon ignored Mitch's teasing and waited for the guard to escort them to the visiting room. As soon as they walked into the room, Devon spotted Shaniece sitting at one of the tables, looking as good as ever. Her bottom lip was shoved into her mouth and he could tell how nervous she was by the way her legs shook underneath the table.

"Oh, I see her," Mitch whispered. "She look better than the picture."

Devon nodded with a smile as he walked toward the table. His presence nearly startled Shaniece, but she seemed to regain her control. All he wanted to do was take her into his arms and hug and kiss her. Knowing he would be out of line if he did, he slowly lowered himself into the seat across from her, his eyes never leaving hers. He could tell she'd been crying, and he hated to think he'd been the reason behind her tears.

"Hey," he greeted.

She continued to silently chew on her lip.

"Thank you for coming," he continued.

There was more silence between them and Devon sighed as he continued speaking. "It's good to see you. You look good."

Shaniece still rested in silence.

"I guess I should start with an apology." He waited a beat before saying, "I'm sorry for everything that I did to you. I lied and tried to make you believe I was someone I wasn't. I don't really have an excuse for what I did. I just really liked you and I knew that if I would've told you who I was, or what I did, you wouldn't give me the time of day."

"What did you want with me?" she asked softly. "You had a girl . . . a woman from what I can tell. What did you need with me?"

"You were different, Shaniece. And around you, I was different."

A dry laugh escaped her lips. "Yeah, that's for sure." She bit her lip once again and tears fell from her eyes. "I trusted you, Devon," she cried softly. "I trusted you to be honest with me, like I was being honest with you. I allowed you into my space and I opened my heart to you. And for you not to afford me the same privilege really hurts. You hurt me really bad," she said.

He couldn't stand to see her cry. He reached across the table for her hands, but she pulled them into her lap and shook her head. He looked around to make sure that no one had seen the sudden exchange. He caught a glimpse of Mitch playing with his son before returning his attention to Shaniece, who held a look of disbelief on her face.

"Are you that worried about your precious reputation?" she asked. "You can't be the real you because you're trying so hard to be the thug that you want to be."

"Shaniece, this is who I am," Devon said, almost pleading for her to accept him as he was. "I'm not tryna be anything."

"Well, I don't hang with thugs or drug dealers or whatever you are," she said, her voice rising slightly above normal level.

She stood to leave, but Devon grabbed for her hand. The sudden movement caught the attention of the guard and he began moving toward the table.

"I love you," Devon said, loud enough for only her to hear.

Shaniece gazed into his eyes, searching for some morsel of truth in his words. "Don't say that if you don't mean it," she pleaded with him in the same soft tone.

"I do." Devon's eyes were full and Shaniece could see the sincerity in them.

She searched his face a few seconds longer, and then looked up at the guard who had instructed Devon to let go of her arm. "It's okay," she told the uniformed officer.

As she sat back into her seat, the officer slowly backed away. Shaniece continued to stare into Devon's eyes, and he hoped that she could see that he was being genuine. "How do you know?" she questioned him.

Devon shook his head and replied, with a shrug, "I honestly don't know how I know. It's not easy to explain, but I just feel it in my heart. You were the only person I was thinkin' 'bout when I got arrested. You been on my mind for the last three months, and every time I got a chance to use the phone, I wanted to call you. I've never been afraid of anything or anyone in my life, but I was terrified of callin' you when I got in this mess. I almost cried at the thought of losing you 'cause of what I did. And when I was tryna get you to come see me and nothin' was working, I was afraid I'd never see you again. Apologizing to someone has never been so important to me before. I still haven't apologized to my mama for most of the things I've done to her, and I know I love my mama. So if apologizing to you was more important than anything to me, then that had to mean something deeper than me just feeling guilty." He breathed deeply and struggled not to reach out for her hands. "I love you, Shaniece. I know I do."

Shaniece's tears were falling by now. "I'm so angry with you," she said truthfully. "But I'm hurt more than anything else. I've tried so hard to get you out of my mind, but I can't. Daddy says that I need to pray for you, but I couldn't even do that. He told me that I need to forgive you first, and that's really hard for me to do. He said that I'm so angry because I love you, and it hurts more when someone you love wrongs you. He's right," she admitted. "I do love you, but I'm so scared of you hurting me again that I don't even want to give you another chance."

"Shaniece, I'm not trying to make promises that I could possibly break," he said, "but I love you enough to try to make a change. I wish you loved me enough to forgive me."

Shaniece lowered her head and Devon wondered if she was praying. He never would have thought he'd fall in love with a woman of God. Growing up, he'd hated church, but he'd go every Sunday now if that was what it would take for Shaniece to give him a second chance. The persona he'd portrayed while with her wasn't one he'd fabricated. It was a side of him that she'd brought out by being so true and genuine. He wanted a chance to prove to her that he could be that same way for real.

"I forgive you," she finally said. "But, Devon, I'm not going to give you my heart so that you can break it again. You've got to change."

Devon sighed, knowing that would be a hard task, but he'd declared that his love for her was so strong that he would try. "I don't want to make any promises."

"I just want you to try," she said. "For me. For your mother. For yourself."

There was silence between them once more, and Devon thought about Shaniece's request. Leaving his old lifestyle would be difficult, but it would've been harder, had he still had access to the streets and to his business. There wasn't much he could do in prison, so maybe it would be easier than he believed.

"When can I see you again?" he asked, his eyes caressing hers.

The look in Shaniece's eyes told him that she knew he was trying to change the subject. He was relieved when she didn't push for him to respond to her previous statement, but rather answered, "I don't know how often I can visit. My dad was skeptical about me coming up here by myself, but he let me, anyway. I doubt he'll let me make it a habit." She was quiet as she allowed herself to fall deep into his gaze. "I know how to write," she said with a smile.

He laughed softly. "I stayed in school long enough to learn how to do that."

"Tell you what, we'll write each other and I'll visit as often as I can." Her face turned serious. "I'm going to be praying hard for you because I want God to save you."

"Shaniece—"

"No, Devon," Shaniece interrupted. "I'm serious. I'm not going to trust you with my heart until you give yours to God. I don't even want you to respond to that, because I know I'm not saying anything you want to hear, and I know you don't have anything to say that I want to hear. So I'm ending this discussion by saying I'm going to pray for your soul, because I feel that's what I need to do."

Devon wasn't trying to convert his entire life. He'd committed to trying to make a few changes, but becoming a holier-than-thou Christian wasn't at the top of his priority list. He nodded and kept his thoughts to himself.

"There are some other things I think would be good for you, but I don't want you to think I'm a control freak," she said with a soft smile.

"You just want what's best for me," Devon summed up knowingly. "That's why I love you."

She blushed this time and lowered her gaze.

"I want for you to wait for me, Shaniece," he told her, causing her to look back up into his eyes. "I need you to."

"Devon, you're going to be here for some time," she began to protest.

"Do you love me?" he questioned, locking his gaze on her.

Shaniece nodded. "But I don't want to live a fairy tale. You'll be in here for *at least* ten years, and though I'm not looking right now, who's to say my Mr. Right won't come in five years."

"He won't," Devon assured, "because unless a miracle happens, I won't be out of here in five years."

She was impressed by his confidence. "As long as you have my heart, I'm not going anywhere," she promised. "But—"

He placed his finger against her lips. "There are no 'buts' or 'what-ifs,'" he said as he affectionately moved his touch from her lips across her cheek and to her chin. "No promises that can be broken."

She suppressed the fluttering in her heart and tried not to allow him to see the effect he was having on her as she nodded. "You want me to wait for you," she stated as she took his hand. "I want you to stay out of trouble. You never know . . . if these people see you doing well, you could be out of here ahead of time. It wouldn't hurt your ego if you went for your GED either. School can keep you out of trouble." She smiled as he made a face. "If you can live in your fantasy, I want to live in mine. You want me to wait for you; I want you to be ready for me when you get out."

Devon raised his eyebrows. "That's something I can definitely work on."

He kissed both of her hands and then savored the feeling of her right hand caressing his cheek. He wanted so badly to kiss her lips, but he knew he couldn't. They were already pushing the limits of prohibited physical contact. As if sensing his thoughts, Shaniece glanced in the direction of the guard to make sure he wasn't looking before bringing her fingertips to her own lips, kissing them softly, and then moving her hand toward his lips, brushing her fingers softly across them. He smiled and hoped that they could survive the restrictions his lifestyle had placed between them.

Chapter 18

"Wait for him?" Tatiana questioned incredulously. "As in put your life on hold for the next ten years or more just so that he won't lose you to another guy?"

"You make it sound so bad," Shaniece said softly, avoiding Tatiana's piercing glare.

"No, *you* agreeing to it was bad," Tatiana nearly shouted. "And I thought you said that you weren't going to go out with him until he got saved. Did you introduce him to Christ during your little visit?"

"Well, no, but we're not officially dating either," Shaniece defended.

"Oh, so you just go around telling random guys that you love them and you'll put your life on hold for them." Tatiana placed her hands on her hips. "Well, why don't you just march up to Craig and allow him to dictate your love life?"

"Dictate? Devon is not dictating anything. I make my own decisions." Shaniece folded her arms across her chest. "And why do you insist on comparing Devon to Craig? I don't even like Craig like that."

"Maybe you should consider liking Craig *like that,"* Tatiana said. "At least he's close to your standards. D is miles away from being what you described as your ideal man." She shook her head. "What happened to wanting a man with a high-school diploma and a college degree? What happened to a *legal* job? And what about honesty and trust? What about God being the center of the relationship?"

"God is the center of my relationship with Devon," Shaniece insisted, purposely avoiding the other points her best friend had made. "I feel like God's the reason why we were brought into each other's lives."

"How can that be, Niecey, when D is not connected to God? The triangle is incomplete, and your relationship with D is unequally yoked. You said yourself that a relationship like that is bound for destruction."

"Tati, why can't you just be happy for me?" Shaniece yelled. "I love Devon! Devon loves me! Why can't you just let me believe that our love can overcome the obstacles in our way?"

"Because it's a *dream* that can never become reality, and you know that."

Shaniece fell back on her bed as she allowed tears to roll from her eyes. Tatiana was right; she was in way over her head if she thought a relationship with Devon would work out without God being in their corner. Yesterday, she'd been so enraptured by Devon's presence that she would've danced around the visitors' room if he'd asked. But today, Tatiana had made Shaniece realize her willingness to comply with Devon's request had been an irrational decision, one in which she allowed her emotions to overshadow her common sense. However, she couldn't deny what was in her heart; she wanted to be with Devon.

"Well, what am I supposed to do now?" Shaniece asked softly. "I told Devon that as long as he had my heart, he'd have me. He has my heart."

Tatiana sat on the edge of the bed and looked down at her distraught friend. "I don't know. That's something you'll have to figure out on your own, but I do know that you can't tie yourself down to this guy. Doing so will only hold you back."

"I can't just tell him it's over after our talk yesterday." Shaniece rose to a seated position. "I don't want to tell him it's over."

"Nothing can be over if nothing ever started, Niecey," Tatiana told her. "I can't believe you got yourself into this mess. D's in prison for selling drugs and he's asking you to wait for him, and you agree to it like he asked you to do something as simple as picking up a few items from the grocery store." She searched Shaniece's eyes. "I'm not completely sure if what you're feeling is love, but I have to take your word for it. I'm not telling you to go back and tell D that you can't see him anymore, but there's no way a relationship is going to work between you guys."

"Well, why can't I see him and work on his spirituality at the same time?"

Tatiana laughed at her friend's childish tone and hopeful eyes. "Girl, it's not just about him not knowing God. That's a big part of it, but that's not what this discussion is all about." She stood and faced Shaniece, who was still seated on the bed. "This is about you living your own life. D gave his up when he decided to break the law, and now he wants you to do the same."

"He doesn't want me to give up my life," Shaniece defended. "He just wants us to be together."

"In ten to twenty-five years," Tatiana emphasized. "So that means you're going to have to turn down every good man who approaches you, because you've made a promise to D to be available when he gets out. Now, I know you're not one to go out looking for a man, but who's to say the man's not out there looking for you."

"Tati, why are you so against this? I made the decision, and though I know you're right in what you're saying, I don't regret the choice I made. As of now, I don't have an interest in anyone besides Devon. So why renege on my promise?"

Tatiana shook her head. "Look, you're grown enough to make your decisions, so you handle this however you want. I'm just letting you know that this whole situation is unrealistic. Fairy tales only happen in Disney movies."

Dear Shaniece,

I miss you so much. Ever since you visited me last week, I've been working nonstop, trying to make a trade to get a couple of stamps so I could write you. I've cleaned toilets and scrubbed floors, and a few other things, just so I could tell you that I love you. I love you, Shaniece, and I hope you won't ever get tired of hearing that, because I don't think I'll ever get tired of saying it. I really do love you, girl.

I want to apologize to you again for all the pain that I put you through. I knew you wouldn't put up with me if I'd told you who I really was. I'm sorry you had to find out the way you did. Honestly, I hadn't planned on telling you, because I never thought our relationship would progress past us being friends who hung out with each other. But after I got arrested, I realized that nothing that I thought was important was as important as you. I want you to know that the person I was when I was with you wasn't just some front that I put up. It was just another side of my personality that you brought out of me by being who you were.

I'll admit that breaking away from the street life is going to be hard, but maybe being in here will help me get myself straight. I've decided to start school. They got this program in here that will let me get my GED. Even though I am doing this for you, I'm just tired of wasting away every day in this cell. I need to do something productive before I go crazy. So I guess this is a start for me. I hope it makes you happy because knowing you're happy makes me happy.

I know you're busy with school and stuff, but please write me back as soon as you get a chance. I hope you'll visit if you get a chance, but I'm content with just hearing from you through your sweet words. I love you, baby, and I hope you'll be waiting for me when I get out of here.

Yours always and forever,
Devon

Shaniece refolded the letter and smiled as she placed it in her purse. She'd read it at least ten times since receiving it in the mail on Saturday. She imagined sitting before Devon and becoming hypnotized by his caressing voice as he spoke the words to her. She could feel his strong hands holding hers as she looked deep into his eyes and he poured his heart out to her, just as he'd done when she'd visited him over a week ago. She was happy, no doubt, but she just couldn't get Tatiana's words out of her head: *"Fairy tales only happen in Disney movies."* Shaniece couldn't deny that she knew she was living a fairy tale, but she was sure that, just like

Cinderella, Snow White, Sleeping Beauty and Princess Tiana, she would live happily ever after.

"Make sure you review chapters six and seven for tomorrow's quiz," Shaniece's teacher said just as the bell sounded, signaling the end of another school day.

Shaniece gathered her belongings and exited the classroom. She hurried down the hall and to her locker. Once she'd retrieved her belongings, she and Tatiana headed toward the student parking area. Tatiana was in a hurry to pick her brother up from day care, so she and Shaniece shared a very brief conversation before she departed. Before Shaniece could leave, though, Craig came out into the parking lot and walked up to her.

"Hey, Niecey," he greeted her with a bright, almost hopeful, smile.

"Hey, Craig," she replied as she placed her books on the passenger-side seat of her car.

"You haven't called me," he pointed out, glancing down at her.

Shaniece avoided eye contact as she responded, "Oh, I've been real busy." She wasn't really lying. Her schedule had been full—school, National Honor Society responsibilities, other extracurricular activities, and thoughts of Devon left her with no time to entertain Craig's continuous infatuation.

Craig nodded as if he understood, but Shaniece knew he didn't. She knew he was hurt at the fact that she hadn't given him the option of taking his relationship with her past the friendship stage, but she didn't feel that way about Craig. She couldn't see herself thinking of him as more than a friend. She knew that she'd promised herself to give him the chance that he deserved, but there was nothing much about him that intrigued her. He was a nice guy who appreciated her, but . . . he just didn't . . . he just wasn't . . . Devon.

"Hey, Shaniece."

Shaniece looked across the concrete at the young boy who'd just saved her from continuing her conversation with Craig. She tried to smile at the familiar face, but she was sure the rolling of her eyes made her smile seem less genuine. "Hi . . . umm . . ."

"Q," the boy replied, once he stood in front of her.

Shaniece nodded as if remembering. "Oh yeah." She glanced at the two guys standing behind him, but she didn't take the time to speak to them, since Q hadn't bothered to introduce them to her.

"Nice ride," Q complimented. "Wanna drive me and my boys home?"

Shaniece smirked. "I don't think so. The bus is every freshman's best friend." She laughed as he smacked his lips.

She watched as Q looked up at Craig with a smirk on his face; the other boys had been glaring at him also. Shaniece wondered what would cause them to be so rude to her friend.

"Do you underclassmen have a problem?" Craig asked with laughter in his tone.

"Naw, we ain't got no problem," Q declared, with his nose turned up at Craig. "But you gon' have one if you don't leave Big D's girl alone."

"What?" Craig asked, glaring at the boy, who was a few inches shorter than he was.

"Boy, stop tryin' to act all hard," Shaniece told Q, giving his shoulder a slight shove. "If you keep on, you gonna end up in jail, just like *Big D.*"

The boy to the left of Q shrugged. "Well, if we got to go out, we ain't goin' out like no punks," he said, with the other boys agreeing wholeheartedly.

Shaniece didn't suppress the heavy sigh as she shook her head. Apparently, these boys had declared Devon as their mentor and role model, but they would see soon enough that that life wasn't all it was cracked up to be.

"I'm gonna go see Big D this weekend," Q informed Shaniece. He glanced at Craig before continuing. "You want me to tell him wassup for you?"

Shaniece could feel Craig's gaze burning into the side of her face, but she avoided looking at him. She didn't want him to know that she wouldn't give him her heart because it belonged to a jailbird. She didn't want him to think that she was one of those girls who passed up the nice guy for the hard-core thug who did nothing but treat her wrong and abuse her, whether physically or emotionally. She didn't want to explain why she chose to treat him as if his feelings didn't matter, while she allowed herself to get caught up with a guy who couldn't give his all to their relationship because he was confined behind prison bars. She couldn't look at him for fear of seeing the truth of Tatiana's words in his eyes.

"Yeah, that's fine," Shaniece finally answered in a soft voice.

"That's a bet," Q said. He gave Craig one final glare before he and the boys walked off toward the school buses, which were preparing to deliver the school's attendants to their respective neighborhoods.

"I'm guessing *Big D* is the reason why we didn't have a follow up date this past weekend."

Shaniece had been in a daze as she watched the boys stroll off the school's campus, so Craig's statement had caught her completely off guard. "I'm sorry?" she questioned confusedly.

"You're Big D's girl," he stated knowingly, with a hint of jealously in his tone.

Shaniece lowered her eyes. "I'm not dating anybody, Craig."

"Yeah, you say that, but I know what's in your heart." Craig's eyes showed his sadness. "Big D—Devon . . . whatever you want to call him—the fact is, he has your heart, which, in my opinion, is something he doesn't deserve."

"Craig, please . . ." Shaniece wanted to stop him before he started something he wouldn't be able to finish.

"Shaniece, what I don't understand is why you'd give your heart to a—a thug, who can do nothing better with his life than have kids selling drugs for him."

Shaniece reeled her neck back in shock. "And just how do you know *anything* about who Devon is and what he does?"

Craig shrugged. "Those li'l wannabe thugs that just tried to threaten me went to my li'l brother's school last year. Q and my brother were both on the track team. . . . That was until Q started working for Devon." He looked down at Shaniece, who continued to avoid eye contact with him. "I know more than you think, Niecey. I know that this is the same guy who hurt you last year, and I know that this is the same guy who has something I wish I had."

"Craig—"

"Shaniece, I've been nothing but real with you, even before you knew how I really felt about you. I've been into you for the longest, and have just had the nerve to let you know in the past two years. I think you're a beautiful, intelligent, and talented young woman, and I feel as if you deserve to have nothing but the best." He moved closer to her. "I feel like you're settling and I kinda understand that, because I know how hard it is to find a decent guy in today's times. But it hurts me to see someone as special as you settling for a guy who doesn't even deserve half the woman you are." He searched her face and cautiously reached up to turn her head so that she'd have to look into his eyes. "I love you, Shaniece, and I just want you to be happy. I want you to be happy with me," he told her softly before leaning in to kiss her tenderly.

Shaniece was momentarily paralyzed in shock by Craig's forwardness, but once that feeling passed, she immediately pushed him away and shook her head. "Craig, I am happy. I'm happier than I've ever been before. Devon makes me happy, and though I'm not officially dating him, I love him more than I can ever express to him, to you, or to anyone else. It's almost unbelievable to me. And though I don't owe you an explanation, I will say this: I'm not settling for anything or anybody. My standards have always and will forever be high. And no guy, not even Devon, will be able to claim me fully until he meets the standards God has helped me set for myself. I know I deserve nothing but the best, and Devon is trying to give me that. Who am I to stop him from trying?"

"I just don't think he's right for you," Craig responded. "But if he's allowed to try from his tiny jail cell, won't you afford me the same opportunity while I'm right here in your face?"

Shaniece shook her head in defeat. She'd shown Craig through her words, but more so through her actions, that she was not interested in pursuing a relationship beyond friendship with him. Even after she'd pondered a relationship with him after Devon had been arrested, her heart was never in it. Her heart had always been with Devon, and there was nothing Craig could do to change that at this point. If he wanted to continue to pursue her, there was nothing she could do about it.

"It's your time wasted, Craig." Her tone was soft, but her words stung his heart.

He nodded. "I'll show you that we truly belong together. You'll see," he said as he backed away, allowing her to step around him and head toward the driver's side of her car.

Shaniece avoided looking at him as she backed out of the parking lot. As she drove home, she spotted Q standing on the corner with his two friends and a couple of other guys. A quick handshake and Shaniece realized what had just transpired. Devon was handling his business, even through his confinement, and she wondered if Craig was right when he said she was settling for less than what she deserved.

Chapter 19

Devon stood at the cell's bars as the dirty beige cart was wheeled down the corridor. The man pushing the cart stopped in front of him and handed him a standard-size envelope before continuing on his way.

"I wonder who sent that?" Mitch spoke sarcastically from his bed as Devon jumped back up onto his bunk.

Devon only smiled as he tore open the envelope and pulled out the handwritten letter.

> *Dear Devon,*
>
> *I miss you so much. I want you to know that I think about you constantly and that I'm praying for you. Every time I think about you spending the next ten years of your life locked away from the free world, I cry for you. Sometimes I feel like my tears are selfish because I just want to be able to see and talk to you every day.*
>
> *Everyone is telling me that you're not worth the wait and I'm sorry to say that sometimes I feel the same way. I see your peddlers all over the streets and it reminds me daily that you're not the type of person I should even be messing with. But then I remember what you promised me. I hope you're trying to*

stay on the right path, because it's my hope that in due time we'll be able to be together fully, not just emotionally, but spiritually as well.

Here's a thought for today: God loves you no matter what you've done. He loves you so much that He sent His only Son to earth to die for you so that you may have eternal life. (John 3:16)

I know you think I'm preaching, but I'm just trying to help. I want you to know that you are worth more than the life you've lived in the past five years. God knows it, I know it, and now you need to know it. Daddy wanted to know if you would mind the Prison Ministry coming to speak with you on one of your visitation days. Let me know and I'll tell him.

I have to go now, but write me back as soon as you can. I know it can be hard to get the money for stamps, so I sent some with this letter. If you'd rather talk, just call me.

Devon, I'm putting a lot of faith in you. Please don't let me down. I love you, and no, I won't get tired of hearing that from you. I hope you won't get tired of hearing it from me.

Always yours,
Shaniece

Devon sighed as he folded the letter and placed it back into the envelope, which he noticed held a full book of stamps. Shaniece's words tugged at his heart, making more urgent the need to make her happy. He couldn't care less what others thought of their relationship. But when he thought of how their words might cause Shaniece to doubt the love she had for him, Devon wanted nothing more than to prove them wrong. She was betting it all on him, and he'd hate himself if he caused her to lose everything just because he wanted to cling to the street life.

"Aye, D," Mitch called from his bunk. "You wanna play ball during rec hour?"

Devon shrugged. "Man, I don't know. I just feel like chillin' today."

Mitch sat up and strained his neck to look up at Devon. "By chillin', you mean sittin' in the yard and readin' them love letters for the rest of the day?"

Devon laughed. "There ain't much else for me to do, now is there?"

Mitch stood as the buzzer sounded, releasing the prisoners to the prison yard to participate in whatever recreation they chose, which usually included basketball or weight lifting. "Man, you need to do somethin'. I mean, it's not much to do up in here, but take advantage of the fresh air. I know I'm tired of being clammed up in this cell with you and this stank toilet." He pointed toward the stall, which sat in the corner of the cell. "For real, man, come hang out. You been here since November, and you ain't did much of nothin' besides eatin', sleepin', and dreamin' 'bout that girl." He pointed toward the picture of Shaniece and Yvonne. "You need to meet some new people. I know you tired of talking to me every day. Now come on."

Devon sighed as he placed Shaniece's letter under his pillow and jumped off his bed. He followed Mitch out into the courtyard.

"Hey, Mitch," one of the guys shouted out as they made their way onto the court. "We need one more for three-on-three."

Mitch nodded. "I got him right here," he said as he pointed toward Devon. "Y'all know Big D." He looked toward Devon and nodded in the direction of the other guys. "D, this is Raquel, and the fellas."

Raquel looked Devon up and down. "So this is the infamous *Big D*. Heard a lot about you, dawg."

"Don't believe everything you hear," Devon replied, slapping hands with Raquel.

"'Nuff small talk. Ball up," Mitch said.

The guys played a rousing game of three-on-three and Devon put his all into the game. He wanted to prove himself before these guys could assume him to be someone he was not. Regardless of how he felt about Shaniece and his promise to improve his lifestyle, it was still important that he received the respect that came along with his name.

By the end of the game, Devon was in need of a good shower. As recreation time came to an end, Devon and the other prisoners headed back inside. Devon turned and looked out into the courtyard. Beyond the high barbed-wire fence, he could see the freedoms of the outside world: the cars that sped along the highway and the pedestrians who moved with determination or just for the sake of enjoying the surprisingly sunny winter day. He breathed deeply. An hour a day, in the confinements of the fence, would have to suffice for the next ten years . . . or more.

As he turned back around to enter the prison, a large male, who had to weigh at least 300 pounds, mostly fat, blocked his pathway. Devon backed up as the guy stood steadfast. Two other guys stood behind him. If Devon didn't know better, he'd say they were trying to send silent threats his way.

"Can I help you?" Devon questioned as he stiffened his stance and showed the guys that he wasn't afraid of them.

"Yeah, you can help me by keepin' your boys off Roc's block."

"Roc?"

"I ain't stutter," the guy retorted. "Roc wanted me to let you know that since you don't know how to handle your b'iness without gettin' caught, he gon' do it for you . . . 'cept you ain't benefitin' from it." He chuckled.

Devon fumed at the thought of some stranger taking over Riverside and his business. He'd worked too hard to let all he'd invested into his business be taken away from him by some coward who waited until he was behind bars to step in and try to claim what wasn't his. He thought of Q, Antwon, and all of his other workers and wondered what they were doing to hold down the fort while he was away. The fact that this strange guy was approaching him with this nonsense told Devon that his employees might have been trying to keep things in order, but their efforts were producing very little fruit. He heard Shaniece's plea for him to give up his street mentality and focus on getting his life in order, but this was his neighborhood, and he'd be dead and buried before he allowed someone to tear down what he'd built up. He had to do something before this got out of hand. He made a mental note to make a few calls over the next few days.

"You tell *Roc* that if he steps foot on my territory, I got somethin' for him," Devon stated before pushing his way past the three gentlemen and heading back to his cell.

***

Q stood at his usual post and surveyed the street. It had been a long night, but at least he hadn't been bored out of his mind. From his position, he could see everything. There had been an insignificant car accident earlier in the day and he laughed as he watched the woman, who'd been rear-ended, fuss about how men were such careless drivers. Instead of calling the police to draw up an accident report, the man, who'd slightly bruised her bumper, sweet-talked the woman out of exchanging insurance information and they ended up exchanging numbers, instead.

Then almost an hour earlier, two girls were about to have it out on the sidewalk over some guy, whom Q deemed unworthy of the two beauties. He chuckled when the girls started fighting and attracted a small crowd. His chuckle grew to all-out laughter when the girls began beating the boy down after they realized that he was standing amongst the crowd cheering them on.

He'd also watched one of his friends attempt to steal something from the corner store that he was standing in front of. He laughed as he watched the Asian store owner chase his friend out of the store with a handgun.

Q had also seen Roc and his entourage riding up and down the blocks in the neighborhood as if they were looking for something or someone. He'd tensed once more when he saw the black Escalade on twenty-six-inch rims slowly move past the corner store for the third time that night. Q wouldn't say he was scared, but he was nervous. He'd been told by one of Devon's most trusted to hold down his post—no matter what or who tried to stand in his way. He was fully prepared, knowing he had the 9 mm gun tucked away safely in his jeans, but he'd never shot anyone before and he wasn't ready to start now.

Selling drugs was one thing, but having to protect himself was another. Devon had always done that for him. From the very first day Q had met Devon, Devon had taken care of Q as if they were brothers. Q had been financially desperate enough to try to steal money from one of Devon's workers, but when he'd gotten caught, he boldly shared with Devon that he and his mother were about to be put out of their house if they didn't catch up on the rent. Instantly Devon had pulled out several hundred dollars and told Q to take it to his mother's landlord. From that day forward, Q vowed to repay Devon for all he'd done for him—from keeping a roof over his head to placing food on his mother's table to putting clothes on their backs—and that's exactly why he was standing in front of the corner store right now. He knew the dangers and the risks of the job he held, but he didn't care. Devon had taken care of him in his time of need, so Q would do the same for him.

Not only would he make sure that Devon's streets were kept in order, but he would make sure that his mentor was kept abreast on any information concerning Shaniece. Q could tell that Devon loved the girl, or else he wouldn't have been so adamant about Q watching out for her. Q could understand Devon's attraction—Shaniece was beyond beautiful, and she carried herself with dignity and grace. He could tell she didn't take anyone's junk, despite the fact that her sweet demeanor initially had caused him to assume she was a pushover. But what Q didn't understand was Shaniece's ability to put up with Craig's inability to understand that she didn't want a relationship with him.

Q had purposely brought up Devon in front of Craig, wanting to see the senior's reaction to the mention of the name itself. He'd known Craig for a couple of years back when he was on his middle school's track team.

Q had been cool with Craig's brother, who was a year younger than Q's fourteen years, but he had quickly found new friends after taking up business with Devon. So he was well aware of the fact that Craig knew who he was and what he was all about, but he couldn't care less. All he cared about was making sure Craig stayed away from Shaniece.

Chapter 20

Shaniece cheered from the bleachers, along with her parents and her brother, as they watched the Riverside Jaguars take on the Tri-Cities Bulldogs. The girls' varsity game was almost over, and Rainelle had been playing with all her might tonight. Shaniece loved the way the team's energy wound up the crowd, and vice versa.

"Defense! Defense!" the crowd yelled.

Shaniece cheered along with the rest of the home team's supporters when Rainelle went for a three-pointer and succeeded effortlessly. The black, purple, and silver pompoms were wildly waved in the air as they watched the Jaguars' score move ahead of Tri-Cities' by five points.

"Man, this is messed up," Keith said as they settled in their seats during a time-out called by Tri-Cities, only ten seconds before the end of the game.

"What?" Cedric asked. "We're winning?"

"Yeah, that's all good and everything, but look at how many people are out here, and look at how many people were at the JV game last night?" Keith pointed out.

Shaniece laughed. "Keith, you're gonna have to get used to seeing only parents at the junior varsity games. No one cares to see a bunch of little kids play ball. They want to see a real game."

"Stop being mean, Niecey," Natalie told her daughter as she patted her son's knee. "Baby, your game was just as great as this one, and those who don't come just because of the title given to the team don't know what they're missing."

"Yeah, they don't know that they're missing a pro-baller in action before he becomes famous." Cedric tried to cheer his son up.

Keith shot Shaniece an irritated look as she hid her laughter behind a series of coughs.

As the game resumed, Riverside was given the ball. For the next ten seconds, the teammates did nothing but dribble and pass the ball. Rainelle threw the ball up in the air just as the buzzer sounded, signaling the end of the game and Riverside's victory. The crowd stood on their feet and cheered as they flooded the courts.

"You were great, baby," Natalie told Rainelle after pushing her way through the crowd.

"Thanks, Mama." Rainelle smiled. "I gotta go, but I'll meet you guys at the car as soon as I get my stuff."

Shaniece and her family walked out of the gymnasium and into the cold night air. She stood next to her mother near the entrance of the school as they waited for Rainelle to join them. Shaniece sighed when she saw Craig coming their way. She'd seen him when she'd first arrived, right after the boys' varsity game. She had hoped that he wouldn't stay for the girls' game, but he had, and, sadly, she wasn't surprised.

"Hey, Niecey," Craig greeted her first, once he'd reached them. "Keith, Mr. and Mrs. Simmons."

"Hey, Craig," Cedric greeted him happily. "How's everything going, son?"

Craig shrugged as he glanced at Shaniece. "Okay . . . could be better."

Shaniece rolled her eyes and prayed that her parents hadn't caught on to Craig's statement.

"So, Craig," Natalie said as she smiled at Shaniece, "what do you have planned for Valentine's Day next week?"

He shrugged once more. "I haven't really thought about it."

"Well, you should come with Niecey to the church's Sweetheart Dance, like you did last year," Natalie continued, to Shaniece's dismay and embarrassment.

Craig looked at Shaniece and studied her reaction. Shaniece was sure the objection that sat on the tip of her tongue was written all over her face. "That's up to Shaniece, Mrs. Simmons," Craig replied.

"I'm sure she would love to go with you," Natalie insisted. "Wouldn't you, Shaniece?"

All eyes turned toward her and Shaniece was speechless. She looked into her father's eyes and knew that he understood her predicament, but before he could save her from answering her mother's question, someone else stepped in and unknowingly rescued her for the second time that week.

"Hey, Shaniece," the now-familiar voice called out.

Shaniece wanted to grab Q and pull him into a bear hug. "Hey, Q." She turned toward her family and introduced them to the young boy just as Rainelle came out of the school building.

"How do you know Q?" Keith questioned suspiciously, knowing that his classmate wasn't someone Shaniece would usually converse with, and not just because he was a freshman.

"Oh, you didn't know?" Craig spoke up. "They have a mutual friend."

Shaniece glared at Craig, with her hands on her hips, before looking at her parents and explaining. "He lives in Devon's neighborhood."

"Yeah," Q confirmed, but with saddened eyes.

Before anyone could respond to his demeanor, gunshots rang out and everyone fell to the ground with fearful screams. Craig immediately grabbed onto Shaniece and she fell into his protective embrace.

"Jesus, Jesus, Jesus," Natalie cried as she clung to her husband.

Cedric pulled his family close as they hugged the concrete ground. "Father God, we come to you asking for your protection right now. Cover us with your blood and keep us safe from all harm. . . ."

As he prayed, Shaniece tried to listen to her father's calming voice, but the sound of gunshots only inches away from her ear succeeded in distracting her. She turned her head slightly to the left and looked upward and was shocked to find that Q was returning fire. As the vehicle, from which the initial gunshots had come, drove on, Shaniece watched as Q and a few other boys ran off campus. She cried for their safety, knowing that whatever had transpired had something to do with Devon.

Q sat down at the table and waited for Devon to be escorted into the room. He'd been waiting for this visit all week, and the need to see his mentor only grew after last night's drive-by shooting. Initially he'd been afraid, but once he saw that the shots were coming from the same black SUV that had been stalking the west side of Riverside all week, Q couldn't help but retaliate in anger. He'd felt the need not only to represent for Devon, but he'd also felt as if it was his responsibility to protect the people in his community.

He couldn't even smile as Devon made his way toward the table, and he knew that his grim attitude would make Devon realize how serious this visit was.

"What's happenin', li'l man?" Devon asked as he relaxed in his seat.

"Roc and his boys are movin' in real quick," Q stated quietly.

Devon smacked his teeth and sat up. "Man, who is this Roc?"

"Roc . . ." Q tried to find the words to describe the man. "He's like the Big D of the east side. He's tryna set up camp in our neighborhood, and last night, at the school, he marked his territory."

"First off, there ain't but one Big D . . . worldwide," Devon declared, dismissing the comparison. "And what you mean he marked his territory?" he questioned, his anger rising.

"Man, they shot up the school after the basketball game last night," Q explained, and tried not to allow Devon's anger to intimidate him.

"Are you kidding me?" Devon cursed. "What are y'all doin' out there? I thought y'all was holdin' it down. Now you tellin' me that this guy, who ain't even from here, is tearin' down everything I've worked to keep up since Kane died. This is straight bull, Q, and I'ma need you to man up." He paused and his eyes opened wide in realization. "Did you say he shot up the school . . . as in *your* school?"

"Yeah," Q said quietly.

"And it was after a basketball game?"

"Yeah," Q replied again, not sure what Devon was trying to figure out.

Devon suddenly banged his fist against the metal table, causing the sound to resonate throughout the room. He sputtered a string of curses before saying, "Shaniece's sister and brother play ball. That means she was there last night. Don't tell me my baby was out there when that fool came by."

Q looked up at the guard who was coming toward their table. "Man, it's cool," he told him when he asked Q if everything was okay. The guard walked away and Q looked back at Devon; his eyes answered the question.

"That's it," Devon stated, trying to lower his voice so that he wouldn't get Q in trouble due to the orders he was about to give him. "I'm ordering y'all fools to tighten up the blocks ASAP. If Roc even sets foot on my territory, I want it locked down, and I want all y'all posted up and packin'."

"Big D, why are you so bent on this girl?" Q asked cautiously.

Devon's jaw clenched and he gritted his teeth as his nose flared in anger. "Boy, why you questioning me? That's my woman, and I don't want her getting hurt 'cause of this fool. Now, what did you do to protect her last night? Or did you forget that I asked you to look out for her?"

"Man, I ain't forgot. I made sure I protected her and everybody else that was out there last night." He lowered his voice. "I had the campus on lock and I put a few bullets in that Escalade. So I been doin' what you asked me to do," he whispered.

"That's what I'm talkin' 'bout," Devon complimented. "So why you asking me stupid questions like that?"

Q shrugged and lowered his eyes. He didn't want to make Shaniece out to be a bad person, because she most definitely was not, but Q wondered if Devon really expected for her to be completely faithful to him when she had Craig and other guys equally as worthy in her face constantly.

"What's the problem?" Devon asked, moving closer to the table.

Q kept his gaze lowered. "The dude I told you that was feelin' her. . . ," he paused. Devon nodded in response, signifying that he remembered Q mentioning Craig. "Well, I made sure I let him know that Shaniece was your woman, but it's like he don't even care. I was talking to them on Monday afternoon, you know . . .

just kinda checking up on her, and that's when I told the dude that he had better watch himself around your girl. Then me and my boys left. Not even a full two minutes later, I saw the guy kiss her. He wasn't all down her throat or nothing, but it was kinda . . . I guess the word is 'intimate.' And when they started shooting last night, he grabbed on her like he was 'bout to take a bullet for her."

"She let him kiss her!" Devon nearly shouted before muttering another round of expletives.

"Well, she pushed him away," Q said, trying to defend her.

"And he be tryna protect her, like she's his woman?" Devon shook his head angrily.

"Look, Big D, I'm not tryna kill what you got wit' Shaniece, but do you honestly think she gon' keep pushin' dudes like him away for the next ten years?"

"Yes," Devon replied defiantly. "She told me she would."

Q sighed. He didn't know what else to say. It all sounded crazy to him and he was only fourteen. If he didn't know it before, he knew now that Devon was seriously in love with Shaniece. Devon's anger was apparent through the expression on his face, but it was his eyes that caught Q's attention. His mother had held the same look in her eyes many times before when she couldn't pay the rent, or the light bill, or when she couldn't put food on the table or clothes on her and her son's back. He'd seen her cry many nights and the look in her eyes had made itself a permanent fixture in Q's memory. That's how he recognized that Devon's eyes were full of despair and sadness.

Q tried to find a way to put the hope back into his mentor's spirit. "Well, she's probably good for her word, then. I only told you 'cause you asked me to keep you filled in."

Devon nodded. "I appreciate it, man," he said as he prepared to leave. "Keep holdin' it down for me where that fool, Roc, is concerned." He stood and began walking away from the table.

"Wait!" Q called out, and Devon turned to face him. "What about Shaniece? You want me to keep checkin' up on her?"

Devon's eyes darkened. "Naw, it's not even worth the trouble," he said before trudging away as if all of the life had been drained from his body.

Chapter 21

"On Friday night, the lives of those throughout this community were placed in unnecessary danger." Cedric spoke into the microphone as he stood behind the podium in the pulpit. "I say 'unnecessary' because I believe the motive behind Friday night's events were juvenile, ignorant, and immature."

Shaniece listened from her position in the choir stand as her father ranted and raved about the shooting, just as he had been doing since Friday night. Shaniece could mimic her father's words in her mind if she wanted, having heard the speech several times since the shooting.

"I don't believe things happen for no apparent reason. I believe that the natural reason behind the drive-by was unnecessary, but the reason God allowed it to happen while we were there is very apparent. This is a wake-up call for our community! It's time for us to band together and keep those who render us as minuscule targets of their violence off our streets.

"With the violence being targeted toward those who are students at Riverside High School, all of our children, including my own, are in a great deal of danger," Cedric continued. "There are three places a child should be able to go for safety: the first and foremost should always be home, then church, and finally school. But with those in the school returning the violence full force lets me know that our children's lives are at stake every time they step onto the campus. Now, since the authorities have done nothing to offer the security we really need, it's up to us to stop this madness before it gets completely out of hand."

"Amen, Pastor," several congregants agreed.

As Cedric continued, Shaniece kept her eyes lowered and silently continued to pray for Devon, Q, and all those involved in what was going on in her neighborhood. The school was the only thing in the neighborhood that was fairly new, and now that the local government had seen the national news, it would probably be another decade or two before another school or other government-sponsored building would be built in their area. But that wasn't an issue that Shaniece was overly concerned with at the moment.

She knew that whoever was responsible for initiating the shooting was trying to lay claims on Devon's territory. That fact had been established by one of Devon's workers, who'd appeared on *11 Alive News* Friday night. The guy had played off his statement as if he wasn't a part of the operation, but Shaniece could see the anger in his eyes and the contempt in his tone. He spoke scornfully of Devon being incarcerated last Thanksgiving and how someone was trying to come in and cause mayhem in their community.

"Big D is a respected figure throughout our community. And now someone is trying to come through and mess up all he's worked for." The guy continued to speak highly of Devon.

The reporter had questioned the man on how anyone could look up to a drug dealer, as many of those standing in the background of the recording did.

"It's not about what he does," the guy explained. "It's about who he is. He was caring and he worked hard to provide for those less fortunate. I can't tell you how many times he's helped me provide for my own family when I couldn't."

Shaniece knew that his statement meant that he'd worked for Devon and the job had paid well, but she watched in amazement as others came forward and told of how Devon had assisted them in finances as well, and how upset they were to see that an outsider, who couldn't care less about those in the community, was causing such danger and destruction.

Shaniece had no idea that Devon had been such a strong tower for her community. Before meeting him in the grocery store nearly four months ago, she had never heard of him. She'd been well aware of the distribution of drugs; that became obvious one day last year when she'd driven one of her friends, who lived on the downtrodden side of Riverside, home from school. The girl lived three blocks away from a crack house and had shared with Shaniece just how many Riverside students took part in the distribution or use of drugs. But despite the illegality of it all, there was no denying the fact that since Devon's incarceration, the community had been going downhill.

As her father began his sermon, Shaniece thought about the upcoming holiday. Valentine's Day was on Saturday and the church's Third Annual Sweetheart Dance was that night. Her parents had given her no choice but to attend, and she had no problem doing so. It was just the fact that she would be going alone that she hated. Last year, she'd invited Craig to accompany her because he'd told her he had no plans for the holiday, and she'd gone the year before with a guy she'd been in a relationship with at the time. This year, she wanted to spend the holiday with the man she loved, but that was obviously out of the question.

Her mother and even her siblings had been putting the pressure on her to ask Craig to the dance. Her father hadn't said much about it, only letting her know that he did want her to have fun at the event. Spending the evening with Craig might not be as bad as it seemed, but Shaniece didn't want to spend the night hearing about how Devon wasn't good for her and how she was wasting her time with him. She'd have to be sure that Craig wouldn't criticize her decision to wait for Devon instead of giving him a chance.

She'd have to go see Devon on Saturday, though. There was no way she'd feel comfortable going out with Craig that night if she didn't at least go visit Devon at some point during the day. Maybe she would buy him a gift . . . or make him a card—seeing as how she had no idea what types of gifts were or were not acceptable for prisoners to receive. She'd probably receive a letter from him at some point this week, but instead of writing him back, she'd visit him. She wanted to feel his strong hands holding hers as they had done the first time she'd gone to see him. She wanted to feel his soft lips against her skin as she had when she'd brushed her fingers across them in order to satisfy his hunger for a kiss. Even if she couldn't touch him, she wanted just to be in his company, if only for a few minutes.

She also wanted to let him know that regardless of the fact that *his* streets were in turmoil, she wanted him to focus on getting himself together. He'd promised her that he was going to try to do better, and she would hold him to that. She was sure that during his visit yesterday Q had told Devon what was going on, and she might not know Devon that well, but she knew that anyone who cared about his reputation would do anything to make sure it remained intact. She realized

Devon was that type of person. She'd have to make him see that it was not worth it. He needed to use his free time to grow spiritually, not remain stagnant in his street mentality.

As Cedric brought the service to a close, he sent up a fervent prayer for the community, asking God to protect them and to keep them through whatever hardships may come their way. He also asked God to have mercy on the lost souls who were ignorant of the hurt they were causing those around them. Lastly he prayed that the community would stick together during this time of need. After the benediction, Shaniece gathered her things and met up with Tatiana and Krystal.

"Are you okay?" Krystal asked Shaniece as they walked toward the exit. "You seemed kinda out of it today."

"I'm okay," Shaniece assured her as they walked toward Tatiana's car. "Tati, when is your mother going to get her car back? You've been driving to church for the past two Sundays."

Tatiana shrugged. "I don't know. Every time she gets it back, something else goes wrong and it has to go right back to the mechanics. She's had me running to the store for diapers and groceries and I'm 'bout tired of it. But with my dad driving trucks every weekend, I have no choice but to tote my helpless mother around. I hope this is the last time, though, 'cause I'm sick of having this car seat in my car." She pointed toward her baby brother's carrier that was strapped down in the backseat.

Krystal laughed. "So who are you guys bringing to the dance on Saturday?"

Tatiana's smile was wide as she replied, "I'm going with Justin Wilburn."

"Oh, okay, girl," Krystal sang as she searched the parking lot for the new topic of their conversation.

All three girls spotted the five-foot-ten, coffee-colored gentleman, who'd just joined the church a few months earlier. He was standing with a group of guys near the church's entrance. As if he could sense their stares, he turned toward them and flashed a blinding smile.

"Mmm, mmm, mmm." Tatiana smiled and waved in response.

"Did you ask him?" Shaniece wanted to know, realizing that it wouldn't be unlike her friend to do something as bold as asking a guy on a date.

"Actually," Tatiana began as she tore her eyes away from Justin and faced her friend, "we asked each other. We were talking one Sunday after church and asked the question almost simultaneously."

"Must be destiny," Krystal surmised.

"What about you, Krys?" Tatiana asked. "Who are you going with?"

"I'm bringing this guy, Tyrie, from my school. He asked me to be his valentine and I told him that I would, but only if he celebrated at my church." Krystal chuckled softly. "He thought I'd lost my mind, but I told him about the dance and assured him that it would be like a regular dance, but without all the bumpin' and grindin'."

Shaniece began to fiddle with her hands as both Krystal and Tatiana looked toward her. She knew she'd have no choice but to tell them what boy she had thought about coming to do the dance with . . . or they could just find out on Saturday. Either way, they'd both have something to say about it, so she figured it would be better to get the conversation over with now.

"I thought about asking Craig again," she stated softly.

Tatiana studied her friend's distraught expression. "Is that what you want, Niecey?"

"I really want to spend time with Devon," Shaniece replied honestly. "But my parents . . . well, *my mother* has suggested that I go with Craig, and I don't see anything wrong with it."

"Other than the fact that he's in love with you, and spending the time with him could give him the impression that you want more than friendship, when in actuality you're just using him to compensate for the fact that the person you want to be with is unable to be with you."

"That's not true, Tati," Shaniece denied rebelliously.

"Yes, it is," Tatiana retorted. "You may not be doing it now, but you're going to abuse Craig's availability to satisfy your desire to have someone around who can hug and hold you, like you want D to do."

"Tati, that's not fair," Shaniece said, nearing tears. "You're predicting something that's not even going to come true."

Tatiana sighed. "Maybe, but just consider it a warning. You, Craig, and I—we're tight," she said as she crossed her index and middle fingers to symbolize their closeness. "And if things go sour between you two, I don't want to be caught in the middle of it."

"You won't," Shaniece assured. "I'll make sure he knows we're just two friends hanging out. I'm not going to lead him on."

"And what does Mr. D have to say about this?" Krystal asked. "He seems like the jealous type."

"Yeah, you know that li'l thug, Q, is going to tell him if he finds out that you went out with Craig," Tatiana pointed out. "Mind you, it doesn't matter if you guys are just going to a dance together or going around collecting cans for community service—he'll take it as Craig trying to steal *Big D's* woman."

"First of all, I am nobody's to claim," Shaniece said, though she liked the thought of being Devon's girl-friend—that is, if he could get his life together. "Second, it's not like Q is stalking me, so he wouldn't know anything about me and Craig, *if* there was something to know."

"Yeah, that's what you think," Tatiana said skeptically. "That li'l boy is sneaky."

Krystal laughed. "You talk like he's a private investigator."

"Shoot. With the way he's been popping up in Niecey's face lately, I wouldn't knock that as a possibility."

"Look, it doesn't matter, because Craig and I are just friends," Shaniece said. "Devon and I aren't working on a relationship; he's trying to get his life together. And, regardless of who I'm with, I'm free to do as I please. Therefore, I have nothing to hide from anybody."

"That's what I'm talkin' about!" Krystal laughed as she slapped hands with Shaniece.

"Besides, I'm going to visit Devon on Saturday before the dance. I'll tell him about me asking Craig to be my date and explain to him that we're going just as friends."

"And what if he still disapproves?" Tatiana asked.

Shaniece shrugged. "What could he possibly disapprove of? It's not that big a deal."

"That's what you say, but he may feel like Craig is a threat . . . and I can't blame him." Tatiana shrugged. "Craig's got a lot going for himself, and if D realizes that he can't compete, he might feel intimidated."

Shaniece rolled her eyes. "Devon has nothing to worry about. I told him—as I've told you before—as long as he has my heart, I'm not going anywhere."

"Are you sure you guys aren't in a relationship?" Krystal asked with raised eyebrows. "Sounds like you've tied yourself to him permanently."

Shaniece shrugged again. "I'm just following my heart."

Chapter 22

Dear Shaniece,
This will probably be my last letter to you. I'm only writing to tell you that I think it's best we not see each other anymore. This is not something I want, but it's something you need. I'm thinking of you and I just feel as if you're wasting your time waiting for me when you have better options. In your letter, you said people were telling you the same thing, and at first, I was gonna do everything I could to prove them wrong, but over the last week, I realized they're right. You deserve better than what I can give you. Besides, I thought that making you happy would be a good enough reason for me to try to do better, but the safety of the people in my neighborhood also means a lot to me. So, right now, I gotta do what I gotta do in order to make sure my streets stay in order and those tryna take over know they're out of place.
I told you that I didn't wanna and couldn't promise you that I'd make a complete turn around and I said that for this exact reason. I didn't wanna let you down because I know how much

faith you had in me, but I just can't let my people fight for their community without any direction. I'm responsible for them, and me not being careful in the first place is what got them into this situation. So I've got to step in and make sure the problem is corrected.

I'm sorry if you're disappointed in me, but this is something I have to do for me—just like I want you to let me go for yourself. You deserve better and I'm nowhere near close to being what you deserve, nor do I deserve you. Please don't take this to mean that I don't love or care about you. There are no words that describe how I really feel about you, but my love for you is what is helping me to let you go. I can't selfishly hold you back from living your life just because I went out and ruined mine. There's nothing that can save me now, so I think it's best we go our separate ways.

Please don't write me back and don't bother to visit me. I hope you can forgive me for wasting your time. And I hope you find what your heart desires . . . what your heart deserves. My love for you still remains, always and forever. Good-bye, Shaniece.

Devon

Shaniece watched as her tears soaked the handwritten letter. She'd been waiting for a letter from Devon all week, and when she'd gone out to check the mailbox this Friday afternoon, she'd expected another letter full of loving words that were sure to touch her in places she'd never been touched before. But this . . . this was not what she'd waited all week to receive. A breakup letter. *You weren't dating him, Niecey,* she told herself. But in her heart she knew differently. Never had she and Devon spoken the words that would make their bond official, but their hearts had shouted volumes over the last couple of weeks. Shaniece and Devon *had* been dating, and she could no longer deny that. But after only a short amount of time, it was over. And why? Because he felt she deserved better. *How selfless of him,* she thought cynically. She crumpled the letter, tossed it onto her dresser, and then sprawled her body across her bed. As she lay there, her mind tried to register what had just happened.

How hard is it for you to grasp? she asked herself silently. *He doesn't want you.*

"That's not true," she retorted aloud. "He said that he still loves me. I just don't understand."

She wondered who'd placed the idea that he wasn't good enough for her into his mind. She thought of all the people who'd told her that she was wasting her time with him: Tatiana, Craig, her mother—without being as obvious as others—and, lately, even Keith and Rainelle had been trying to get their sister to seize other opportunities with a guy who would love her enough to allow her to grow without holding her back in order to satisfy his selfish desires. Now Devon was agreeing with them all. *Maybe they're right.*

Even with that conclusion, Shaniece's heart was still unsettled. She thought that if she waited for Devon, no matter how ridiculous it seemed, he would do all he could in order to change for the better. Last week, he was telling her that he was going to start school, and that it would be easy for him to make a positive transition, since he was locked up, away from the streets that had held him hostage since he was fifteen years old. Now, only eleven days later, he was telling her that protecting his name and his streets were more important than trying to rise above his ignorant state of mind.

She just didn't understand. She realized that Devon had been an important figure throughout the community, but if the lifestyle he'd led had caused him to be deprived of his freedom, why would he still want to hold on to it? She had to find answers to the questions that were clouding her mind. He'd said that he didn't want her to call or visit, but she'd stick to her Saturday afternoon plans. Tomorrow, she would visit Devon and find out what was going on in the back of his mind.

The sound of her ringing cell phone caused Shaniece to quickly dry her tears, as if the caller would notice them once she answered the phone.

"Hello," she answered gruffly.

"Hey, Niecey," Craig greeted. "Did I wake you up?"

Shaniece didn't feel like talking to Craig; she wished she'd checked her caller ID before picking up the phone. She buried her head in her pillow and inhaled deeply before responding, "No. What's up, Craig?"

He was silent for several moments before asking, "Are you okay? You sound like you may have been crying."

"Craig, you apparently called me for a reason. I'm sure it wasn't to analyze the tone of my voice," Shaniece snapped.

"Maybe I should just try you later, when you're not so moody."

She wanted to apologize, but she felt like being angry, and if she couldn't take her frustrations out on Devon, Craig would have to do. "*Moody?* For your information, Craig, I am *not* moody. I'm fine. Now either you tell me why you've decided to call me this *wonder-ful* afternoon, or just forget you have my number, because I'm not trying to hear whatever you have to say later." Tears began to trail her cheeks once more, and she tried to get her emotions under control.

"Niecey?" Craig said cautiously. "Whatever's wrong . . . I'm sorry. If you're still upset with me for being so against your relationship with Devon, then I'm sorry. If I'm bothering you or pushing you to put up with my feelings for you, then I'm sorry. I just want us to be friends . . . like we used to be."

Shaniece only cried harder, knowing that Craig was hardly the root of all her animosity. He'd been such a good friend to her. He'd been there for her when she needed him to be. She remembered last Friday night when the drive-by had occurred; Craig had immediately protected her. He cared about her well-being. But she'd been pushing him away—for Devon. Just a fleeting thought of her *ex-boyfriend* made her writhe in distress.

"Whatever I did, Shaniece—"

"I'm sorry, Craig," she cut him off, giving in to her urge to apologize. "You haven't done anything . . . except be a better friend to me than I've been to you." She paused to gather her emotions before continuing. "I know I've been really rude and disrespectful toward you and your feelings for me and I want to apologize for that. I've been so wrapped up in my own feelings that I never took time to consider yours, and I'm really, really sorry. I just hope you can forgive me."

"Shaniece," Craig breathed her name, "you know I do. Now, I've told you before, and I'll tell you again, I love you, and you can always come to me when you're feeling like you're feeling now."

"I know," she answered, sniffling.

"So, do you feel like telling your *friend* what's got you so torn?"

Shaniece wasn't sure if she should share with Craig the issues she was having with Devon. Considering the fact that her friend was in love with her and had told her repeatedly that Devon didn't deserve even half the woman she was, Shaniece was sure he'd be biased in any advice he'd give her.

"C'mon, Niecey. I promise I'll listen and be fair when I respond to whatever's going on," he said as if he'd known what she'd been thinking.

She did want advice. *You could always call Tatiana for that,* she reminded herself. But why do that when Craig was willing and ready to listen to *anything* that might be on her mind? She disregarded what her head was telling her and allowed her heart to vent to her friend.

"I got a letter from Devon today." She became quiet, fully expecting Craig to begin making assumptions of what could have been written in the letter. But he remained quiet, so she continued. "He basically cut me off and told me that I deserved better than him." She paused once more, knowing that Craig would jump in and say, "I told you so." He remained quiet. "He also said that he couldn't try to better himself when there were people trying to come in from the outside and take over his territory. So since I deserve better, and since he doesn't want to do what he has to do to stay out of trouble, he doesn't want to talk to me, he doesn't want me to call him, and he doesn't want me to visit him." She began to tear up again.

"I just don't understand this at all, Craig. He told me that his love for me was so strong that he would at least *try* to do better. What happened to that?" she asked rhetorically. "What? Did his love weaken overnight and cause him to decide that I wasn't worth it, after all? And it's not just me he should've been doing it for. He should want it for himself, shouldn't he? I mean, who wants to go around for the rest of his life selling drugs and being on the run all the time? I know he was always watching his back when he was out running the streets. Why would you want to live your life, not knowing if you'd make it to the next day due to the fact that a drug deal can go completely out of whack at any moment?" she rambled. "And then to put other people's lives in danger as well. . . . It's just so stupid!

"Was I asking too much of him?" she questioned. "Was I just living a fantasy I knew could never be reality? Maybe I was playing myself for a fool? I was trying to save someone who just didn't want to be saved," she concluded.

The line was vacant of sound as Shaniece waited for Craig to respond to her rampage. When he said nothing, she spoke again. "Go ahead and say it, Craig."

"Say what?" he asked, his tone normal as if they were having a regular, everyday conversation.

Shaniece sighed, and if she didn't know Craig as well as she did, she would've assumed that he hadn't even been listening to her. "You know what I'm talking about. I know you want to say that you told me so, so go ahead and say it."

Craig chuckled softly. "You know me better than that," he told her. "I'm not into making you feel bad about the decisions you make for yourself."

"Does that mean you don't have anything to say about what I just told you?"

"No, I've got a lot to say about it, but the majority of it would be directed toward Devon, not you," he said, and she could hear the hostility in his tone. "But I do

think that you just need to let him go. And I'm not saying that because I don't like him. I truly feel that's the
only way you're going to move past this."

"But I really wanted to go see him tomorrow," Shaniece
said. "You know, just for the holiday. I haven't seen him
since the first time I visited, and I thought tomorrow
would be a wonderful time to see him again."

"And you still want to go . . . even after receiving that
letter?" he asked, almost disbelievingly.

"I know, it seems stupid, but I just want to look into
his eyes and hope to see that the look in them would
contradict everything he wrote in the letter."

Craig was silent again, and Shaniece knew that her
desire to hold on to what she and Devon shared disappointed him.

"I'm sorry, but that's how I feel," she said in response
to his silence.

He breathed deeply. "I know, and, trust me, I completely understand. Every time you tell me there's no
chance of us moving beyond friendship, I search your
eyes and your soul and pray that they'll show that your
words are nothing but lies to cover up your true feelings. I know you probably think I'm a sucker for even
continuing to pursue you, especially when it's crystal
clear that your heart belongs to another guy, but I can't
change the way I feel." He paused. "And neither can
you, so that's why I'm telling you to follow your heart.
If you feel you need to see him, then that's what you
need to do."

"Thank you," Shaniece replied with a smile. "I really
appreciate you letting me vent, and I want you to know
that I love having you as my friend. You're a really good
one."

"Thank you," he said.

She dried the remainder of her tears and decided to change the subject. "So I know you're not psychic and you had no idea about the letter. And I'm most certain you didn't call to hear me cry and ramble on about Devon. What was your reason for calling me?"

Craig laughed and replied, "I was actually calling to see if I was invited to the Sweetheart Dance again this year?"

Shaniece smiled. "Are you asking me to ask you to be my date to the dance, Craig?"

He was quiet as if thinking about her question. "Yeah, I think I am." He laughed again.

She laughed with him. "I was planning to ask you, anyway," she said to his surprise. "I don't want you to think I'm just using you as a substitute for Devon," she added, remembering the words Tatiana had spoken on Sunday. "I just would like to spend the evening with my good friend."

"I know you wouldn't do that," Craig assured her. "So, do we have a date?"

"Yes, the dance is at seven, so you can pick me up at seven-thirty."

He laughed. "Great. We'll be fashionably late."

"That's the plan," she agreed. "So I'll see you tomorrow."

"Okay. Just make sure you're ready to have fun. There will be no tears to shed tomorrow night . . . unless, of course, you're laughing so hard, you end up crying."

She chuckled. "I promise, no tears . . . at least until I see you dancing."

"Oh, you got jokes!" Craig laughed. "We'll see who owns the dance floor, come tomorrow night."

"We will."

"That's a bet," he said as he prepared to hang up.

"Oh, and, Craig . . ."

"Yes, ma'am," he answered teasingly.

"Thank you again." Shaniece spoke gently to her friend.

"That's what friends are for," Craig replied.

Shaniece said good-bye, ended the call, and placed her cell phone back on her nightstand, with a slight smile on her face. She'd go see Devon tomorrow afternoon and hopefully straighten everything out. But regardless of how her meeting with Devon would go, she planned on coming home from the dance tomorrow night with a smile on her face.

Chapter 23

Devon wasn't surprised that he had a visitor today. He knew his mother would be thinking of him on Valentine's Day, so he'd expected her to come visit him this afternoon. He shuffled his way into the visitors' room and looked around, but didn't see his mother. The guard pointed toward the table closest to the entrance, and Devon's face went blank. He hadn't noticed Shaniece sitting there, because she had her head buried in her hands. He stared at her as she continued to quietly sit with her face hidden. He didn't feel like talking to her, and he was certain he'd made that clear in his letter—apparently, she hadn't caught on to the obvious.

He turned toward the guard. "Man, I don't want my visit today," he said quietly.

"You sure?" the guard asked. "If you don't see her, then you can't see anybody. You only get one visit per day," he said, as if Devon needed to be reminded of the rules.

"I'm sure. Take me back to my cell."

Just as Devon was about to leave, he heard her soft plea, "Devon, please come talk to me."

He stopped at the sound of Shaniece's sweet voice and forced himself not to look at her. There were only two other prisoners in the room and he didn't want to cause a scene. He had two options: he could completely ignore her and return to his cell, foregoing his chance to spend some time in a room without the horrible odor of musk and urine, or he could sit, face-to-face, with the woman he loved, even if he was still adamant about his decision not to see her anymore.

He took a deep breath and turned to face Shaniece. *God, she's beautiful,* he thought as she returned his gaze, her brown eyes piercing his soul. She looked as if she'd been crying, and he knew exactly why. He turned toward the guard, and, knowingly, the guard allowed him to approach the table. Devon took a seat and tried to pretend as if Shaniece's presence wasn't causing his heart to race.

"Hey," she said softly.

He forced himself not to look into her eyes. "Wassup?"

Shaniece reached into her pocket and pulled out the letter he'd sent her the day before. "Wanna tell me what this was all about?"

He glanced down at the folded piece of paper and noticed that it had been crumpled. He was sure Shaniece had almost trashed it in her anger. Turning his head away, he silently shrugged.

"Oh, so you can't talk now?"

Devon was surprised by the tone of her voice. Each time he'd spoken with her, she'd always been calm. Even when she did raise her voice, her tone never held the level of anger it held now.

"What is this crap?" she asked, tossing the letter onto the table.

"Look, Shaniece, if you gon' sit here and act like this, I'ma go back to my cell," he told her, his eyes still turned toward the bland walls to the right of him.

"Devon, how do you expect me to act when you send me something like this?" she asked. "Do you know I waited all week for a letter from you? I wanted it to be filled with words telling me how much you love me and want to do better so we can be together."

He could tell she was fighting hard to keep from crying.

"Imagine how I felt when I got that and read what you wrote. I had just sent you a letter, telling you that people had been telling me that I shouldn't be with you, or that I was wasting my time with you, but I wasn't listening to them. I told you how much faith I had in you, and that I couldn't wait for the day we would fully be together. I promised you that I would wait, and you promised me that you would try to stop acting like an idiot and get your life in order. It's like you took what I wrote and turned it around, as if I had told you that *I* didn't want to be bothered with you anymore."

"Niecey, I'm just being realistic. What we got ain't no TV show or some romance novel or movie. . . . It's real. We not gon' live happily ever after, and we need to be real about it. I'ma be in here for *ten years,*" he stressed, still avoiding eye contact, "and *that* depends on how I act. You're young and just about to live your life fully on your own. It ain't right for me to hold you back, when you got so much to live for."

"Didn't I say the same thing when you asked me to wait for you? I told you I didn't want to live a fantasy and that was a long time to put my life on hold for you, but *you* promised me that it'd be worth it. Now you're saying the exact opposite." Shaniece sat back with her arms folded. "So what was the point of going through all the 'I'm sorry and I'ma try to do better because I wanna make you happy' mess that you told me the last time I came to see you?"

"That was then" was all he said.

"And what? This is now?" she retorted angrily, shoving her pointer finger toward the letter that still sat on the table. "So basically what you're saying is that you didn't mean any of it. Which means you didn't mean anything you said that day, including a statement that sounds a little like 'I love you.'"

"*No*, Shaniece," Devon interjected firmly, finally looking directly into her eyes. "Don't even do that. Don't try to turn this around, as if I'm just a big liar and I never mean a word I say."

"Well, it's kinda hard not to do that when you've done nothing but lie to me from the day we met," she shot back.

"Look, I'm not 'bout to sit here and argue with you. I don't have nothin' to prove to you. I know how I feel, and I know that I love you, regardless of what you think," he declared. "If I didn't love you, I would keep asking you to put your life on hold for me, but I do love you, so I'm not gonna ask you to do that. Why can't you see that I'm thinking of you?"

"Because you're also thinking of yourself," she told him. "You're not doing this just so I can live my life. You're doing it so that you can continue to live yours. You wanna handle your business and not feel bad about having me hold on to a promise you knew from jump you couldn't keep. And that is selfish."

Devon threw his hands up in frustration. "Do you want me to keep making a promise to change, when I know I can't?" he questioned. "Stop tryna use my lifestyle as an excuse for wanting to save me."

"Devon, that's not what I'm doing. I was only trying to show you a better way to live. Is it truly worth it for you to do all you can for your community, through illegal means, and still end up going to hell?" An incredulous look passed over Devon's face that caused Shaniece to instantly regret her words.

"You know, judging someone when you're not in a position to judge is just as much of a sin as me trappin'," Devon told her as he gazed deep into her eyes.

"I'm sorry," Shaniece replied sincerely. "I'm just upset because you didn't even give us a chance. I mean, what happened that just made you change your mind about us and about helping yourself?"

He shook his head. "I just came to my senses."

Shaniece pursed her lips. "And who helped you do that? Q?" she questioned knowingly.

"Not intentionally," Devon answered. "He was just telling me about the shooting—that's when I realized I had to do something about what was going on in my streets. Then when he told me you were there, I got scared. I was pissed because I wasn't there to protect you. Then Q told me about ol' boy who's been pushin' up on you . . . some guy you hang with on the regular."

"Craig," Shaniece interjected, knowing full well that Devon was talking about him. "He's just my friend."

"Yeah, Q told me you wasn't feelin' him like he was feelin' you, but that don't change the fact that he's there, in your face every day, and I'm stuck in here." He sat up and took her hands. "He's a better option, and I'm cool with that," he lied.

Shaniece tested the waters. "So you'd be cool with the fact that he's going to be my date tonight for my church's Sweetheart Dance?"

Devon released her hands and returned to the slouching position in his chair. He couldn't stand the fact that tonight—the night on which couples, families, and friends celebrated the love they shared—this guy, whom Shaniece only saw as her friend, but who loved her just as much, if not more than Devon did, would be dancing in her arms. The thought made his skin crawl and he wanted to shout out to her that he wouldn't be cool with it at all. But if he truly wanted to show her that he was serious about them going their separate ways, he'd have to make her believe that going out with Craig was best for her.

"If that's what makes you happy," he replied, with a shrug.

"I was happy with you," she said, to his surprise. "But that doesn't matter anymore."

"I just don't want to be the reason you don't take advantage of better opportunities."

"And you don't want to feel like a punk for letting your people fight for their community by themselves," Shaniece added. "I guess I have to accept that. But it doesn't mean that I'm going to give up on you. I'ma keep praying for you, like *I* promised."

"Do what you gotta do," he said as he pushed away from the table. "Have fun with your friend tonight." He stood and prepared to leave.

"Wait," Shaniece said as she reached into her purse and pulled out a peach-colored envelope. "Happy Valentine's Day," she said as she handed him the card.

He took it and nodded his head. "Good-bye, Shaniece." He turned and walked toward the guard, who led him back to his cell.

"Who was your visitor?" Mitch asked Devon once he was back in the confines of his cell.

"Someone I wasted my time seeing," Devon replied forcefully.

He didn't want Mitch to know about his breakup with Shaniece. It would only bring about a series of questions he didn't feel like answering. He avoided looking at his roommate as he jumped onto his bunk. He knew that if Mitch just looked into his eyes, he'd see the hurt and anger Devon was experiencing. Hurt from the thought of never again being able to call Shaniece his lady. Anger from the realization of another man getting and taking advantage of the chance to make her happy and love her fully, like he wished he would've done from the very first day he'd met her. But it was his decision to let her go; therefore all of his hurt and anger was his fault, and his alone.

He looked down at the card that she'd given him before he'd left her sitting at the table. He was almost afraid to open it, for fear of regretting his decision more than he already was. Slowly he tore open the envelope and pulled out the card. Opening it, he realized it was a blank card on which Shaniece had handwritten a personalized note, only making it harder for him to read. He hesitantly adjusted his eyes to the words in front of him.

Before you, I never gave love a second thought
I was told to offer myself because I never knew what I'd receive
But out of fear, I refused to open my heart
Its walls were never to be penetrated, I believed.
Before you, I was alone, never lonely
It took a moment to get used to the thought of companionship
But you proved yourself worthy
And I felt the need to at least offer my friendship.
Before you, the limits of my trust were never tested
I was beginning to believe that things were too good to be true
But I realized forgiveness would be my greatest obstacle yet
Overcoming it allowed me to see the true colors in you.
Before you, I never thought fairy tales were real
It seemed what we had belonged on the movie screen

But your touch, your love, your presence alone
It all brought to life a fantasy that set our love free.
Happy Valentine's Day, Devon
All my love, Shaniece

Devon kept his eyes glued to the poetic piece that described the stages of their relationship and fought hard to keep the tears pressed behind his pupils. *She had to have written this before she got my letter,* he thought, knowing full well that had she purchased the card after receiving his letter, the words would've been full of anger and contempt, instead of the love and care that Shaniece felt in her heart for him.

He knew that Shaniece loved him, but her words had shown that her feelings ran much deeper than that. The depth and meaning of her words once again made him realize how much faith and trust she'd placed in him. And once again, he'd shattered it all in one day.

Chapter 24

"Niecey," Rainelle said as she knocked on her sister's closed bedroom door.

"Yes," Shaniece responded from inside her closet.

Rainelle opened the door slightly. "I just wanted to let you know that Keith, Mama, Daddy, and I are about to head to the dance," she said. "Daddy said to make sure you turn the alarm system on and lock up before you leave with Craig."

Shaniece waited a moment before saying, "Okay."

She waited until she heard her sister close her bedroom door before emerging from her closet and taking a seat on her bed. She hadn't wanted her sister to see that she was still lounging around in her deep red terry cloth bathrobe—that would have surely caused Rainelle's thick eyebrows to rise in concern. Shaniece didn't need to be interrogated. She didn't want her sister to know that she was contemplating not going to the dance this evening. She just hadn't mustered up enough nerve to call Craig, thirty minutes before he was to pick her up, with a lame excuse as to why she couldn't go. It wasn't that she didn't want to go out with Craig, or that she didn't want to go to the Sweetheart Dance. She just didn't want to go to the dance with someone who wasn't her sweetheart.

For the last four hours, she'd thought about her visit with Devon, and for the last four hours, all she could see was the disappointment he'd tried to hide when she'd told him about her date with Craig tonight. She'd thought that a mention of her going out with another guy, even if it was casual, would snap Devon back into his senses and make him realize that he didn't want her to be with anyone but him, and him with her. But he hadn't; he'd shrugged it off. Though Shaniece knew that it meant more to him than he'd let on, it still hurt to see him react so nonchalantly.

This is why I should've never gotten involved with him, Shaniece scolded herself. She had been content with her single status and had felt the last thing she needed was a boyfriend to complicate her life. Her last relationship, nearly two years ago, proved that. Jordan Daye had taught Shaniece that no matter how trusting, loving, and caring a guy said he was, or seemed to be, there was always a chance he'd find something to nit-pick about.

With Jordan, it had been that Shaniece spent so much time studying and actively participating in school, she couldn't see his *needs* weren't being met in their relationship—as if a sixteen-year-old boy had an inkling of an idea what he really needed. That was the reason why, instead of just ending the relationship and saving Shaniece a lot of heartache, he'd started cheating on her with someone who would satisfy him. Shaniece always felt that Jordan had been selfish by not breaking up with her before he'd started to see the girl, who'd gladly done what Shaniece had refused. When caught in the act, Jordan told Shaniece that he hadn't wanted to hurt her by breaking up with her just because she wouldn't sleep with him—an explanation Shaniece had thought to be very ridiculous. How could he have thought he'd be hurting her if he broke up with her, because she wouldn't give in to his requests, but didn't believe he would be hurting her by seeing another girl behind her back? It didn't make sense, and from the day she broke up with Jordan, she vowed not to enter another relationship unless she was truly ready. Spending her time emotionally torn over a guy, who was hardly worth one tear, wouldn't happen again.

Now here she was again, crying over a guy who swore he was thinking of her when he'd decided to break her heart. While it had taken Jordan nearly two months to find something wrong in his and Shaniece's relationship, it had taken Devon all of two weeks to realize that he didn't want to change who he was, even if it would make the girl he loved happy. And now that Shaniece thought about it, maybe Devon was right in saying it was for the best. It was best that they separate now, rather than doing so later when their feelings for each other would have grown into something neither of them would have been able to control.

Shaniece nodded as she walked back into her closet. *It is best,* she tried to convince herself. "It is best," she repeated her thoughts aloud. "I'm not going to mope about this. It's for the best, and I need to move on."

Just as she spoke the words that would take her on a journey down a different path, without Devon holding her back, her cell phone rang its tune. She smiled and sang along with Chrisette Michele's "Be OK," as she felt it was fitting for her new frame of mind.

"Hello," she answered, just before the call was sent to her voice mail.

"Hey, Niecey," Craig greeted.

Shaniece immediately thought he was calling to cancel for some reason or another. "Hey, is everything okay? You're not trying to ditch me last minute, are you?" she asked, hoping that he wasn't. Despite the fact that she'd thought of doing the same, only five minutes earlier, she'd gotten over the apprehension. Now the thought of staying home with nothing else to do, besides think about Devon, was not appealing to her.

He laughed. "No. I just had this feeling that maybe *you* might not be up to hangin' with me tonight."

"Actually, I'd thought about not going, but I can't think of anything else I want to do more than go out tonight," she assured him.

"But do you feel good about going out with me?"

Shaniece thought about his question and knew that she was still a little nervous about spending the evening with Craig. Devon's disappointed expression flashed through her mind and she almost gave in to the sad brown eyes taunting her thoughts, but she refused to allow him to ruin this night for her. She'd go out with Craig, and she'd love it. "I feel *great* about it, Craig," she replied, to his surprise and pleasure.

"Wonderful, that's all I wanted to hear." She could hear the smile in his tone and was sure his entire face was aglow. "I'll be by to pick you up in about twenty minutes."

"Sounds good to me," Shaniece replied before saying good-bye and disconnecting the call.

She actually felt better as she rushed back into her closet and pulled the long-sleeved pink sweater dress from the rack and placed it on her bed. She searched through her small collection of shoes and found a pair of pink T-strap heels to match. She ran through the routine of dressing herself, and then protecting the cleanliness of her clothes by slipping back into her robe as she went into the bathroom to pin her hair up, chignon style. She then applied a bit of loose powder to her face, eyeliner under each of her eyes, eye shadow on both of her eyelids, and lip gloss to her lips, in order to enhance her natural beauty.

By the time she'd slipped into her shoes and grabbed her dress coat and silver clutch, Craig was standing on her doorstep, ringing her doorbell. She tried to calm her nerves, as they seemed to heighten at the sound of the chimes ringing throughout the house. She didn't know why she was so nervous. She felt the way she had when she went on her very first date. She felt jittery, just like she had the night Devon was supposed to take her out the weekend after he'd shared dinner with her family.

Ugh, why am I doing this! she screamed within herself. She refused to think about Devon tonight. Tonight, she was going to have fun without feeling guilty. Tonight, she would remember what it was like to go out and enjoy being with her friends.

She opened the door and greeted her date with a sweet smile. "Hey, Craig."

"Shaniece, you look beautiful," Craig complimented.

"Thank you," Shaniece replied as she admired his black slacks and red dress shirt, with spit-shined dress shoes. "You look great, yourself."

He didn't try to hide his reddened face. "Thank you. Are you ready to go?"

"Yes, just let me set the alarm and lock up."

Shaniece had expected to see the church's dining hall decorated in the traditional red or pink Valentine's décor, but she was pleasantly surprised to see that the Events Planning Committee had been less predictable than they had in the last two years. She was awed by the purple and gold streamers, balloons, and ornaments that embellished the room. Tables were positioned around the perimeter, some dressed in purple tablecloths, others dressed in gold. On each tabletop sat a lit vanilla-scented candle, surrounded by purple and gold heart-shaped confetti. Everything was simple, but elegant.

The party had already begun, which was no surprise to Shaniece. She was sure her father had ordered the DJ to start the music exactly at seven P.M., even if he, his wife, and two youngest children had been the only ones present at that time. And if she knew Reverend Simmons as well as she knew she did, the party would end abruptly at eleven o'clock. So Shaniece decided she'd take advantage of the time and have as much fun as possible.

"Hey, girlie." Tatiana waved as Craig led Shaniece toward the table for six, where Tatiana, Justin, Krystal, and Tyrie were seated. "We saved you guys seats."

Shaniece smiled toward her friends as Craig assisted her into her chair. "Thank you," she said to him.

After Craig took his seat, Shaniece introduced him to those who didn't know him, and Krystal did the same with her date. A look at Tatiana's nearly empty dinner plate caused Shaniece to realize she hadn't eaten since picking over her breakfast that morning. She excused herself, and Craig followed. They moved down the buffet, and Shaniece tried to keep from piling her plate to its max. She laughed as Craig seemed to have no problems helping himself to the baked chicken, gravy and rice, corn on the cob, and warm rolls.

"What? No dessert to top it all off?" Shaniece teased with a laugh as she motioned toward the various cakes and cookies at the end of the table.

"Oh, don't worry," Craig told her with his most serious face, "I'll be back."

Shaniece laughed again as she followed him back to their table. Before they could reach their seats, though, they were stopped by Shaniece's mother. Shaniece rolled her eyes heavenward, knowing Natalie was not going to let them get away without first telling Craig how good he looked, and then introducing him to everyone at her table as Shaniece's *special friend.*

As Natalie gushed over Craig, Shaniece wondered why her mother was so bent on her and Craig becoming an item. Shaniece was sure that her mother was aware of her love for Devon, regardless of the tension between them, so she couldn't understand why her mother was pushing her daughter to move in a direction she didn't want to go. Shaniece wasn't sure if her mother completely disapproved of Devon because since learning of his incarceration, Natalie hadn't spoken to her about the young man, whom she'd given the "okay" to go out with Shaniece. So Shaniece wasn't sure if Natalie even cared that her daughter had been upset for the past two days.

"Okay, Mom," Shaniece said as she grabbed Craig's arm. "We're going to go sit down now."

Natalie shot her daughter a knowing look, but she smiled as she said, "That's fine, honey." Then she turned to Craig. "Save me a dance, Craig?"

Craig smiled and nodded. "Of course, Mrs. Simmons. I hope you all have a nice night," he said, addressing the group of adults at the table before walking off with Shaniece.

"I'm sorry, Craig," Shaniece remarked as they made their way back to their table. "My mom would've kept you tied up all night with questions and conversation."

Craig smiled. "It's a'ight. Your mom's cool," he said as they reached their table. He then leaned down and whispered, "But I'd much rather spend the evening with you."

Shaniece smiled as he ushered her to her seat before taking his own. She looked at Tatiana, who had probably been watching them as they conversed. Shaniece made a face at her friend, who laughed out loud, drawing everyone else's attention toward her.

"Inside joke," Tatiana said as she pointed between her and Shaniece, who only shook her head, with a soft smile on her lips.

"So why isn't anybody dancing?" Craig asked. "It's almost eight."

Their eyes turned toward the dance floor and Shaniece laughed. "There are people dancing," she stated.

"Yeah, old people," Tyrie blurted out, and looked at Krystal. "And all they playin' is this old-school music. Krys, you told me this was gon' be fun."

Krystal laughed. "It is fun . . . once you get into it."

Tatiana smacked her lips. "Or we can do like we did last year and sing Mr. Cedric into letting the DJ play a few contemporary songs," she said, looking at Shaniece.

Craig laughed. "Oh yeah. Y'all did do that last year. Y'all had Mr. Simmons in tears with . . ." He looked at Shaniece. "What song did y'all sing? Y'all took it way back too," he recalled, trying to remember the selection the girls had performed last year.

Tatiana answered, "It was BeBe and CeCe's 'Lost Without You,' and Mr. Cedric was tow up." She laughed. "So, Niecey, Krys, how are we going to make it happen this year?"

Shaniece rolled her eyes and turned her face away from her friends. "Shoot, y'all better get with the program and *whoop it up* with the mothers and the deacons."

Krystal pouted and looked at Shaniece with sad eyes. "C'mon, Niecey. I wanna have a good time, and though Teddy Pendergrass, Al Green, BeBe, CeCe, and Commissioned are cool, I wanna hear some Smokie Norful, Musiq Soulchild, Monica, Mary Mary, and Kirk Franklin."

It seemed as if all eyes had turned toward Shaniece and she folded her arms as she squirmed nervously in her seat. She loved singing and knew just the song that would break her father's ban against the more contemporary love songs, but singing it would probably bring tears to her own eyes. It was one of her parents' favorites, though, and Shaniece knew she had to sing it if she and her friends wanted to have any chance of partying to new-school artists.

"Fine," she replied, sighing. "Where's my dad?"

Krystal laughed and pointed toward the dance floor. "Over there, doing the two-step with your mom."

Shaniece turned toward the floor full of older adults and her jaw dropped at the sight of her parents dancing together. She noticed their wide smiles and was sure that they had no idea how embarrassed their oldest daughter was at that very moment.

Tatiana's loud cackle drew more attention. "Aww, get it, Reverend!" she yelled out, adding to Shaniece's embarrassment. "Come on, girl." She got up and pulled Shaniece out of her seat.

Krystal and Shaniece followed Tatiana as she danced her way toward Shaniece's parents. Shaniece turned toward the guys sitting at her table and caught them laughing—at the fact that she was so embarrassed, she was sure.

"Excuse me, Mr. Cedric and Ms. Natalie, we have a small request," Tatiana said, interrupting their dance. She turned to Shaniece. "Gon', Niecey, ask 'em."

Natalie stood with her left hand on her hip as she and Cedric waited for their daughter to respond. "What is it, girl? You messin' up our groove," Cedric said in all seriousness.

Shaniece shielded her eyes as she hung her head. "Lord, this is not happening." She softly laughed. "Daddy, we wanna hear some new stuff," she told him.

"Is that so?" he asked, with his arms folded over his protruding chest.

"Yes. Look"—she swept her arm out, drawing his attention toward the tables full of extremely bored teens—"no one's dancing because y'all are playing this old music."

"So we thought we'd sing one more song for the adults and then let the DJ switch it over for us, young'uns," Krystal piped in.

Natalie glanced up at her husband and poked him in his side. "Let 'em sing their song, Ceddy. This is an event for the kids, and I think we've had enough fun for one night."

Shaniece nudged Tatiana to keep her from laughing at the affectionate nickname Natalie often called her husband—usually in private. Tatiana coughed and struggled to keep a straight face.

"All right," Cedric replied after some thought, "but I wanna hear a good one."

"Thank you." Shaniece hugged each of her parents. "Trust me, you're gonna love it."

Chapter 25

"'One look in your eyes and there I see just what you mean to me. . . . Here in my heart I believe your love is all I'll ever need. . . .'"

As Shaniece sang the well-known Luther Vandross love song "Here And Now"—her parents' wedding song—Tatiana and Krystal backed her up. Shaniece struggled to keep her tears at bay. The song spoke of a love that was real and true . . . a love Shaniece wanted to share with Devon so badly that it gnawed on her nerves. She wanted to forget about him, but she couldn't control what she felt in her heart.

She just didn't understand how God would allow her to fall in love with someone she was apparently not meant to be with. And Craig, being so awkwardly placed into the picture, only caused the matter to become even more confusing. She wasn't sure if Craig was the man she was supposed to love, or if she was supposed to wait for Devon to regain his common sense and listen to his heart, leading him back into Shaniece's arms. Or was she even supposed to be thinking about indulging in a romantic relationship? And if her and Devon's romance was not meant to be, then why was he constantly tugging at her heart? What was it about him that continued to draw her interest, when it had been established long ago that he was not the one for her?

She watched her parents embrace each other in dance and longed for the love they shared. They had been together for nearly twenty years, and though they had their share of trouble, their love for each other continued to grow stronger, carrying them through each day.

Shaniece glanced at Craig, and his stare was so intense, it seemed as if his heart was speaking to hers. His eyes said that he loved her no matter where her heart resided, and she hated that she couldn't return his deep affection. No longer could she hold back her tears. As she brought the song to an emotional end, she wiped her hand across each of her cheeks and smiled out to the audience. She was so caught up in her emotions that she didn't even become disgusted when her parents shared a lingering kiss. The partyers cheered as they basked in their spiritual parents' love.

Shaniece wiped the remainder of her tears as she walked toward her parents and hugged each of them.

"Thank you for the song, baby," Cedric said, placing a kiss on the top of his daughter's head. "You really made our night." He hugged his wife's waist.

"You're welcome," Shaniece replied as she moved to hand him the microphone. "Now can you make mine?"

Cedric rolled his eyes and sighed as he accepted the device that would help turn the party around. "DJ, let's make this a party for the young people," he said, inciting cheers from all sides of the building as the DJ removed the old-school records and replaced them with the latest by Kirk Franklin.

Dozens of teens and young adults rushed the dance floor as the older generations moved to fill the now-empty seats around the tables. Shaniece smiled as Craig motioned for her to come and dance with him.

"Your voice is amazing," he said as she began to move to the beats of "Still In Love."

"It does have its advantages." She smiled.

They danced to several upbeat tunes before the DJ slowed the music down. Shaniece moved away from Craig and thought about taking a seat. She searched her friend's eyes and noticed that he was waiting for her permission to lead them in a slow dance.

"We could sit this one out, if you want," Craig offered with questioning eyes.

Shaniece shook her head. She'd promised herself that she would have fun tonight without allowing her hesitance concerning her being out with Craig to keep her from doing so. He loosely slipped his right arm around the small of her back and enclosed her right hand with his left. Shaniece felt a mixture of comfort and protection, just as she had the night of the shooting. She didn't know what it was then, and still didn't recognize the feeling now. But it was a sensation she could definitely get used to.

"How was your visit?" Craig suddenly asked as he released her hand and placed his other arm around her waist.

Shaniece followed his lead and placed both her hands behind his neck, but pulled back slightly so she could look into his face. "I got answers to my questions," she replied.

Craig studied her expression before asking, "Are you still unsettled?"

"Yeah." She didn't even try lying. "I just feel like there was a reason Devon was placed into my life. I thought it could have been to fill the void in my heart where I'd wanted a romantic love to reside. But apparently that's not the reason, and now I'm more confused, because I know that our purpose for being brought together hasn't been fulfilled."

Craig looked deeper into her eyes and said, "Just keep praying. God will reveal to you His purpose for your relationship with Devon."

Shaniece smiled, surprised at her friend's advice.

Craig shrugged in response. "Hey, just because I have feelings for you doesn't mean I can't be a good friend and offer sincere advice when you need it," he told her.

"Well, I appreciate it." Shaniece moved her arms from around his neck and grabbed his forearms. "Craig, I understand how you're feeling about me and all, but I'll admit that I'm not sure how I feel about you. I mean, as a friend, I love you and would do just about anything for you." She lowered her eyes. "Then I get close to you, like right now, and I feel this surge of protection, like I know you won't ever hurt me."

"You know I won't, Niecey," he said softly.

"Yeah, but I'm afraid I'll hurt you," Shaniece told him. "I don't like messing with people's feelings, and I think I may be doing that to you. And if I'm not doing it now, I may do it in the future. Never intentionally, though. But inside me, I have this longing for companionship, and with you around, ready and willing to offer me what I want, I'm afraid I'll use you for temporary satisfaction, knowing that my feelings for you don't come close to yours for me."

Craig took his forefinger and lifted Shaniece's head so that her eyes reached his. He gazed at her for what seemed like forever before silently pulling her into his chest and continuing their dance.

Shaniece was thankful that Craig hadn't responded. She knew he wasn't angry at her for being honest with him, but she wasn't sure if he was hurt by her words or not. His embrace told her that he was content with being her friend—at least for now. His strong arms promised always to protect her, no matter the status of their relationship. Shaniece relished the sincerity of the moment and prayed that she wouldn't ruin her relationship with Craig just because of her desire for romance.

"Excuse me, Niecey."

Shaniece heard her mother's voice behind her and she pulled away from Craig.

Natalie looked up at her daughter's date for the evening and smiled coyly. "I believe this handsome young man promised me a dance?"

Craig blushed and released his hold on Shaniece. "That I did, Mrs. Simmons. Shaniece, do you mind?" he asked.

"Be my guest." Shaniece moved out of the way so her mother could step in.

Before accepting Craig's outstretched hand, Natalie hugged her daughter close and whispered, "Your father would like to dance with you."

Shaniece looked past her mother's shoulder and spotted Cedric standing a few feet away, rocking back and forth on his heels and twiddling his thumbs. She laughed at his imitation of a young boy waiting for the girl of his dreams to accept his invitation to dance.

As Natalie and Craig began to dance, Shaniece walked over to her father. She smiled teasingly as she leaned into him. "Mom's looking mighty hot tonight, Daddy. Are you sure you want to dance with your daughter and allow her to sway in the arms of a younger man?" she asked.

Cedric laughed as he placed his left hand on Shaniece's back and held her hand with his right. "I'm pretty suave myself, so your mother better watch her back."

Shaniece chuckled and nodded. "Yeah, you both look good. This turned out really nice," she added as she looked around.

"It did, and you look absolutely beautiful," he complimented. "Craig's a lucky young man, and he knows it."

Her smile was faint and the words slipped from her mouth before she had a chance to stop them. "I wish Devon would've realized it."

"Niecey, baby—"

"I know, Daddy," Shaniece interrupted. "I need to move on and just leave Devon alone. But it's so hard when he has my heart. And it hurts even more that he so easily took his away from me, as if I was unworthy of possessing it. I'm trying to understand it all, but it's taking some time."

"And it should," Cedric said, pulling her into a hug as they continued swaying to the music. "But I wasn't going to tell you to get over this or move on."

"You weren't?" she questioned as she looked up at him.

He shook his head. "No, I was going to tell you that I was sure Devon had realized how blessed he was to have you, but he also realized that he is not the best man for you—at least not now. He needs to get himself together."

"But, Daddy, that's what I was trying to help him do. I was supposed to be his motivation to stay on the straight and narrow, but he cut me off so that he could waver and live however he wants."

"Baby girl, Devon needs to get himself together without your help. He is a distraction to you, and he has come to comprehend that. You all being together may have helped him, but it was only going to hurt you. You were so caught up that you weren't focused on yourself, but so bent on changing him. Devon has to *want* to change, and you were unknowingly forcing him by giving him an ultimatum. God gave us a choice to accept

His Son, and the decision is left up to each individual alone. Devon has to decide, on his own, to accept the Christian lifestyle." He moved so that he could catch her eyes. "Do you understand that?"

Shaniece nodded. "I just wish there were something I could do."

"Pray," Cedric said, as if the action could be that simple. "Pray that he sees the error of his ways before his time runs out. Sister Yvonne was just in counseling with me the other evening and I had to tell her the same thing. She's just as distraught as you, blaming herself for her son's ignorance. It's not your job to change people. It's your job to help push them in the right direction. If that person doesn't wish for your help, you can still do what God wants for you to do by praying for His child. God will take care of the rest."

Shaniece knew her father was right. . . . He always was. She needed to take his advice and just let Devon and their relationship go. She needed to give it all to God and let Him handle the situation as He so chose. If Devon was going to make a change in his life, he needed to be the one to initiate it. Shaniece needed to step back and let Devon breathe so that he could clear his mind, which would allow God to show Devon what His will for his life was. She'd still pray relentlessly for Devon's salvation, just as she'd promised, and hope that God would take heed to her requests for him to become her brother in Christ. No matter how she had to do it, Shaniece was determined to save Devon.

Chapter 26

Q was ready for a showdown. It had been nearly four months since Devon had gotten locked up, and Roc was steadily moving in on Devon's territory. Q gathered with several other workers and prepared to defend what was rightfully Devon's. They were the most loyal of the employees, and Q knew they could handle anything Roc tried to throw at them.

"Everybody packin'?" Mase, one of the older peddlers, asked as they all sat in the living room of his house.

Everyone answered accordingly, and Mase nodded in approval.

"A'ight," he said. "Everybody post up and make sho' you holdin' it down, should that fool roll up on you. To all the youngsters, this ain't no joke," he stressed. "The life of everybody in this room is at stake, but we doin' this fo' Big D. He done so much fo' us that we owe him this much. These are his blocks, and ain't nobody fixin' to come up in here and take it. We fightin' fo' what's ours . . . fo' what belong to Big D. Y'all got that?" His voice raised a bit as he glared at the younger guys, whose ages ranged from fourteen to seventeen.

The boys nodded, making sure they took heed to what their elder was saying. This was serious business, and Q, along with the other peddlers, was ready to defend Devon's name, even if it meant sacrificing his life.

***

Devon sat in the cafeteria eating lunch with Mitch and Raquel. When he'd first been incarcerated, it had taken Devon nearly three weeks to get used to the prison food without feeling the urge to regurgitate the meal. Immediately he'd thought of Trina's "home cooking" and how he'd complained that it was less than satisfying. He'd give anything to be able to sit in front of a plate of her baked chicken, string beans, and wild rice. The pastelike mashed potatoes and tough meat loaf made the meals, which Trina put her time and effort into, look like five-course dinners from a four-star gourmet restaurant.

"You all right, Big D?" Mitch asked as he watched Devon idly use his fork to stir the mashed potatoes around his plate.

Devon didn't bother to look up from his tray. "I'm straight," he answered dully.

His answer couldn't have been more of a lie if he'd stared his cellmate directly in the eyes and spoke the same words. He was completely out of his element. It had been nearly a month since he'd last spoken to Shaniece. Per his request, she hadn't tried to contact him in any way, form, or fashion. No letters, no impromptu visits, not even a "hello" sent by his mother, who continued to visit him at least once a week. *This is what you asked for, man,* he thought. But it wasn't what he really wanted. He sighed aloud as he pushed his tray away and sat back in his folding chair.

"D, what's up wit' you?" Raquel asked, almost annoyed.

"You need to talk or somethin' 'cause, if so, askin' is better than making me guess what the deal is," Mitch added.

Devon shook his head. "I told you I'm straight. Just a li'l tired."

Tired is right, he added in his mind. He was tired of thinking about Shaniece when she'd clearly forgotten about him. She was probably cuddled up with her *friend. Craig.* The way she'd said his name, when he'd questioned her about the male associate, who was nearly attached to her hip, made his heart ache and his eyes flash with anger. There hadn't been a hint of desire or such in her voice that would have made Devon think Shaniece thought of Craig as more than a friend. A smile hadn't even graced her lips as she spoke of him. Devon hadn't seen the same sparkle in her eyes, nor had he heard the affectionate tone she often used when his very name flowed from her lips. It hadn't been any of those things that caused Devon to become so irate when Shaniece had said Craig's name. It was the mere possibility that there was another guy ready and waiting to take Devon's spot if it even looked as if he was about to make a wrong move.

He wanted to call Shaniece and tell her that he'd changed his mind—that he didn't want to live without her and that she was more important than saving his reputation by making sure that his neighbors weren't affected by the one who called himself Roc. But he couldn't, because he knew that if he did, his conscience would receive no rest until he rectified the problem he'd created for his neighborhood when he decided to be so careless in handling his business. He thought about his line of reasoning and wondered how giving up his neighborhood for the sake of his relationship with Shaniece would be any different from him giving up Shaniece for the sake of his neighborhood. Either way, he received very little sleep at night.

Devon looked up at Mitch and Raquel, who were both still looking in his direction. "What?" he asked them in annoyance.

Mitch shook his head and looked away. Raquel continued staring at Devon as if searching his soul for something, but he also decided against responding. They definitely knew something was wrong, but Devon hadn't mentioned anything that would lead them to believe his unhappiness had anything to do with his situation surrounding Shaniece. Mitch had questioned Devon when he noticed that his cellmate had stopped raving about the girl he loved, but Devon simply shrugged off Mitch's concern. Devon knew Mitch wasn't dumb; his friend had to know that something was going on by the way Devon continuously re-read Shaniece's letters and gazed at her picture for hours at a time.

"Who was your visitor today?" Mitch asked Devon.

Devon sighed, but he kept his eyes lowered. "My moms came up here to see me before going to Bible Study," he told Mitch.

"When was the last time you saw your honey?" Mitch continued to question.

Devon looked up at him and squinted his eyes. "When's the last time you saw yours?"

Mitch chuckled and held up his hands in surrender. "A'ight, you got it."

"Man, I know you ain't all down and out over no female," Raquel stated, almost laughing at the thought.

Devon glared at his other acquaintance. "Don't start with me today, man. I ain't in the mood."

"Well, that's good to hear," a deep, gruff voice said from behind.

All three men turned toward the large male who'd interrupted their dinner. Devon recognized him as the man who'd approached him after recreation hour several weeks ago. The two guys, who'd been with him during their first encounter, were still standing behind him as if they had nothing better to do with their time.

"Man, what you want?" Devon asked the guy.

One of the man's sidekicks cackled and mockingly said, "Rip, I think *Big D* here is havin' a bad day."

"Yeah," sidekick two agreed. "You think it got something to do with his business?"

Devon's jaw clenched as he stood, with his fists tightened by his sides, in front of the guys. "Look, if y'all lookin' for trouble, you 'bout to get it."

Rip laughed. "Oh yeah, trouble is comin', but not for us." His eyes narrowed and his face became like stone. "You call your boys off Roc's territory, or this exchange of b'iness won't take place on friendly terms."

"I told you, my boys got the 'hood on lock. Ain't no way that punk 'bout to step in like he own it," Devon declared confidently.

Rip laughed again. "Like I said, call 'em off, or it ain't gonna be pretty."

"Yeah, and if Roc need us to take care of you in the process, it won't be a pro'lem," sidekick one said.

Mitch and Raquel stood at that statement and the two groups of men faced off.

"I wouldn't go around makin' threats if I was you," Mitch said in Devon's defense.

"Trust me, *shorty,*" Rip began menacingly, "we don't make idle threats."

Just then, three officers walked over and ordered the two groups to separate.

Before obeying, Rip looked back at Devon and said, "Call your men off, Big D. It'll be best for everyone involved."

The guys walked off as quickly as they'd come. Devon stood in place, fuming at the encounter that had just transpired. He couldn't believe this was happening. He hadn't had to worry about anyone challenging his reign over Riverside in the past, when he was out running the streets. But as soon as he was out of sight, and unable to fully defend what rightfully belonged to him, someone wanted to step in and test his limits. He'd make sure things remained in order, though. There was no way he'd allow Roc to take over.

"Big D, what was that all about?" Mitch questioned.

"Man, just some punk tryna take over my operation," Devon said, throwing his hand in the direction that Rip and his sidekicks had gone as if waving off their threats. "I ain't worried about it, though. I got my workers on top of everything."

"But what about you?" Raquel asked.

"What about me?" Devon asked incredulously.

Mitch glanced at Raquel knowingly. "You need protection, man."

"*Protection?* From what?"

"Not from what," Raquel replied. "But from Rip and his boys. You might've been the man wherever you came from, but up in here, you either stand up for yourself or you have someone do it for you."

"I ain't worried about him," Devon replied, sitting back down at the table.

Mitch and Raquel followed. "Look, you ain't got to be worried about him. But up in here, you gotta protect yourself, and it's easier when someone or a group of people have your back," Raquel explained.

"So what you saying? You want me to join a prison gang?" Devon asked.

Mitch pointed toward the mark below his left eye. "It wouldn't hurt."

Devon studied the delicately drawn cross under his friend's eye and then turned toward Raquel and noticed, for the first time, that he had the same tattoo in the same place. "What does that represent? Some cult?"

Mitch laughed. "No, it's just a group of guys who decided that as long as we're locked up in here, we gon' stick together and make sure all of our *brothers* are taken care of."

"I talked you up to Lee—he's over us—and he said he'd have the group look after you," Raquel informed them.

Devon contemplated the thought. It wouldn't be the first time someone had his back. And making sure he remained alive for the duration of his sentence wouldn't be as much of a chore if he had someone watching out for him. But something about joining a prison gang just didn't appeal to him. He'd been an individual for the majority of his life, and he wasn't about to change now. He'd taken care of himself for the last few months he'd been incarcerated, and he was almost certain he could continue to do the same for at least the next nine and a half years.

"Naw, man, I ain't tryna get caught up in the gang hype. I'll be cool takin' care of myself," Devon claimed.

"Suit yourself," Mitch said. "But make sure you watch out for Rip, 'cause it don't look like he playin' no games."

Chapter 27

God, I'm coming to you tonight just asking that you please keep your loving arms around Devon. He needs you whether he knows it or not. I know he's having a hard time in the situation he's in right now, but let something positive and fruitful come out of this negative experience for him. Allow him to see how merciful and loving you are for just giving him the opportunity to see another day. Lord, please don't let him get caught up in what's going on out in his community, but let him see that his soul is in more danger. Let him hear you calling for him and I pray that he finds comfort in your embrace.

Lord, I love him and I only want the best for him. It's hard not being able to see or talk to him, like I want to, but I'm dealing with it because I know it is for the best now. And I know you have something great in store for both of our lives. I love you and I praise your name. Amen.

Shaniece wiped her eyes as she raised herself from the altar and returned to her seat in the sanctuary. She'd been on her knees, praying for her family, her friends, the community, and Devon for the last half hour. Intercessory prayer always took place before the Wednesday night Bible Study at Creekside. In the past, Shaniece had found it hard to remain in prayer position for so long a time. But for the last few weeks, she'd taken her father's advice and she'd been praying every chance she got. Tonight, she noticed that she was one of the last congregants to return to their seats as the prayer time came to a close.

She settled in her seat between her mother and brother. Natalie gently squeezed her daughter's hand as Cedric took his place behind the podium in the pulpit. Shaniece smiled slightly as she picked up her Bible and placed it in her lap. As her father opened up the lesson with a quick prayer, Shaniece shot up one more request to her Heavenly Father in Devon's favor. *Keep him, Lord.*

She listened intently as her father spoke about how prayer can turn any situation around for the better. Shaniece was glad she'd brought her notebook tonight, because she was sure her father was going to say something she'd definitely need to remember.

"In First Samuel, Hannah longed for a son. She prayed day in and day out and even promised God that if He blessed her with a child, she'd give her child back to Him," Cedric said. "When King Herod placed Peter in prison, with the intent to persecute him, the church prayed earnestly for his release. And Anna, in Luke, showed great patience while praying to see the Messiah, until she was over eighty years old.

"The thing about praying is . . . you can be consistent in your praying, but you have to be patient, and you have to believe that God hears your prayers and is going to give you an answer, whether it's 'no,' 'yes,' or 'just wait.' Not only was Hannah consistent in her praying, but she was patient, and God not only blessed her with one child, but gave her five more children. Anna was certainly patient, waiting nearly all her life for her prayer to be answered. And the church . . . well, they were patient, but when God answered their prayer and brought a freed Peter right to their doorstep, they were doubtful. You have to have faith in God that He will exceed abundantly above all you can ask or think. Prayer and faith go hand in hand. Prayer without faith that God will answer you is like being a law student who expects to pass the bar exam without studying for it. It's not very effective."

Prayer and faith. Faith and prayer, Shaniece thought. *I have to have faith that God will take care of everything. The community . . . Devon . . . He has it all in His hands. I need to stop worrying.*

After the service came to a close, Shaniece walked out to her car. She'd decided to drive tonight, wanting to make it to the service on time for prayer, and with her brother and sister holding her parents up, the entire family would've been late. She spoke to a few people as she unlocked the door to her vehicle. As she was about to get in, she saw Tatiana standing by her car with her baby brother in her arms. Justin was standing next to her.

Shaniece quietly watched the couple; they had been dating since Valentine's night. Justin grabbed Samuel's chunky hand and shook it, while the two-year-old gave his sister's boyfriend a toothy grin. He helped Tatiana get Samuel situated in his car seat and then he stood with her next to the driver's-side door. Justin gazed deep into Tatiana's eyes and they exchanged a few words. Shaniece couldn't help but smile as her best friend's grin grew wider at whatever Justin was telling her. Then Shaniece's eyes began to mist as she watched Justin gently place his palm against Tatiana's left cheek before leaning in and placing a delicate kiss against her right. Shaniece held her breath, as if she was being kissed, and didn't release it until Justin pulled away from Tatiana. She watched as Justin helped Tatiana into her car, and then he waved as she drove out of the church's parking lot.

Justin spotted Shaniece as he was walking back toward the church. He gave her a smile, but it waned when he saw the salty liquid in her eyes.

"Shaniece, are you okay?" he asked, walking closer to where she stood.

Shaniece tried to smile as she nodded her head. "Yeah, I'm fine," she said, her voice slightly shaking. "You and Tati look really nice together."

Justin's smile grew wider, and Shaniece was sure he was blushing. "Thanks. Tatiana . . . she's really different from the other girls I've dealt with. She's real about her relationship with God, and I really like that."

Shaniece nodded again. "That's my best friend. You've made her really happy in the last few weeks. She can't stop talking about you."

"Well, she's made me happy too." He paused, and then a look of concern washed over his face. "Are you sure you're okay?"

Shaniece wanted to tell him that she was, but her eyes continued to water. She was sure that if she opened her mouth, she'd burst into more tears.

Justin cautiously moved toward her and awkwardly placed one arm around her shoulders, pulling her into his chest. "You know, whatever it is, you can take it to God in prayer, just like your dad was saying. And when you pray, make sure you pray without ceasing, and with the belief that God will answer your prayer." He pulled back and searched her face.

She gave him a smile. "Thanks. I really needed that." She wiped her eyes. "I need to head home before my parents come out here and think that I've just been hanging around the parking lot for the past ten minutes."

He laughed. "All right."

He held the door open for her while she climbed into her car. Before shutting the door, she looked up at him and said, "Justin, could we keep this little emotional breakdown between us? I don't want Tati worrying about me."

"No problem," he promised. "Drive safely," he said, closing her door. He waved as she drove off the lot.

Shaniece inhaled deeply. She couldn't believe she'd just broken down in tears in front of someone she hardly knew. But Justin had been there for her just like any of her closest friends would have, and she thanked God for his presence when she most desperately needed someone to provide her comfort.

She really needed to get herself together, though. She couldn't lose her cool every time she saw a couple enjoying the love they shared. She would need to gain a strong grip on her emotions, or else she'd be in tears every day of the week. Of course, she missed Devon, but she had to get over him or she'd never be able to move on with her life. That was a fact she'd known since Valentine's night. She desired a romantic love that would make her weak in her knees and cause her heart to skip, but Devon wasn't the man she'd share that love with. She had to come to terms with that before she lost sight of herself.

Knowing that she needed time to herself, and even more time to ponder her thoughts, Shaniece decided to take the long way home—through Devon's neighborhood and back around to her side of town. Shaniece's high school acted as the center point for the community, bringing together the low-income, high-crime zone, in which Devon had lived, with the middle-class, family-oriented area, where Shaniece resided.

She drove past the run-down buildings that were covered in graffiti and the unkempt lawns of the one-story homes. She drove slower than the speed limit of thirty-five miles per hour as she continued down the potholed street. She glanced around and noticed that several people were still hanging out on front porches and standing at the corner of intersections, despite the fact that it was nearly ten o'clock at night. She passed by the only corner store that seemed to be open at this time of night and was momentarily shocked when she saw her young acquaintance Q standing near the store's Dumpsters. She slowed down and hardly second-guessed pulling into the store's parking lot. She shook her head slightly when she noticed Q stiffen up when she stopped her car in front of him. She rolled down her window and gave him a warm smile.

"Shouldn't you be at home?" she asked him.

Q chuckled softly. "Don't you live on the other side of Riverside? What you doin' way over here?"

"Just came from church," she told him. She looked around and her smile dropped. "Q, let me take you home."

He shook his head. "Naw. I 'preciate it, but I'm workin'."

Her eyes showed her disappointment. "It's too late for you to be out here just standing around."

"I ain't standin' around," he insisted. "I told you I'm workin'." He looked around nervously. "Now, you need to get outta here, for real."

Shaniece glared at him intensely and then studied him from head to toe. She could see that he was nervous and was sure something horrible was about to happen tonight. "Look, Q, whatever it is you've gotten yourself into, you can get out of it. Please let me take you home."

"No!" he said forcefully. "Shaniece, I ain't playin' wit' you no more. I'm out here for a reason, and I ain't 'bout to punk out."

"What are you talking about?" Shaniece asked. "I'm trying to help you, Q. Please just come with me."

She could see his angry tears. "Shaniece, I'm serious. You gotta get out of here, *now!*"

"I'm not leaving unless you come with me," she told him in all seriousness as she climbed out of her car. "Do you think your mother would want you out here, putting yourself in danger just for a few bucks?"

His eyes narrowed. "My mama need for me to do whatever I gotta do so we can have some food on our table. My mama know what Big D's all about, so I ain't gotta hide nothin' from her. You live on the other side, so you don't know what it's like to go without. You got a nice house, with nice furniture and nice clothes. You got parents who can provide for you."

As she looked into the eyes of the less fortunate child, Shaniece was starting to feel bad about the things with which she'd been blessed. "I just wanna help you, Q. I don't want you to end up like Devon. You can have a better life, if you just try."

"Shaniece, you can't save somebody if they don't wanna be saved," Q said.

Tears filled her eyes at the tone of his voice. He sounded just like Devon, who'd been trying to tell her the same thing when they'd broken up. Maybe she should listen to the young boy, knowing he had way more street smarts than she ever would. But it was something about him . . . something about Devon . . . something about this entire community that made her want to step in and rectify all of their problems. She'd never felt this way before meeting Devon, but after he'd entered her life, everything changed. She felt the urge to help all of those in need . . . even if they didn't realize that they were in need.

"I just feel like I'm supposed to help," she said softly. "Like God put me here to help you all." She looked around.

Q sighed. "God ain't never sent nobody over here to help before, so why now?"

She shrugged. "Time could be running out for you. I don't know." She tilted her head and gazed at him somberly. "You should give Him a chance, like He's trying to give you."

Q turned away from her, and she could tell that he was trying to keep his emotions at bay. He looked back at her and shook his head. "I pray every night that I stay alive out here . . . and I been stayin' alive. That's good enough for me."

"But you need to let Jesus into your heart so that you can get away from this life altogether. So you don't have to pray that you stay alive out here. So you don't have to worry about anything anymore. So you can just give everything to Him, and let Him handle it all."

Q's tears showed Shaniece that her words were sinking in, but he remained stiff in his stance. Before he could respond, gunshots rang out in the distance. Q jumped and wiped his eyes before grabbing his gun from his pants. Shaniece's eyes opened wide and tears began to stream down her brown cheeks.

"Q," she said calmly, "please don't do this."

"Go home, Shaniece!" he yelled as his eyes searched the streets. "They're coming, and you don't need to be here when they get here."

"But, Q—"

"Big D would kill me if he knew you were out here when these fools came by," he stressed. "*Please* go home."

Shaniece hesitated before quietly getting back into her car and shutting the door. She took one more look at Q, who was still standing stiffly with his gun in hand. He nodded for her to leave, and she sent up a prayer for his soul before she regrettably drove off. She was barely down the next street before she heard more gunshots. They continued like the sound of fireworks being shot off as she resisted the urge to go back to the corner store.

Tears clouded her vision as she drove toward her home. Praying the entire way, she felt a sinking feeling in her heart, and she knew that Q had just been given his last chance. She could only hope that he'd taken it, even if he'd had to submit his soul with his very last breath.

Chapter 28

"This morning, we would like to take a moment of silence in memory of Quincy Bollard, who was a freshman here at Riverside," Principal Hutchinson's voice announced over the school's intercom system. "Quincy was shot and killed last night in front of One Stop Corner Store. He was only fourteen years old." The principal released a heavy sigh. "So let's please have a few moments of silence. . . ."

Shaniece lowered her head and tried hard to keep her tears from spilling into a pool on her desk. She'd cried all night long after returning home. Her parents had made it home before she had, but before they could yell at her for not being at home when they'd gotten there, Shaniece had fallen into her father's arms in tears. It had taken her forever to explain her tears, due to the fact that she couldn't stop crying.

"He's gone, I just know it," Shaniece had continued to say over and over as she nearly choked on her tears. "I tried to help, but I was too late."

Shaniece knew her parents had thought she was delirious when they made her retire in her room so that she could get some rest. But no matter how many hymnals her mother sang or prayers her father recited, she just couldn't sleep. It wasn't until this morning, when the overnight news story headlined, that her parents finally understood why their daughter had continued to cry through the night.

Three people had been shot and killed last night, Q being amongst the bodies found throughout the neighborhood. The shooting had been drug related, of course, and reporters said the police had no leads. They'd highlighted Q's story, along with another young dealer named Antwon, whom Shaniece had never met before. It had been horrifying to watch Q's mother fall into a friend's arms in tears while the reporters tried to get a statement from her.

A few young people came forward and tried to share a few words about Q. A couple of girls couldn't get out one word as they held on to each other for consolation. But a few guys were able to keep back their tears as they talked about their young friend. Shaniece knew that the guys were way too old to be hanging out with a fourteen-year-old and figured that they were a part of Devon's operation. She could tell they were angry about both Q and Antwon's deaths, and she could see the look of revenge in their eyes. She definitely knew that this war between Devon's crew and whoever it was that was moving in on his territory was far from over.

As the moment of silence came to an end, Shaniece kept her head lowered, not wanting her classmates to see the tears in her weary eyes. Her parents had suggested that she stay home today, saying that she hadn't received any sleep and was too emotional to be able to focus on her schoolwork. But Shaniece had refused, knowing that if she stayed home, she'd have time to dwell on her friend's death. Now as she listened to her principal make an announcement about the counselors being available to students who might need to talk about their feelings, Shaniece knew that the topic of every other conversation today would be Q's death.

By the time her lunch period had rolled around, Shaniece had had to make a trip to the bathroom three times in order to shed her tears in private. She wasn't functioning properly and she knew that she needed to go home and get some rest. She moved through the lunch line and sighed when she heard two students talking about Q.

"Man, I just never thought it would happen like this," she heard a young boy say. "Q was my boy, and I just can't believe he's gone."

The girl seemed to be slightly upset as she replied, "Q tried to get with me. I wish I woulda gave him a chance. I just feel so bad—"

Shaniece glanced back at the couple and shook her head before exiting the line without purchasing a lunch. She was tired of hearing about Q, and listening to some girl who was sincere in her remarks, but ignorant of what was most important—where Q's soul would spend eternity—was causing Shaniece to become sick to her stomach. She'd completely lost her appetite. She plopped down into a seat at her usual lunch table and buried her head in her hands. Not even a full minute later, she felt the presence of her two closest friends on either side of her.

"You okay?" she heard Tatiana ask.

Shaniece inhaled deeply and tried to hold back her tears. "No, not really," she said honestly, but her hands were muffling her voice.

Craig placed his arm around her shoulders. "C'mon, let's go to the courtyard."

They helped Shaniece stand, and all three of them made their way out toward the grounds designated for seniors to enjoy their lunch if they chose not to eat in the cafeteria. The area was spacious, and as the weather began to change, the grass was returning to its rich green coloring, and soon the trees and flowers would be in full bloom. The sun was shining and the weather was mild, so the trio didn't hesitate to find a seat at one of the wooden tables. They were all quiet for a few moments as the sounds of birds chirping carried on the light breeze.

Shaniece finally broke the silence. "I was with him last night . . . right before the shooting," she told them. "I was trying to get him to let me take him home. He was just standing on the corner, waiting for somebody to come by asking for some dope." Tears welled in her eyes. "I begged him to come with me, because I knew something was gonna happen, but all he seemed worried about was getting me out of the area. He knew those guys were coming by, and he still wouldn't leave." She began sobbing. "I tried—I tried so hard, and I thought I was getting through to him. I was trying to introduce him to Christ, and I was so close. I thought he was going to come with me. I thought he was going to let me help him, but then we heard gunshots. It was like he didn't even think twice when he pulled a gun from his pants. He was so ready to defend Devon's grounds. I was begging for him to come, but he was so set on getting me out of there. So I left, and not long after, I heard more shots. I knew he was gone. I just . . . I knew he didn't . . . make . . . it," she said between deep intakes of breaths. "I should've . . . made him . . . come. God, I shouldn't have left him!"

Tatiana held her as Shaniece cried and she spoke a soft prayer in her friend's ear. After her prayer, she said, "Niecey, you've got to let this go. You've done your job, now let God do His. You can't beat yourself up about this."

"I'm not," she said, knowing she was lying. "I just wish I could've done something to help."

Craig's mellow voice calmed her. "Shaniece, you could've done everything in your power to try and help Q, but it wouldn't have changed things if he didn't want your help."

"I can't save someone who doesn't want to be saved," Shaniece whispered against Tatiana's shoulder. "That's what he told me."

Tatiana pulled back. "He's right," she replied. "You'll tire yourself out if you keep wasting your energy on people who aren't appreciative of your efforts."

Shaniece wiped her eyes. "I know. I should've learned that with Devon."

"Does he know?" Craig asked. "About Q, I mean?"

Shaniece shrugged. "I don't know. I'm sure one of his workers would've told him by now. Plus, that place is hooked up with cable, so he's probably seen it on the news or something." She sighed. "I haven't spoken with him since Valentine's Day."

"I know this is going to be painful news for him. Are you going to go see him?" Tatiana asked. "You know, just to make sure he's okay?"

Shaniece looked up at her and shook her head. "No, no. I'm not going up there to see him. Doing that would just make me emotional and place unnecessary stress on me. He asked me to stop all contact with him, anyway, so it would be a waste of my time." She shook her head again. "No, I'll just keep doing what I've been doing for the past month—stay on my knees, praying for him and everybody else involved in this mess."

"Are you going to be okay? Or do you need to go home?" Craig asked.

She sighed as she pulled at her ponytail, which she'd barely had enough strength to put her hair into this morning. "I don't know. I didn't get much sleep last night and I'm really tired. I might check myself out early." She nodded solemnly. "Yeah, most likely."

"That's probably best," Craig agreed.

"I'll take notes for you in class," Tatiana offered.

Shaniece smiled as she stood. "Thanks. I'm gonna go ahead and leave now," she told them.

Since that Shaniece was eighteen, she was legally permitted to check herself out of school. By the time she reached home, she'd called both her parents at work to let them know that she'd left school early. Both agreed that she needed to rest and should try to catch up on lost sleep. She immediately changed out of her jeans and fitted T-shirt into an oversize nightshirt before climbing into her bed. Inhaling deeply, she wondered what was happening to Q's spirit. She pictured him standing before God, and God revealing to the young boy all he'd done during his lifetime, whether good or bad. Was Q nervous or was he confident that he was going to spend eternity with Jesus? In his last few moments of life, could he have completely submitted himself to the Holy One? And if he hadn't, what was going through his mind as his body lay motionless in the middle of the dark, lonely street? Had his short-lived life flashed before his eyes? Did he think about how his family and friends would feel without him in their lives? Did he regret not leaving with Shaniece when he had the chance? Did he still think highly of Devon and the life that his mentor had introduced him to?

Shaniece was sure that Q realized, now, that the life he'd led had not been all it was cracked up to be. She wanted to believe that his death would be a wake-up call for all those involved, including Devon, but Shaniece was no fool. This horrible happening was most likely just the beginning of an even greater disaster.

Chapter 29

Devon walked into the visitors' room and awkwardly smiled at his mother. Taking a seat at the table, he took her outstretched hands.

"How are you doing?" Yvonne asked him, searching his face for the truth.

He shrugged. Finding out that Q had been murdered last week was like finding out that his very own brother was gone, never to return. Q had been like a younger sibling to Devon, and knowing that both him and Antwon were dead cut his spirit deep. He still hadn't cried, knowing that would only bring satisfaction to his opponents. So having to suppress his tears had caused his animosity to spiral almost out of his control, and he was fully ready for battle. He was prepared to avenge his young mentees, regardless of the consequences.

"I'm holdin' up," he replied.

"I hate you have to spend your birthday in this place," Yvonne stated.

Devon shook his head somberly. He'd hardly acknowledged the fact that he'd turned twenty today. "Nothing to really celebrate anyway."

Yvonne handed him an envelope. "Well I got you a card and I put some money on your book."

"I 'preciate it," he said, taking the card. "How was the funeral?"

Devon hated that he'd missed both Antwon and Q's funerals, but because neither was in his immediate family, he was not allowed to attend. In his place, he'd requested that his mother attend the home going services. Antwon's funeral had been a couple of days after the shooting and had been a small gathering of family and "coworkers" at a local funeral home. Q's service had been a larger gathering at Creekside Church, held on the Tuesday after the shooting had occurred.

"Antwon's was nice and intimate," Yvonne told him. "There was a short eulogy and a simple viewing of the body. But Q's service was much larger and longer. Our choir sang a couple of songs as the family came in." She paused. "Did you know he had family besides his mother?"

Devon shook his head. "When I met him, he was trying to steal money from one of my boys, so I figured if he had to steal money just to keep his lights on, he must not have any other family to help him and his mother out." He shrugged. "But you know how that goes. When a family member dies, people come from all over, even if they haven't spoken to the person in years."

Yvonne nodded in agreement. "But he has a lot of family—grandparents, aunts, uncles, cousins, and all. Anyway, Reverend Simmons did the eulogy and . . . Shaniece sang a solo."

Devon stared into his mother's eyes. "How is she?"

His mother inhaled deeply and released a heavy sigh. "Not well at all. She cried through the whole thing. She took Q's death hard. Before she began her song, she told the congregation that she'd been with Q before the shooting."

"What?" Devon gasped. "She was out there?"

"Yep, she was with him. She said she was trying to get him to come with her. . . . She was trying to save him, basically, but he was determined to stay out on the streets."

"Was she upset with the reason why he was out there?" he asked nervously. He couldn't stand the thought of Shaniece holding Q's death against him, just because Q had been doing the job Devon had assigned him.

Yvonne shrugged. "I don't think so. She just said that she continues to cry and pray for all of those involved in the ongoing conflict." She lowered her eyes. "Devon, you need to stop this before more people are killed."

Devon shook his head immediately. "No, doing that will only make things worse. First off, it would make it seem like Q and Antwon's deaths were in vain. They were fighting to keep our neighborhood in order, and if we stop now, those guys are gonna take over and everybody else will be at risk. It's not just about my business," he said in a lowered voice. "It's about making sure the whole community is safe from any harm and danger that would come if Roc and his crew took over."

She squeezed his hands and gazed into his eyes so that her son would see how serious she was being when she said, "That community is in danger now. There have been shootings every night since Q and Antwon died. No one else has been killed, but I heard on the news this morning that three more guys have been injured."

Devon sighed. "I understand what you're saying, Mama, but these guys know what they're fighting for. I'm not making them do anything; they're just making sure that the community is safe."

"Baby, the community will never be safe as long as drugs are constantly distributed throughout the blocks, and it pains me even more to know that you're behind it." Tears threatened her brown eyes, but she willed them not to fall. "You've got to stop this before it really gets out of hand."

"I'm sorry, Ma," he said.

Yvonne sighed and released the grip she had on his hands.

"It's not that I don't want to," Devon quickly explained. "It's just that I can't. What's done is done, and just telling my guys to step off isn't going to work. It's out of my hands now."

Silence rested between them, and Devon knew his mother was disappointed in him. He wanted to say something that would allow hope to spring back into her eyes. Anything that would make her believe there was a chance for this war to be over, but he didn't want to give her false hope. Besides, he wasn't so sure that if there was something he could do to stop what was going on, he'd actually step in and do it. He wanted his people to be protected, and he knew for a fact that if he didn't fight back, his community would be destroyed.

"Have you at least been praying?" Yvonne finally asked.

Devon laughed as he brushed his hand over his face. "You know that's something I've never been good at."

"Well, we need all the prayers we can get, so you better prepare those knees of yours for the task," she told him. "And have you given anymore thought to letting the prison ministry come out to visit you?

He pursed his lips and shrugged. "I don't know 'bout all that, but I'm hoping this ends without anyone else on my end getting hurt," he changed the subject.

"I want this to end without anyone else, period, getting hurt, including you."

"What's that supposed to mean?" Devon asked defensively, knowing that his mother couldn't possibly have a clue as to what was going on between him and Roc's accomplices inside the prison.

"I don't know. I really don't know, but I feel like just because you aren't out there doesn't mean you aren't in as much danger as everyone else. I've been praying for you, as has Shaniece and her family. I want you to know that you have a choice."

"A choice?"

"Yes, Devon. You have a choice of how you wish to live out the rest of your life. You can continue relying on your boys out in the streets," she said, pointing toward the exit behind her, "and hope that they truly will have your back when it comes down to the wire. Or you can give your life, including all of the baggage and issues that come along with it . . . you can give it all to God."

Shaniece rested on the front steps of her porch as the cool March breeze encircled her. She pulled a couple of leaves off one of the bushes that embellished the front yard. She was waiting for several of her friends to come by her house for a small get-together. Bowls of chips and several jars of dip were awaiting them in the kitchen. The pizza and hot wings would be arriving any minute. Tatiana had been by earlier to help make the spacious den area cozy enough for everyone to be able to relax and enjoy the evening. She was now waiting for her best friend to return from picking up Justin and the movies they'd all be able to enjoy for the evening. Craig had called and said that he was only minutes away from arriving, and Krystal would be coming a little late.

Shaniece sighed, knowing she really wasn't feeling up to having these people at her house tonight, but her parents were so sure that this was what she needed in order to come out of her pity party. She knew that she'd been blaming herself for Q's death, which had occurred almost two weeks ago, but didn't she deserve to wallow in her sorrow? She'd known what Q was into before that night, and she should've tried to reach out to him before it was too late. Why had she waited until that fateful night to say something to him, when she'd been given multiple opportunities before? She didn't know, and she was continuously beating herself up for it.

She looked up as the Pizza Hut delivery car and Craig pulled up to her house at the same time. She stood and waited for the delivery guy to approach her. Craig stepped out of his car first and walked toward the house.

"Looks like I'm right on time, huh?" he laughed.

She gave him a faint smile in return. "Hey, can you help me with these?" she asked, pointing toward the six boxes of pizza and two orders of wings the delivery guy was holding in his hands.

"Sure," Craig said.

After Craig and the delivery guy had brought the pizzas and wings into the house, Shaniece paid and tipped the employee; then she headed inside to find Craig snooping through the food.

"Can you wait until everyone else gets here?" She laughed.

"I was just making sure you had the Supreme for me," he said, closing the lid to one of the pizza boxes.

"Yep, I got everybody's favorite, plus one extra plain old cheese pizza."

Craig grabbed a handful of Doritos from one of the bowls on the table. "So what are we doing tonight?" His eyes questioned her.

Shaniece moved around the kitchen, shifting random items into their place. "Music, movies, a little conversation. I really don't care, as long as you guys have fun."

"You should try having a little fun yourself," he said to her.

Shaniece turned away from him as she leaned against the counter. She stared out the bay windows and watched as the wind blew, causing the trees' limbs and leaves to sway in the breeze.

"Niecey, I'm serious." Craig spoke to her as he walked toward her. "You need to loosen up and allow yourself to live."

"I'm breathing, right?" Shaniece retorted sarcastically, rolling her eyes.

He smirked. "You know what I mean. Stop worrying about everybody else's problems. Stop stressin' over stuff you have no control over." He stood in front of her, blocking her view of the outside world.

Shaniece forced herself to keep her eyes lowered toward the white-tiled floor. Looking up at him would only cause her to burst into tears, something she didn't want to do, especially since her friends could possibly walk in on her having another emotional breakdown. Besides, she'd cried enough in the last two weeks. It was time to pull herself together and get over it.

"I know" was all she could muster past the lump in her throat. Anything more would have been accompanied by tears.

Craig opened his arms for an embrace, and Shaniece didn't hesitate in accepting it. She'd needed a good hug since that night, and tonight she was able to relish in the feeling of someone helping her support the weight of all her problems. She inhaled deeply and waited a beat before releasing her breath.

"Thank you," she said softly as he released her.

He shrugged. "You're welcome. Now, where's Tati, Justin, and Krystal? I'm ready to eat."

She laughed. "Krystal is gonna be late, because she's working, but Tati and Justin should be here soon."

They both moved into the den and Shaniece handed Craig the remote. He settled for watching ESPN as they waited for Tatiana to arrive. Moments later, the doorbell rang and Shaniece moved to answer it.

"Hey, girl!" Tatiana nearly shouted as she walked through the front door. She held two bags of DVDs in her hands and set them on the coffee table.

Shaniece shook her head as she looked toward Justin. "I'm sure you're used to that by now."

He laughed as he lugged in two 2-liter sodas. "Hey, Shaniece. How's it goin'?"

"Good. You can put those on the kitchen table," she told him. "Thank you."

"Hey, Tati, what movies you got?" Craig asked.

"The ones I bought," she playfully retorted in response as Justin returned from the kitchen.

Justin took a seat next to Craig. "Man, how do you deal with her?" Craig asked him.

Justin was about to respond, when Tatiana stood to her full height and placed her hands firmly on her hips. He laughed as he watched her eyebrow twitch and the warning in her eyes increased. He turned and looked toward Craig. "Only with God," he muttered, keeping his smile in place.

"*Anyway,*" Tatiana said, rolling her eyes. "Niecey, where's the rest of your family?"

"Mom's helping Dad at the church for tomorrow's service," Shaniece explained as she rested on the love seat. "And Rain and Keith are out playing ball with some friends. They all thought I could use this time to chill with you guys."

"That's for sure," Tatiana said as she looked through the family's CD collection. "So which should come first, movies or music?"

Craig rolled his eyes. "Man, I don't care as long as we can eat."

Shaniece chuckled as Tatiana moved away from the CDs and began to peruse the bag of DVDs. Shaniece looked around and knew that she'd be able to relieve her mind of any troubling thoughts while she shared a fun-filled evening with her closest friends.

Chapter 30

As Devon was pointed toward his visitor for the afternoon, he quickly did a double take, knowing that the person waiting to see him was truly not who he thought it was. He moved slowly, locking his eyes with hers, allowing her to see the shock he felt from seeing her. By the time he sat down, he came to the realization that he wasn't losing his mind.

He narrowed his eyes and glared at her. "Wassup?"

Trina barely smiled when she replied, "You apparently. Your name's all up and down the streets."

Devon smirked. "I know. I got it handled, though."

"Do you?" she asked, almost worriedly.

"Why do you care?" he asked. "You ain't even out there no more. I know you chillin' with one of your girls out in the burbs."

"That don't mean I can't care, D," Trina stressed. "That's my home, and everybody I know is in trouble."

"Look, if this is what you came up here to talk to me about, then please don't waste your time," Devon told her. "I said I got it covered, and that's all you need to know, or you'll probably be the next one buried."

He could see the sadness in her eyes and it troubled him because he knew that she was genuinely concerned. But he couldn't let anyone else become a victim due to his role in the situation.

"Well, you look good," she told him. "How are they treatin' you up in here?"

He shrugged. "As good as could be expected. What about you? How you been?"

She lowered her eyes and spoke softly. "I miss you, D."

He choked back his laughter. "Really? *You* miss *me?* That's why for the last five months I haven't heard from you. Not that I was expecting to ever see you again, but for you to just be sittin' around, feeling this way and never sayin' nothin' to me about it, is unbelievable."

Shaking her head, Trina replied, "I tried not to think about you, but it was hard. I never thought I would miss you so much, but I do, and I hate it because I know you've hardly thought about me while you've been in here. I figured you and that girl would've hooked up."

Devon turned away from her questioning gaze and thought before saying, "We did . . . for a while. But we were just too different."

She nodded as if she understood. "You still love her, though."

His gaze shot toward her. "Why would you say that? I mean, like you really know what I'm feelin'."

She chuckled softly. "D, you can't even talk about the girl without looking like you 'bout to have an emotional breakdown. Trust me, I know how that feels."

"Look, Trina, I'm sorry for the way things ended between us. I was insensitive and selfish, but I just couldn't help the way I was feeling."

"It's cool," Trina told him. "Although I still have feelings for you, I actually appreciate you leaving me that night. It was something that needed to be done long before it happened. We were just . . . *too different."* She paused a moment and then inhaled before saying, "I apologize for telling your friend all your business the night you were arrested."

"Shaniece," he corrected. "Yeah, she told me that she found out from you, but you know what? . . . It's cool."

Trina was surprised. "*Yeah, right.* I know you were ticked when you found out I'd told her."

"Yeah, I was, at first. But I stopped trippin' over it 'cause even though Shaniece knew what I was all about, she accepted me. Well, she accepted me with the promise that I would change."

"You told her you'd change for her?" she asked, even more shocked than before.

Devon laughed at the thought. "Yeah, I did. I promised that I would at least try, and I did for a minute, but then some fools who roll wit' Roc came up to me talkin' junk. Then Q told me about some dude who Niecey had up in her face at school. . . . It was just too much for me and I pulled out . . . kinda like I did you."

"At least you didn't hurt her."

"Well, I don't too much know about that either. She was pretty upset when I broke it off with her, but I knew I was doing what was best . . . for both of us."

They were silent for a moment and Devon watched as Trina studied him. He could tell she was reminiscing and he couldn't help but smile. He hadn't been in the presence of a woman, besides his mother, since Valentine's night, and even then it hadn't been a pleasurable visit. He was locked up all day with a guy who seemed to have a problem with his bowels, always having to use the toilet, which caused the entire room to smell like a sewer. Then he spent any free time outside of his cell with guys who continuously scratched themselves and reeked like a hamper full of two-month-old dirty laundry. It had been a while since his nostrils were pleasured by the scent of exotic fragrances.

Slowly he extended his hands across the table. Trina looked at him apprehensively and he nodded to reassure her. She slipped her hands over his and breathed deeply as he tightened his grip. He relished the feeling of her soft skin against his as he intertwined their fingers together. She smiled as he closed his eyes and slowly brought her right hand to his face and rubbed it across his cheek and lips. In the darkness behind his eyelids, he saw himself holding Shaniece and enjoying the feel of her touch. The last time he'd enjoyed her touch was when she'd first visited him. His desire for a closer connection heightened, and his emotions began to overshadow the physical gratification he was receiving from Trina's touch.

"Mmm, I love you, Shaniece," he whispered as he placed a gentle kiss against the back of Trina's hand.

Immediately Trina snatched her hands out of his grasp, bringing Devon back to reality. "Boy, you better get right."

Devon's eyes showed his regret as he apologized. "Dang, Trina. My bad. I'm sorry. I—I don't know what I was thinking."

"Well, I do, and you need to get yourself together," she told him fiercely.

He could tell that she was upset, but he was surprised that she hadn't left him sitting at the table by himself. "I know. I haven't even seen Shaniece since Valentine's Day, when we broke it off with each other. I miss her so much."

"Why don't you just call her?" Trina asked, making it sound like it was an easy thing.

Devon shook his head. "I can't. I told her not to contact me in any way, and I feel like I need to do the same."

"So you're just gonna sit around and be miserable?"

He was surprised with Trina's interest in his relationship with another woman. He had never thought he'd see the day when his ex-girlfriend actually cared about him being happy, but here she was, sitting in front of him, trying to get him out of his funk.

"I know what you're thinking," Trina said. "Why am I concerned about your love life? And I don't really know myself, but I've learned that sitting around, moping about something, isn't going to do you any good. I should've visited you months ago, but I was too scared of being rejected. Plus, I was still upset with you for the way you treated me throughout our relationship. So I allowed myself to be unsettled, because I was too afraid to contact you." She shook her head. "If this girl is really that special, you gotta do something about it."

Devon thought about her words and knew that they made a lot of sense, but he knew that things were better now for both him and Shaniece than they ever would be if the two were together. "She is that special, and that's why I'm keeping my distance."

They were silent once again; then Trina began preparing to leave. "Well, it was nice being able to see you again, D," she said. "But I need to be going. I have to head to work before I'm late."

He smiled. "Oh, you got a job?"

She nodded. "Yeah, I finally decided to put my degree to good use."

"Congratulations. I'm happy for you." He laughed. "Trina—makin' her own paper. Who would've thought?"

She laughed with him. "Don't try me. But seriously," she said as she stood to her feet, "keep your head up. I know that all this stuff goin' on out in the 'hood is affecting you, so I'll be praying for you and everybody else."

Devon raised his eyebrows in surprise. *"You? Praying?"*

She chuckled softly. "Yeah, it's a new thing I've been trying. It works pretty well. Maybe you should give it a shot."

He shrugged and replied, "Thanks for comin' to see me, Trina."

"You're welcome." She smiled and blew a kiss in his direction before adding, "Take care of yourself, D."

He nodded as she walked away and out the doors. As he was led back to his cell, he reflected on her last words. "*. . . I'll be praying for you and everybody else.*" He shook his head, wondering if this whole prayer idea was really all it was chalked up to be.

Chapter 31

Mitch watched as Devon ran back and forth against the length of their cell. He tried to keep from laughing, but he could tell that his cellmate was going through a serious sexual withdrawal. He was surprised that it had taken Devon so long to become victim to what the inmates called NASH, or Needing a Sexual Healing, Syndrome. Mitch had gone through it himself almost a month after he'd been incarcerated. But after becoming aware of his situation and settling for using alternative techniques, he had grown accustomed to living with the self-diagnosed disorder.

When Devon had finished running nearly a mile in the small room, he dropped onto his hands and proceeded to do several sets of push-ups.

"Well, at least you'll be able to take on Rip and his boys," Mitch said, taking notice of the muscle weight Devon had gained in the last several months.

"Man, shut up!" Devon retorted, pushing himself up and down in a rapid motion. He hadn't even bothered to keep count of how many repetitions he'd completed. "I can't believe I let myself get caught up with her like that."

"Why can't you?" Mitch asked. "You been up in here since November, and I know you ain't been hookin' up with nobody in here. . . ."

Devon stopped in the middle of a push-up and looked up at Mitch with annoyance masking his countenance.

"Let me let you know right now," Devon stated evenly, "I'm not like that. Never have been, never will be. I don't care if I don't get none for the next ten years that I'm in here—I refuse to be that desperate for intimacy."

Mitch laughed hysterically. "My bad, man. I'm just sayin' it's normal for you to feel how you're feelin' right now. You ain't seen your girl in almost a month and the only woman who been up here to see you in the last four weeks is your mama. So when your ex-girl come up here, you bound to feel somethin'." He shook his head. "The problem comes in when your new girl finds out. She don't look like no 'hood chick, but she don't seem like she one to play wit' either."

"Trust me, she ain't," Devon mumbled as he continued exercising with more vigor.

"So why you tryin' her?" Mitch questioned.

Devon jumped up and looked squarely at his friend. "Look, this ain't really none of your business, so why don't you just drop it 'fore you get handled."

"I know you didn't just threaten me," Mitch retorted. He liked Devon and all, but he wasn't up for being bullied. He was used to defending himself and didn't mind showing Devon that he wasn't in the least bit intimidated by his massive size. He glared at his cellmate and his attitude calmed when he saw the anger on Devon's face, but the remorse in his eyes. "Man, what's your problem?" Mitch asked, knowing Devon's emotional outburst had nothing to do with their conversation.

Devon sighed. "Me and Shaniece not together no more," he confessed.

Mitch was shocked. "What? When did this happen?"

"Valentine's," Devon answered. "I wasn't gonna tell you, but every time you say somethin' to me, you mention her and I be 'bout to choke you to death. I figured that I couldn't do that, since you really didn't know what was goin' on. But now you know, so don't mention Shaniece no more, 'cause I don't wanna hear about her."

"Dang, D. I mean, what happened? You seemed happy with her?"

"I was," Devon replied. "But sometimes you gotta put someone else's happiness over your own."

"So she wasn't happy with you?"

Devon squinted. "No, actually she was."

"Then what you said didn't even make sense," Mitch told him with a smirk.

"Yeah, but it sounded good." Devon laughed. "Anyway, I knew her being with me wasn't best for her. So I guess I should say that she was good for me, but I wasn't all that good for her. She wanted me to change, but I can't have my 'hood screwed up like it is and pretend like I had nothin' to do with it. So I cut it off with her."

"And now what? You tryna rebound with your old chick?"

Devon shook his head. "No, no! It ain't like that, man. When I was tryna feel Trina, I was thinkin' 'bout Shaniece, so I'm not tryna hook up with her on the rebound. It's just been a while, that's all."

"Well, that I can understand," Mitch stated.

"I'm sure," Devon replied as he lay down on his back and began doing sit-ups.

Devon couldn't believe he'd allowed himself to get caught up with Trina like he had. And the worst part about it was that he'd known exactly what he was doing, but he hadn't realized that his mind would start playing tricks on him. When his mind's eye told him that it wasn't Trina who was seated across from him, but Shaniece, he lost all control.

Leaving the visitors' room, Devon was squirming in his jumpsuit, and when locked back up in his cell, he immediately began pacing the room. Soon his pace became a sprint, lasting for nearly a half hour. Exercise had always been the only thing to calm him down after being teased in such a fashion. He'd learned the trick one night when Trina had left him hanging in the middle of the night to go tend to one of her emotional friends. Though the series of workouts helped to keep him from losing his mind, they were hardly a cure when he was seriously in need of intimate affection.

Devon saw Mitch settle back onto his bunk with a letter he'd received earlier in the day. His cellmate released a heavy sigh as his eyes roamed over the contents of the letter.

"What up?" Devon asked as he stopped doing sit-ups and sat with his hands around his ankles.

Mitch shook his head. "Got this letter from my baby mama," he said as he used his thumb and forefinger to rub his eyes. "She tryna take away my visitation rights."

"Why?" Devon asked. "I mean, you ain't did nothin' to her or the child, have you?"

"Naw," Mitch answered angrily. "'Parently, she got some new guy who wanna marry her, but he don't want my son being brought up here to see me in this place. Then she gon' tell me that he wanna take care of Austin, but not if his name ain't legally tied to him."

"What?" Devon replied. "That's stupid. He wanna adopt li'l man or somethin'?"

"That's what this letter says, but you know, I ain't 'bout to let that happen. That's my son, and just 'cause I can't take care of him, don't mean somebody else fixin' to come take him from me."

"So what you gon' do?"

Mitch shrugged as if defeated already. "Man, I don't even know. I guess I'ma need a lawyer or somethin' 'cause I know Shari, and if she serious about whoever this guy is, then she'll make this a legal issue." He cursed under his breath. "I really don't need this right now. She know I love my son and she gon' bring drama like this to me. She bein' so foul right now." He was seething. "I know she doin' this just 'cause I asked her to stop comin' up here and using my son as a way to see me. That's why my mama been bringing Austin up here for the last year."

"Why don't you wanna see her?" Devon asked.

"Like I said, she always bringin' drama," Mitch responded. "One time, she came up here to visit me—I think it was almost two years ago—and it had to be on a day she wouldn't have usually come, because I wasn't expecting her like I usually would've. I'd already had my visit for the day, and one of the officers told me that when she came all the way up here with my son and found out she couldn't see me, she went off, threatening the officers and stuff. He said that when they told Shari that I'd already had my visit and she couldn't see me, she demanded to know who'd come to see me without her knowledge."

Devon laughed. "That's some *Fatal Attraction* junk, right there."

"Then when she came to see me on a day I would've expected her, she was questioning me like I owed her an explanation. She thought I was seeing someone else, and she basically gave me an ultimatum: either I stop seeing whoever was coming up here to see me, or she won't ever bring my son back up here to see me."

"And your decision was . . . ?"

Mitch smirked. "I told that chick that I would see whoever I wanted, including my son. And I would very much appreciate her not bringing my son up to see me. . . . Instead, I'd like her to drop him off at my mother's and let someone wit' some sense bring my boy up here."

"I bet she flipped." Devon laughed, trying to imagine the altercation that had surely followed.

Mitch chuckled. "Yep, so much that I had her escorted out."

Devon was cracking up. "Man, I wish I woulda been there."

"It wasn't pretty, that's fo' sho." Mitch folded the letter in his hands and placed it back in its envelope. "I only seen her a couple of times since, and then she was tryna get me back, sayin' how sorry she was and how much she needed me."

"Now she wit' this other guy." Devon shook his head.

"Yep, and I hope she happy, but she ain't 'bout to take my son from me. He really the only reason, besides my mama, that I'm tryna get outta here as soon as I can."

"I feel you. My mama is tryin' so hard not to let me know how scared she is for me. She keep hidin' behind her prayers and stuff, but I know she worried."

"Duh, fool." Mitch laughed. "That's why she prayin'. If she wasn't scared for yo' behind, she wouldn't be on her knees for you."

Devon shrugged. "Well, I ain't worried 'bout nothin', so I don't see why she is. Besides, prayin' ain't really gon' do much if somebody gon' try somethin' wit' me. God can't make somebody love me if they hate me, you know?"

"Yeah, but I ain't gon' front. Prayin' is the only thing that's got me through these four years."

Devon sucked his teeth. "You on this prayin' thing too?" he asked in disbelief.

First his mother, then Shaniece, Trina, and now Mitch; all the people he came in contact with knew something about this philosophy called prayer. Were they all out of their minds, or was there really something about praying that would cause even the least sanctified person to put a small amount of faith in it?

Mitch chuckled and rubbed his chin. "I gotta be," he replied. "I ain't got nothin' else to lose . . . except my life, and like I told you earlier, I gotta be around for my family." He pulled a small Bible from under his pillow.

Devon laughed. "You read that thing?"

Mitch nodded in all seriousness. "I ain't claiming to be all holy or nothin', but this Book"—he held up the Bible for Devon to see—"has gotten me through some serious stuff."

"Are you saved?" Devon wanted to know.

Mitch paused as if in deep thought before bursting into laughter. "I guess you say if I gotta think that hard, then I must not be. But, technically, I am."

"Technically?"

"Yeah, I asked God to come into my heart when I was seventeen. But when I got to college, I was havin' a hard time keepin' up. I stopped focusing on the books and got caught up in some stuff I really didn't want to get out of, and it drew me away from God. By the time I was twenty, I was so far behind in school that I just quit and started foolin' around with some guys who weren't 'bout nothin'. By twenty-two, I was Shari's unborn baby's father and locked up for bank robbery. It wasn't till last year when I got with Lee and his crew that I realized I needed a little more than muscle to stay sane in this place."

"You sayin' a prison gang got you hooked back up with God?"

"It's not really a gang," Mitch defended. "It's more like a brotherhood. All the guys in it are Christian or have a firm belief in God."

"So y'all go around beatin' the crap outta everybody who ain't a Christian?" Devon asked, only half joking.

"We ain't about fighting with the others," Mitch told him.

"But you and Raquel was ready to throw down the other day when Rip and his sidekicks was threatening me. Then y'all was tryna get me to join this group, like y'all was some type of gang who'd defend me if it come down to it."

Mitch nodded. "Well, we do take care of our people, but we try not to do it by fightin'. Me and Raquel was 'bout to stand up for you just 'cause you our boy. It ain't have nothin' to do with the group, and Lee would've killed us if he'd found out.

"Lee been locked up for 'bout twenty years for murder and he ain't gettin' out no time soon, so he thought it was best he turn his life around before his time ran out. And he tryna help everybody else do the same while they can. We was askin' you to join our crew 'cause we thought you could use the spiritual protection. It had nothin' to do with our crew tryna fight Rip and his crew. That was on me and Raquel, and like I said, Lee don't know nothin' 'bout it."

Devon shook his head as if trying to clear his thoughts so he could better understand all the information Mitch was giving him. In all the time Devon had spent with Mitch, Devon would've never known his friend was serious about spirituality. Even Raquel didn't seem like the type who'd be in church on a Sunday morning. This was a little too much for him, knowing he'd been running from church and God all his life. It would be hard to deal with it, now that he was sharing such a tiny space with someone who claimed to have faith in the God Devon had been hiding from for years.

"Look, I ain't preachin' to you or nothin' because like I said, I'm hardly a saint and I'm still workin' on my relationship with God. But you gotta be in here for a long while, so why not hook up wit' some people who could help you through this?"

Devon shrugged and released a heavy sigh. He wasn't ready for all this religious stuff, and he definitely wasn't going to try to change for anybody. He'd tried that with Shaniece and it hadn't worked out, so he knew it wasn't going to work with a group of guys he hardly knew. Besides, unless God could remove Roc and his boys from this earth and produce a miracle that would save the people in his community, there wasn't much else He could do for Devon.

"I'll think about it," Devon finally answered, knowing he would, but doubting he'd actually take Mitch up on his offer.

Chapter 32

Shaniece held on tightly to Yvonne's left hand as her mother's grip on her right seemed to cut off all blood circulation in her fingers. She and the five other women in her circle were in prayer position, holding on to each other as they prayed without ceasing. Creekside's regular Bible Study night had turned into a prayer service when, nearly thirty minutes after the service had started, gunshots interrupted the peaceful gathering. Shaniece knew the war was getting worse if they were able to hear the battle from the church, which sat several neighborhoods away. That would mean that the warfare was spreading beyond the west side. It was very close to disturbing the everyday peace of the suburbs.

Immediately Cedric called for his "prayer warriors" and the atmosphere was turned completely around. The name of Jesus filled the sanctuary as worshippers fell down on their knees, crying out for God to bring harmony back into their community. They asked for those who were causing calamity throughout the neighborhoods to be brought to the throne of God and shown the error of their ways so that they might realize their wrongs. They prayed that not even one more life be thrown into the hands of Satan and those, who must fall, don't leave the earth without God in their hearts.

The shooting had stopped almost five minutes after it had started, but the congregation had been praying nonstop for nearly an hour. Shaniece had tears falling from her eyes, knowing that the reason behind the shooting was the same as it had been back when firearms were aimed at the grounds of her school. Devon's role in all of this wouldn't leave her mind and she prayed that he, too, would realize how senseless this was and put an end to it.

After a while, Shaniece could no longer formulate the words to pray as tears overflowed her eyes and sobs erupted from deep within her stomach. She cried for the entire community—for those who lived on the poorer side of the school, and even those who lived within her neighborhood and were just an arm's length away from the troubles that haunted their entire community. She recalled a scripture in the Bible that read, *"And when you pray, do not keep on babbling like pagans, for they think they will be heard because of their many words. . . ."* Shaniece nodded as she recalled Matthew 6:7.

Taking heed to the Word, Shaniece began to whisper her simple prayer over and over. "Keep us, Lord." She began mumbling the words softly at first, but soon her prayer became earnest and her voice louder. "Keep us, Lord."

"Yes, yes." Natalie spoke in agreement with her daughter's prayer.

"Keep us all, Lord," Shaniece asked one final time before releasing her prayer to the heavens, knowing that God would answer.

Cedric stood in the pulpit and spoke, in a powerful voice, a prayer that stirred up the spirit in the church, causing those who weren't on their knees to fall to the floor in worship, and those who had already been kneeling to lower their faces to the ground as they continued to solicit God's divine intervention. After another fifteen minutes, Cedric began to bring the prayer service to a close. There wasn't a dry eye in the church, and as they were preparing to depart from each other, some were still speaking in tongues and calling out Jesus' name.

Shaniece wiped her tears with a tissue, handed to her by an usher. She gathered her belongings and turned to join her family, who was still at the altar, conversing with several members. Before she reached them, Yvonne approached her and pulled her into a firm embrace.

"Thank you," Yvonne said tearfully. "Thank you for praying for my baby . . . for us all."

Shaniece could feel the woman's tears in the crook of her neck, only causing more of her own tears to seep through her closed eyes. "You're welcome, Ms. Yvonne. I'm always praying for us, especially for Devon." She pulled back and looked directly into the woman's eyes. "I'm really worried about him."

"Me too," Yvonne agreed with a nod. "I told him he needs to be praying, but he keeps saying that everything's out of his control now. Even if he wanted to stop all this madness, he couldn't."

Shaniece shook her head. "I don't believe that, but then again, it could be true. If Devon backed out, there would still be someone to take his place, trying to fight this battle until they were victorious."

"When's the last time you had contact with him?"

Shaniece rolled her eyes to keep the rest of her tears at bay. "Valentine's Day. We stopped contacting each other after that."

Yvonne could see the simmering hurt in Shaniece's eyes and decided to comfort her. "He asks about you all the time, if it's any consolation."

Shaniece smiled wearily. "You tell him that I'm still praying for him and that I no longer hold anything against him."

Yvonne nodded. "I'll do that." She stood back and gazed at the young woman before her. "Shaniece, you are truly one magnificent woman of God. Your faith and trust in Him is so much stronger than most people your age. Your prayers, no matter how simple, are powerful beyond human belief. God is really using you as His vessel."

Tearfully Shaniece thanked Yvonne for her kind words and encouragement before excusing herself. She walked toward the back of the line of people waiting to greet her father. There were about three more people in line before her, so she decided she'd greet Cedric like a regular member would.

She saw her mother shaking her head in amusement just as she was about to approach her father. After the last member was acknowledged, Shaniece plastered on a smile in preparation for her father's greeting, but as she moved toward him, he turned toward his wife and said, "All right, Natalie, it's getting late, let's head out."

Rainelle, Keith, Natalie, and a few lingering members burst out laughing when Shaniece folded her arms and whined, "Daddy!"

Cedric chuckled deeply as he turned toward his daughter. "I'm just playing with you, baby." He hugged her and kissed her forehead. "Thank you for your prayers tonight."

She bashfully batted her eyes. "You're welcome."

As the family headed out the door and toward the parking lot, they bid final greetings to those members who were still fellowshipping. The drive home was quiet as the soft melodies of CeCe Winans streamed from the speakers. Suddenly Cedric turned down the music.

"Aww, c'mon, Daddy, that's my favorite song," Rainelle complained.

Cedric glanced at his youngest daughter in the rearview mirror. "I just want to talk to you guys really quick."

Natalie glanced at her husband and gently caressed his right hand, which rested on the armrest between them.

"You guys know that I've been making my rounds on the west side," Cedric began.

"Yeah," Keith replied. "Larry told me that his dad's been going with you almost every other weekend to minister to those people," he said, speaking of one of his friends in the church.

Cedric nodded. "That's right. A few of the brothers and some of the women in the church have been joining me in reaching out to the people in our community. Now, I want to reach the youth, but it's hard. They just see us as a bunch of adults trying to tell them how to live their lives."

"Well, that's probably because that's all they've ever heard come out of an adult's mouth," Shaniece explained. "If you want to reach them, you've got to use people they can relate to."

"Exactly," Cedric agreed. "That's why I want to start bringing some of you guys with me."

"*Us,*" Rainelle asked, almost nervously. "Daddy, I would love to help and all, but I don't know about going over there. It's not like our side of the community."

"Which is exactly why you need to reach out to them," Natalie interceded as she turned slightly to look at her children.

"This isn't about you, sweetheart," Cedric continued. "It's about doing God's business. Now, I'll need you guys' help in rounding up more of the youth, because I want to start a program that will bring in the troubled kids off the street and into our sanctuary."

He looked toward his oldest child. "Shaniece, if you don't mind, I'd like you and a couple of others to be like the CEO of this program. Maybe you and Tatiana and one other person. I want strong heads with compassionate hearts so that we can be smart about reaching out to the ones in need."

Shaniece nodded. "I guess I can do it."

"You guess?" Natalie questioned. "What's the matter with *knowing* that you can do it?"

Shaniece allowed her shoulders to drop with a heavy sigh. "I don't know, Mama. It's just that I haven't been so good at trying to help other people. When I had the chance I blew it, so why even try anymore?"

"Shaniece, what are you talking about, girl?" Keith blurted out. "You always give the best advice, and you're always helping somebody."

"Yeah," Rainelle agreed without hesitation. "I mean, I don't always come to you with my problems, but when I do, I never regret it."

Shaniece gave her siblings a soft smile. "Thanks, guys, but giving advice on regular everyday problems and trying to lead someone spiritually are so different."

"Look, if you're still on this thing with Devon and Q, get off it!" Keith spoke in an almost harsh, nearly fed-up tone.

"Keith, stop it," Natalie reprimanded, and then turned, with concern filling her eyes, toward Shaniece. "Niecey, baby, is that what you're worried about?"

Shaniece blinked back tears. "Mama, I had so many chances and I never took them. I was too busy characterizing Q by his age and using him as a liaison between Devon and me that I didn't realize until it was too late that he was in need of a savior." She shook her head somberly. "And I was too wrapped up in trying to change Devon so that I could be with him that I forgot that I should've been trying to get him to change so that he could have a relationship with God." She reached up and wiped the water escaping through the corners of her eyes. "It's been proven that when God gives me chances, I don't take them. So why even continue to mess up other people's lives?"

The car became completely silent as Cedric pulled into the family's driveway. He shut off the car, but no one even moved to exit, knowing that Cedric had something to say in response to Shaniece's confession.

He turned around as far as he could in his seat so that he could look into Shaniece's eyes. "Niecey, you are human, and God understands that. That is exactly why He gives us so many chances. We're not perfect, and God doesn't expect us to be. He knows we can be the most selfish, disobedient people, and He loves us regardless.

"God forgave you for not doing as He'd intended for you to do when you began seeing Devon. He also forgave you each time you didn't seize the opportunity to speak a word into Q's life. Now, you need to forgive yourself and stop being afraid of what God has in store for you. Your fear of evangelism is hindering God's Kingdom work, so you definitely need to pray that you get past this spirit of fear that you have concerning this situation.

"As far as Q and Devon are concerned, leave it up to God. Your last few moments with Q could've changed his life dramatically. He could be sitting at the right hand of Jesus right now, praising God for having sent you his way that night. We don't know," Cedric said, shrugging. "And we shouldn't have to worry about it because it's not our place. And Devon can still be saved.

You may have even planted a seed in his life in the little bit of time that you had been around him. All the seed needs is a little water. As a matter of fact, Sister Yvonne has asked me to accompany her on her next visit to see him. He hasn't responded well to the idea of having the prison ministry visit him, so his mother wants me to speak with him concerning a few things. I'll give him a few words of encouragement, and if he wants, I'll even pray with him." He gave his daughter a smile. "Now, does that make you feel any better?"

"I'd feel better if you came home from your visit with Devon and told me that he received Christ right there on the spot," Shaniece said.

Cedric shrugged. "I could, but sometimes things do take time, and as long as God is merciful toward him, Devon still has time," he told her. "Now, will you help me plant seeds in the lives of the other hundreds of people who need to be saved, or are you gonna stay stuck on things of the past?"

"Now you're trying to make me feel guilty." Shaniece laughed.

"Maybe." Cedric shrugged. "But we're not getting out of this car until you agree to help me." He sat back in his seat, with a leisurely sigh, as if he had all the time in the world.

"Oh my goodness, Shaniece," Rainelle yelled. "Please say 'yes' so we can go in the house."

"I know, 'cause I'm tired," Keith added.

Shaniece laughed. "Okay, Daddy," she said through her giggles.

"I'm sorry, what did you say?" Cedric called, placing his hand up to his ear as if he hadn't heard what Shaniece had said.

Natalie hit her husband against his arm. "Ced, you heard the girl say 'okay,' now let us out of this car."

They laughed as Cedric unlocked the doors and they exited. As they walked toward the front door, he hugged Shaniece's side and kissed her cheek.

"Thank you, baby girl," he said. "God never gave up on me, and He's not gonna give up on you. You are destined to be a powerful woman of God."

Chapter 33

Saturday evening found Shaniece and Craig, along with Tatiana and Justin, enjoying each other's company on a double date. They were seated in the dark theater, nearly falling out of their seats in laughter, watching the newly released comedy starring Martin Lawrence. When the credits began to roll, the foursome exited the theater, still laughing at some of the scenes from the movie.

"Craig, that was a good choice," Tatiana complimented as they moved toward the food court, housed along with the movie theater in the mall.

"Yeah, man," Justin agreed. "I was scared Tatiana and Niecey would get up in here and try to get us to watch some sappy chick flick."

"Excuse me," Shaniece countered. "For your information, I like comedy, action, and scary movies way more than I like romance. If it would've been left up to me, we would've gone for something a little more frightening than Martin Lawrence."

They laughed as they bypassed the fast-food counters and headed for the Applebee's restaurant.

"My bad," Justin said, chuckling. "I guess my baby's the only one here not into anything besides romance."

Tatiana eyed Shaniece. "I wouldn't be so sure about that."

Shaniece placed her hands on her hips. "We are talking about movies."

The guys exchanged confused glances, but they didn't bother to ask what their dates were talking about.

"Y'all always got some inside conversations goin' on," Justin said.

Craig chuckled. "Man, I've known them since middle school and I still never know what they're talkin' 'bout."

After being shown to a table, Tatiana immediately asked if Shaniece would accompany her to the ladies' room. Shaniece agreed, knowing Tatiana wanted to talk about how Shaniece had been feeling about the evening so far.

"Craig, if the waiter comes by, would you mind ordering me a glass of water with lemon?" Shaniece requested.

"Sure, no problem," he replied.

"Yeah, baby, could you order wildberry lemonade for me?" Tatiana put in her order.

Justin nodded as he and Craig took their seats while the girls walked off toward the restrooms.

"Excuse me, but when did Justin become 'baby'?" Shaniece wanted to know as soon as they entered the lavatory.

Tatiana laughed as she gazed into the mirror and teased her Shirley Temple curls. "I don't know. It's been like that for a while." She turned toward her best friend with a wide smile on her face. "I'm really happy with him."

"I see." Shaniece chuckled. "I'm happy for you."

Tatiana searched her friend's eyes and knew that Shaniece was being sincere, but she also knew that Shaniece was slightly envious of her and Justin's relationship. Tatiana could see the longing in Shaniece's eyes every time Justin pulled her close, whispered in her ear, or did something as simple as holding her hand. It almost caused Tatiana to feel guilty about being so content in her relationship, knowing that it was something Shaniece was longing for.

Shaniece noticed her friend's gaze and smiled wearily. "Girl, I know what you're thinking, but I truly am happy for you," she insisted with a light laugh.

Tatiana nodded. "I don't doubt that you're being honest. I'm just scared that you're unhappy with your life."

"Why would you even think about something like that?" Shaniece asked, forcing herself to continue looking into Tatiana's eyes so her friend wouldn't think she'd struck a nerve.

Tatiana shrugged. "I know how much you wanted a relationship with D and never really got the chance to explore that with him."

"Yeah, but I've gotten over that."

"Really?" Tatiana questioned. "You're completely over what you guys had?"

"Well, maybe not completely," Shaniece admitted. "But I'm getting there. I realized that I was brought into his life to lead him into the right direction. I was so caught up in my own desires that I missed out on a great opportunity. But now that I'm no longer distracted, I can focus on doing God's will. I'm content in praying for Devon and for our community and helping my dad reach out to those who need us."

Tatiana smiled. "Well, I guess that answers my question, huh?" She looked back into the mirror. "So what about Craig?"

"What about him?" Shaniece asked as she touched up her lip gloss.

Tatiana rolled her eyes. "Don't act, Niecey. What's going on between you two?"

"Nothing," Shaniece answered, with a laugh. "We're just friends. Trust me, if it was more, I wouldn't have asked you and Justin to come along with us tonight."

"I'm sure Craig would've loved it that way," Tatiana retorted playfully.

"Well, it will be a while before he has it his way . . . *if* he ever has it his way."

"Uh-huh," Tatiana hummed as she headed toward the door. "We'll see how long it takes him to sweet-talk you into letting him have it *all* his way."

"Tati, has anyone ever told you that your friends are the family you choose for yourself?" Shaniece questioned rhetorically. "'Cause you're about to be disowned."

Tatiana laughed as she walked out of the restroom with Shaniece on her tail. The girls were still laughing when they approached the table.

"What's so funny?" Craig asked as both he and Justin stood so that the ladies could take their seats inside the booth.

"We were just discussing the significance of the Burger King slogan," Tatiana answered, still chuckling.

Justin shook his head. "I'm not even gonna ask."

"We ordered an appetizer," Craig informed them just as the waitress, who'd been assigned to serve them, approached the table with their drinks.

"Oh," the tall, curvaceous woman said as she placed the drinks on the table, "you guys weren't lying when you said you had dates."

Shaniece eyed the dark-haired woman, who looked to be at least thirty. She could see the flirtatiousness in the waitress's eyes and was inwardly disgusted. Shaniece then looked across the table at Tatiana, who had the same guarded look on her face.

"And we also told you they were beautiful," Craig remarked, interrupting the silence.

"We weren't lying about that either," Justin added, placing his hand on top of Tatiana's.

The girls' faces softened and smiles replaced their deep frowns.

The waitress took the hint and shrugged as she asked, "Are you all ready to order?"

"No, we're not," Tatiana replied sweetly, but with an edge in her tone. "Could you please give us a minute?"

The woman shrugged again before walking off.

"Is she new?" Shaniece asked. "She has no professional courtesy."

"I don't know what her problem is," Tatiana announced, allowing everyone at the table to become aware of the fact that she already didn't like the woman, "but she's gonna find herself without a tip and maybe a job if she don't get right."

"Baby, calm down," Justin told her. "Remember, she's the one handling our food."

Tatiana rolled her eyes as she picked up her menu. She was mumbling under her breath about someone getting hurt if she found anything in her food. The others just laughed as they searched their menus for a desirable entrée. By the time they had received their appetizers, they were ready to order. Once their food arrived, they ate and enjoyed each other's company.

"Tati, have you gotten your prom dress yet?" Shaniece asked, noting that their school's junior/senior prom was not too far away.

Tatiana smacked her lips and rolled her eyes. "No, because Justin doesn't like the color I picked out. I wanted lavender, but he wants red."

"Because, girl, you look good in red," Justin tried to compliment, but didn't hesitate to add, "and so do I."

Tatiana rolled her eyes. "But do you know how many red dresses are gonna be worn to the prom?"

"I hate to tell you, Justin, but it's usually the girl's decision," Shaniece informed him. "She picks out the dress of her dreams and her date coordinates his tux."

"That's cool and all, but I'm not tryna rock no lavender," he declared defiantly. "Especially since whatever we wear to your school's prom, we're gonna wear to my prom. Money is tight."

"Well, y'all need to figure something out, because prom is only a few weeks away, and waiting until the week before to get everything would be a big mistake," Craig shared.

"I know that's right," Shaniece agreed. "I remember last year when my parents waited until March to tell me I could go to prom and I had to rush everything. Not only did my dress cost nearly a hundred dollars more, but I had to find a last-minute date."

"That wasn't a complete disaster." Craig smiled.

"Yeah, good thing Craig didn't have a date."

"How convenient," Tatiana smirked.

Craig narrowed his eyes in her direction and gave her a knowing look. "Tati, you knew before anyone else that I was either going with Niecey or I was gonna go solo dolo."

"Dang, Craig!" Justin laughed. "You had it bad."

Shaniece lowered her head and focused her attention on her meal.

"So, are y'all going together this year?" Justin pried.

Shaniece could feel Craig staring at her, but she kept her head lowered. No doubt, she'd thought about going to the prom with Craig, and not just because she felt as if she had no other option, but she knew she would have a good time with him. There was only one thing keeping her from allowing herself to do so, though. She could no longer deny that she was starting to buy into Craig's affection. He was so sweet and caring; he loved her and treated her with the utmost respect. She was starting to like him more for it, and it excited her a little, yet frightened her a lot.

"If he asks me," Shaniece answered softly before Craig could respond.

After dinner, Craig drove to Shaniece's house, where Justin had left his car and Tatiana was staying for the night. The couples separated for good-byes. Tatiana stood with Justin next to his car, while Shaniece and Craig stood under the porch light.

"Were you serious about what you said earlier?" Craig questioned.

"What did I say?" Shaniece teased.

Craig didn't crack a smile as he looked into her eyes. "Niecey, please don't play with me. Were you serious or not?"

Shaniece wiped the smile from her face. "Look, Craig, I'm not trying to use you, and I'm not playing games with you. I was very serious about what I said earlier."

He smiled. "Well, then, would you like to go to prom with me?" He bit down on his bottom lip before teasing, "And you can wear whatever color you want. You know you look good in anything."

She laughed as she lightly touched his arm. "I'd love to go to prom with you. And I had a good time tonight also."

"I could show you many more good times if you allowed me to," Craig suggested.

Shaniece's gaze was immovable. "That would be nice, but I'm only willing to take baby steps. I want to make sure that what I'm feeling is for real, and I want to be sure that I'm over what I shared with Devon before I start anything with you." She blinked slowly. "I don't want to ruin our friendship."

He nodded. "I understand." He leaned down and kissed her softly on the cheek. "Good night, Niecey."

Shaniece blushed as Craig stepped off the porch. "Good night."

As he got into his car and drove off, Shaniece waved good-bye. She was just about to call for Tatiana's attention, and then she realized that her best friend and Justin were sharing a very intimate kiss, which Shaniece didn't want to get told off for interrupting. So she went into the house, leaving the door unlocked for Tatiana to come in once she said good night to her boyfriend.

Natalie was coming out of the kitchen just as Shaniece was about to head up the stairs toward her room. "Hey, Niecey, where's Tatiana?"

Shaniece stifled her laughter. "Still outside with Justin. She should be coming inside in a minute."

"Yeah, well, if she doesn't, I don't mind playing 'Mama.'" Natalie laughed. She began walking toward her bedroom, but suddenly stopped as she turned toward her daughter. "May I talk to you for a minute?"

Shaniece hesitated before nodding. "Sure."

"Just give me a second," Natalie requested. "Let me get this tea to your father and I'll be back."

Shaniece sat on the sofa and waited for her mother to return. When Natalie rejoined her daughter in the living room, she took Shaniece's hands into hers.

"Shaniece, I love you and I only want what's best for you. You do know that, right?" Natalie questioned with uncertainty.

Shaniece nodded. "I know, Mama, and I thank you for that."

"But I don't want you to think that I don't trust your judgment. I know it seemed as if I was against your relationship with Devon, especially after he was arrested. But when I think of my little girl spending her life with the man of her dreams, I just never imagined that it would be someone like him. I know he's a good person, but he doesn't lead the greatest lifestyle. I wanted better for you, and I knew he wasn't the best you could do." She paused and searched her daughter's eyes. "I'm sorry if it ever seemed like I was trying to run your life or was making my opinion a little too obvious about whom you should spend your time with, but I was only trying to help."

Shaniece smiled. "Mama, I understand what was going through your mind. I've come to realize that I do deserve better, and it was a shame that even Devon came to terms with that before I did. I do still care for Devon, but I'm moving on and focusing on the real reason he was brought into my life. I'm praying for him, and the only relationship I hope to have with him in the future is a spiritual one."

Natalie's grin was so wide, and Shaniece knew that her mother was proud of her for recognizing that God had called her for a higher purpose in Devon's life.

"God is doing mighty work in your life. I can't wait to see His will in full effect."

"Me too, Mama," Shaniece agreed as she embraced Natalie.

Just as they were releasing each other, Tatiana walked through the front door.

"Oh, look what the cat drug in," Natalie kidded. "I thought I was gonna have to come out there and pry you two lovebirds apart."

Tatiana blushed as she averted her starry-eyed gaze. "Hi, Ms. Natalie."

"Uh-huh," Natalie teased. "Has Mr. Wilburn headed home, or do I need to go check to make sure that he's not waiting for you to sneak out after everyone's asleep?"

Tatiana laughed as she adjusted the backpack on her shoulder. "He's gone, and he asked me to tell everyone good night."

"All right," Natalie sang, and she stood from her seat. "I'm going to bed, and you girls should do the same." Her gaze shifted between the two teens as she shook her head. "I don't know why I'm wasting my breath, though, because you'll stay up all night talking. Just make sure that you're able to get up for church tomorrow."

"Good night, Mama," Shaniece said as Natalie walked toward her bedroom. "Tell Daddy good night for me."

"Okay, good night, girls. Sweet dreams," Natalie said before disappearing behind her bedroom door.

Shaniece turned toward Tatiana and the girls stared at each other for a moment before bursting into laughter.

"I'm sure you'll have plenty of sweet dreams," Shaniece said to her friend as they headed up to her room.

"Yeah, well, if you keep it up with Craig, you'll have this same smile on your face too."

Shaniece turned toward Tatiana—her mouth wide open, not hiding the broad grin on her face.

Tatiana laughed. "Maybe sooner than later."

Chapter 34

Devon stood, looking at the passing cars through the barbed-wire fence. How he wished he were in one of those cars, driving leisurely without a care or destination in mind. He'd have a CD blasting and the windows down as he cruised the interstate for the simple sake of enjoying the ride . . . the freedom of being able to go wherever his heart pleased without limitations or hindrances. And if he could have Shaniece in the passenger seat, he'd be even more content. He sighed as he thought about how much of his life he'd thrown away in exchange for money and a lavish lifestyle. He was starting to believe that it truly hadn't been worth it.

He would give anything just to be able to walk out on his own front porch and enjoy the afternoon spring breeze. If he could just walk around his neighborhood, even with the possibility of being attacked or approached in a disrespectful manner, he'd revel in the freedom. If he could get just one night of peaceful sleep in his comfortable king-size bed, instead of having to rest his stiff back on the metal springs, which he'd have no choice but to call his resting place for the next ten years, he'd sleep as if there were no tomorrow. If he could shower without freezing to death or worrying about losing his grip on the slippery soap—which could turn a time of cleansing into an experience he'd have nightmares about every time he closed his eyes—he'd stay under the steaming hot water for hours without worrying about how much the water bill would place a hole in his pocket as a result. If he could enjoy a decent meal, instead of consuming the processed foods of the prison, only to vomit later on, he'd savor the aroma and every bite and swallow of his food. If he could just go back to that night when he was supposed to have enjoyed one of the most talked-about plays, which had been through town and around to at least twenty other cities by now, he would have stuck to his plans instead of detouring, if only for a second, to make a few dollars. He had so many regrets—things he wished he would've said or done—and he'd have plenty of time to think about them, now that he'd given up the opportunity to do the things he'd put off for so long.

Suddenly a sharp punch to the back of his head sent him out of his thoughts and plunging forward. Before falling, he caught his balance. But before he could turn around to find out who'd assaulted him, the gentleman stood before him, allowing him to see his face for only a second before slamming his fist into Devon's right eye, sending him plummeting into the ground. Devon found the guy's foot and swung his own leg around, causing the guy to lose his balance. Devon jumped up and began punching the guy in his face and any other place his fists would land.

Soon another gentleman joined the fight and placed a strong grip around Devon's neck, pulling him off the other guy. Devon found himself helplessly fighting back as the nearly 300-pound guy shoved one large fist after another into Devon's body. Devon was clueless as to where Mitch had come from, but, somehow, his midget of a roommate had managed to jump onto the second guy's back, trying with all his might to strangle him as Raquel stepped in and punched the life out of his jelly-filled stomach. The alarm that signaled a yard fight blared, and Devon knew all of the other prisoners had dropped to the ground in response. Soon officers would be ordering him and his attackers to separate, or they would be taken to solitary. Devon wanted to get as much revenge as possible before that occurred, so he returned his attention to the first guy who'd jumped on him and proceeded to finish him off. But when he looked into the eyes of the man, he realized he was nose to nose with a seemingly familiar face.

"Remember me, punk?" the guy asked, his grin cocky.

Before Devon could respond, officers pushed through and grabbed onto the five guys who'd been involved in the altercation.

"Break it up!" they shouted as they held up their batons in preparation to discipline anyone who refused to comply. "Back to the cages."

As Devon headed inside, he caught up with Raquel and Mitch. "'Preciate the backup."

"I told you we gotcha back, dawg," Mitch replied.

"Just tell me what that was about?" Raquel asked.

Devon shrugged. "Man, I don't even—"

His response was interrupted when the familiar guy brushed past him as he walked back into the prison. He turned toward Devon and glared at him with much animosity. "Say somethin' else 'bout me, fool," he challenged. "I got somethin' fo' ya!"

Devon was about to jump in the guy's face when he suddenly felt someone grab onto his arms. He turned around and was boiling with rage to find another unfamiliar person gripping him like he was a child. Before he could say anything to the older-looking gentleman, the sound of Rip's voice caught his attention.

"What up, *Devon?*" he taunted. "That sho' is a nice, sissy-soundin' name." He had his arm around the guy who'd assaulted Devon. "I told you we'd take care of you if we had to. And this is only the beginning," he informed him before looking down at the guy next to him. "You remember my folk, Rico, don't cha?"

Devon was seething as he watched a sneaky smile spread across Rip's face. He tried once more to move in their direction, but the man behind him had yet to release his hold. So he watched in anger as Rip and Rico simply laughed and walked off.

"Man, let go of me," Devon demanded as he shook himself from the man's grasp.

He turned to face the guy, who was about five feet eleven inches in height and was significantly larger than Devon in muscular build. His head of silver hair and the lines in his face gave away his age. His eyes showed years of wisdom, and his calm demeanor gave off a father-like persona.

Devon glared at the man. "Why you grabbin' on me like that?"

"Fighting is not going to get you anywhere in life," the man simply said. He then turned toward Raquel and Mitch. "I thought these two would've learned that by now."

Devon turned his gaze toward his friends. "Who is this grandpa?"

Mitch seemed to be holding back laughter as he made introductions. "*Devon,* this is Lee."

"Don't try me, *Mitchell,*" Devon spat, hoping his glare had let his cellmate know that he had no problems taking his frustrations out on him if he felt that he had to.

"Move it! Move it!" a nearby guard ordered those prisoners who were lagging behind.

"We don't have time to talk now, but later. . . ." Lee spoke in a soft manner as the guard ushered them toward their cells.

Devon didn't speak another word until he was back behind the bars that had held him prisoner for months now.

"Look, I don't know who that old dude was, but I don't 'preciate him puttin' his hands on me like he my daddy!" Devon spoke harshly to Mitch as he lay in his bunk.

Mitch smacked his teeth. "You oughta be happy Lee lookin' out for you, but I guess you won't understand, unless you get yourself into another situation like you did out there."

"Whateva!" Devon said, his voice rising. "Rico ran up on me first. I ain't gon' mess wit' nobody unless they mess wit' me first. Shoot, he the one who should be happy somebody like Lee around, 'cause he was 'bout to get beat down."

"You tellin' me that fool ran up on you for no reason?" Mitch asked disbelievingly. "You ain't did nothin' to him?"

"Did I stutter?" Devon snapped. "You should know better than me that dudes in here will run up on you for no reason."

"He said you was talkin' 'bout him?"

"How I'ma talk about somebody I hardly even know?" Devon questioned.

"So you do know him?" Mitch questioned as though interviewing Devon for a news article.

Devon hit his fist against his bed. "Dawg, why you askin' me all these questions?" He cursed angrily.

"Look, you can calm all that down," Mitch stated as his anger began to rise as well. "I just wanna know what I'm fightin' for. Next time I'll just chill and let ol' boy handle his b'iness."

"Ain't neither one of y'all gon' have business if y'all don't shut up," another prisoner yelled from across the hall.

"Man, you don't want me to put these hands to ya!" Devon shouted.

"Big D, just cool it, man," Mitch warned.

"Naw, I'm tired of this," Devon said as he sat up on his bed and cursed again. "I'm sick of y'all fools actin' like y'all can talk to me any kinda way. Y'all don't know me! I ain't 'fraid to handle mine."

Laughter came from several cells. "Young buck, you need to chill 'fore somebody bring you down a notch."

Devon didn't recognize the voice, but he could tell whoever had spoken the words was huge. The voice was gruff and held heavy breaths. "God, I need to get outta here 'fore I lose my mind," he spoke aloud to himself.

"D, he's right," Mitch said in a much calmer tone than before. "Man, you gotta calm yourself down. You too new to be so hot up in here like you are. I ain't never seen nobody have so many enemies before their first year is even close to bein' up."

"Yeah, that's just somethin' you gotta deal wit' when people always hatin' on you."

Instead of responding to Devon's remark, Mitch returned to his initial question. "Who is Rico?"

Devon hesitated before releasing a sigh. "I used to work wit' that fool when I was comin' up under my mentor, Kane. Rico 'bout a couple of years older than me and he got me locked up when I was seventeen. I was wit' him when he got caught in a bust and I spent 'bout four weeks in jail before I was able to get out. He was there for a good six months before he got off."

"So why he pissed wit' you?" Mitch questioned. "Seem like you should be the one havin' a beef wit' him, not the other way around."

Devon shrugged. "I ain't had no contact wit' him since Kane died. He left the operation after I took it over. I knew he was mad 'cause Kane let me take over instead of givin' him the job, but I didn't think he'd hold a grudge over it for almost three years."

"But he said you was jawin' 'bout him?" Mitch reminded Devon.

"My best guess is that fool, Rip, got somethin' to do wit' this," Devon surmised. "He probably found out I had history wit' Rico and started some junk so he could scare me. It ain't gonna work, though. All he done did was pissed me off more."

"Well, just put that on ice, 'cause tryna handle it ain't gon' do nothin' but prolong your parole hearing when it do come around," Mitch advised.

Devon wanted to be receptive toward Mitch's warning, but it was hard when his conduct was continuously challenged by those who hated him the most. There was no way he could calm down if he was provoked time and time again. He'd never let anyone disrespect him before, and he didn't plan on allowing it now, even if that meant losing out on being granted parole once his ten years were up.

Chapter 35

Shaniece stared ahead at the single-level house, with its unkempt lawn and fading paint. A broken window to the far left caught her attention, and the dark-colored drapes were pulled together tightly as if the resident wanted nothing to do with the outside world. The entire house seemed dark and unwelcoming, and Shaniece felt like taking the unspoken warning and running as far away from this place as she could. But she had to do this. She'd promised her father that she would try. Even though she'd made that promise with the thought that he would be right by her side, she'd keep it if it killed her.

She turned toward the group of teens—some were excited, most were apprehensive—that had agreed to play active roles in the new ministry that Cedric had formed. The looks on some of their faces nearly mirrored hers and she wanted to burst into laughter at the fact that they were all so nervous about reaching out to people who truly needed their help. Shaniece couldn't believe that as long as they'd lived in this community, they hadn't taken this approach before. If they had, maybe they wouldn't be going through the issues that they were dealing with now.

"Okay," Shaniece breathily said as she tightened her grip around the Bible in her hands. "Everyone has their materials?" she questioned, holding up the Bible and small book on witnessing the Gospel. "And their two partners?"

The others nodded silently. "Remember," she continued, "*do not* go into anyone's house. Make sure you introduce yourselves and the organization that you're with. Explain what we're doing, and make sure you, as well as the person you're speaking with, is comfortable. Don't worry if you don't get to speak with anyone today. The goal is just to try reaching out to them. You do your part, and God will handle the rest," she encouraged, and smiled when she saw some of the teens relax their shoulders. "All right, let's get started."

The teens scattered, some more quickly than others. They studied their surroundings before approaching the chosen home, some with enthusiasm, some with caution. Shaniece turned toward Tatiana and Krystal, who both wore bright smiles, bringing more assurance into Shaniece's spirit. She hadn't even thought twice about which people to choose as her partners when her father suggested that all volunteers be grouped into threes. These girls were her support group, and without them, she wasn't sure she'd be able to go through with the project.

"You guys ready?" Shaniece asked them.

Tatiana rubbed her hands together anxiously. "You know I am," she answered as Krystal silently nodded with her smile still in place.

The girls approached the house they'd been standing in front of. They walked past the weeds scattered throughout the grass and the broken-down car that rested in the driveway on cinder blocks. Shaniece shook her head, correctly assuming that the tires had been stolen—most likely for money or drugs.

Shaniece stepped onto the porch and breathed deeply before reaching up to knock on the door. She caught a glimpse of someone peeking out the window, but when no one came to the door, she decided to try again. She glanced back at her friends before knocking one more time.

"Who is it?" a female voice shouted.

Shaniece's voice shook nervously. "Umm . . . my name is Shaniece and I'm with my friends Tatiana and Krystal. We're part of the youth group from Creekside Church of God in Christ. We were wondering if it would be okay for us to speak with you."

"You're from Reverend Simmons's church?" the woman questioned.

"Yes, ma'am," Shaniece replied. "I'm his oldest daughter," she added, hoping to draw the woman toward the front door.

They heard the sound of feet shuffling and soon the door was being unlocked. When the woman revealed herself, Shaniece immediately recognized her as Q's mother. She wore the same distressed look on her face as she had the day of her son's funeral, and the weary smile she plastered across her face caused her youthful countenance to appear ten years older.

"Ms. Bollard?" Shaniece spoke with surprise in her tone.

"Please, it makes me feel really old when you refer to me as 'Ms.,'" the woman replied. "You all can call me Monique."

"Monique." Shaniece smiled. "How have you been?"

Monique lowered her eyes and shrugged her shoulders somberly. "I'm trying to make it," she answered.

The girls remained silent, but they nodded compassionately.

"Would you like to come in?" Monique offered.

Shaniece glanced back at her friends before replying. "Well, we're out here with a group of kids from the church, and we're not supposed to go into the houses—"

"Please," Monique interrupted. "I'm not very comfortable being out here on the streets where my son was murdered."

Shaniece gazed at the petite young woman, who'd easily dropped ten pounds in the last month. Without even consulting with her partners, Shaniece motioned for them to move into the house. Tatiana and Krystal hesitated before following.

The four women settled in the small living room, and silence fell between them. Tatiana glared at Shaniece and nudged her in her side. The look in her eyes told Shaniece that they were not supposed to be closed up in this woman's house. Shaniece replied by allowing her glare to tell her best friend that if she had felt it would be unsafe for them to be here, she wouldn't have stepped over the threshold. Besides, this was Q's mother, and it was obvious by her demeanor that their visit to Monique was right on time.

"Would you all like something to drink or something to snack on, maybe?" Monique asked, breaking into the thickness of the silence.

"No, thank you," the girls quickly responded.

"So what brings your youth group out this way?" Monique questioned.

Tatiana took the liberty of answering. "Well, with everything that's been going on over here, Reverend Simmons decided to implement this program where we go out and try to reach out to our very own neighbors. He's been around here with some of the older church members, but decided that he'd need the youth to draw in some of the kids. So that's why we're . . ." Tatiana stopped speaking when she realized that there were no kids inside this house.

"We're not just trying to reach children; we're up for speaking with anyone who's willing to listen," Krystal quickly added.

Monique forced a faint smile to her lips as she looked down at her coffee table. Several photo albums lay on top, and one rested with its pages open. She gently lifted the album as if it were a precious piece of jewelry and handed it to Shaniece.

"That's Q when he was born." She spoke as she pointed toward the photograph of her holding Q in her arms, and a man standing over them. "That's his father, Tyrese." She pointed toward the man, who looked as if the last thing he wanted to be doing at that moment was taking a family photo. "As you can see, he's not a smiling man." She chuckled softly. "That was the first . . . and the last picture we took as a family."

"Oh" was all Shaniece could push past her throat.

"I was twenty and a junior at Spelman when I got pregnant with Q," Monique continued. "Tyrese was twenty-three and a grad student at Emory. I was so young and naïve that I didn't realize how far away I'd allowed Tyrese to pull me from my studies until I wound up pregnant. He promised he'd take care of us and we'd want for nothing. He was going for his doctorate and I'd soon graduate and get a job that paid well enough for us to live however we wanted." She chuckled again, but this time there was no amusement in her tone. "I played myself for a big-time fool. Q was barely six months old when Tyrese transferred universities, leaving me no way to get in contact with him. I was devastated, and I had no idea how I was going to raise Q by myself.

"Thank God for my parents, though. They stepped in when I needed them most and they helped out until I graduated and found a decent job. Q and I were doing well, until I got laid off five years later and couldn't find another job that paid well enough to keep the nice apartment we were living in. I couldn't run back home to my parents 'cause I was trying to prove to myself that I was an adult and could do this without intruding on other people's lives. So I moved out here." She looked around the small house. "This neighborhood wasn't that bad when I first moved here. It wasn't the burbs, but it was better than it is now. Then things changed as the economy got worse. Pushers started to appear on every corner and soon crackheads were walking down the streets. I hated that I had to raise my son in such conditions, but it was the only option I had at the time without fending off of family, and things only grew worse. I'd always had behavioral problems with Q, but I thought he'd outgrow them. All throughout day care and elementary school, I would receive calls on my job from someone asking me to come pick my son up because he was being disruptive or picking on another student. By middle school, I was being called to pick him up for suspensions of three, five, or ten days. When he got into the eighth grade, he decided to join the track team. I was thankful, because I knew the track coach was a no-nonsense kind of man. I figured he'd be a good influence on Q, and he was."

Monique inhaled deeply. "*Then* Q got caught up with Big D." She locked eyes with Shaniece. "But as much of a surprise that it may be, D was just as good of an influence on Q as the track coach had been. He made sure Q stayed in school and that he kept up at least a C average. He told Q that I was all he had and that he needed to respect me as his mother and provider. And I let Q hang out with D for those reasons. The fact that D helped Q bring money into this house was a plus as well. I was being selfish by taking the money and allowing my son to put himself in harm's way, and that's where I failed," she admitted as her voice broke. "If it weren't for my selfishness, my son would be here today." She wiped her eyes and tried to pull herself together.

Shaniece immediately moved to console Monique. "Please don't believe that."

Monique shook her head. "It's true. I'd always told him, even before he started trappin', that he would be the man of this house, and when the time came, he'd have to step up to the plate and help support this family. When we were in desperate times, he did exactly what I told him, in the best way that he knew how."

Shaniece wanted to say more to comfort her, but Monique had a good point. As Q's mother, she should've made sure her son held a level of morals and standards so that when he had begun looking for a job, it wouldn't have been one that would eventually lead to his death. Shaniece couldn't imagine allowing her child to hang out on the streets until the early morning, waiting for someone to approach him about purchasing illegal substances. The boy was hardly old enough to be left alone at the mall, let alone out on the streets full of troublemakers and dangers.

Shaniece looked toward Tatiana and Krystal for assistance.

"Monique," Krystal cut in, "can I ask you something?"

Monique wiped her eyes and nodded solemnly.

Krystal breathed deeply and asked, "Do you have a personal relationship with Jesus?"

Monique looked around the room at the three young girls and her shoulders slumped. "No, but I'd never really been exposed to one either." She shook her head. "My parents adopted Christianity as their religion of preference, but we never went to church or read the Bible. Although we had our own personal morals and values, growing strong in our religion wasn't at the top of our priority lists."

Shaniece nodded as if she understood as Krystal continued speaking to Monique. "Do you believe in the foundations of Christianity, such as Jesus being sent by God to die for our sins, only to raise three days later, so that when our earthly lives come to an end, we may have a chance to live eternally with Him in heaven?"

"I don't know," Monique whimpered helplessly. "I mean, how do I know that Christianity is the right religion? What if in actuality Buddha or Allah is the true god?"

Krystal hesitated, giving Tatiana a chance to jump in and help. "How is it that you have a chance to wake up every morning? Who helps you to keep this roof over your head? How is it that you can walk or drive down these dangerous streets on a daily basis and return without so much as a scratch to your knee? Who was it that has kept you for these last few weeks, when I know you've wanted to give up after Q's life was taken?"

Shaniece leaned in and whispered, "Who was it that your son continuously prayed to while he was out on those streets? Who was it that kept your son safe in His arms day after day, and night after night, until it was his time to go?"

"Certainly, it was Someone bigger than all of us. Someone who promised never to leave or forsake us. Someone who loves us beyond human comprehension. Someone who said that if we trust and believe in Him, He will give us eternal life with Him. All you have to do is believe," Krystal finished.

All four women had tears in their eyes as the three young girls, along with Monique, all remembered and realized how much God had done for them in their individual lives. How He cared for and loved them. How He'd kept them throughout each day and convicted their hearts when needed.

"I know," Monique said softly. "It's been Him. It's been Jesus all along." She wiped her eyes.

Shaniece held out her hand, offering it to Monique to take. "We'd like to pray with you, if that's okay?"

Monique answered by taking Shaniece's outstretched hand. The other two girls followed suit, and Shaniece led them in prayer, hoping that after today, Monique would come to believe God would continue to carry her through all of her trials and tribulations. She could make it through today, tomorrow, and every other day that she would be facing for the rest of her life.

Chapter 36

Devon threw his head back in exasperation as he noticed his visitors for the afternoon. He shook his head as he glared deeply into his mother's eyes, letting her know that if she was planning on bringing her pastor, she should have given him a heads-up. As he moved toward the table, he studied Reverend Simmons's attire and wondered why ministers always had to be decked out in their clerical garb when they visited inmates. It always baffled him, but it seemed to get God's chosen ones special treatment, so maybe they knew something he didn't.

His mother immediately gasped at the sight of his battered face once he reached the table. He knew she was going to delve into what had happened, but he didn't feel up to discussing it, and he'd be sure to let her know that.

"Devon, baby, what happened?" Yvonne asked as she tried to reach out to touch his face.

Devon pulled away. "Nothin'," he replied.

Yvonne frowned deeply. "Devon, how can you say nothing happened, with your eye blackened and your lip busted like that?"

"Ma, I only get a quick minute out here and I really don't wanna spend this visit talkin' 'bout somethin' that ain't important." Devon knew his words were harsh, especially since he knew how much his mother worried about him, but he'd been made fun of all week about the fight and how someone he hadn't seen in nearly two years came out of nowhere and jumped him. He'd been so fed up that he'd almost gotten in an altercation this morning, but Mitch had calmed him down before he could do something that would've landed him in the hole.

"Well, you remember Reverend Simmons, don't you?" Yvonne asked quietly.

Devon barely nodded.

"How have you been, young man?" Cedric asked.

Devon shrugged. "I'm makin' it."

"I brought Reverend Simmons with me today because I felt he needed to speak to you about what I've been trying to tell you since you were born."

Devon remained silent, knowing he didn't have anything to say in response to his mother's explanation of Cedric's presence. He honestly wanted to get up and leave, but with nowhere pleasurable to go, he decided he'd stay seated and halfway listen to what the preacher had to say.

"The last time I had a chance to speak with you," Cedric stated, "I asked you about you not having received salvation. I recall quite clearly you saying that you hadn't made such a change in your life due to the fact that if you did, there were some things you'd have to give up that you didn't want to let go of. Do you still feel that way?"

Devon shrugged and sat back in his seat. "Man, I'm so tired and confused right now that I don't even know how I feel about much of anything. All I know is that I'm sick of being up in here."

"You may not know it, Devon, but being confused could be a good thing," Cedric informed him. "It means your heart is searching for answers."

Devon shrugged again, as if he knew the assumption to be true, but he didn't want to discuss it further.

"I'm going to ask you a couple of questions, and I want you to think about them before you answer. Is that okay?" Cedric asked in a tone that suggested he would ask his questions whether Devon felt like answering them or not.

Devon shrugged once more, and Yvonne eyed her son, silently telling him to straighten up and show a little more respect than he was.

Cedric was obviously ignoring Devon's insolence as he continued speaking. "You do believe in God—as in the one, the only, true living God—right?"

Devon nodded. "And to answer any more of your questions, I also know about God's Son, Jesus, who was sent to die and rise again for my sins. I know that all I got to do is ask God to come into my heart and my life will be changed forever. I know that if I drop dead right now, I will most likely go to hell for the life I've been leading. I know all that stuff."

"And you still don't feel the need to change your life?" Yvonne questioned, nearing tears.

"Like I said before, I really don't know how I feel about anything." Devon shrugged as if he really couldn't care less about clearing his clouded mind.

Yvonne tossed a worried mother's look toward Cedric, who simply consoled her with his eyes. Devon watched as Cedric turned toward him and silently made unyielding eye contact. Devon knew breaking the stare would cause the reverend to believe that Devon felt threatened by his authority, but if he boldly held the contact, the reverend would think Devon was trying to be defiant by undermining his stature. Devon decided to hold the stare, but he blinked a couple of times when Cedric straightened his posture.

"What is it that you want out of your life?" Cedric questioned after a moment of silence.

Devon thought for a few seconds as he let the question permeate his brain. "I don't know. It's not like I really have a life, being up in here."

"Okay, if you weren't locked up right now," Cedric began, "what would you be doing?"

Devon chuckled, remembering that he'd been thinking about how he'd stop taking the simplest things in life for granted if his life could just return to normal. "Taking a walk around my 'hood."

"May I ask why?"

"'Cause I ain't never done it without being terrified of being arrested," Devon answered without hesitation. "I figure if I can walk around the block, just because I wanna enjoy the air, then life would seem normal."

"What is normal to you?" Cedric continued to question.

"Me bein' free," Devon responded, taken somewhat aback. He acted like the answer was clearly written across his forehead for Cedric to see. "Me bein' able to do whatever, whenever. Me livin' my life how I want to . . . without any limitations."

Cedric squinted his eyes before asking, "Son, do you truly understand the concept of being free?"

Devon shrugged. "What's there to understand? Being free is not havin' someone tell you when to go outside, when to eat, when to sleep. It's being able to see my mom—or even Shaniece—whenever I want, not when someone says I can be released to see them. It's being able to say what I want, without fear of being placed in solitary or being jumped. Well, I coulda said somethin' on the streets and got jumped, but at least I'd feel free enough to fight back."

Cedric listened attentively and nodded as Devon spoke. He sat in silence and contemplated his response before speaking. "Okay, you do understand the concept of being free, in the worldly sense. Now I'd like to know if you realize what it means to be *set free,* in a spiritual sense."

Devon dropped his shoulders in a heavy sigh and rolled his eyes toward his mother. Yvonne continued to sit in silence as she'd been doing for the last several minutes. Her glare told her son that he needed to hear what Cedric was trying to tell him. Yvonne had spent a portion of Devon's life trying to help him understand the love God had for him, but she hadn't been so successful. If there was anything her pastor could do to help her son see the light, Yvonne would be eternally grateful.

"To be set free means never having to worry about a thing." Cedric continued as if he couldn't care less if Devon wanted to listen to him or not. "It means allowing God total access to your mind, body, and spirit. Romans 12:1–2 says that we should offer our bodies as a living sacrifice, holy and pleasing unto the Lord; and in doing so, we should no longer conform to the patterns of the world, but we should be transformed by the renewing of our mind through Christ Jesus. That means because Jesus died for our sins and rose again so that we can have eternal life, we should die to ourselves and live for Him. When we sacrifice the pleasures of this world for Jesus, we are rewarded eternally. I tell you that nothing, not one physical thing in this world, can compare to what God has in store for those who give their lives to Him."

Cedric placed a Bible on the table and pushed it in Devon's direction. "I'd like you to have this."

Devon hesitantly stared at the Bible. "Why? What am I supposed to do with it?"

Before Cedric could respond, Yvonne blurted out, "Read it, Devon! You need to read it, for God's sake."

Devon stared at his mother in surprise. She seemed fed up with his blatant ignorance of where his life was headed, and Devon almost wanted to apologize.

"Sister Yvonne, you can't force the Word down his throat," Cedric told her in a nurturing manner. "This is why so many people refuse to seek God as the answer . . . because those trying to share the Gospel present themselves or the Word in a manner that turns people away from God. I know you're tired, and even more worried, but your job is to seek the Lord on his behalf, not to force him into doing it for himself."

Yvonne nodded and apologized to Devon. Devon remained silent, amazed at how calm and patient Cedric was being with his mother, and even with him. He wondered if God had anything to do with that.

Cedric again motioned toward the Bible and said, "I've marked some scriptures for your reference. I think that they would help you better understand why your mother's so worried about you and why God is the answer for anything you're going through, including this very experience." He jabbed his finger into the table.

Without speaking, Devon reached up and placed his palms against the top of the Bible and slowly pulled it into his lap.

"We have to get going now, but I will make plans to visit you soon," Cedric promised, and Devon knew that he could accept the pastor's word as truth. "Oh, and before I let it slip my mind, Shaniece wanted me to send her love and let you know that she's still praying for you," he informed Devon, not surprising him. "Would you like for me to give her a message from you?"

A moment passed, and Devon thought about what he wanted Shaniece to know. There was so much that passed through his mind. He wanted her to know that he still loved her and that he wanted to be with her without restrictions. He wanted to tell her that if he could turn back the hands of time and make right all the wrongs he'd done during the time they had known each other, and even before they'd met, he would. He wanted her to understand that he wanted what was best for her, and if it meant giving her up, then so be it. He needed her to always remember that he'd never forget how she'd changed his outlook on life in just being herself, even when he pretended to be someone he was not.

"Just tell her I said . . . thank you," Devon finally answered.

Cedric nodded as he rose from his seat and helped Yvonne up as well. "Now, if you ever need to talk, feel free to give me a call at home or at the church, *anytime,*" he said as he handed Devon a business card.

Devon accepted the card. "Thank you," he said.

He got up and turned to leave, but before he could, Yvonne reached out and grabbed him. She pulled him into her arms and hugged him as if her life depended on it. Devon could hear her heavy breaths against his chest and knew she was fighting tears. He closed his eyes as he relished the embrace, knowing he needed it just as much as she did.

Yvonne pulled away and wiped the tears that tempted her eyes. "Take care of yourself, Devon. And please, please read this book," she begged as she gripped the Bible, which he still held in his hands. "I love you."

"I love you, too, Mama," he said. He nodded toward Cedric before making his exit.

Chapter 37

For Christ's love compels us, because we are convinced that one died for all, and therefore all died. And he died for all, that those who live should no longer live for themselves but for him who died for them and was raised again. . . . Therefore, if anyone is in Christ, he is a new creation; the old has gone, the new has come. . . . We implore you on Christ's behalf: Be reconciled to God. For He made Him who knew no sin to be sin for us, that we might become the righteousness of God.

Devon narrowed his eyes and pulled the Bible closer to his face. His eyes were tired from reading all day, but for some strange reason, he couldn't put the book down. It had taken him a week to even open the Bible that Cedric had given him during his visit. But out of pure boredom, Devon had cracked open the pages and searched for the highlighted passages the reverend had recommended he read. As he finished reading the fifth chapter of the book of 2 Corinthians, Devon moved on to the sixth chapter. He'd begun reading the New Testament, per Cedric's request through a note stuck inside the Bible. But he knew that as soon as he finished, he would backtrack to the old books of the Bible, just to see how everything started. He was so intrigued, as if everything that he had read was fantasy. In his soul, though, he felt its truth.

All throughout the Gospels, Devon was amazed at the wonders of Jesus' life. The Savior's conception and birth, and the miracles He performed, fascinated him. He wondered how the blind could see, the crippled were healed, and the unbelievers believed—all from just following this man. He was confused by the torment and crucifixion, and he couldn't understand why anyone would want to go through such turmoil just to save the lives of others, some of whom could care less about His life. But at the same time, Devon was thankful, because he realized that the only thing that could have kept him for the past several years, while he ran the streets, was God's grace and mercy.

His mind wandered back to the day his mother found out he was dealing drugs. She'd caught him standing on a street corner one day as she came home from work for her lunch break. When she pulled her car up next to him, he didn't even bother to pretend that he was just hanging out.

"Why aren't you in school?" had been the first words out of her mouth.

Devon had shrugged and answered honestly, "'Cause I'm workin'."

"Workin' for Kane?" Yvonne had asked for clarification, as if she already didn't know.

"We need food" had been Devon's reply.

"I don't want you doing this," Yvonne stated, but they both knew there was hardly anything she could do to stop him.

That same evening, they argued about the new career Devon had chosen, and in the end, Yvonne gave up trying. About two weeks after Devon stopped going to school, he came home from his assigned street and found a small backpack with a week's worth of clothing in it. He banged on the door of his mother's home and pleaded with her to let him in. Yvonne wouldn't even come to the window. Devon recalled sleeping on the front porch that night, but he promised himself that he wouldn't do so again.

Staying with Kane the year preceding his death afforded Devon the opportunity to see what it would be like to live a more luxurious lifestyle, but he also witnessed just how dangerous the job could be. He recalled so many times when Kane's property was the victim of a drive-by shooting in the middle of the night. The first time Devon had been shot at, he stood on the corner trying to sell crack to a neighborhood friend, when the young boy used his older brother's gun in order to get out of paying him. Devon immediately snatched back the merchandise before taking off, full speed, to avoid the bullet. It was the scariest day of his life, and when he told Kane about it, his mentor simply said, "That's the game, li'l homie." At the time, Devon had thought about his mother and the comfort she would've given him. But now, he thought about how God had saved him that day. He could've died out on the streets, like Q or Antwon. The times he'd been locked up, caught in cross fire, and participated in street fights—all for the sake of keeping his business in tact—seemed significant now, because God had spared his life on all occasions.

The overwhelming feeling in his heart couldn't be explained as he continued reading the words printed on the pages of one of the oldest books in history. The recreation bell sounded, and Devon almost didn't want to go outside, but since he had to, he carried his new companion with him.

"I see you really into that, huh?" Mitch chuckled.

Devon only smiled as he placed the book under his right arm and headed toward the courtyard. Instead of joining Mitch and Raquel in their usual game of three-on-three, Devon sat against the fence and opened the Bible so that he could continue reading:

As God's fellow workers we urge you not to receive God's grace in vain. For he says, "in the time of my favor I heard you, and in the day of salvation I helped you." I tell you, now is the time of God's favor, now is the day of salvation.

Devon continued reading, but that scripture remained in his mind, replaying itself over and over. *"I tell you, now is the time of God's favor, now is the day of salvation."* As he continued on to read the subsequent scriptures that described the hardships of God's servants, he wondered if he should take that scripture literally. If so, that meant today should be the day he turned his life around. *Am I ready for that?* he almost asked aloud.

As he pondered that question, he continued reading: *Do not be yoked together with unbelievers. For what do righteousness and wickedness have in common? Or what fellowship can light have with darkness? What harmony is there between Christ and Belial? What does a believer have in common with an unbeliever?*

Immediately he thought of Shaniece as he read 2 Corinthians 6:14–15. She was a believer and he was not, he pondered. To Devon, that meant that she was wrong to even think about having a relationship with him. The Bible compared their relationship as if Devon was wicked and Shaniece was righteous, and they should never mix.

That's why we didn't work. We could love each other all day, but if we're not equal in this faith thing, then what does it mean? he questioned himself. *Apparently, nothing,* he decided.

Devon was slowly beginning to understand why his life was as messed up as it was. He was a young black man with absolutely nothing going for him. He had become a statistic—he had no job, no money; he was locked up, without steady faith and almost no hope for the future. Devon hadn't even thought about what he would do once he got out of prison. It was as if he thought he would be incarcerated for the rest of his life, and maybe that was the truth. Maybe once he was released, he'd be arrested again for trying to regain control of his business, or for attempting to murder the trespasser in his neighborhood. Both crimes had crossed his mind on more than one occasion. He realized that he was so willing to do whatever he had to do in order to remain a prominent fixture in his neighborhood, and if it meant returning to prison, once released, then so be it. Now guilt consumed him as he thought about all the trouble he'd caused the inhabitants of Riverside when he thought he had been protecting them. He was the reason there was a crack house down the street from his lavish townhouse. Because of his business, some of his high-school friends, whose futures had been as bright as the sun, were now bums who preferred doing nothing if the activity would not reward them a quick fix. Due to his desire to live a more abundant life than the one he lived as a child, he'd disappointed and worried his mother to tears. He had lost the only girl he'd thought about changing his life around for, because he had decided that she wasn't worth the change. Apparently, there wasn't anyone or anything that meant enough to him that would cause him to want to change.

Then he read the scripture again: *Be reconciled to God.*

"'Be reconciled to God,'" he whispered aloud, with a heavy breath. "'Be reconciled to God.' Am I ready for that?" he questioned again. "'Be reconciled to God.' 'Be reconc—'"

Suddenly darkness spread over him, and the sunlight that had allowed him to read the words within the Bible was overshadowed. He looked up and caught a quick glimpse of Rip's large body, along with his three accomplices, standing over him just before Rip rammed his fist into Devon's face. The force knocked Devon over and caused the Bible he'd been reading to fall from his grasp. Immediately Devon tried to stand to his feet and fight back, but it was no use. The four men began to charge toward him relentlessly, aiming with their fists and feet.

"You wanna run yo' mouth 'bout me!" Devon heard Rico seething before he shoved his heel into Devon's groin.

He felt like a paralytic who could do nothing for himself as he lay crumpled on the ground while his assailants continued to assault him. Soon Mitch and Raquel joined the altercation, trying at least to tame Rip and two of his companions. The sirens began to blare around the courtyard as Devon saw his friends throwing punch after punch, while Rico was now kneeling over him, spitting curses and launching blows as if he had enough energy to last a lifetime. Then he proceeded to bang Devon's head against the concrete ground a couple of times before releasing him. Devon hollered in response.

"Be reconciled to God."

His head pounded relentlessly, but he heard those words replay in his mind just before his attention was drawn toward Rico, who jabbed a makeshift blade into his side. "Aaahhhh!" he screamed in agony, drawing more attention to the fight.

Rico stood up and sneered, "Guess you won't be gettin' back to yo' business no time soon." He laughed, but before he could turn away, Rico was grabbed by two officers.

"Well, that's strike three, Rico," Devon barely heard one of them say as he continued to scream. "Twenty-five to life is what you just bargained for."

Rico sputtered curses as he tried, but failed, to kick Devon in his stomach as he was being apprehended. "Murkin' this fool was just about worth it."

Devon writhed in pain as his trembling hand felt for the weapon that was shoved into his flesh. All he felt was blood, and he knew he'd feel the same if he reached toward the back of his head. He heard prisoners standing around him; some were making compassionate comments, while others mocked him.

"Dang, Big D, you can't go out like this," one said.

"Man, that fool deserved it wit' all that cockiness," another commented. "Big D ain't so big at all now that somebody done took him down a few notches."

Devon moaned as the pain spread throughout his body, and he gave up on moving. He lay still, as if comatose, and waited for officers to have him transported to the medical facility.

"Father God, I ask that you put your arms of protection around this child," Devon heard a calming tone speak over his body. He tried to open his eyes to see who it was, but when he did, it caused his head to pound with excruciating pain. "Heal his body and make him whole again . . . not just physically, but spiritually as well. Give him a mind to want to change and live his life for you. Whatever it takes, Lord," the man pleaded. "Show him your grace and mercy. Now is the time of your favor, Lord. Today is the day of Devon's salvation. Please, just give him one more chance."

"Now is the time of God's favor, now is the day of salvation," the scriptures replayed in Devon's mind. *"Be reconciled to God."*

"That's enough, Lee," another guard spoke up. "Prayin' ain't gon' do much for this one."

Devon's breaths became short and quick, and he felt himself losing consciousness. Just before he blacked out, he heard Lee whisper, "God is a miracle worker. Just believe, son."

Chapter 38

Shaniece nearly tripped over her own feet as she rushed to her father's SUV. She heard her mother telling her to be careful, but she wished the rest of her family would follow her lead and rush as if someone's life depended on it. *Devon's life does depend on it,* she thought.

Yvonne had just called the Simmons home while they'd been enjoying their dinner. She informed Cedric that she'd received a call from Emory University Hospital Midtown, telling her that her son was in their intensive care unit. Devon had been stabbed and had received severe head trauma; he would be undergoing emergency surgery. Reportedly, removing the blade from his side would be risky, but leaving it in place would cause uncontrollable hemorrhaging that could possibly result in the death of her only child. When Cedric had passed the news on to his family, Shaniece had nearly choked on her steak.

Now she waited impatiently in the car as her siblings walked out of the house, with their parents behind them. Shaniece wanted to reach toward the steering wheel and give the horn a harsh push, but she wasn't in such a hurry that she'd lost her common sense. So she remained seated, with her arms folded and legs shaking, as she bit down hard on her bottom lip in order to keep from crying.

Cedric pulled out of the garage and placed his emergency flashers on so that getting to the hospital would take less time as he sped down the road. Shaniece couldn't believe Devon had been hurt like this. She wondered what had happened to cause such an altercation to occur between him and whoever had been angry enough to stab him in his side. Had he been provoked? Or was he the one to provoke his attacker? Was this his fault or was it his destiny? Was this how his life was supposed to end?

But he's not saved yet, Shaniece cried inside. She hadn't had a chance to see him turn his life around, and that's what she'd been praying for over the last several months. Though she hadn't been able to see or talk to him since Valentine's Day, she remained on her knees on his behalf. Anytime she could shoot up a quick prayer for Devon while in class, while studying for a test, or while enjoying lunch, she would. And when she had enough free time at home, she wasn't unfamiliar with lying prostrate before the Lord, crying out to Him to continue working on Devon's heart, mind, and spirit.

Her father had said that after visiting with Devon, he held hope for the young man's soul. "He sat there and listened to what I had to say," Cedric had informed Shaniece last week. "And he took the Bible I gave him. I'm sure with all the free time he has, he'll be reading it."

But what if he hasn't? she continued to worry. Devon was a stubborn soul; Shaniece had learned that after he'd given up on changing his life for the better. If he didn't want to do something, he wouldn't do it, regardless of the incentives that came along with it. Just the thought of him being without salvation, and possibly on his deathbed, brought tears to Shaniece's eyes.

"Niecey, are you okay?" Keith asked quietly when he noticed her tears.

Shaniece silently nodded as she reached into her purse for her ringing cell phone.

"Hey, girl," Tatiana sang when Shaniece answered.

"Hi, Tati," Shaniece replied softly.

"Girl, what's wrong?"

Shaniece could never hide anything from Tatiana. Even through the phone, Tatiana could hear her discontentment. "Devon's in the hospital. He's been stabbed and he's not in good condition."

"What hospital is he in?"

"Emory," Shaniece replied. "We're on our way now."

"Okay," Tatiana said. "So am I."

"Thank you, Tati. And please pray for him."

"Of course," Tatiana answered before ending the call.

Shaniece was happy that Tatiana would be there with her. She knew her family would be more concerned with keeping Yvonne's emotions under control. Shaniece would need the extra comfort from her best friend as she waited for news concerning Devon's condition.

Once they reached the hospital, they were directed toward a waiting room, where Yvonne was already resting, until a doctor could come and speak with them.

"Sister Yvonne," Cedric greeted her.

She looked up at him with tears in her eyes. "Thank you for coming, Pastor." She proceeded to hug each individual. She seemed to hold on to Shaniece a second longer before releasing her. Then she gave them a quick update. "Devon is already in the operating room and undergoing surgery to remove the blade. They've already done some work on his head. He's lost a lot of blood." Her tears began to flow as she added, "They don't know if he's gonna make it."

Shaniece gasped and sank down into the nearest chair as her father took on the responsibility of reassuring his parishioner. "Doctors don't have the final say. God is in control, now and forever, and if it's His desire for your son to live through this, then it is done." He took her hand and then reached out for his wife. "Let's pray."

Shaniece could barely stand, so she leaned against her brother for support as her father prayed for Devon. Shaniece inwardly whispered a prayer of her own, beseeching God to have mercy on Devon and allow him at least one more chance in life. Shaniece knew there was so much he had to live for, even if it meant he'd be living behind bars for the next several years. Just like there was work for Shaniece and her friends to do outside of the prison, there was work for Devon to do while he was incarcerated.

Before the prayer ended, Tatiana, Craig, Justin, and Krystal joined the circle. Shaniece released her tears, out of happiness that her friends were there in support of her. She praised God for the fact that they didn't hesitate to pray for Devon. When they all said "Amen," Shaniece hugged each of her friends. Craig took Keith's position as Shaniece's comforter as they all rested in the waiting room.

"Thank you, guys, for coming," Shaniece said as she wiped away several tears. "I must look a mess."

"Girl, you're fine," Tatiana assured her, handing Shaniece a tissue. "Everything's gonna be okay."

Shaniece nodded. "Did you pick all of them up?" she asked, wanting to get her mind off Devon.

Tatiana pursed her lips and nodded her head. "I called Craig, because I figured you wouldn't mind him being here for you," she replied as Craig nodded. "But then Krystal called me about going shopping, so I had to fill her in, and she wanted to come for the ride. Then Justin called to ask me about going out tonight and I told him about Devon, because I didn't know how long I'd be up here. And he asked to come along for support, even though he barely has a clue as to who Devon is."

Shaniece smiled toward Justin and he slyly winked at her. She figured he recalled having to comfort her that night after Bible Study and figured Devon had been the reason then. She silently thanked him for keeping her secret.

"I'm glad you all are here," Shaniece told them. "But you don't have to waste the rest of your evening here. Devon just went into surgery, so there's no telling how late we'll be here."

Craig shook his head. "It's no problem, Niecey. I'm good for an all-nighter."

"Yeah, girl," Tatiana agreed. "Tomorrow's Saturday, and my day was pretty much free anyway. With the exception of choir practice, I don't have anything to do."

Justin suddenly looked offended. "Oh, so I guess weekends aren't our thing anymore?" he questioned Tatiana.

"Tati, don't cancel your plans just to stay here," Shaniece told her best friend.

Tatiana sucked her teeth and pushed up against Justin's chest. "Girl, please, Justin knows we didn't have nothin' planned for tomorrow."

He smiled. "Yeah, she's right."

They shared a lighthearted laugh and then settled in quietness as they waited for good news. A while later, Shaniece noticed Monique come into the waiting room, along with a rather tall, attractive young woman. Monique immediately noticed Shaniece and walked toward her.

"Hi, Monique." Shaniece smiled weakly as she stood to greet Q's mother. "How are you?"

Monique smiled as she reached out to hug Shaniece. She then greeted Tatiana and Krystal, then spoke a quiet "hello" to the guys. "I'm good. Not too happy about being in this hospital, though," she said to Shaniece. "I came to see D. I got a call from one of my son's friends and he told me he'd been stabbed."

Shaniece struggled to keep her tears at bay. "I know. He's why we're all here," she said softly. She motioned toward her family, seated across the room. Her father was still praying with Yvonne. "We've been here with Devon's mother for almost forty-five minutes and haven't heard anything. But we know that he's still in surgery." She noticed the woman who'd walked in with Monique had a reflective expression on her face. Shaniece looked at the woman and smiled.

"Oh," Monique suddenly spoke. "This is Trina Williams. Trina, this is Shaniece Simmons. She went to school with Q."

"Nice to meet you." Shaniece was slightly taken aback when Trina simply stared at her as if she were an alien from another planet. It took several moments, but the girl finally mustered enough courtesy to reply.

"You too," she said, and then she moved to a seat in the far corner of the room.

Monique gave Shaniece an apologetic smile. "She's been solemn since I called her about this," she whispered. "She and D used to date, and she loved him very much."

Shaniece shot a quick glance toward Trina, who was sitting with her hands clasped in front of her and her eyes closed tightly as if she was praying.

"She's taking this extremely hard, and I don't really know how to comfort her," Monique continued.

Shaniece gulped before she answered. "Just tell her to keep praying for him like she's doing right now," she whispered tearfully, thinking of how Trina must feel, meeting her at a time like this. "God will work it out."

Monique nodded as she moved toward where Trina sat. Shaniece sank back into her seat, allowing Tatiana to comfort her this time.

"She knows who I am." Shaniece spoke quietly as she watched Monique whisper in Trina's ear. "That's why she was looking at me like that. I feel like *the other woman,*" she confessed.

"Don't worry about it." Tatiana spoke in the same quiet manner. "Don't even focus on her or your past with Devon; just remember why we're here. He needs all of the prayers he can get right now."

Shaniece tensed when she saw Trina look in her direction as Monique continued to whisper. Their eyes locked, and Shaniece felt as if their souls were communicating. The harsh look in Trina's eyes was overshadowed by the hurt that was in her heart. They knew nothing about each other; yet they had so much in common. They'd both been hurt by someone they loved dearly, and it was bringing them closer—without them even knowing it. Trina stood and moved toward Shaniece; there was a determined sparkle in her eyes.

"I know this chick ain't 'bout to start no drama in this hospital," Tatiana said, barely moving her lips. Her comforting tone had suddenly become harsh, and her stance was guarded, as if she thought Trina was about to confront her.

"Baby, calm down," Justin told her, already sensing her temper rising.

Trina stood before them and gazed at Shaniece. "Could we talk in private, please?"

For some reason, Shaniece didn't hesitate in agreeing. She told her friends she'd be back and then walked out of the room, with Trina behind her. They stood in the hall, which was bustling with doctors and nurses—all of them would be working late into the evening as they cared for helpless patients. The two women were quiet for a moment, but Trina soon stated her reason for the confrontation.

"I hate to say it, but it's a relief to be able to finally put a face with the name," she said as she seemed to size up Shaniece. "Since D and I broke up that night when he was supposed to see you, I've wondered who is the girl that made him want to give up someone like me. I mean, I figured we had a good, steady relationship. We dated for a year, lived together for several months. We had our drama, but with the lifestyle D was living, it was bound to happen. I thought we would last forever, but even if you weren't in the picture, I don't think that dream would've come true."

"I'm sorry," Shaniece offered. "If I would've known from the beginning, I would've never even thought about dating him. I promise, I'm not the type to step in on someone else's territory."

Trina managed to chuckle in response. "I can tell. And I don't hold anything against you, because I know you had no idea what was going on," she assured. "D was my life while we were together. It took us breaking up for me to realize that my focus on him was my downfall."

Shaniece nodded in understanding. She had experienced the same thing while she'd been with Devon. She had been so focused on trying to get him to change so that they could be together that she'd lost focus on what was most important—him changing so that he could lead a better lifestyle in Christ. It wasn't until they stopped seeing each other that she realized her mistake, and she thanked God for the wake-up call.

"I've been praying for D and our neighborhood," Trina continued. "And when Monique told me what you said to her, it really reassured me that I was doing the right thing. I didn't call you out here to confront you about D or anything. I just wanted to say thank you, because I'm really new at this praying and faith thing, so sometimes I'm not sure if it's working."

Shaniece smiled, almost out of relief that Trina wasn't about to tell her off for stealing her boyfriend and ruining her chances at a happy future. She was thankful that she'd been able to encourage the young woman in her walk with God. "You're welcome. This has been hard for me too," she admitted. She felt the need to explain. "Devon's relationship with me was extremely short, but in the time that I got to know him, I fell for him. In the process, I tried to change him, and it didn't work, because I was basically giving him an ultimatum. He saw that his community was in danger and decided that getting his streets in order was more important than our relationship. He felt I deserved better, and that he was only holding me back from living my life. He was right, but I didn't realize it until later. Recently I've been praying that Devon gets right with God before it's too late. I've had my doubts as well, even now, but I'm still praying and hoping that God doesn't take him like this." She folded her arms. "I saw you praying, and it gave me a little more hope, so that's why I told Monique to give you that message. I'm glad it did some good."

"It did," Trina replied. "I guess being with D has allowed both of us to connect with God in a way we never have before, huh?"

"I never thought about it like that, but I guess you're right," Shaniece agreed. "Before Devon, I was just going through the motions of being a Christian. My heart was after the wrong things, and my prayers weren't really personal anymore. Devon changed all of that."

"Maybe we owe him more than we think," Trina said just as a doctor strolled past them and into the waiting room, where everyone else was waiting.

Immediately they followed her, and Shaniece hoped she came bearing good news.

Chapter 39

"Lord, I stand in your presence, wanting you and needing you and . . . I am here and I surrender all of me so I can see. . . . Your will is where I desire to be. Take all of me. . . ."

Devon could hear the voice as if the angel singing were sitting right in front of his face. But as he looked around, he saw no one. All he saw was an open field of grass. No trees, no flowers, no other life whatsoever. He had no idea where he was, but it almost didn't matter. The field was wide open, and there were no restrictions; that's all that mattered to him. For once, since being locked up, his heart held no inkling of fear of what might happen to him. This place, as unfamiliar as it was, provided him with the peace he'd been searching for. He heard the songstress again and the voice became more familiar. Though quavering as if she was crying, she sounded just as beautiful as she did the first day he'd heard her sing to her Heavenly Father.

"Shaniece," he whispered.

He searched his surroundings once more and realized, again, that he was alone. He rested in the field and wondered how long he'd been here. He really couldn't remember when or how he got to this place, but it felt like he'd been there for a while.

Suddenly dark clouds hovered over the field, drawing Devon's attention toward the once crystal clear skies. He looked around for shelter, but found none. *Great,* he thought. *I'm stranded in the rain.* He searched the heavens as the clouds became so dense he could hardly see the sun that had warmed him a few seconds earlier. Then lightning struck, and in the flash, Devon saw a younger version of himself, standing on the corner of one of the busiest intersections in his neighborhood. He was making sale after sale. In between sales, he searched the block for lurking police officers. As he relived the moment, his heart raced and his palms became sweaty. It reminded him that he had lived in fear every single day that he stood on that block. Suddenly the image disappeared. Seconds later, a roar of thunder followed.

He heard the words to the unfamiliar song again. They spoke of God being the light in the darkness of night. The voice that sang this time was different, but hardly unfamiliar. It had soothed him to sleep many nights as a child and had kept him sane in those times when he was losing his mind.

"Mama!" he called out, and his voice echoed as if he was in a large building with cement walls. There was no response.

Another flash of lightning followed and he caught a vision of his mother crying. It made him remember the many nights he'd come home, long after midnight, to find her asleep on the couch with remnants of tears she'd shed the nights before. The image showed him how worried his mother had been for him for most of his life, and it placed a heavy burden on his heart as thunder roared throughout the field.

With the third strike of light came an image of Shaniece on her knees praying, almost relentlessly. He knew it was his name upon her lips as she looked upward with tears streaming down her face. He shook his head as he thought of all the drama he'd put her through at the start of their relationship. All the lies he'd told and the promises he'd made that were never carried out. They haunted his mind as he watched Shaniece's image disappear with another clap of thunder.

Lightning flashed again and he immediately was brought back to the night he and Trina broke up. The arguing and her tears hadn't stopped him from walking out the door. But when the image quickly shifted, and he saw Trina standing at an altar inside a church, his mouth dropped in surprise. Her hands were lifted and a woman was standing before her with her hand placed against Trina's shoulder. Trina was mumbling, and Devon figured she was repeating whatever the lady was saying in her ear. The image wasn't new to him, but he would've never guessed that Trina would be on the receiving end of salvation. He suddenly realized that his decision to walk out that night had changed her life. Immediately the image faded at the sound of thunder.

This time, he heard Shaniece's voice blend in perfect harmony with several female voices as they admitted to God that they were lost and broken without Him. They sounded so heavenly as they sang of how much they needed Him, but Devon could hardly enjoy listening as another strike of lightning sent him into a fit of tears. No matter how hard he tried, he couldn't take his eyes off Q's lifeless body lying in front of the corner store. He saw his friend's chest slowly rise and fall as his wide eyes stared into the heavens. Devon couldn't believe that he'd been the cause of the young boy being murdered so callously. He could use the excuse that Q and his mother needed the money—as he'd done when he began working for Kane—but now that didn't seem like such a good reason for a fourteen-year-old boy to be selling crack when he should've been in school.

Without realizing it, Devon had sent Q on the same path he decided to take when he was the boy's age. The only difference was Q hadn't lived long enough to make a change.

Devon wiped his tears and squinted toward the image when he realized Q's mouth was moving slowly as if he was talking to someone. It took a moment, but Devon was able to make out the phrase: *"God, save me . . . please."* A second later, Devon watched as Q stopped breathing and his spirit was lifted from his body into the dark, cloudless skies.

Shaniece's voice stood alone once again as she sang of how gracious God was and how He made her life worth living. The image of Q disappeared as quickly as it had come as thunder sounded once more. Devon continued to cry, but he felt joy in his heart for his young friend, who had apparently been shown God's grace in the last moments of his life.

Devon used to wonder how he made it through some of the situations he had gotten himself into throughout his life. The times when he'd been shot or beaten. The times when he'd misplaced some of Kane's merchandise and survived having a gun shoved into his temple as a threat on his life by the very man he looked up to as a father. The times when the cops searched him from top to bottom and somehow couldn't find the gun tucked away on his person, or when the dogs never detected the drugs hidden within his clothes. The times he'd been the one to threaten someone's life or to give an enemy severe wounds in order to keep his business running without trouble. He never understood how he got by in those times of trouble, but now he didn't have to wonder anymore. The song that he heard in his head, and the words upon Q's lips, said it all. God's mercy, along with those who cared enough to stay on their knees, had kept him for twenty years.

His eyes clouded with tears as he repeated Q's plea. "God, save me . . . please."

With each repetition of the phrase, the sky became clearer. And he heard the voices sing once more. *"Lord, have mercy; Lord, have mercy . . . have mercy, have mercy."*

Shaniece wiped her eyes and smiled toward Yvonne. "I haven't sung that song in a while."

Yvonne nodded. "That's definitely one of my favorites," she spoke of Kirk Franklin's "The Appeal."

"You ladies sounded wonderful. I'm sure God and Devon were pleased," Cedric complimented.

Tatiana looked toward Krystal and laughed. "They should be. I don't think we've sounded like that before."

"That was God's touch," Natalie replied.

Shaniece looked toward Devon, who had yet to awake after his surgery. He had bandages wrapped around his head, and the stands that surrounded him fed fluids into his body. If Shaniece pulled back the covers that hid Devon's body, she'd take notice of the stitches that held the large wound in his side together. It had been about an hour since the doctor had informed them that Devon's surgery was complete. He'd had a few setbacks while under the knife, but he'd made it. She was still monitoring his vitals, so they wouldn't be able to see him just yet. While they'd been waiting, Trina introduced herself to Yvonne, and Yvonne requested that the young woman join with them in praying as they continued to wait. Thankfully, about thirty minutes after that, they'd been given permission to visit Devon, even though he was still unconscious. At first, the doctor refused to allow all of the visitors in at once, but once Cedric spoke with the woman privately, stressing the fact that they would like to pray over his body as a unit, she permitted his request.

From her position next to Yvonne, Shaniece noticed water seeping through Devon's closed eyes. She stepped closer to the hospital bed and reached out to touch his face as the first tear became visible.

"He's crying," she said softly, gaining everyone's attention.

"Crying?" Keith looked skeptical. "He could be sweatin', Niecey. It is kinda hot in here."

"I know tears when I see them, Keith," Shaniece shot back. "And sweat doesn't pour from your eyes."

"S—sa—save . . . me."

Trina fell on her knees and scooted toward the bed as if hearing Devon speak was about to give her a heart attack. Immediately Cedric began to pray.

"Devon," Yvonne called his name, almost frantically.

In response, Devon muttered the phrase again. "God," he breathed. "Save . . . me, please."

"Oh, Jesus," Yvonne spoke, nearing tears. "Please, Jesus," she pleaded.

Devon continued to whisper the phrase over and over again as tears ran down his brown cheeks. His family and friends began to encourage him, though he was still unaware of his surroundings.

"Yes, Devon, receive Him!" Shaniece cried as Trina croaked, "Help him, Lord."

The Spirit filled the room as even Rainelle and Keith joined in the prayer that was slowly pulling Devon into consciousness and toward eternal salvation. Justin and Craig joined hands and began forming the prayer circle as Devon's cry persisted. Each individual prayed his or her own prayer with such persistence that Devon's tears seemed to flow more freely. Fifteen minutes of corporate prayer ended when Devon seemed to have a breakthrough.

"Thank you." He breathed the words out.

Yvonne moved toward the head of the bed, where she'd been sitting earlier. She reached out toward her son, and he gazed at her like he never had before. Shaniece could see the mixture of the emotions, regret and appreciation, in Devon's eyes as he connected with his mother.

"Devon," Yvonne said softly. "How are you feeling?"

Devon smiled and shrugged. "Good . . . great and saved."

"Oh, thank you, Jesus!" Yvonne cried out with raised hands. She began to shout in place as she continued to praise God.

Cedric chuckled. "Sister Yvonne, I know this is a long-awaited prayer answered, but please don't have us kicked out of this room."

Yvonne slowly calmed down, but tears still filled her eyes as she repeatedly whispered, "Thank you, God."

Shaniece could hardly stop smiling as she gazed at Devon, who slowly raised himself up to a seated position. He seemed so different now than he had when she last saw him. His muscles seemed more defined, his face lined with fatigue, but his eyes were filled with joy. Aside from his physical attributes, she noticed how warm and sincere his spirit felt as his eyes locked with hers.

"Shaniece." He smiled as he spoke her name. "It's good to see you."

When he motioned for her to come closer to him, Shaniece nervously studied her surroundings. Her father nodded as if giving his permission, and when she spotted Trina sitting next to Monique, the young woman simply shrugged. Then she glanced toward Craig, who was standing behind her. They'd been spending a lot of time together lately and she didn't want him to feel threatened by Devon's actions, no matter how passive. Craig's eyes showed no doubt or fear, so Shaniece slowly moved to the spot opposite where Yvonne stood. She and Yvonne took Devon's outstretched hands and waited for him to speak.

"It's good to see all of you. It's been hard to be really happy bein' behind bars all day, every day," Devon admitted. "But seeing all of you brings me unexplainable joy. I heard your prayers and your song." He looked between Shaniece and Yvonne. "But it wasn't just you two," he observed. His eyes slowly traveled around the room and he searched the faces of those unfamiliar to him.

"That would be Tatiana and Krystal," Shaniece replied, pointing toward her girlfriends. Then she introduced the rest of her friends. "And that's Justin . . . and Craig."

Surprisingly, Devon didn't flinch at the mention of the guy he'd been in competition with. "I appreciate y'all bein' here. Thank you for believin' in me," he said to them. "For believin' in God for me. For prayin' for me like my life depended on it, 'cause it really did." He looked around the room, then chuckled softly. "Man, Trina, I can't say I ain't surprised to see you here, but I heard your prayers for me too."

"Well, you know, when I have a little time, I like to slip one in there for the people I love." Trina smiled wearily.

Devon nodded and then looked at Monique. Shaniece knew he hadn't seen her since he'd been incarcerated, so the apology in his eyes was of no surprise. "I'm so sorry, Monique. I never meant for anything bad to happen to Q."

"I know, D," Monique interjected. "I don't blame you. It's my fault. I should've—"

He shook his head. "Monique, neither of us should blame ourselves," he admitted. "God had His hand over Q the entire time. He's definitely in a better place."

"How do you know?" Monique squinted as if she didn't believe him.

He hesitated as if he wasn't sure how he knew where Q's soul resided, but his confidence returned when he replied, "Trust me and believe that God does perform miracles. I'm *living* proof."

Yvonne's tears continued to flow as she listened to her son speak about the major change in his life, and Shaniece couldn't help but rejoice with her because she realized that all of their prayers had been answered. She had been wrong all along. She wasn't sent into Devon's life simply to present him to Christ. It was evident that not only had God saved Devon, but he had used him as a vessel to promote spiritual growth in the lives of her and her family and friends. Her mind traveled back to the day she met him in the grocery store. It was because of their meeting that Shaniece's fervor for serving God and reaching his people had been restored. She had discovered her divine purpose in life through Devon, and she praised God for their blessed meeting.

Group Discussion Questions

1. What was your favorite part of this story? Why?

2. If there was one outcome of a scene or event that you could change, which would it be? How would you change it, and why?

3. Why do you feel Devon did not immediately reveal his true self to Shaniece when they first met?

4. Shaniece's parents and friends willed her not to start a relationship with Devon for several reasons, but mainly because he was not Christian. 2 Corinthians 6:14 reads, "Do not be unequally yoked with unbelievers. . . ." How important do you think it is for a couple to be spiritually connected under the same belief system?

5. Did you believe Devon's vow to change for Shaniece was out of love or desperation to keep her within his reach? Why do you believe Shaniece took his word for truth even after his past transgressions?

6. Craig's infatuation with Shaniece seemed overbearing at times. How do you feel about his attraction toward her? Do you feel as if the saying "Nice guys finish last" is illustrated here? If you had to make a choice for her, would you choose Craig or Devon as her mate? Why?

7. Devon's absence in the community led to chaos in the streets. Would you say Devon's presence and actions within the community truly held things together? If so, in what way? If not, why don't you believe so?

8. Mitch tried to introduce Devon to a group of guys who would "protect" him during his sentence. How do you feel about prison gangs? More specifically, how did you feel about the particular group that sought Devon?

9. Q's interaction with Shaniece was very brief, but extremely impactful. Do you truly believe that Q accepted Christ before it was too late? How do you feel about the belief, many Christians hold, concerning accepting Christ just before your last breath and being rewarded eternal life?

10. Shaniece was determined to change Devon in order to be with him. How permanent do you think change is when it's done for someone or something else instead of one's self?

11. Trina made a significant life change by the end of the novel. What role do you believe Devon played in that? Did your perception of Trina change by the end of the novel? If so, how? Do you feel she was a better partner for Devon than Shaniece was?

12. The neighborhoods that Shaniece and Devon lived in were separated as though two different worlds, but it was evident that these worlds were more connected than most initially realized. How is it that such a division in class and socioeconomics can

occur in neighborhoods that are geographically so close together?

13. Shaniece realized her life's purpose through her encounter with Devon. What significant role has an individual played in your life? What discoveries were made through the relationship?

Notes